The Bitmores

The Bitmores

JUANITA TISCHENDORF

Hard Cover: ISBN:978-1-7350712-3-7
Paperback: ISBN:978-1-7350712-4-4
E-Book: ISBN:978-1-7350712-5-1

DEDICATION

To those who have repetitious lives, may you experience the delights and dangers of adventure.

BOOKS BY JUANITA TISCHENDORF

The Coronavirus Effect Story
FICTION

Three Little Girls (Murder in Rochester, NY)
Based on a True Story

Circle of Seven
Fiction – Thriller

Love Will Find A Way
Fiction – Romance

Playground In My Mind
Fiction - Thriller/Suspense

All The Missing Pieces
Fiction – Thriller/Suspense

Body Of Evidence
Fiction - Thriller/Suspense

Don't Look Back
Fiction – Thriller/Suspense

The Selfie
Nonfiction – How To

Mastering Childhood To Womanhood
Five book series
Nonfiction – How To

Over My Head
Nonfiction - Biography

An Unfair Advantage
Nonfiction – Biography

The Madman The Marathoner
Nonfiction – Biography

ACKNOWLEDGMENTS

To The Bitmore Street Residents

I ask the indulgence of the people who live on Bitmore Street in Irondequoit who may read this book. I have changed the geography of your street for the mere purpose of writing my story, a story I needed to write because of a house that inspired me. For years I have walked by the house on the corner of Bitmore Street and List Avenue, wondering who lived there or if any one did. I wondered why this house was so different from the others as it stood alone in style. I had no answers to my wonderings, so I wrote my own. You will not recognize more than the name and the location of your street, but you may, as I have, wondered about the house's story.

CHAPTER 1

Everything changes and that is a fact. When he was growing up the first day of spring was always on March 21, now suddenly spring comes on March 20. That does not mean snow days are over. The meteorologist announced that several inches of snow was expected to fall on Sunday and early Monday. The forecast could change slightly over the weekend, but an update on Friday afternoon predicted three to four inches of snow in the city. So, to get ahead and save himself from more work later, he was out pruning the trees.

It was a tedious job, to say the least, but it had to be done and it was a good day to do it. It was just beginning to warm up and now, it was nearing fifty-five degrees, one of the best weather days yet. He was a young man, in his mid-thirties and on the small side. His name was Cameron Bitmore.

When he finished pruning the two trees in his yard, he raked the twigs and dried branches into a pile, retrieved the garbage bag he had brought out with him and started gathering the debris by handfuls, careful not to stab a finger as he placed them in the bag. When it was cleared to his satisfaction, he picked up the bag by the top and carried it in his arms, pressed against his stomach until he reached the garage bin where he sat it down. He opened the lid of the bin and carefully retrieved the bag and lifting it up over his head, he lowered it down into the bin, then lowered the hinged top back in place.

With a look of satisfaction, he went to the back of the garage and wheeled out the lawn mower and put on his ear plugs and safety glasses before turning it on and commencing his next job.

It was the suburbs and if it had not been for the fact his lot was on the corner, he would have neighbors close on either side and across the street. He was glad of that and that his house was different from those around him. It sat on a plot like thousands of others in Rochester, but he enjoyed the area and the change in scenery even if it meant a lot of yard work year after year and season after season.

In Summer, the green leaves on the forest of trees scattered along every roadway and in patches between each dwelling, offered shade that increased his work as he had to deal with the grass dying when it was too shaded and being burnt out when they shade was defeated by the sun. Those days meant not only mowing the lawns but watering the grass and the flower gardens he had planted. That and keeping the herb garden well-watered, kept him busy most of the day.

Autumn brought its own chores of trying desperately to keep up with the leaves as they fell wherever they cared and did it dramatically, each and every day. Yet, there was beauty to be seen as the leaves turned color before they descended; each taking on a new look as if sprinkling jewels on the ground. He raked, bagged, and kept after it, along with mowing so that the grass below looked well-manicured.

In Winter, the view was of snow, lots of it, covering the sidewalks, yard, and roads and then he had to shovel the walkways, use a snow brush to clean off the car, then pull out the snow blower to clean the driveway. On those days as his body ached, he managed to take the time to take in the beauty of the sun turning the snow into a sparkling wonderland and the trees with a layer of snow clinging to the bare branches, looking majestic.

Then in the Spring the green grass with patches of yellow from the shade of the large oak and elm trees started to replenish itself on his 0.30 acres that made it an easy job of mowing but also meant his neighbors would be wanting to talk. But what he liked most about mowing was it gave him time to deal with his own thoughts and do it without interruptions as he walked back and forth across the lawn and hopefully moving in straight lines.

This Spring was like every other spring as he looked around him, from house to house that matched each other in style and design, with the only differences being the color of the siding or the color of the doors and shutters. Only his house was different; one of a kind.

Finished mowing, Cameron stood regarding his home. The house was a 1524 square foot single family dwelling with 3 bedrooms and 3 bathrooms located on the corner of Bitmore Drive and List Avenue. Built in 1989 it was a comfortable establishment with forced air heating, central air conditioning and a real wood burning fireplace and he was the first to admit it did need updating since nothing much had been done since the day it was built. As he stood staring at the exterior, he wondered how many people would be interested in purchasing a single-story ranch house with dark wood exterior walls and a black roof.

Cameron sighed and wheeled the lawnmower back to its spot in the garage and went to the side of the house and uncoiled the hose that was encased in its home and screwed the end to the outdoor spigot. He painstakingly watered the lawn and shot water over the branches, then saturated the spaded circles of earth under the trees. Seeing the results of dead leaves on the sidewalk and driveway, he aimed his water at the concrete walk and blacktop. When the whole area was damp and smelled like rain, he turned off the water, pulled the hose through his hand, then went to the hose box and began cranking it until the hose disappeared within. His job done, he took a last look around. As always, his gaze fell on the spot where he had first made the discovery. He stood there staring for some time and then finally went into the house.

The living room he stepped into corresponded to the lawn he left. It was mostly green from the green walls with a picture of a landscape on one and a good sized tv on another, it reeked of country, only seated in the suburbs. He looked at the plaid drapes that edged the windows and allowed his eyes to descend to the green rug on the floor. His gaze continued over the familiarity of the room from the fireplace to the sofa in front of the fireplace, flanked by two chairs all of these having straight backs and oak tables holding lamps with stained glass shades, two floor lamps that match with green silk shades. As he continued his visual, he smiled as he swung his head from wall to wall where one displayed the three sisters at sunset with cow skeletons in the foreground, and one of a cowboy on horseback, herding cattle on the plains.

He lowered his eyes to a side table where there was a coffee table book placed at an interesting diagonal. One might object that this living room was cold and at the same time stuffy, and that it would be quite oppressive to live in. But he was proud of it, especially the pictures which he had convinced himself were tasteful. This was his personal taste, and though not shared by others in the household, he managed to keep it that way."

He hurried through, whistling and went toward the back of the house to a bedroom, which had an en suite. The décor was done in baby blue with a comforter, ruffled pillows, and floral drapes. It reeked of obvious feminine touches and because of so much furniture, there was little floor space left. He whispered incongruently, "Marriage is about compromise. Yes, marriage is about compromise." He took off his work clothes, gave them a sniff and hung them in the closet and stepped naked into the bathroom.

With the door shut it was like a sound chamber as he began to whistle. The room was immaculate, its green lower tiles casting off the light along with the white tiles above. In this room, like every other room, everything was in its proper place, and in his masculine viewpoint everything worked. He pulled back the green shower curtain and stepped over the edge of the green tub that matched the green toilet and sink. The man turned on the spigots and twenty seconds after that stepped into a shower of exactly the temperature he wanted, washed himself clean, watched the water swirling as it went down the drain, and stepped out, still whistling a tune he would be hard pressed to give a name.

After combing his hair, he dressed in gray flannel slacks and pulled a white golf shirt over his head. He checked his appearance in the full-length mirror on the back of his closet door. The expression on the face that stared back at him showed his appreciation of himself and he turned and headed down the short hallway to the kitchen. Taking a deep breath in preparation of the same onslaught faced every day, he is happily surprised that she is busy concentrating on a cake she is icing and not preparing to argue about how the house needs updating.

She was a small woman, considerably younger than himself; but if questioned about her appearance he would be hard pressed to categorize it. He moved closer and saw there was a smear of chocolate on her face. He looked down to take in her loose green top. He lowered his gaze further to her tight-fitting crop pants hugging her rather voluptuous hips. At the moment she was studying a design in a magazine and when he walked closer, he saw it contained pictures of wedding cakes. The one that held her interest, he read the description below the picture aloud. "A thick creamy white frosting covering the top of the cake and heavy ivory fondant covering the lower tiers. The middle tiers of the cake are coated with satin like ruffles and pastel flowers. The lowest tier of the cake contains small gold flakes, adding an extra bit of glimmer to the cake."

Cameron stopped, looked at her creation that was even to his unpracticed eye visually stunning. He continued watching her work, in obvious deep concentration, then said, "That looks nice." Before the words were out, he knew that to be an understatement, for it was a massive undertaking, eighteen inches across the middle and four layers high, covered with a sheen like satin.

He knew when she was creating one of her masterpieces, she barely saw or heard anything around her so he stood a moment after his lame comment, then shifting his body said, "Well, don't see there's much else I can do around here. Guess I'll take a walk down the street."

Immediately Bridget's head raised and with the spatula in midair she finally acknowledged his presence. "You will be home for dinner?"

"I'll try to make it, but if I'm not home by six don't wait for me. I may be tied up."

"What does that mean?"

"It means if I'm not home by six…"

She interrupted him. "That doesn't do me any good. I am making this cake for Mrs. Reece. She needs it today. She will pay me when I deliver it and I plan to go to the store and pick up something for dinner. So, if you are not going to be home, I'll get something the children will enjoy."

Cameron thought about it. Images of her trying to get this monstrosity out of the house and into the back of her van humored him, but he said, "Then count me out."

"That's all I want to know."

There was a dour note in her voice that was obviously out of key with his humor. He tried to soften the mood. "I trimmed the trees and cut the grass. Looks pretty nice out there."

"Are you going to water the grass?"

"I did water it."

He said this with quiet gratification, for he had set a little trap to soften her mood, and she had fallen into it. But the silence that followed had a slightly ominous feel to it, as though he himself might have fallen into a trap that he was not aware of. Uneasily he added, "Gave it a good wetting down."

"Pretty early for watering isn't it?"

A puzzled expression appeared on his face.

"Most people, when they water the grass, wait till later in the day, and later in the year."

Not wanting to be outdone, he added, “Come on, Bridget, what are you getting at?”

She turned, to face him with her face red with anger. “She’s waiting for you, so go on.”

“Who’s waiting for me?”

“I think you know.” He stared straight into her glare, her eyes unblinking.

“If you are talking about Elizabeth Donahue, I haven’t seen her for a week and she never did mean a thing to me except somebody to golf with when I had nothing else to do.

“That’s practically all the time, if you ask me.”

“I wasn’t asking you.”

“Well, I’m not stupid. You golf with her and then you need to rest so you go to her house where you have a drink or two and then unbutton that red sweater, she is always wearing without a bra under it to entice weak men like you. You have sex, sleep and then take some time to get some nourishment and then, then you say something like, “Oh, will you look at the time. I must get back. You kiss and say goodbye.”

His face muscles tightened, but before words were spoken, he stopped himself. Breathing through his nose, he took a deep breath to calm himself and spoke softly. “Oh, all right, all right.”

He delivered the words in a lofty, resigned way so as not to fuel the fire and then walked across the kitchen.

“Wouldn’t you like to bring her something?” Bridget asked with sarcasm dripping from her words and the spatula swinging dramatically from her hand.

"Bring her…? What do you mean"?

"Well, there was some batter left over, and I made up some little cakes I was saving for the children. But fat as she is, she must like sweets so here, I'll wrap them up for her."

His resign to remain calm, escaped him as he yelled, "Go to hell, Bridget, go to hell?"

Bridget felt helpless, totally inadequate. She thought of asking him to think of the children, and in the next instant knew that it had nothing to do with the children. Of course, she had an alternative. She could get a divorce. But all her instincts shied away from the thought of leaving him. Where would she go? She could go to the house in the country where her mother and father lived, the place where she had been born, the only place she thought of as home. There the neighborhood had trees, but more space between the homes, sitting on vast well-manicured lawns. More appealing was that inside the walls were all white with no carpets on the hard wood floors. She sighed as she pulled herself out of her reverie. No, Not yet. Later, perhaps she could leave him, but not yet.

Bridget heard the refrigerator door being closed and it jerked her back to reality and she heard his last pathetic words.

"There is no work out there, Bridget."

That got her going and she started in on him again. "Have you heard of fidelity or morals? Do you know that men work to support their family and take any job that will help him meet that obligation instead of spending his days with a home wrecker?"

In his own defense he added, “She’s not a homewrecker.”

“No, of course you wouldn’t see it that way. Mrs. Donahue is married and wants to take on my husband too.”

“Stop it Bridget. Spending time with her is peaceful. She doesn’t constantly nag me over things that are out of my control.”

It was the same argument they had constantly with little originality or satisfaction on either side. Presently he had enough. He closed the refrigerator door then started across the kitchen floor but before he reached the doorway, she stopped him.

“Where are you going?”

He paused but remained quiet.

“Tell me. Are you going to Elizabeth Donahue’s?”

“Suppose I am?”

“Then you might as well pack right now, and leave for good, because if you go out of that door, I’m not going to let you come back. If I must take this knife to you, you’re not coming back in this house.”

She lifted a large knife out of a drawer, held it up, put it back, while he watched contemptuously. “Keep it up, Bridget, keep it up.”

“I mean it. You go to her this afternoon, and that’s the last you’ve seen of this house.”

“I go where I goddam please to go.”

“Then pack up, Cameron.”

He could feel the color drain from his face as he stared into her eyes. He fought to gain control, but he was beyond restraint now. “Okay, then, I will.”

“You better do it now. The sooner the better.”

“Okay, okay”

He stalked out of the kitchen. To occupy her mind, she filled a paper cornucopia with icing snipped the end off with a pair of scissors and started to ice the cake.

By then he was in the bedroom, pitching his suitcases from the closet to the middle of the floor. He was noisy about it, perhaps hoping she would hear him and come in there, begging him to change his mind. If that was his wish, he was disappointed, and there was nothing for him to do but pack.

He worked systematically. First making sure he packed his suits, dress shirts, ties, and shoes. All of these he wrapped tenderly in tissue paper and placed in the bottom of the biggest bag. His mind drifted as he continued to pack.

His life had been a comedy of blunders since day one with a little sprinkle of infallible. Cameron, in life, learned the value of a dollar, but not in the way that would make him prosper. Instead, it was a lesson learned in how to get what he wanted.

It kept him from being lazy and made him feel important. That, along with the blessing of his handsome face could get him far, only something always stood in the way of success. When he reached his teens, he was like every other teenager working in fast food restaurants to earn money. Then an uncle had died and left him a farm, one of the few remaining in the Irondequoit suburb of

Rochester where nothing much changed to bring the place into the 20th century. But then, at his young age it did not matter because he owned a farm. So, living the country life he wore his jeans and flannel shirts every day as he tried to operate the farm, but without much success even though he had knowledgeable workers who had been part of his inheritance and were paid from an account overseen by the lawyer.

His heart was not in farming, so after the initial idyllic wore thin, he gave little thought to any advice and expended little effort to keep the farm going. The problem was that farming took time…lots of it and he just was not a farmer.

Finally, he gave up trying to earn a living from the land and worked odd jobs in town to earn money to live on. This time the tides changed from hope to despair and then back again. What he had not been told was that his uncle, knowing farming was not the type of living that one could just fall into and make good had installed a backup plan. Along with the three hundred acres he had set aside a nest egg for his nephew with detailed instructions on how to not only farm the land, but how to make the money last until he began to see the fruit of his labor. Maybe if he had known about this ahead of time, he might have made a success of it, but the lawyer was told not to share this with his nephew before he had a chance to prove himself capable or….

No matter, he did what any young man would do. He enjoyed himself with his newfound windfall. It was the fruit of his labor that the land did not provide and in the end, he was broke and on the verge of losing the farm.

He screwed up, but instead of going down, he went up. He was visited by three men who made him a proposition and he accepted. Almost overnight, with his three hundred acres that were in the exact spot where people wanted to build, he went from farmer to landowner. He and the three gentlemen formed a company, called Bitmore Homes, Inc., with himself as president. He named a street after himself, and on Bitmore Drive, after he married Bridget, built this very home that he now occupied, or would occupy for the next twenty minutes. Although at that time he was making a great deal of money, he declined to build a pretentious place. He wanted to blend in and not stand out because by now he knew the pattern of his life. Yet it was a little better, in some ways to what was the norm in those days. It had three bathrooms, one for each bedroom, and certain features of the construction were almost luxurious, even if his ideal of decorating was unfashionable.

As he looked around him, he saw it all as a mockery now. Just as always, on the heels of his success came failure and like always, he did not try to make it better so the place had been mortgaged and remortgaged, and the money from the mortgages long since spent. Allowing himself a little recompense he admitted that the community was well thought out and the houses had been solidly built.

The failure was all his. Instead of putting his money in a bank, he had invested it in AT&T, and for some years had enjoyed daily vindication of his judgment, for the stock soared majestically. He thought himself capable of handling his finances on his own and he did, for a while. But like farming, investments took time and attention; the two things he knew least about. So, not one to stay on top of it, the stock went from their peaks in October 2007 until their closing lows in early March 2009 when the Dow Industrial Average, Nasdaq Composite and S&P 500 all suffered declines of over 50%, marking the worst stock market crash since the Great Depression era.

His plunge to ruin was rapid. In September he had been rich, and Bridget had been happy. In November, he had had to sell the spare car to pay current bills. He did not worry as many of his friends were in the same plight, and he could joke about it, and even boast about it.

Yet different from before, this roller coaster of success had gone on for some time. He had become so used to crediting himself with vast acumen and thus never admitted each high point in his life was all luck, due to the land inheritance and the location of his land rather than to his own personal abilities. So, he still thought in terms of the vast deeds he would do when things got better. As for seeking a job, he could not bring himself to do it, and despite all he told Bridget, he had not made the slightest effort in this direction. So, by steady deterioration, he had reached his present status with Mrs. Donahue.

She was a lady of uncertain years, with a tidy income from two dead husbands and she supposedly had a live one, only no one knew for sure. This left her with a lot of time on her hands that she loathe spending alone. She needed Cameron. She listened to the tales of his grandeur, past and future, fed him, golfed with him, and smiled coyly when he lifted her sweater. Cameron had to admit he was addicted to a life of living in a dream world, with no worries beyond the moment as he watched the seasons come and go.

He kept looking at the door, as though he expected Bridget to appear, but it remained closed. When little Isabella came home from school, he stepped over and locked the door. In a moment she was out there, rattling the knob, but he ignored it. He heard Bridget call out to her. He heard Isabella's footsteps as she hurried down the hall. He heard the front door opening and knew the other child was waiting for Bridget. That would be their daughter Chloe.

His last bag packed, he unlocked the door and walked dramatically to the kitchen. Bridget had returned and was again at work on the cake, which by now was a thing of overwhelming beauty. She did not look up. He moistened his lips, asked, "Is Chloe home?"

"Not yet she isn't."

He knew this to be untrue, but maybe it was since he had not really checked to see who she was talking to.

"I laid low when Isabella came to the door just now. I did not want to have her see me packing. I did not see any reason for either of them to know about it. I do not want you to tell them I said goodbye or anything. You can just say…" He paused. "You can just say…"

"I'll take care of it."

"Okay, then. I'll leave it to you."

He hesitated to wait for that piece of good news to show itself, but when it didn't' come he said, "Well, goodbye, Bridget."

He stood, watching her walk over to the far wall where she stood with her forehead leaning against it. All was still until she began beating her fist against the wall and tearfully said, "Go on, Cameron. There is nothing to say. Just go on."

When she turned around, he was gone. As she walked back across the kitchen the tears came, and she stood away from the cake, to keep them from falling on it. She heard the SUV being backed out of the garage and gave a low, frightened cry as she ran to the window. They used it so seldom now, except on Sundays if they had a little money to buy gas, that she did not expect him to take it. And so, as she saw this man slip out of her life, the only dear thought in her head was that now she had no way to deliver the cake.

CHAPTER 2

She was putting the final touches on the cake and started removing stray flecks of icing with a cotton swab wound on a toothpick, when there was a rap on the screen door, and Lucy Steele, who lived next door, let herself in. She carried her age well with streaked blonde hair in a pixie cut and a figure that still showed signs of how shapely she was in her younger days. Most interesting about her was the way of changing her serious expression to an inviting smile which had one wondering if the permanent creases on her forehead might have come from care, or from knowing her well, might have come from liquor. Her husband was in the trucking business, but they were more prosperous than most truckers were at that time. There was a general opinion that Steele trucks often dropped down to Lake Ontario, where certain low, fast boats stood waiting with questionable cargo.

Seeing the cake, Mrs. Steele raised her hands to her cheeks and her mouth dropped open. She moved closer. It was indeed worth the stare which her large brown eyes gave it. All its decorations were now in place and next to it stood a tester slice from a smaller version she had made. It had an aroma, a texture, a totality that proclaimed high distinction. It was a cheerful rainbow cake with vanilla icing and created in seven layers of purple, blue, green, yellow, orange, and red.

In awe, Mrs. Steele murmured, “I do not see how you do it, Bridget. It's beautiful, just beautiful.”

“If you have to do it, you can do it.”

“Well, it’s amazing.” After a long final look Mrs. Steele got to what she came for. She had a small plate in her hand, with another plate clamped over it, and now lifted the top one. “I thought maybe you could use it. I fricasseed it for dinner, but Ashton’s had a call to Canada, and plans on eating dinner there.” She paused. Her face taking on a dreamy expression. “He’s asked me to go with him. This will not be as good when we get back, so…”

“Yes, thank you. That’s so kind of you.”

Bridget got a plate, slid the chicken on it, and put it in the refrigerator. Then she washed Mrs. Steele's plates, dried them, and handed them back. “Thank you, Lucy. I appreciate it.”

“Well, I've got to run along.”

“Have a nice time.”

Turning her head as she stepped out the door, Lucy said, “Tell

Cameron I said hello."

"Ah, I will."

Lucy stopped and turned toward Bridget. They had known each other long enough that she knew something was wrong. The choke in her voice as she replied was unmistakable.

"What's the matter, Bridge?"

Bridget grabbed a Kleenex from her pocket and dabbed her eyes before she turn to face her friend. "Nothing."

"Come on, Bridge. I am your friend and I know something is wrong. Tell me, what is it?"

Hesitating at first, Bridget finally allowed herself to say it aloud, "Cameron…Cameron's gone."

"Gone? Gone where?"

Bridge sniffled as Lucy made her way closer. She was aware they were having problems, but she figured they would get over it. But now, as she tried to comfort her friend, she knew this was serious. "You mean for good?"

"Yes. Just now. He left."

"Come on Bridge, sit." While she helped her friend seat herself at the counter she continued. "Cameron walked out on you, just like that?"

Her sniffling came louder now as she covered her face and spoke into the Kleenex. "I probably pushed him to this. I should have known it was coming."

Talking almost to herself, Lucy's voice in a stern whisper replied, "Well what do you know about that? He left you for that blonde haired bimbo. How can he even look at her?"

"She's what he wants."

"I say good riddance, but I think you still love him. I don't know how, but you do."

Crying openly now, Bridget replied. "I do, I do." She paused, blew her nose, and continued. "Oh, what's the use of talking? If she likes him, all right then, she's got him. I tried to get him back, but he made his choice."

"Why now. Why when you are having money problems would he leave. Why not try to get everything in order before he left."

"I did pester him, I nagged him, he said. But I cannot take this lying down. It has been going on too long now and I do not think it will stop, no matter what I say or what I do. I tried to be considerate. I know men cheat, but I think this is beyond cheating. God, Lucy, he takes her out in public. He doesn't treat her like a secret anymore."

Lucy continuously nodded her head. What Bridget was saying was so true. Everyone knew Cameron was having an affair. "What are you going to do?"

As if that thought was foreign to her, Bridget repeated it. "What am I going to do?"

A grim silence fell on both women. Then Mrs. Steele shook her head. "Well, you've joined the biggest army on earth. You are now officially part of the great American institution that never gets mentioned on Fourth of July. I'd say make him pay, but he is penniless…" Lucy went over and gave her friend a hug. "Oh Bridget. I will help all I can, but you need to pull yourself together. You have two small children to support." She lifted Bridget's face adding, "The dirty bastards."

"Oh, Cameron's all right."

"He's all right? He's a dirty bastard and they're all dirty bastards."

"It takes two. I accept that I am partly the fault."

"So, what. You wouldn't pull what he pulled."

Bridget heard the front door slam open, and she quickly pulled herself together as she held up a warning finger.

Mrs. Steele nodded and asked if there was anything she could do, today. Bridget wanted desperately to ask if she could give her a lift with the cake, but there had been one or two impatient taps on an automobile horn from across the yard, and she knew it was Lucy's husband. She did not want to cause her friend any problems, so she said, "Not right now."

"Okay, my friend, I'll keep in touch, and you call me if you need anything."

She watched as Lucy headed for the side door, off the kitchen. "Thanks again for the chicken."

The child who now entered the kitchen did not scamper in, as little Isabella had a short time before. She stepped in primly, sniffed contemptuously at the scent left by Mrs. Steele, and put her schoolbooks on the table before she kissed her mother. Though she was only eleven she was something to look at twice. In the jaunty way she wore her clothes, as well as the beauty around her face, she resembled her father more than her mother in skin tone and her hair was bouncy and straight: It was something that Cameron's family was always pointing out that Chloe was a Bitmore, even though they swore they were not prejudice or cared less for Isabella who had a perfect combination of both races with curly hair that danced when she walked and had a mind of its own. Even her smile was identical to that of Cameron's.

Chloe's hair, which was a coppery brown, and her eyes, which were light brown like her mother's, were even more vivid by contrast with the scramble of light freckles and light tan skin which formed her complexion. But the most arresting thing about her was her walk. Possibly because of her high, arching chest, possibly because of the slim hips and legs below it, she moved with an erect, arrogant haughtiness that seemed comic in one so young.

She took the slice of cake her mother gave her and smiled as she recounted what she had learned during her piano lesson.

Bridget returned her smile. Seeing her daughter so happy made the expense of the lessons worth it. Cash had been tight during the last year and a half and paying fifteen dollars an hour for her daughter's lessons made it even harder, but her daughter's lessons she refused to cancel. Chloe was a satisfactory pupil, for she practiced faithfully and showed lively interest. She had picked out a piano she wanted but, when they lost their socks on the stock market crash, it was never paid for. So now, Chloe practiced at her Grandfather Bitmore's place. He had an old grand piano and loved to hear his granddaughter play.

Chloe would scoot over to his house right after school to practice what she had learned during her lessons and on this account always arrived home from school somewhat later than Isabella.

'Counting Stars', by One Republic had been the first piece that Chloe had accomplished during her lessons, but now she shared with her mother she had played the classical solo, 'Chopin's Nocturne Op. 9 No. 2'. She told her mother that she found the music soothing and she felt she played it well, though at first this classical piece presented a challenge as it had a variety of notes in various sequences. But it did not matter as her interest in doing it well paid off.

Bridget was more fascinated by the way her daughter spoke in the clear, affected voice that one associates with stage children, and indeed everything she said had the effect of having been learned by heart, and recited in the manner prescribed by some stiff book of etiquette.

Chloe finished her recitation and walked over to have a look at the cake. "Who's it for, Mother?"

"The Reeces."

"Oh, you mean for Tyler, the paper boy."

Young Reece's after school job was soliciting subscriptions for the newspaper, which Chloe saw as one step up from begging. Bridget smiled. “He'll be a paper boy without a birthday cake if I don't find some way to get it over there. Eat your cake now, and then run over to Grandfather's and see if he minds taking me up to Mrs. Reece's in his car.”

“Can't we use our car?”

“Your father's out with it, and he may be late. Run along now. Take Isabella with you, and Grandfather can drive you both back.”

Chloe stalked unhurriedly out of the kitchen. Bridget waited a few minutes, listening for the front door to close. Several minutes later she heard it and the sound of Chloe calling her sister. A minute or two later she was back. She closed the door carefully and spoke with even more than her usual precision. “Mother, where's Father?”

“He had to go somewhere.”

“Why did he take his clothes?”

Bridget had let it slip her mind. Chloe had an odd passion for her father's clothes that she constantly inspected to see if there were any new additions. She did this regularly so when they had a school event, or a piano recital she could tell him exactly what she wanted him to wear. Obviously, she had done that today. In her heart she knew it was impossible to fool Chloe anyway, but she tried.

“He’s gone away.”

"Where?"

"I don't know."

"Is he coming back?"

Bridget hesitated. Was it too much on an eleven-year-old to say her father had left them? Before she had a chance to decide, Chloe said, "For good?"

Bridget said, "Not sure."

She felt heartbroken, as she stood wanting Chloe to come over to her, so she could take her in her arms and tell her about it in some way that did not seem, so shame faced. But Chloe's eyes were cold, and she did not move. Bridget could not help admiring her beautiful daughter for her promise of talent and even her snobbery which in their society could lead to superior outcomes in later life.

But Chloe doted on her father for his grand manner and fine ways, and if he disdained gainful work, she was proud of him for it. In the endless bickering that had marked the last few months, she had invariably been on his side, and not afraid to let her mother know that. Now she said, "I see, Mother. I just wanted to know."

Presently Isabella came in, a chubby, curly haired little thing, five years younger than Chloe, and the picture of her mother. She began dancing around, pretending she was going to poke her finger into the cake, but Bridget stopped her, and told her what she had just told Chloe. She began to cry, and Bridget gathered her into her arms, and talked to her as she had wanted to talk in the first place. She said Father thought the world of them both, that he had not said goodbye because he did not want to make them feel badly. She told her girls that it was not his fault, but the fault of a lot of things she could not tell them about now but would explain later. All this she said to Isabella, but she was really talking to Chloe, who was still standing there, gravely listening. After a few minutes Chloe evidently felt some obligation to be friendly, for she interrupted to say, "If what you don't want to say right now is about Mrs. Donahue, Mother, I quite agree." Chloe frowned and added, "I think she's distinctly middle class."

Bridget was able to laugh at this, and she seized the chance to gather Chloe to her and kiss her. Then she sent both children off to their grandfather's. She was glad that she herself had not said a word about Mrs. Donahue and resolved that the name should never pass her lips in their presence.

CHAPTER 3

The grandparents were special to Bridget as well as to the children. Papa Bitmore arrived with the car and an invitation to dinner, and after a moment's reflection, Bridget accepted.

The Bitmores had to be told, and if she told them now, after having dinner with them, it would show there were no hard feelings, and that she wanted to continue relations as before. But after the cake had been delivered, and she had sat around with them a few minutes, she detected something in the air. Whether Cameron had already stopped by, or the children had made some slip, she did not know, but things were not as usual.

She loved Spencer and Lily Bitmore and would not hurt them for the world. But she had no choice. As soon as dinner was over and the children had gone out to play, Bridget helped Lily clear the table. In the kitchen she put the food away while Lily rinsed the dishes and placed them in the dishwasher.

It was easy to surmise that Lily Bitmore, being a caring, smart, and rightest woman would have raised Cameron properly. Even knowing that Cameron had a personal relationship with Spencer, Bridget knew he was not at fault either for how Cameron turned out. The children as well as Bridget loved the grandparents who seemed to have a unique trait in that they never lost their sense of humor. That she counted on now.

Spencer and Lily had raised Cameron in a modest home in the country, not far from the development. When they first heard of Cameron selling the farmland, they never expressed an opinion or showed disillusion and when Cameron 'gifted' them with a house in the development, they accepted, never once allowing him to doubt it was what they wanted.

They were simple people who had worked at Kodak and now lived nicely on pensions they received. When Cameron came to them with the idea to invest in the stock market with him, they had graciously thanked him, but declined. As a result, they were comfortable enough and had turned the house into one of coziness where they planned to live out their twilight years.

While they worked, Bridget filled the grandparents in on what the children had been up to, especially Chloe. She knew how she sounded when she talked about Chloe, and she hoped the grandparents did not see her as favoring one child over the other. If she had given it more thought she would have known that was something papa and mama could not fathom. Instead, they saw it as the older child developing a personality that pleased her mother, while the younger one was still a baby.

With the dishes in the dishwasher, it was time. Whenever possible, Spencer and Lily liked to spend the evening on their patio that faced the backyard. Bridget knew their ritual and went to get a bottle of wine and three wine glasses. Lily had a tray already with cookies and crackers to take out with them and they went out the back door. Spencer was already seated on the patio, watching the children play with the children next door.

It was here that Bridget broke the news. A silence fell on them, a glum silence that lasted a long time. Lily had her glass of wine and sat in the chair swing. She kept sipping the wine and looking across at Spencer. Bridget tried to think of something to say to ease their pain, but at that moment she knew to be silent. Lily became more animated, touching the floor with the toe of her shoe and forcing the chair to rock back and forth. As she rocked, the bolt in the patio ceiling squeaked with each movement back and forth.

Then she spoke, in a bitter, jerky way, looking neither at Bridget nor at Spencer. "It's that Donahue woman. I knew from the moment I first laid eyes on her she was up to no good. The idea, carrying on like that with a married man and her own husband…" She couldn't bring herself to finish the thought.

Once she started there was no stopping her. "And the filthy way she keeps house. And going around like she does with her breasts wobbling every which way, forcing every man she passed to find it hard not to look her way."

"Lily... calm down." Spencer could see she was getting agitated and not thinking about what she said. Hearing the tone in her husband's voice she looked over at him, her eyes glassy from tears. "Why did she have to pick on my boy? Wasn't there enough men out there that were single." Lily sobbed. "Tell me, why."

Bridget closed her eyes and listened, and Spencer sat down his wine and went over to his wife."

It was all about Mrs. Donahue, and in a way, this was a relief. But then a sense of vague apprehension stirred within her. This evening, she knew, was important, for what was said now would be written indelibly on their hearts. For the children's sake, if no other, it was vital that she be truthful. She would have liked to leave the blame on this woman, but Mrs. Donahue was not the only one at blame. This went a lot deeper.

When Lily was somewhat calm, Spencer returned to his seat. Bridget took a deep breath. "It's not just Mrs. Donahue."

"What?" Shocked, Lily looked at her daughter in law in awe. "Who is it, then?"

She knew at that moment that they were being parents. They needed to shift the blame away from their son and whether or not they knew he played a role; it was not obvious. Bridget spoke with caution. "It's a whole lot of things, and if they hadn't happened, Cameron wouldn't any more have looked at her than he would have looked at any woman." Now Bridget went on. "It's what happened to Cameron's business. And the awful time we had getting along. And the way Cameron got fed up. And…"

“Wait! You mean to tell me this is Cameron’s fault?”

Bridget waited a minute, for fear the coarseness in Lily’s voice would find an answering one in her own. Finally, she said, “I’m not saying it was anybody's fault. Remember when the stock market hit its peak in October of 2007?” Both Bitmores nodded. “Well Cameron had invested everything and when the bottom dropped out in March 2009, everything was gone. Only Cameron could not accept it was all gone. Cameron couldn't change his ways either.” She stopped, then staunchly plowed on with what she dreaded saying, and yet felt had to be said, “But I might as well tell you, Cameron wasn't the only one that got fed up, I got fed up too. He did not start this thing today. I did.”

There, it was said. Now Bridget waited for the backlash.

“You mean you put Cameron out?”

The rasp in Lily's voice was so pronounced now as she began to sob uncontrollably. Bridget was not sure it was not being able to accept the reality of the situation or that she was infuriated by the fact she had thrown Cameron out. She sat quietly waiting her punishment.

After five minutes of complete silence and Lily able to control her sobs, she said, “It had to come.”

“It certainly did have to come if you went and put that poor boy out! I never heard of such a thing in my life. Where's he at now?”

“I don’t know.”

All the love she had felt from these two people, now seemed

nonexistent. It was never more obvious than hearing her mother-in-law say, “And it's not even your house.”

Bridget needed a reprieve. “It'll be the bank's house pretty soon if I don't find a way to raise the money to pay the taxes.”

“Hush, both of you,” Spencer said.

Bridget gave them time to think and finally added, “I’m not defending her or am I blaming it all on Cameron because he thought he had done the right thing. All I'm trying to say is that what had to come happened and if it came today, and I was the one that brought it on, it was better than having it come later, when there would have been even more hard feelings about it.”

Lily said nothing as the swing moved back and forth again. It was obvious she was angry. It was Spencer who tried to soften the wounds. “That stock market crash had certainly hit a lot of people hard. I was glad we didn’t put any money in it.”

Bridget waited. She had said all she intended to say and now wanted to leave but gave it a few minutes so her departure would not seem like a put off. Finally, she stood. “I need to be getting the children home.” Spencer stood up and opened the patio door. They watched as Bridget gathered up the children, not offering her a ride. When she started toward the sidewalk, Spencer stepped out the door and said, “You need anything right now Bridget?”

“Not right now. I earned what I needed this month.”

“Believe it or not, I’m sorry. “Goodnight, Bridget.”

So, moving the children along, Bridget began to feel a hot resentment against the Bitmores not only for their complete failure to get the point, but also for their ignoring the plight she was in and that of their grandchildren. As they turned the corner and arrived at Bitmore Drive the night chill settled in and she felt the cold not only on her skin, but in her heart.

After putting the children to bed she went to the living room where she sat in a chair where she could look out the window. She sat there in the dark looking out at the familiar scene, trying to shake off the melancholy that was creeping over her.

Finally, she went to the bedroom and turned on the light. It would be the first time she had slept in here since Cameron started his affair with Mrs. Donahue. For several months now, she had been sleeping in the den on the pull out sofa. She tiptoed in there now, got her pajamas and carried them back to the master bedroom. She undressed and put on her pajamas, then sat in front of the dressing table and started brushing her hair, Then she paused, staring at her reflection.

She was a shade under medium height, and her small size, brown hair, and shocking green eyes made her look considerably younger than she was, which was twenty-five. About her face there was no distinction whatever. She was what is described as 'nice looking', rather than pretty but this did not quite do her justice. There was much more to her than met the eyes.

Cameron had seen it and was attracted to her. They met just after her father died, when she was in her final year of high school. After the garage business had been sold and the insurance collected, her mother had toyed with the idea of buying a Bitmore

Home, using her small capital as a down payment, and taking in roomers to pay the rest. That was what brought Cameron around and Bridget, admittedly was excited by him, mainly on account of his dashing ways.

On the day of the grand tour of Bitmore Homes arrived, Mrs. Spears was unable to go, and Cameron took Bridget. He picked her up in his Corvette and had the top down so that the wind blew her hair and gave her a feeling of excitement she could not explain. When they arrived at the development, Cameron stopped at the Bitmore Model Home, which was really the main office of Bitmore Homes, Inc., but was furnished like a home, to stimulate the imaginations of customers.

The bookkeeper had gone by the time they arrived, and Bridget inspected everything, from the great living room in front of the cozy bedrooms at the rear, lingering longer in these than was perhaps advisable.

Cameron was very solemn on the way home, as befitted one who had just seduced a minor, but ignoring that he suggested a reinspection on the following day. A month later they were married. Bridget quit school two days before the ceremony, and Chloe arrived slightly sooner than expected. Cameron persuaded Mrs. Spears to give up the idea of a Bitmore Home to be used as a boarding house, possibly fearing this would lower the image of the development. As a result, Mrs. Spears went to live with Bridget's sister Eleanor, whose husband Maxwell Temple had a ship business in Washington.

All that ran through her head as she stared into the mirror. She returned to examining her reflection. She had to admit her figure got her attention in any crowd. Her neck was long, and her shoulders drooped, but gracefully. Her bra ballooned a little, emphasizing the firmness of her breast and her hips were small, like Chloe's, and suggested a girl, rather than a woman who had borne two children. Her legs were beautiful, and she was quite vain about them. Only one thing about them bothered her. In the mirror they were flawlessly slim and straight, but as she looked down on them direct, something about their contours made them seem bowed. So, she had taught herself to bend one knee when she stood, and to take short steps when she moved, bending the rear knee quickly, so that the deformity, if it existed, could not be noticed. The results was a very feminine walk, like that of a show horse. She did not know it, but that walk made her bottom switch in a provocative way. Or possibly she did know it.

The hair finished, she got up, put her hands on her hips and surveyed herself in the mirror. For a moment she felt her appraisal was not merely for her benefit, but that she was taking stock to see what she had to offer against what lay ahead. Leaning close, she bared her teeth, which were large and white. She stood back again, cocked her head to one side, struck an attitude. Almost at once she amended it by bending one knee. She sighed as she went to turn off the overhead light and out of force of habit crossed to the bedroom window and looked over to the Steeles to see if they were still up. Then she remembered they were away. She also recalled what Mrs. Steele had said… the great American institution that never gets mentioned on the Fourth of July. She snickered, sourly as she got into bed.

Unexpectedly she caught her breath as Cameron's smell enveloped her, but before she could react, the bedroom door opened, and little Isabella ran in weeping. Bridget held up the covers, folded the little thing in, snuggled her against her stomach, whispered and crooned to her until the weeping stopped. Then, after staring at the ceiling for a time she fell asleep.

CHAPTER 4

For a day or two after Cameron left, Bridget baked nonstop, making cakes and pies. This was a close neighborhood and as such she knew that the word must be out, she was going it alone. Her thoughts often turned to Cameron and what she would say to him when he dropped by to see the children. She heard herself saying, "Oh, we're getting along all right no need for you to worry. I have all the work I can do, and more. Just goes to show that when a person's willing to work there still seems to be work available."

Lately she was given to rehearsing things in her mind and having imaginary triumphs over people who had upset her in one way or another. It eased the thoughts of reality that she had to deal with, but soon she began to get frightened. Several days went by, and there were no orders. Then there came a letter from her mother, mainly about the AT&T, which she had bought outright and still held, and which had fallen to some absurd figure. She was quite explicit about blaming this all on Cameron and seemed to feel there was something he could do about it and should do. And parts of the letter that was not about the AT&T was about Maxwell Temple's ship business that was going bankrupt. When Maxwell, married her sister, Ellie, her mother was so happy and willing to help them get their feet on the ground by investing in his idea for a Washington DC Dinner Cruise and in honor of her attitude toward their marriage, she suggested naming it Cloud 9. When she married Cameron, her mother was happy, but because Cameron had money and a business, she saw Bridget as the one to help the family.

Bridget broke into a hysterical laugh as she read this. And in the same mail was a brief communication from the gas company, headed 'Third Notice', and informing her that unless her bill was paid in five days service would be discontinued. Yes, she could help the family all right.

She had been careful with her money and still had some left from the cake she made for Mrs. Reece. That and her current earnings was enough to pay the gas bill. Without wasting a moment, Bridge immediately went online to the gas company and made a payment with her credit card. She logged into her bank and checked the balance and then called an Uber to take her to the store where she bought a chicken, a quarter pound of hot dogs, some vegetables, and a quart of milk. The chicken, first baked, then creamed would cover meals over the weekend. The hot dogs were a luxury. She disapproved of them, on principle, but the children loved them, and she always tried to have some around, for bites between meals. The milk was a sacred duty. No matter how difficult things got, Bridget had two rules and that was to always have money for Chloe's piano lessons, and for all the milk the children could drink.

It was a Saturday morning, and when she arrived home, she found Spencer Bitmore there. Though Mr. Bitmore was not fond of Bridget, and now was less fond of his son, Cameron, but both adored their granddaughters. They also felt they could come and go anytime they wanted and had their own key to prove it. She had barely taken her coat off when he approached her. “Listen Bridget, I’ve come to take the children over to our house for the weekend.” She started to protest.

“No, listen, Bridget, I know they have school on Monday and will take them myself.” He paused then added, “They can come home from there.”

Bridget was not stupid. He was probably planning an outing with them and Cameron would seem to appear quite by accident. She resented him trying to play her, but then reason took hold.

The children would be fed well for two whole days and that would allow her purchases to feed them into the following week.

Isabella and Chloe were not far away, and they came running into the room saying, "Mother, can we go, can we go?"

She trusted the grandparents and knew they loved the children so they would be safe. After giving it some thought, Bridget acted quite agreeably about it. "Of course, you can go." She looked directly at Spencer. "It would be a treat for them."

"Girls, come on, help me pack a bag for you." She barely got the words out of her mouth before the girls ran pass her and went into their room. She joined them to make sure they packed the necessities and then gave each of them a hug, telling them to be good girls and she would see them on Monday.

"They're all set, Spencer. I'll pick them up after school."

She watched them walking on either side of their grandfather, each holding a hand. She stood in the doorway as he helped them into the car, heard him tell them to fasten their seat belts and then put the bags in the back. Once Spencer was behind the wheel, he turned to say something to the girls, and she saw them wave. She waved back and watched as they drove away.

Around five that evening the bell rang. She had an uneasy feeling it might be Cameron, with some message about the children. But when she went to the door it was Greyson Hobbs. Greyson, one of the three gentlemen who had made the original proposition to Cameron which led to Bitmore Homes, Inc. He was a handsome man with black hair that had gone grey at the temples. There was something about his eyes, though, that bothered Bridget. They made him always look as though he was frowning and that the fact his lips were always meeting, added to that unpleasant feeling. Bridge guessed him to be around forty and knew he worked for the receivers that had been appointed for the corporation. She knew this because when the position had opened, Cameron had told her about it.

"So, what is a receiver?"

"Well, a receiver is a person appointed by the courts to manage debt consolidation for a company."

"You mean, like a liquidator?"

"Sort of, only a receiver's duty is to the bank, while a liquidator is concerned with all of the affairs of a company and all of its creditors. I want that job."

"What one."

"I want to be the liquidator. They suggested me for receiver, but I turned it down."

That became another source of irritation between Bridget and Cameron, for she thought he should have taken the job, and if he had gotten off his high horse, he would be employed right now. But Greyson had been offered the job and accepted it. Bridget put on a smile and opened the door.

"Hello, Bridget. Is Cameron around?"

"Not right now he isn't."

“Do you know where I can find him?”

“No, I don't.”

Greyson stood thinking a minute, then turned to go. “All right, I'll see him Monday. Something came up about the title, and I thought maybe he could help us out. Ask him if he can drop over, will you?”

Bridget stood in the doorway and realized what this could mean. “Wait Greyson.”

Straightening out a title would mean Cameron would have a job, if only for a little while. That meant income and who knew, maybe a permanent position. She had to see he got a chance.

Greyson looked a little surprised, when he turned to face her and started walking back to the house. Bridget stood aside and he stepped into the living room. As soon as he entered, Bridget closed the door behind her.

“Listen, if it’s important, Greyson, you'd better look Cameron up yourself.” She swallowed her pride and stood up firm. He's not living here anymore.”

“What?”

“He’s left.” Bridget looked directly in his eyes and added, “We had a fight and he left.”

“Where?”

“I don't know exactly. He didn't tell me, but you might try his dad, Spencer Bitmore, he may know.” She paused, thinking. “Oh, they might not be home, they have the kids for the weekend and may have taken them somewhere."

"Do you know, where?"

She could send him to the beach and find out that Spencer had not planned to have Cameron show up there. That would delay the matter and they might find someone else. As much as she dreaded it, she had to tell him.

"Listen, Greyson, I think Margret, ah, Maggie Donahue might know. If she does not know where he is, she at least knows how to reach him."

Greyson looked at Bridget wonderingly. Of course, it did not come as any surprise to him. He did not know exactly what to say or how to act so he just stood staring at her, then finally spoke. "When did it happen?"

"A few days ago."

"You mean he left you?"

"Not the best choice of words, Greyson, but, yes, something like that."

"For good?"

"As far as I know."

"Well, what a mess."

"It's for the best."

Greyson shuffled from one foot to the other. "So, you're living here all alone?"

"No, I have the children. They're away with their grandparents for the weekend, but they're living with me, not with Cameron."

"Well, this is a hell of a note."

Greyson looked around, feeling relaxed and no longer in a hurry to find Cameron. He swung out his arm toward a chair and watched first as Bridget nodded her okay and then let his eyes take in the rest of her. When his gaze returned to her face, he could see she was nervous and looked elsewhere while she sat down on the sofa. He cleared his throat and casually asked, "So, what do you do with yourself?"

"Oh, I manage to keep busy."

Bridget was not comfortable with how this conversation was going. "I figured that while the children were occupied, I would get some cleaning and shopping done." She paused. "Oh, yes, and I have some baking to do."

"Baking?"

"Yes, I bake… I have a pastry business."

Cautiously Greyson said, "Well, it's Saturday. You should just take it easy. I am sure this was not a shock to you; what with him leaving, but it will not do you any good to work yourself to death. I wouldn't mind spending time with you."

"Spending time with me? I never felt once that you liked being around me Greyson."

"You were… I mean, you were with my business partner. That would not have been Kosher," he said, smiling widely as he said it.

To his surprise Bridget laughed. Not sure why, but glad she had not taken it in the wrong way, he laughed too.

Bridget felt a little tingle, as well as some perplexity that this man, who had never taken the slightest interest in her before, should begin making advances the moment he found out her husband had left her.

“Well don’t fear, little lady, Greyson is here.” From there the conversation took on an intimate sense and a need to feel wanted weld inside her and she replied flirtatiously. Even while they engaged in this sensual conversation, she knew it was wrong, but it made her feel giddy knowing he found her attractive. Presently he sighed, “I’m busy tonight, but look.”

"Yes?"

“What are you doing tomorrow night?”

It shocked her, hearing the words coming out her mouth. “Why, nothing that I know of.”

“Well then?”

Suddenly she felt shy about the whole thing, but she wanted the attention. “I don't know why not.”

He got up and she followed suit. “Then it's a date. That is what we will do. We'll step out.”

Bridget smiled sheepishly. “If I haven't forgotten how to have fun.”

“Oh, you'll know how,” he said, his eyes saying much more as he continued. “When?”

“Half past six, maybe?”

“That suits me fine.”

“Oh wait, Make it seven.”

"Seven o'clock it is, then."

CHAPTER 5

Around noon the next day, while Bridget was watching the kitchen television and folding the laundry, Mrs. Steele knocked gently and without invitation, entered through the kitchen door.

"Hi, Bridget. I came to invite you to a party tonight."

Bridget lowered the sound on the television and turned to face her friend.

If there was anyone more observant than Lucy Steele, Bridge did not want to meet them as her friend said, "What's going on with you? You look guilty my friend." Moving in a little closer she added, "So, tell me, what's up."

Being a grown woman, whose husband had left her should have been enough to remove any shame, but Bridget was not used to the situation and could not help feeling guilty. She attempted a smile of confidence, but knew it was not up to par, so she blurted out, "I have a date." She took a deep breath. "I have a date and can't come to your party."

Lucy stared in astonishment. "A date? Gees, aren't you the fast mover."

"I've got to do something besides sit around and feel sorry for myself."

"Do I know him?"

"Greyson Hobbs."

"Greyson, I see." Lucy paused thinking then said, "Well, bring him."

There was something about the way Lucy responded that put Bridget on edge, but no matter. The one thing she had learned long ago was that the worst poison to a relationship was to allow a friend to interfere before giving it a chance. Bridget did not inquire, and Lucy did not explain. "I'll see what his plans are."

Lucy fingered a napkin on the counter as she moved closer to her friend, trying to find the words to say what she wondered in the nicest way possible. Finally, she blurted out, "I didn't know he was interested in you."

"Neither did I Lucy. I do not think he was. I did not think he'd ever looked at me. But the second he heard Cameron was gone, well it was almost funny the effect it had on him. You could see him get excited.

"Well, that explains it. You are an innocent. The second he realized that shall we say, your image changed. In his eyes you were no longer a wife and mother, but a young breathtaking and available woman.

"Oh, come on Lucy, really." Bridget laughed.

"Stop laughing. I am serious.

"You're serious?"

"I am. And they are. Let me explain something to you baby girl. There are several types of women who scare men away. First there is the control freak who must regulate his every thought and desire. Then there is the woman who wants a superhero to take charge and solve her problems. Then there is the tease who can be interesting at first, but that gets old fast." Lucy paused as she walked even closer to her friend. "Then there is the type of women who tracks the money, working the relationship like a business. Just as annoying is the woman who constantly cares about her man: how he is feeling, what he wants to wear, what he wants to eat, and so on. And finally, there is the one who wants to be adored and loved. Her life is a pedestal, and next to her there must be servants. The thing is, she cares less about love than she does about being adored and put on a pedestal."

Bridget looked at her friend with amazement. "I know you have more experience than I do, but none of those seem bad."

"They're not. But it is not what a man is looking for, in shall we say, a casual relationship."

"So, what type of woman is a man interested in, Lucy."

"You mean what behavior in a woman? It is a strange question, because every woman thinks she is a great actor who can be anything. Only that role becomes your daily behavior. Women want to please men, but do not understand that they can exaggerate their abilities."

Bridget was confused now as she could not perceive Lucy's reasoning. "Okay, so it's everything in moderation."

"Not exactly, its every man will see a woman's actions differently and the one type that attracts them instantly is the innocent one. The one who has not learned how to play the game. But if you want to keep them interested, let them explain their behaviors first before you decide what they mean. It is safer that way. All you have to do is play the game and follow his lead so that both are on the same page."

Bridget pondered the advice for some time while Mrs. Steele made her way to the Keurig and poured herself a cup. Presently she asked, "Is Greyson married?"

"Why, not that I know of." Bridget gave it some thought, then said, "No, of course he's not. He was always bragging about how lucky the married ones were on income tax day."

"Why is that… never mind." Lucy then said, "Maybe you shouldn't bring him over."

A little shocked, Bridget replied, "Well, as you like."

Worried her friend was taking it the wrong way, Lucy explained. "Oh, it's not that he's not welcomed, as far as that goes. But the party is for business friends of Ashton's, who are not married and are all right guys, trying to make a living same as anybody else. They are all about having fun and not looking for anything serious and I think you should be on that same wavelength; at least to start."

“Do you think I'm taking Greyson seriously?”

“You ought to be if you're not. He is fine, upstanding, viewed as a decent man, with good looks and you think he is single. More importantly, he has a good job and can show you a good time.”

“I don't think he'd be shocked at your party.”

“I didn’t say that. It is not a question of whether he would be shocked at my party, it's a question of the impression you make. What are his plans, as far as you know them?”

“Lucy, the man just asked me out to dinner.”

“When?”

“Seven tonight.”

Bridget watched the expression on her friend’s face turn to horror.

“What? What is it?”

“That's mistake number one, baby. That puts you in his debt. Instead, I'd sit him right down and fix dinner for him here.”

“What? Me work when he's willing to…”

“As an investment, baby, an investment in time. Now shut up and let me talk. Before I start, let me say I am paying and supplying whatever is needed for your date.” Seeing Bridget’s puzzled expression, she said, “I've become inspired. So just listen. It's going to be a perfectly terrible evening, weatherwise.” She waved a hand at the window, which had turned gray, cold, and overcast, as it usually does at the peak of a Rochester spring. “It won't be a fit night out for man nor beast.”

“Just the same, that was his idea.”

"Not so fast, baby, let us pause and examine that idea, Why would he want to take you out? Why do they ever want to take us out? As a compliment to us, they say. To show us a good time, to prove the high regard they have for us."

Lucy pauses. "Baby, they're a pack of goddam liars. In addition to being dirty bastards, they are also goddam liars. There is practically nothing can be said in favor of them, except they are the only ones we have. They take us out so they can get a drink. Secondly, so we can get a drink, and succumb to their designs after we get home, but mainly so you will feel obligated."

"No, I don't think…"

"Listen Bridge, he knows your husband and he has met you before. What he knows is what he is working with now. So, you turn the tides, and he is confused, and you are now on equal ground." Lucy could see she had reached Bridget and cautiously added, "Listen, I know things are tight and all this is my idea so like I said, I will supply what you need."

Before Bridget could protest, Lucy ducked out the screen door and ran across the back yards. Bridget returned to folding her laundry. When she folded the last piece, Lucy returned with a basket, grinning from ear to ear. She sat the basket on the counter and pulled the contents out, talking as she did so.

"This is gin and scotch. All the gin needs is a little orange juice, and it will make a swell cocktail, but whether he asks for gin or for scotch, be sure you cut it down plenty with ice. Now this other, is the wine and it is not top shelf, but will do fine. I brought you both red and white. I suggest you lean on the wine more than the gin and scotch."

Seeing that Bridget was getting ready to interrupt, Lucy raised a finger to quiet her. "That's the trick, baby. Offer the wine first and the high-priced hard stuff last. Fill him up on it as much as he wants because the more, he drinks of that, the less he'll want of Scotch." She pauses and pulls out the rest. "Here's three extra reds and white wines, just because I love you, and if things don't go as you want, you might need a few drinks later."

Lucy worked her way beside Bridget and put an arm around her. "With fish, chicken and turkey, give him white, and with red meat, give him red." Lucy again pauses, a puzzled expression on her face. "What are you having tonight?"

"Who says I'm having anything?"

"Now listen, have we got to go all over that? Baby, baby, you go out with him, and he buys you a dinner, and you get a little tight, and you come home, and something happens, and then what?"

"Don't worry. Nothing will happen."

"Oh, something'll happen. If not tonight, then some other night. Because if it does not happen, he will lose interest, and quit coming around, and you would not like that because I can see you are flattered, but more than that, you are already interested in this man. Once you get a taste that there is still a life for you, you will not want to lose it and besides, the more you like him, the more you want more. It's a part of us, just like it's a part of them, only not so much as it is with them."

"Goodness Lucy, it's just our first date… our first. Besides, it has been a long time since I have been with a man, any man."

Lucy thought a bit and said, "You need to think about yourself, and also your children." Again, Bridget starts to interrupt, and Lucy holds up her finger.

"I'm being perfectly honest and open here. Things are tough all around. People are low on cash… maybe not as low on cash as you are, but low anyway. So, you need to help yourself and this is the way to do it. You cook him an innocent home meal and offer him wine and he will see you in another light than a soon to be divorcee. He will see you as a woman. He will then make up his mind to see you again and just as you know things are tight, he knows it too and will want to help. This will move things along quicker before your financial situation becomes embarrassing and scares him away."

Lucy has a look of defiance as she continues. "Listen to me Bridget, you play it right, and inside of a week your financial situation will be greatly eased, and inside of a month you'll have him begging for the chance to help you get a divorce. Setting the stage for a home life with a beautiful woman like you, will interest this man Greyson more than having someone on his arm when he goes out."

"You think I want to be kept?"

"I wouldn't say it that way, but Yes."

CHAPTER 6

For a while after that, Bridget did not think of Greyson. After Mrs. Steele left, she went to her room and wrote a few letters, one in particular to her mother, explaining that Cameron was no longer living in the house and she had a lot on her plate to deal with. She clarified by saying she had to keep baking pastries if she wanted to survive the new phase her life had entered. When she finished writing the letters, she was surprised to see that it was almost four o'clock.

Bridget stood and stretched as she stared out the window. It had started to rain. She laughed. It was as if Lucy had magical powers. Shaking her head side to side, she headed to the kitchen.

She stood there a moment checking out her supplies. She had oranges, vegetables, and chicken. There were lots of spices and pastry supplies. Bridget stood tapping a gingerroot against her chin as the menu began to form in her head.

She moved aside the milk in the fridge and saw she had a container of whipping cream. That made her smile. Soon she was off to the races.

Humming she turned on the oven and began making pie crust and pressing it firmly into the pan before going to the pantry to retrieve a can of apple pie filling. She poured the filling into a bowl and added her special touches before filling the pie crust and carefully putting on the top layer which she decorated with cute little leaves around the vent opening she cut into the top. When the edges were pressed to perfection, she put it into the oven.

While that was baking, she stuffed the chicken and put the white wine into the fridge to chill.

Around five, she took the pie out of the oven. Her pie was perfect and cooling on the counter and the fixings for the whip cream were assembled. Around six she laid a fire, feeling a little tinge that most of the wood consisted of the dead limbs Cameron had sawed off the oak trees the afternoon he left. That feeling evaporated fast when she heard herself say, “Serves him right.”

She did not build the fire in the living room. She built it in the den, which was on the other side of the chimney from the living room and had a small fireplace of its own. It was really supposed to be one of the three bedrooms in the house and had its own bathroom, but she had fixed it up with a sofa, comfortable chairs, and photographs of the banquets Cameron had spoken at, and it was here that they had done most of their entertaining.

The fire ready to light, she went to the bedroom. She climbed into the shower and washed her body and her hair. When she stepped out, she dried herself and wrapped her hair in a towel while she put on her deodorant and lotioned her body.

The bathroom was warm and felt warmer as she blew dry her hair. Using the curling iron, she gave it just a little lift before she began putting on her makeup. She chose a printed dress, put on a pair of pantyhose, and slipped her feet into a pair of simple pumps. Then, after surveying herself in the mirror, admiring her legs, and remembering to bend the right knee, she went to the den. Around ten minutes to seven she went around closing the blinds and turned on several lamps.

Around ten after seven, Greyson rang the bell, apologetic for being late, anxious to get started. For one long moment Bridget was tempted, by the chance to go somewhere, to sit under soft lights, perhaps even to hear music but her mouth seemed to step out in front of her and take charge in a somewhat gabby way. “Well, my goodness, I never even dreamed you'd want to go out on a night like this.”

“Isn't that what we said?”

“But it's so awful out. It has been so cold and dreary and when I saw it was raining, I decided it would be better if I fixed us something here and we could go out, some other night?”

“But I wanted to take you out.”

Anticipating this reaction, Bridget, with conviction said, “All right, but at least let's wait a few minutes, for this rain to let up a little. I just hate to go out when it is coming down like this."

She led him to the den, lit the fire, took his coat, and disappeared with it. When she came back, she was balancing a tray on which were two glasses and a pitcher of orange blossom cocktail. She had settled on making this after reading that compared to other classic cocktails like the martini, these orange blossoms were quite light, and the sweet vermouth took some of the acidity out of the drink. It was a nice surprise and when it all came together, it was a very pleasant drink.

"Well say, that's nice."

"Thought it might help pass the time."

"You bet it will."

He took his glass, waited for her to take hers, and said, "Here's to us," and sipped. Bridget was startled at how good it was. As for Greyson, he was downright reverent at praising her. "What do you know about that? It's made perfectly." He took another sip. "How did you learn to make drinks?"

It was quite simple really, Bridge thought. 3/4-ounce gin, 3/4-ounce sweet vermouth, 3/4-ounce orange juice. Easy peasy.

"Oh, just picked it up."

"Not from Cameron."

"I didn't say where."

"Cameron's drinks were God awful. He was one of these home laboratory guys and the more stuff he put in it to make it his own, the worse it tasted."

Suddenly Bridget, not wanting to appear accomplished on making drinks, said, “Well, if I must be honest, I looked it up on the internet.”

“Looked what up?”

“How to make this drink,” she said as she refilled his glass.

She could see that he liked her honesty. When Bridget sat the pitcher down, he looked at her admiringly as he thanked her for the refill. “I couldn’t say no to another one of these. It’s perfect.”

He watched as she took her seat. “Aren’t you going to have another?”

Bridget not much of a drinker under any circumstances, had decided that she needed to be cautious. She had the rest of the evening to get through. She smiled sweetly and shook her head. “Oh, one’s all I have.”

“Don’t you like it?”

“I like it all right, but I’m really not used to drinking.”

“You’ve got to get educated.”

“I know that, but we can attend to that part a little bit at a time. Tonight, the rest of it is all yours.”

He laughed excitedly, strolled over to the window, and stood looking out at the rain. “You know, I’m thinking about something. Maybe you were right about not going out. There’s something about rain when it’s cold that seems to take the spirit out of the evening.” He turned around to face her. “Did you really mean it, what you said about making something for dinner?”

“Of course, I meant it.”

Greyson's forehead wrinkled. "It feels like I'm putting you to one hell of a lot of trouble, though."

"Don't be silly, it's no trouble at all. And I bet you get a better meal here than you would at any restaurant. That is something you might have noticed, all the time you have been coming here. I am a wonderful cook.

The wrinkles on Greyson's forehead deepened. "Quit kidding me. That was the hired girl."

"No, that was me. To prove it, I invite you into the kitchen to watch…that's if you want to watch."

"I sure do."

Then follow me, Mr. Hobbs."

Greyson picked up his drink and trailed behind her. In the kitchen she pointed to the breakfast stools at the island, and he took a seat. Here he could watch her every move as she turned on the oven and while it was heating, went to the fridge and removed a chicken. She melted some butter in the microwave and brushed it all over the bird. When the buzzer on the stove went off, she expertly opened the oven, slid in the chicken, and quickly shut the door so as not to let out too much heat. Lastly, she set the oven timer.

That done she wrapped the potatoes in foil, keeping the top open and popped them into the oven with the chicken, then pulled out a strainer that contained peas. She brought that over to the counter. "Here, help me shell these."

Watching her, he easily managed the feat and with then both

shelling in no time the job was done. She put them into a pan with seasoning and sat the pan on a cold burner.

"That's it for now. Let's go back to the den."

If there was one thing she had learned from Cameron, it was men liked to talk about themselves. "So, Greyson, tell me about your job with Bitmore Homes."

Greyson did not need any further encouragement. He was off and running. Living in a materialistic world he, like most working people liked to celebrate his success at every opportunity. He knew well how to put a positive spin on his position and make the job sound exciting.

Bridget listened intently but had to interrupt. "Sorry Greyson hold that thought. I need to put the vegetables on to boil." She stood and paused to pick up the pitcher. "Here, let me pour you another cocktail."

Bridget was wearing a ruffled blue apron over her dress that she forgot to take off once dinner was prepped. When she leaned over to pour him another drink he said, "I sure would like to give those apron strings a pull."

"You better not."

"Why not?"

"I might tie it on you and put you to work."

"Unless you forgot, you have already."

Bridget smiled as she agreed. "Would you like to eat here? By the fire?"

"I'd love it."

Bridget went over and removed thinks off a small table sitting under the window. “If you can move that over by the fireplace for me, we can use it and those two chairs over by the wall.”

“No problem.”

She left him to it while she went to the kitchen and turned on the burner under the peas. That done, she pulled out the chicken to let it rest and removed some of the juices so she could make a sauce. While the sauce finished thickening, she removed a loaf of bread and placed it in a wicker breadbasket. Then took the butter, salt and pepper and placed them on the counter. She checked on the sauce and found it was ready so got out silverware, glassware, warmer plates, and napkins. These she put on a tray and carried into the den where she arranged them.

She smiled at Greyson then left to get the wine. Greyson had watched her set the table and when she headed for the kitchen, he followed behind her. “Well, this looks like a fancy dinner and I agree will probably taste better than one we could get at a restaurant.”

“I told you. Maybe you weren't listening.”

Greyson smiled. “From now on, I’m nothing but ears.”

Back in the kitchen she plated the food, wiping away any drips and carried them into the den.

The dinner was a success. The food was perfect, and the aroma of the chicken added to the homey feel. She poured them each a glass of white wine to drink with the dinner and as if part of the plan, the flames from the fireplace danced off their glasses.

Greyson was quiet as he kept his fork busy. She watched him as he ate and once, she was sure he was enjoying the meal, she started eating. As was always the case it took less time to eat than to prepare. Soon Greyson leaned back in his chair and raised his glass in a toast to her. “To Bridget who can cook as good as she looks.”

Bridget smiled demurely and clinked her glass against his. She gave them a few minutes to enjoy the wine then stood. “The meal isn’t over. I made dessert.”

“You’ve got to be kidding. I am so full I don’t know if I can eat another bite.”

“Well, it’s freshly made apple pie, but we don’t have to eat it.”

Greyson’s face changed from that look of satisfaction to that of a child in a candy shop. “Oh, no, I’ll make room. Need help?”

“Thank you, yes. You can get the coffee while I plate the pie.”

Greyson laughed.

“What’s so funny.”

“Plate the pie. Most people say get the dessert, or cut the pie, but you say, plate the pie.”

“Well, if you must know, back in the day I worked in a restaurant which is where I learned that and much more.”

Bridget showed him to the Keurig and while he filled the cups, she ‘plated’ the pie. “Would you like ice cream or whip cream?”

"No, I want room for each bite. It smells wonderful, Bridget."

With her back to him as she picked up the plates, she allowed herself a smile of pride. Once seated at the table, Greyson immediately took a bite and them looked across at her. "This is unbelievably great. My mother use to made pies."

She could hear a sentimental tone to his voice as he talked between mouthfuls telling her about his mother and from there, he shared his history and Bridget listened attentively. With the meal over, Greyson stood and moved over to the sofa and insisted that she sit beside him. She did. He reached over and turned out the light on the end table and in the firelight, he put his arm around her. Bridget reached behind her to untie the apron, but he stopped her. "No, leave it on. I've grown used to it."

He squeezed her shoulder and Bridget lowered her head to his shoulder, but when he touched her hair with his fingers she got up. "I've got to take these things out to the kitchen."

Shocked by the turn of events, but still interested, Greyson shook it off and replied, "I'll put the table away for you."

"Thanks."

"Bridget, where's the bathroom?"

"It's right behind you. I'm going to clean up the dishes and then put on something a bit warmer."

"Wait a second, let me help you get these things to the kitchen."

"Well thank you, kind sir," she said playfully. Together they carried everything back to the kitchen in two trips. Greyson hung back to help put the food away and on the last trip they returned to the den where, Greyson smiled, pointed toward the bathroom door, and soon disappeared.

What with the rain, and the general clammy feel of the night, the print dress was becoming increasingly uncomfortable, despite how nice she looked. She went to the bedroom, slipped out of it, and hung it up in the closet. But when she reached for her dark blue woolen sweater, she heard a noise and swung around. He was standing in the door, a foolish grin on his face. “Thought you might need a little help.”

“I don't need help, and I didn't ask you in here.”

She spoke sharply, for her resentment at this invasion of her privacy was quick and real, plus animated by the fact she was standing behind the closet door in nothing but her panties and bra. That is at first. Her outburst was dramatic, and her elbow nudged the closet door, forcing it to swing open.

She heard Greyson catch his breath and whisper, “Wow.” The word flew pass his lips before he had a chance to stop it. Now as she stood embarrassed at her near nakedness, he was bewildered, and stood staring at her and at the same time trying not to look at her.

Clumsily Bridget took the woolen sweater off its hanger and slipped it over her head. Before she could adjust it, however, she felt his arms around her, heard him mumbling penitently in her ear. "I am sorry, Bridget. I am sorry as hell. But it did not play out like I figured it would. I swear to God, I came in here for nothing but to pull those apron strings. It was just a gag, that's all. Hell, you know I wouldn't pull any cheap tricks like that on you, don't you?" And as though to prove his contempt for all cheap tricks, he reached over and turned out the light.

Bridget's mood soften. She was no longer angry, just a little puzzled by this turn of events. She had not a clue what she wanted to do now as her thoughts jumbled incoherently.

Greyson felt his self-control fading. All he sensed or felt was her and he was lost to himself. He heard himself gasp in wonder as his fingers squeezed her soft skin, pulling her closer. Stunned, Bridget was just as confused as she felt her body respond to his. She looked up into his face and felt herself get wet with excitement.

Muscles trembling, Greyson managed to move them over to the bed and brace her as he lowered her down. Then, like two teenagers, they ripped at their clothes, no longer wanting to keep anything between their bodies. They moved in unison from the minute he entered her, feverishly pressing deeper and deeper until finally they both released their passion.

It was over, but instead of talking, they seemed to avoid any contact. They must have slept because Bridget abruptly opened her eyes when she felt the bed move. She turned her body over toward the other side of the bed and saw Greyson leaning against the headboard. Feeling her body heat rise, she thoughtlessly kicked off the covers, and felt the coolness of the air as it flowed around her naked body.

Her movement forced the covers to fall off Greyson and she watched as he reached down and pulled the covers back over him.

He was silently ostentatiously glum as he stared into the darkness of the bedroom. The shyness she felt before was now gone and Bridget managed to say, “Penny for your thoughts.”

Without changing his posture, he replied, "I'm thinking about Cameron.”

Greyson had had his fun, and now he was getting ready to get out from under. She waited a moment or two, tried to sound casual as she asked, “And what about Cameron?”

Greyson turned his head slightly. “I think you know.”

Bridget retorted. “If Cameron left me, and he's out of my life, why do you have to do all this thinking about him, when nobody else is?”

“We're good friends. Incredibly good friends.”

“But not so good that you wouldn't block him from getting a job he was entitled to have. You played all the politics you knew how, to get it for yourself.”

“Bridget, you don’t understand.”

“Yes, I do you double crossed your so-called friend and I don’t like that.”

“I don't care whether you like it or not. It was their choice.”

“Oh yes, at least a dozen people came to Cameron, and warned him what you were doing, and begged him to go down and put his claim in, and he wouldn't do it, because he didn't think it was respectable. And then he found out what was appropriate at the same time he learned what a pal you were."

"Bridget, I give you my word…"

"And what's that worth?"

Things between them had taken an evil turn. She jumped out of bed and began marching around the dark room, bitterly reliving the history of Bitmore Homes, the incidents of the crash, and the results that put a wedge in her marriage.

Greyson started a slow, solemn denial.

There was no way back from the path she had taken. "Why don't you tell the truth? You have had all you wanted of me, haven't you? A drink, a dinner, and other things I would prefer not to mention. And now you want to leave so you start talking about Cameron. Funny you didn't think about Cameron when you came in here, wanting to pull those apron strings, You remember them, don't you?"

"I didn't hear you saying no."

"No, I was an idiot."

She drew breath to say he was just like the rest of them, and then add Lucy Steele's flowerful phrase, 'the dirty bastards', but somehow the words didn't come. There was some core of honesty within her that could not quite accept Lucy's interpretations of life; however, they might amuse her now. She did not really believe they were dirty bastards, and she admittedly had set a trap for Greyson. If he were wriggling out of it the best way, he could there was no sense in blaming him for things that were rapidly becoming, too much for her. Despairingly she said, I am sorry,

Greyson.

"Hell, that's all right."

"It's just that I've been upset lately."

"Who wouldn't be?"

Bridget watched as Greyson got dressed and wrapping herself in the bed sheet, she stood and walked with him to the door.

"Be sure to lock the door behind me?"

"I will"

Greyson leaned over and kissed her on the cheek. And that is how the evening ended.

The next morning, Bridget was glumly rinsing the dishes and putting them into the dishwasher when Mrs. Steele tapped lightly on the kitchen door and then invited herself in.

"Coffee?"

"Yes, thank you. Bridget you missed a great party. It's just what the doctor ordered."

"Oh, I'm glad it all went well," Bridget said as she stood on the other side of the island, sipping her coffee, and giving Lucy her undivided attention.

Lucy gave her a rundown of the highlights of the evening and when she was done, she picked up her cup, rinsed it out and started to put it into the dishwasher. Seeing the extra dishes reminded her that Bridget had her own evening.

"So, Bridget, I see you took my advice," she said pointing at the dishwasher."

"I did."

"Tell me everything."

Bridget trusted Lucy and shared every detail of the evening, even the point where it all turned around.

"Lucy."

"Yes?"

"I thought we had shared something meaningful until he played his get out of jail card."

"Well, you don't mean he actually left the money on the bureau, do you?"

"All but."

Mrs. Steele sat at the island. When she looked up Bridget saw a look of puzzlement on her face. There did not seem to be much to say. It had all seemed so pat, so simple yesterday, but neither of them had played the scenario to the end, beyond dinner and drinks. A wave of helpless rage set over Bridget. She picked up the empty wine bottle, heaved it into the pantry, laughed wildly as it smashed into a hundred pieces.

CHAPTER 7

Bridget knew she had to get a job. There came another little burst of orders for cakes and pies, and she filled them, but all the time she was thinking, in a sick, frightened kind of way, of something she could do, some work she could get, so she could have an income, and not be put out of the house when she could not pay the interest due on the mortgages Cameron had put on the property.

While the children were at school, she studied the help wanted advertisements in the paper and on the internet, but there were hardly any that would pay what she needed to survive. There were notices for cooks, maids, and chauffeurs, but she skipped quickly by them. Next, she read the ones under the headings of "Opportunity," "Salesmen Wanted," and these she passed over entirely. But occasionally something looked promising and today was one of those days. It read, "Woman, young, pleasing appearance and manners, for special work." She answered it.

Each day she checked her email, anxiously hoping to see a reply and was excited a day or two later when she got a response, sent by a man, asking her to meet him at an address in Webster. She put on a print blouse with her best suit, made up her face and went into the garage where her car sat. She had not driven it in forever because she could not afford to waste money on gas or repairs. But this was important, so she climbed in and using her GPS, found her way to the address.

She checked her face in the mirror before stepping out of the car. She walked slowly up to the front door and adjusted her jacket before pressing the doorbell. When the door opened, she smiled sweetly.

Inside the doorway a man stood wearing a sweatshirt and jeans. He stepped aside to let her in. He guided her to a seat, and all the time she felt his eyes on her.

"So, Miss..."

"M…" she started to say, Mrs. but stopped. "It's Bridget, call me Bridget."

"Okay, Bridget, I am a writer." From that point he prattled on saying nothing about what he wrote. He was quite vague, though he said his research was extensive, and called him to many different parts of the world, where, of course, she would be expected to travel with him.

Bridget smiled, but in her head she thought, strike one. There was no way she could leave her kids and travel, but she still thought she might figure out something satisfactory to them both.

He was equally vague about her duties. So, she listened and mentally surmised that she would help him collect material, file documents, and verify citations. That sounded doable on her part and she nodded. It was then he added that she would take charge of his house, dress seductively, and follow his directions. If she could do all that and keep the clients coming, she could easily make a couple thousand a week.

Bridget tried not to show her astonishment as it dawned on her what the job really was. She started shaking and could not stop. It would solve her money problems for sure, but she was not that desperate. Following her instincts, she quickly got up from the chair and headed toward the door.

"Don't you want the job."

Bridget shook her head and hurriedly pressed the door handle latch. Soon she was standing on the stoop, trying to stop shaking. The ad, nor his email had mentioned the salary or the details so she couldn't have known. What angered her more was that she had wasted an afternoon and wasted gas.

It was her first experience with the escort service advertiser, though she was to find out it was fairly common. Not wanting to have it happen again, she did her research and found out that usually they used a ploy, calling themselves a writer, an agent, or a talent scout who had found out that for a cheap online ad he could have a daylong procession of girls at his door, all desperate for work, all willing to do almost anything to get it.

Cautiously, Bridget answered more ads, got repeated requests to call, and did call until her body and her shoes began to show the strain. She began to feel a bitter resentment against Cameron, for leaving her when nothing came of the ad answering. She would be too late, or not qualified, or disqualified on account of the children, or unsuitable in one way or another.

She made the rounds of the department stores and became dismally familiar with the crowd of silent people in the hallway outside the personnel offices, and the tense desperate jockeying for position when the doors opened at ten o clock. At only one store was she permitted to fill out a card. This was at Sears and she was first through the door, and quickly sat down at one of the little glass topped tables reserved for interviews. But the head of the department, addressed by everybody as Mrs. Boole, kept passing her by.

Bridget grew furious at this injustice. Mrs. Boole was rather good looking and seemed to know most of the applicants by name. Bridget was so resentful that they should be dealt with ahead of her that she suddenly gathered up her purse and started to flounce out without being interviewed at all. But Mrs. Boole held up a finger, smiled, and came over. “Don't go. I am sorry to keep you waiting, but most of these people are old friends, and it seems a pity not to let them know at once, so they can call at the other stores, and perhaps have a little luck. That is why I always talk to new applicants last.

Bridget sat down again, ashamed of her petulant dash for the door. When Mrs. Boole finally came over, she began to talk, and instead of answering questions in a tight-lipped defensive way, as she had at other places, opened up a little. She alluded briefly to the breakup of her marriage, stressed her familiarity with all things having to do with kitchens, and said she was sure she could be useful in that department, as salesperson, demonstrating or both.

She felt comfortable with Mrs. Boole and felt if she did not have a job, at least she had not alienated the woman. Mrs. Boole smiled at her and said, "There's nothing open right now, but I'll remember what you said about the kitchenware, and if anything comes up, I'll know where to get hold of you."

Bridget left happy to have been given a chance to interview and suggest her skills. She was halfway down the hall before she heard her name being called. Mrs. Boole was standing in the hallway and came toward her nervously. She took Bridget's hand, held it a moment or two while looking down at the street below. "Mrs. Bitmore, there's something I've got to tell you."

"Yes?"

"There aren't any jobs."

"Well, I knew things were tight, but…"

"Listen to me, Mrs. Bitmore, I wouldn't say this to just anybody, but you seem different from most of the applicants that come in here. I do not want you to go home thinking there is any hope. There is not. In this store, we've taken on just two people in the last three months and those were to replace two people who left."

"But why…" Bridget started to ask.

"We see everybody that comes in, partly because we think we ought to, partly because we want to have possible applicants on file to fill positions when and if they open. There just are not any jobs, here or in the other stores either. I know I'm making you feel bad, but I don't want you to be hoodwinked."

Bridget patted her arm and smiled. "Well, my goodness, it's not your fault. I think I knew that, but when you do have something…"

"Oh, don't worry. I will call or email you. And, if you are down this way, will you drop in to see me? We could have lunch."

"I would be only too glad to."

Mrs. Boole hugged her, and Bridget left, feeling strangely happy. When she got home there was a notice hanging on the door, asking her to call a number.

At first, Bridget was afraid it was to notify her she was being evicted and was not going to make the call, but then something told her to make the call anyway.

She dialed the number. A familiar voice answered, "Mrs. Bitmore, it was like something in a movie. You had hardly stepped into the elevator, honestly. In fact, I had you paged downstairs, hoping you hadn't left the store."

"Oh, Mrs. Boole. What is it Mrs. Boole?"

"Can you come back to the store?"

"When?"

"If it's not inconvenient, right now."

"I'm on my way."

Bridget shut the door and made sure it locked before going back down the sidewalk and climbing into her car. She knew that it had to be important. Mrs. Boole knew her situation and would not make the request for nothing. Bridget drove feeling hopeful this was going to be her last interview.

At the store, she introduced herself and was shown to Mrs. Boole's private office this time. She thanked the guard and walked in. Mrs. Boole sat behind her desk, and Bridget sat in the chair beside it. Mrs. Boole began immediately, "I was watching you step into the elevator when this call came from the restaurant."

"You mean the store restaurant?"

"Yes, the tearoom on the roof. Of course, the store does not have anything to do with that. It is sublet, but the manager likes to take people from our lists, just the same. He feels it makes it easier for him since we do a lot of checking before we place a name in our file. He figures he gets a better class of people this way."

"And what is the job?"

Bridget's mind was leaping wildly from cashier to hostess to dietician. She did not quite know what a dietician was, but she felt she could fill the bill. Mrs. Boole answered at once, "Oh, nothing overly exciting. One of his waitresses got married, and he wants somebody to take her place. They supply a uniform so you won't have to worry about messing up your clothes."

Mrs. Boole had a faint smile on her face as she added, "It's a job and not a career but those women do very well for a four-hour day; they're only busy at lunch, of course and it would give you plenty of time with your own children, and home."

The idea of putting on a uniform, carrying a tray, and making her living from tips made Bridget positively ill. She ran her tongue around inside her mouth to keep herself under control. "Why, thanks ever so much, Mrs. Boole. I realize, of course, that it's quite a nice opening, but I doubt if I'm really fitted for it."

"Mrs. Boole's face turned red as she sucked in her breath before uttering a word. "Well, I'm sorry, Mrs. Bitmore, if I got you down here for nothing. I know the name, Bitmore, but still somehow got the idea that you wanted work."

"I do, Mrs. Boole, but…"

"No worries, it's perfectly all right, my dear."

Mrs. Boole was standing now, and Bridget was edging toward the door, her face feeling hot. Then she was in the elevator again. By the time she was out on the street, she hated herself, and felt that Mrs. Boole must hate her too. She probably thought her a fool. Silently she whispered, "Well I guess I won't be asked to join her for lunch…"

As she drove home, Bridget realized that she could not do this on her own, she needed to register with an employment agency so that she did not waste time. As soon as she was in the door, she went to her office and turned on the computer. She spent hours searching for a good agency that fit her interest. To decide which agency, she consulted the internet and unlike jobs, there were lots of agencies and lots of information about their success rate in finding jobs. She carefully explored their websites and settled on Superior Group as it had been in business for some time and offered a range of positions that interested her. Located in Corporate Woods, she called and made an appointment. She was to meet with a Miss Turner.

On her appointment day, Bridget dressed appropriately, and this time had a prepared resume that listed her skills. She had even watched a video on how to interview. She felt ready.

Superior Group had a suite of offices and the receptionist guided her to Miss Turner, who turned out to be a trim, little person, not much older than Bridget, and a little on the hardboiled side. With no pleasantries, she motioned Bridget to a chair at a small table in the office and Bridget walked over and sat down.

"Do you know how to use a computer?"

"Yes."

"Good. That makes it easier." The woman leaned over Bridget, pressed the space bar and a form appeared on the screen. Fill this out."

After that one initial direction, Miss Turner, turned and went back to her desk.

Bridget felt as though she had entered the twilight zone and was back in high school. Miss Turner, who never introduced herself or gave up her full name, now sat behind her desk as though monitoring her to make sure she did not cheat. It bothered Bridget at first, but then, she had not interviewed in years and so far, no one did it the same way. With a silent sigh she began.

Bridget surveyed the form. It seemed to her an absurd amount of information about herself from her age, weight, height, and nationality to her religion, education, and exact marital status. Most of these questions struck her as irrelevant, and some of them as impertinent. However, she answered them. When she came to the question: what type of work desired, she hesitated. What type of work did she desire? She leaned closer to the monitor as if the answer laid somewhere inside. She thought vigorously. Any work that would pay her something was what popped into her head, but obviously she could not say that. She wrote. 'Secretary'.

Then she came to the great yawning space in which she was to fill in the names and addresses of her former employers.

Regretfully she wrote, not previously employed. She felt doomed to failure as she sat looking at the computer screen, then noticed there was more information below. She scrolled down and read descriptions and requirements for positions and it came to her. One of the positions said she needed only a high school diploma or GED to qualify. That along with any skill inputting data into a computer met the qualifications for the position. It also said she might be able to work from home. Bridget took out her cell and found a description of the position.

Quickly she moved the cursor up to where she entered 'Secretary'. She highlighted the word and typed, 'Data Entry'. Then she clicked, 'Save'.

She stood up.

"Finished?"

"Yes."

"Come sit here." Miss Turner pointed to the chair by her desk and as she took a seat, she could tell that Miss Turner had the image of her form on her computer. Bridget sat quietly but felt confident as she waited.

"You haven't got a chance."

Bridget, shocked, not sure she heard correctly asked, "What did you say?"

"You heard me."

"Why not?"

"Do you know what data entry is?"

"Yes. Yes, I do. It's different from job to job, but basically its typing hard copy information into a computer program designed to organize the information in a way that's useful."

Miss Turner gave her a crooked smile that said it all. She had seen Bridget with her cell and she had recited what she found verbatim. Now Mrs. Turner looked at Bridget and felt she knew her. This woman needed a job, but she was without skills to earn a decent living. She was pretty and had a great figure so she would probably make it where she, Miss Turner had not. She did not have those additional physical qualifications for success. That realization was what hardened her.

"Yes but reading what it is and being able to do the work is totally different." She paused, plastering a smile on her face. "Well, I am going to be honest with you. I think you would be more successful at getting a job as a receptionist. All you would have to do is sit out front where everybody can watch you do it. You know, be the one that tells them to have a seat, and the manager will see you in just a few minutes. Beyond that you get to dress up and will probably have time to polish your nails. Salary is on a fluctuating scale of how much you want to keep the job."

Bridget could barely stay seated as one insult after the other came out of this woman's mouth. Miss Turner looked across the desk and saw her expression. "Forgive me, I'm sorry. I am having a bad day and you happened to enter it. You really do not have much in education and experience to land a data entry position. For that matter, Receptionists is a dying job position, so that may be out too."

Defiantly, Bridget stared directly at Miss Turner. "Receptionist isn't the only thing I can do."

Miss Turner looked at the screen again and then looked at Bridget. "Sorry, but yes, it is."

"You're not letting me tell you how I see my skills working for me."

"If there was something else you could do, you'd have put it down in great big letters. When you say data entry and have no education or experience, I cannot honestly send you out on interviews for that type of job. You have a better chance at a receptionist position, that is what I know. There is no more after that, and no use wasting my time, and me wasting yours. I'll file your application, but being totally honest, I'm telling you again, you haven't got a chance."

The interview, obviously, was ended, but Bridget's blood boiled and for all those who came after her she made a little speech, a sales talk. As she talked, she warmed up to it, explaining that she was married before she was seventeen, and that while other women were learning professions, she had been making a home, raising two children, not generally regarded as a disgraceful career. Now that her marriage had broken up, she wanted to know if it was fair that she be penalized for the course her life had taken and denied the right to earn her living like anybody else. Furthermore, she said, she had not been idle all that time, even if she had been married. She kept her house clean, furnished it on her own and worked hard at making pleasing meals. "Why I in fact am earning a little income selling bake good to my neighbors." She paused to take a breath and said, "If I can learn to do all that, I can learn to do other things." Again, she paused. "And, what I do, I do well."

Out of breath, she headed toward the door.

"Sit down, Miss Bitmore. You had your say, so let me."

Miss Turner moved across to the other side of the desk so that she was next to Bridget. She turned her monitor screen around and punched a few keys and the screen broke into small images of forms; each with a color check in the corner.

"I told you you're not qualified okay, you can look here and see what I mean. These are employers, people that call me when they need somebody. They call me because I level with them and save them the trouble of talking with people who are not qualified for the job. I sell people over this desk just like cattle and exactly for the same reason. I save my time by putting a color check on the side. It's a way of keeping an order since I need to save the records of everyone who walks through that door." Miss Turner looked at Bridget. "You can see there are a lot of applicants for jobs in my files so to save me time I look at the requirements from the employers and quickly can remove all ineligible people beyond the level of the position they are asking for by my additional notes and I match them up." Miss Turner zoomed into a form from an employer with a green check and then, press several keys and forms appeared on the screen with matching green checks.

"See those greens? That means 'No Married Women'."

Seeing Bridget about to speak she holds up her hand and continues. "It's not me, it's them," she said looking at the employer sheet and pointing to their requests. Bridget sees it says no married women.

"Why, may I ask?"

"Because right in the middle of rush hour you might get a call that your son has the flu, and out you run, and maybe you come back the next day and maybe you come back next week. These people, these employers, they are not much interested in your kid having the flu. And another thing that interest them less is the thought of a homemaker wanting spending cash and figuring she would earn some by taking a job. She becomes bored and quits and the employer has to start the hiring process all over."

"Do you call that fair?"

"I call them green. I go by the forms."

"Well, that's not me."

"Do you owe money?"

"Not your business."

Bridget thought guiltily of the interest that would be due July 1st, and Miss Turner, seeing the flicker in her eye, said, "Thought so."

"Miss Bitmore, there are positions with more applicants than jobs available and I've heard all the sob stories. There are stenographers with scientific experience, nurses, laboratory chemists, doctors whose private practice fell apart and now need positions in a hospital. There are men and woman with all kinds of impressive work experience and degrees that few can only dream of. Anyone of them could take charge of all the office work for a small firm."

Bridget watched as she presses keys and another group of

forms appear. “Here are salespeople, men and women, every one of them with an A1 reference which means they are superior at their job. They're all laid off since there's no goods moving.” With a look of sympathy she added, “I don't see how I could put you ahead of them. And here is a preferred list. Look at it, a whole file of men and women and every one of them a real executive, or auditor, or manager of some business. They are all home, sitting by their phones, hoping I will call. I will not call. I have nothing to tell them. What I am trying to get through your head is, You do not have a chance. Those people, it hurts me, it makes me lie awake nights, that I have nothing for them. They deserve something, and there is not a thing I can do. But there is not a chance I would slip you ahead of anyone of them. You're not qualified.”

Bridget was not sure exactly how she felt after that soulful rendition, but she asked the only question she had left to ask. “How do I qualify?”

Bridget's lips were fluttering as she tried desperately to still them and the tears threatening to spill from her eyes. Miss Turner looked quickly away, then said, “Can I make a suggestion?”

Keeping her voice steady she replied, “You certainly can.”

“I wouldn't call you a raving beauty, but you've got a great shape and you say you cook fine and keep a clean house. Why don't you forget about a job, find yourself a man and get married while you’re still young enough?”

“I tried that”, she lied.

"Didn't work?"

Bridget spun her tale. "I don't seem to be able to kid you much", irony apparent in her voice. "It was the first thing I thought of, and just for a little while I seemed to be doing all right. But then, I guess reality set in when he remembered I was a package deal with two little children. So, like no, something beyond my control disqualified me."

"He said that?"

"No, that wasn't what he said, but I knew it was the case."

"Hey, stop already. You're breaking my heart."

"I didn't know you had a heart."

"Neither did I, but it still doesn't matter."

She had tried. Miss Turner dismissed her, and Bridget found herself outside the building without a job. She believed the cold logic of Miss Turner's harangue and it flowed through her body making her knees go weak. Before she had thoroughly prepared herself for an interview, she felt less despondent, but now she had done her research and was properly prepared. How could it still end in disaster?

Bridget leaned on her car wondering what to do next, then steadily she walked around to the driver's side and slid behind the wheel. There she allowed the flood to begin. She cried until she could not cry anymore and then searching in her purse, took out a Kleenex and wiped her eyes and nose. In the silence of her car, she said to herself, "Careful my dear, you might have to sell this car and you don't want your DNA all over it." That somehow lightened her mood.

Bridget drove home and went straight to her bedroom to change and have another cry before her daughters came home. That evening she heated up a can of pork and beans and made biscuits for the children. This was a rock bottom meal, but her daughters loved it.

Talked out of feeling sorry for herself, the next day she doggedly registered at three more agencies. She took to doing desperate things in the meantime, like turning suddenly into business places, as she was passing them on the street, and asking if they had an opening which she imagined was the way it was done in the 80s or even 70s. Just like they did back then, she went into places near her home and ask to meet the owner or manager of the place. It worked at bars and restaurants, but not so much in other workplaces.

One day she entered an office building and beginning at the top floor, called on every firm. All the time the thought of July 1st haunted her, and she could no longer cover up her exhaustion with makeup. No matter what she put on, it looked frumpy as she had lost so much weight. She lived on oatmeal and bread, reserving for the children the eggs, and milk. She tried to expand her customer base to make more money, but there was one limiting factor. She was only one person.

One morning, to her surprise, there was a text on her phone from Miss Boole, asking her to come to her office that day at nine o'clock. That sounded urgent and urgent meant she had a job for her. Bridget stopped frosting a cake and ran into her bedroom to put on a fresh pair of slacks and a nice sweater. It took her about four minutes to complete her ensemble, put on some make up and smooth her hair. She quickly went to the garage and almost forgot to open the garage door before backing the car onto the street.

She drove carelessly, not checking her rearview mirror or slowing down much before stop signs or lights. She could not help it. What if she arrived too late and Miss Boole gave the job to someone else? What if… It just kept on coming until she pulled into the parking lot and hurried through the doors, waving herself by the receptionist without introduction. As if she had some magical powers, the elevator doors opened as if summoned and she climbed inside.

In the hall, she walked quickly, patting her hair, and trying her best to appear calm before she entered through Miss Boole's door and at the door, she took a deep breath before crossing the threshold. The first thing she saw was the clock. It was exactly nine o'clock. She plastered a smile on her face as she walked across the floor. Miss Boole waved her to a seat. "Something has come up."

"What is it?"

“Housekeeper.”

“Oh.”

“It's not what you think, so don't employ that tone of voice. I usually do not handle domestic help, but I was over in Pittsford the other night, and got talking with a lady that is going to marry a plastic surgeon, who does not have a staff to handle the house. She does not know how it is being done, but she is not going to be the workhorse. She wants a housekeeper. So, on account of all that domestic efficiency you were telling me about, I told her about you, and I think it's yours if you want it.”

Again, when Bridget started to speak, Miss Boole raised her hand. “Let me finish. You will have your own quarters and children are okay.” The pay is good, above what you would expect for a live in.”

“I hardly know what to say.”

“Make up your mind. I've got to let her know.”

“Why did you think of me, for this?”

“Didn't I tell you? You broke my goddam heart.”

“Yes, but it's the second time lately I've had an offer of this kind. Not long ago a lady offered me a job as a waitress.”

“And you turned it down?”

“I had to.”

“Why?”

“I can't go home and face my children if they know I've been working all day at taking tips, and wearing a uniform, and mopping up crumbs.”

"But you can face them with nothing for them to eat?"

"I'd rather not talk about that."

"Listen, Miss Bitmore, this is just one woman's opinion, and it may be all wrong. I have my own little business, and it is not very great. I am not rich, but I make ends meet. But if that goes, and I must choose between my stomach and my pride, I am telling you right now, I am picking my stomach every time. I mean, if I had to wear a uniform, I'd do it."

Miss Boole paused and finally decided to say what she was thinking. "Miss Bitmore, you have had it easy and have an image you want to protect. I understand that. Doing one of these menial jobs would be like starting over and might make your children think less of you. But whatever the reason, you need to let it go."

Bridget was quiet and when she spoke, she said, "I'll go over there, as a courtesy to you."

Miss Boole was annoyed and showed it. "What have I got to do with it? Either you want this job, or you don't. If you do not, just say so and I will call up and tell her. But if you do want it, for God's sake get over there and act like you mean it."

"I said I'll go, as a courtesy to you."

Miss Boole got out a card and fiercely wrote a note on it, her eyes snapping as she handed it over to Bridget.

"All right, you wanted to know why that lady offered you a job as waitress, and why I recommended you for this. It is because you have let your life slip by without learning anything but cooking, and setting the table, and now that is all you are good for.

So, get over there. It's what you've got to do, so you may as well start doing it."

That speech unnerved her, but she was determined to keep her word. She climbed into the car and turned on the ignition. Nothing happened. She tried again and had the same results. Shaken, Bridget got out and seeing a bus stop, she went over to it, making it just as the bus pulled up. Before climbing on, she asked it the bus went anywhere near 19 Sunset Blvd in Pittsford.

"Yes, Miss. If you take a seat up front, I'll let you know when to get off."

Bridget sat in the side bench where the driver could see her. She tried to relax, but she was too keyed up. She saw a sign that said Route 252, just as the bus pulled up to a stop. "Miss, this is where you get off. You need to walk up a little further and you will see the street you are looking for."

"Thank you. Where can I get a bus back?"

He pointed across the street.

"Thank you."

Bridget stepped out on a major highway that was unfamiliar to her, and where he let her off, there was no sign of the street, and she started wandering around an unfamiliar neighborhood, trying to get her bearings. The houses were big and forbidding, with driveways that went on a distance before the house, and lawns that were endless. She could not find the courage to approach such a dwelling without being invited.

Of pedestrians there were none, and she plodded around for the better part of an hour, peering at each street sign, losing all sense of direction in the winding streets. She got into a hysteria of rage at Cameron, for if he were a better man, he would have told her how to reach him and he could come and take her to the house instead of her wandering about with no one and no place to ask for directions. Then she remembered that Cameron had to sell his car.

All she could see was bare pavements and frowning trees. Finally, a laundry truck pulled up, and Bridget waved it to a stop. She asked if he knew where 19 Sunset Blvd was, and he did. "Climb in and I'll take you there."

Bridget stood at the stepwell of the van, holding on to the two handles at either side as he drove down the street. She saw the sign before he alerted her and she turned and thanked him, then carefully disembarked.

She stood in front of a French Country Mansion. It was well constructed of stone and stucco with a tiled roof and sat on over an acre of land. It was surrounded by a low stone wall. Bridget went up to the door and a man appeared. When she asked for Mrs. Witmore he bowed and stepped aside for her to enter. Then he noticed she had no car and froze. "Housekeeper?"

"Yes, I was sent by…"

"Go around back."

In one instant she was a welcomed guest and then dismissed as a servant as the man closed the door and she madly trudged around to the back. She searched and found a doorbell near the back entrance and pressed it. Shortly the door opened, and she was told to wait. She was in a foyer where she could see the kitchen where two women stood watching her. When she was about to address them, a man came and asked her to follow him. He took her pass wide doorways before light paneled rooms and beautiful furnishings until finally stopping at a small circular area that held a desk and several chairs. Here he stopped and told her to wait. All around her were shelves filled with books and she started over toward then when she heard someone enter. She turned to see a tall woman dressed in a long flowing dress and sat down in the nearest chair.

"Miss Bitmore."

"Yes."

"I received a call from Miss Boole and know all about you."

The way she said it, made Bridget uncomfortable, but she smiled sweetly.

Seeing the startled look behind the smile, Mrs. Witmore decided to encourage it. "First, my dear, Bridget you need to learn that it is customary to remain standing until told to sit."

Bridget had turned and taken a seat when she heard Mrs. Witmore enter. She shot up as though her legs were made of springs, her face hot, her mouth dry.

Holding back a smile, Mrs. Whitmore responded. "It's

perfectly all right, but on little things, especially with inexperienced woman, I find it necessary to begin at the beginning. Do sit down. We've many things to talk about, and it'll make me quite uncomfortable to have you standing there."

Suddenly feeling like a small child, Bridget obeyed.

"Bridget, sat down, while Mrs. Witmore spoke grandly of her plans for reorganizing the house. Apparently, it was her intended husband's house, and it would be hers in a couple of months after they got married. She went on to say that Bridget would have her own quarters, above the garage. She herself had two children by a former marriage so she liked children, though Bridget's children were not permitted to enter the main house under any circumstances. She rattled on but Bridget was no longer listening. She could not think of putting her children in a situation where they were being treated like servants. She could imagine what the grandparents would think or do. They would have excellent grounds to take the children from her. A surge of pride swept over her and Bridget stood up. "I don't think I'm the person you want here, Mrs. Witmore."

"The Mistress terminates the interview, Bridget." This was said in an angry voice and though she turned, Bridget kept walking. "Mrs. Bitmore, if you don't mind. I'm terminating this interview."

It was Mrs. Witmore's turn to shoot up as though her legs were made of springs, but if' she contemplated further instruction in the relation of the servant to the Mistress, she thought better of it. She found herself looking into Bridget's squint, and it flickered somewhat ominously. Pressing a button, she announced coldly, "I'll have Harris show you out."

“I'll find my way, thank you.”

Picking up her handbag, Bridget left the library, but instead of turning toward the kitchen, she marched straight for the front door, closing it calmly behind her. She floated to the bus stop on air, rode into Irondequoit without seeing what she was passing and at the first familiar sight, got off the bus. She knew instantly where she was and also realized she had quite a distance to walk before making it home.

When she reached East Ridge Road, everything began spinning around, and the sunshine seemed unnaturally bright. She knew she had to sit down, or topple over, right there on the sidewalk. Two or three doors away was a restaurant, and she hurried into it, It was crowded with people eating lunch, but she found a small table against the wall, and sat down.

After picking up the menu and dropping it quickly so the girl would not notice her trembling hands, she asked for a turkey sandwich, with lettuce and a glass of water. Bridget waited an interminable time for her sandwich. The girl puttered about, complained of the service that was demanded of her, and the little that she got for it, and Bridget had a vague suspicion that she was being accused of stealing a tip.

She was too near collapse for argument, however, and beyond

repeating that she wanted the water right away, said nothing. Presently her order arrived, and she sat apathetically munching it down, The water cleared her head, and the food revived her, but there was still a quivering in her bowels that did not seem to have anything to do with the walking, fretting, and quarreling she had done all morning. She felt gloomy indeed, and when she heard a resounding slap, a few inches from her ear, she barely turned her head. The girl who had served her was facing another girl, and even as Bridget looked, proceeded to deal out a second loud slap. “I caught you, you dirty little crook! I caught you red handed, right in the act!”

“Girls! Girls!”

“I caught her! She has been doing it right along, stealing tips off my tables! She stole a couple dollars off the table before that lady sat down, and now she stole a couple more right here and I seen her do it!”

In a moment, the place was like a beehive, with other girls shouting their accusations, while the hostess tried to restore order. Finally, the manager came flying out of the kitchen. He was a rotund little man, with flashing black eyes, and he summarily fired both girls and apologized profusely to the customers.

When the two of them sullenly paraded back to the kitchen, Bridget was so lost in her reflections that she did not fully catch what was happening. It was not until the hostess appeared in an apron, and began serving orders, that she woke up to the fact that she was faced with one of the major decisions of her life. They needed help, that was plain, and needed it now. She stared at the water glass, twisted her mouth into a final, irrevocable decision. She told herself she would not do this kind of work even if she was starving. She put a dollar on the table. She got up. She went to the cashier's desk and paid her check. Then, her body took charge as she turned around and headed for the kitchen.

CHAPTER 8

The next couple of hours, to Bridget, were a waking nightmare. She did not get the job quite as easily as she had supposed she would. The owner, whose name was apparently Hartalkar, but whom everybody addressed as Mr. Chris, was willing enough, especially as the hostess kept screeching in his ear, "You've got to put somebody on. It is chaos out there. It's a disaster about to turn into a major catastrophe."

These were the two on her side, but the girls had another objective in mind, not that they did not like Bridget, but that they liked Emily. So, they started a campaign by vetoing the decision to hire her, that is, unless Emily was taken back. "Emily was just defending what was hers and shouldn't be punished for that. It's so unfair."

Emily, she gathered must have been the girl who had waited on her, and the antagonist in the fight, but as all of them apparently had been victims of the thefts, they seemed to regard her as their representative in a sense and did not propose to have her made a sacrifice.

They argued their case in quite noisy fashion, letting the counters pile up with orders while they screamed, and made inappropriate gestures at Mr. Chris. Arms swung about recklessly with one sending a plate with a club sandwich in flight. Its weight becomes the force as it begins a journey in the air almost in tack as the toothpicks do their job. The results of what they had done was apparent on the faces as jaws dropped and eyes grew big as saucers. Only one person had her wits about her, and it was Bridget. Bridget caught it before it fell. The sandwich was entirely wrecked, but having respect for food, Bridget set the plate on the counter and with deft fingers she put it back together again, unaware that she was being watched.

The chef, a man of massive size stood watching the scene unfold. His chef hat hid his hair, and he resembled the stay fresh marshmallow man with his round face and black eyes. Bridget became aware of her audience when someone shouted their appraisal, “Wow, way to go new girl, huh Archie.”

Archie had watched the sandwich disaster unfolding with little emotion, but when the reconstructed sandwich was back on the counter, he was impressed and could not help but give her a curt nod. He then looked around the kitchen and began banging on the steam table with the palm of his hand.

The kitchen went silent. Archie turned toward Mr. Chris and

without saying a word, Mr. Chris turned to the girls. “Hokay, hokay.”

The question of Emily settled, a commotion began with one waitress hurrying to the back, yelling as she went, “Emily, hold up. You’re not fired… Emily.”

At the same time the hostess grabbed Bridget by the arm hustled her back to the lockers, where she unlocked a door and held out a menu. “Take off your dress and while I’m finding a uniform to fit, study this menu, so you can be of some use, that is if you want the job…” She turned and looking directly at Bridget she added, I assume you want the job.”

“Yes, I want the job.”

“What size do you wear?”

“Six.”

“Have you worked in a restaurant before?”

“No… I mean not lately. Not since high school, that is.”

“Right now, it doesn’t matter. Study the menu, especially the prices.”

Bridget took off her dress, hung it in the locker, and stared at the menu. The breakfast menu seemed standard with a few specialties that she scanned quickly. The prices started at $7.95 and if someone was going all out, Shrimp and grits for $12.95. Lunch offered Nachos at $10.95, Wings from $9.95 Chicken Tenders $9.95, Shrimp for $10.95 and Burgers starting at $9.95 and up to $11.95.

She started to ask about the ninety-five-cent ending on each price but kept quiet. Instead, she quickly reviewed the soups and salads and their prices before checking out the main courses that included chicken, steak, seafood, and pork; all reasonably priced in the $10.95 to $15.95 range. The Bar served most mixed drinks at $5.00 and beer at $3.00. Again, she paused wondering if she would have to make drinks as well. She almost laughed aloud when that thought came to her. "Better have a quick computer. Better be connected to the internet," she whispered under her breath trying not to smile.

The menu was basic, with all kinds of extras to be added along with fancy names. It seemed simple enough, but this woman, she wondered, could not be asking her to memorize the menu in its entirety. Not even a genius could do that, and she was not a genius.

In a minute or two the hostess was back with her uniform, a pale blue affair, with white collar, cuffs, and pockets. She slipped into it. "And here's your apron. This is your uniform, and you are expected to wear it every day, cleaned and pressed. You pay for the uniform and if you need another, you pay for that as well. The cost will come out of your first check."

"How much?"

"Fifteen dollars."

Bridget nodded, surprised that she liked the look and the feel of the uniform. That and after the scene earlier, glad she would not have to go home with food or food stains on her clothes.

"Okay, the pay is seventeen dollars an hour and you keep all your own tips."

Bridget started to ask were they not required by law to turn them in, but the hostess said. "You keeping them makes the bookkeeping job easier. Okay?"

Bridget nodded again.

"Any questions?"

"Just one."

"What is it?"

"What is your name?"

"Oh, sorry, its Ida. And yours?"

"Bridget…Bridget Bitmore."

They started for the dining room but going through the kitchen Ida kept talking. "I'm giving you a light station. Three, four, five, and six; all those little booths against the wall that hold two. Singles and twos are easier. All those that I bring over to your station now are your customers. Those you see seated and eating now are someone else's. I'll take care of them myself so there is no cross over on tips."

They reached the dining room and a waitress walked toward them. From earlier events, she knew this to be Emily. Emily discussed the customer situation in Bridget's newly assigned station. Three of the tables were occupied by customers who had given their orders before the fight started, the fourth by a pair of women who had just come in. All were getting annoyed at the delay in service, but still Bridget was not permitted to start.

Emily led her to the cashier, a blond-haired stern-faced woman who appeared to be in maybe her mid-fifties and thoroughly annoyed. Bridget hoped, that under different circumstances she might be pleasant but who now was ruthless as she spoke to Emily. "My job just got harder from all of that going on. I have enough to do with having to make sure the orders are written and paid for properly, in case you have forgotten…" she leaned forward dramatically, her large bosom demanding attention as she did so. "When I don't have customers, I am the one who has to sweep floors." She shifted her gaze to Bridget. "Thanks to you missy, it won't be as bad as it might have been."

She turned back to Emily telling her of the complaints she had received, and of the five people who had already walked out. Emily cut her off and told her to issue Bridget a new book. Then hearing the sharpness in her voice she turned **back** and said, "Ida, don't worry, it's all being taken care of so don't worry."

With a smirk, Ida turned back to Bridget and in a business-like manner informed her, "You've got to account for every check. In here you mark your number."

"What's my number?"

"You're No. 9." Holding the page so that Bridget could follow, she continued pointing to spaces. "Here you mark the number of the table, here the number of customers on the check. Down here, put down everything they order." She paused and stared sternly at Bridget. "And the first thing you got to learn is don't make no mistakes on a check. It's all booked against you, and if you make a mistake, its deducted, and you got to pay for it."

With this ominous warning in her ear, Bridget at last approached the two women who were waiting to have their orders taken, handed them their menus, and inquired what they were going to have. They replied they were not sure they were going to have anything and wanted to know what kind of place this was anyway, to let people sit around without even asking them if they minded waiting. Bridget, almost in hysteria by now with what she had been through that day, felt a hot impulse to take them down a few notches, as she had done with Mrs. Witmore. However, she managed a smile, said there had been a little trouble, and that if they could just be patient a minute or two, she would see they were served at once. Then, taking a quick lunge at the only thing she remembered about the menu, she added, "The roast chicken is awfully good today."

Slightly mollified, they calmed a little and nodded. They both ordered the chicken. Bridget started to walk away but one of them said loudly, "Wait Miss, I'm not done."

Bridget adjusted her face and turned back around. "Sorry."

"See there's no gravy on mine in any way, shape, or form. I hate brown gravy."

"Yes, Miss. I'll make a note of that."

"And we both want tomato soup."

"Is that it."

"Yes. Why are you just standing there?"

Bridget started for the kitchen, barely missing a girl who

appeared at the door marked, 'Out'. Swerving in time, she dived through the 'In' door and called to Archie, "Two roast chicken plates. One without gravy of any kind."

Just as she started to leave, the ubiquitous Emily was at her elbow, calling frantically to Archie. "Hold one gravy, hold it." Then she pulled Bridget aside and half screamed at her. "You got to call it right. You cannot work anywhere without learning the lingo that the Chef requires you to use. You must keep the Chef on your side.

"Sorry. So where do I learn the, ah, lingo?"

"Practice and listening. Remember this for instance, if there's any trimmings they don't want, you don't call it without them you call it hold them."

"Yes, Miss, and thanks."

"You're welcome. Yes, to make it here or anywhere, first and foremost, you got to be in good with the chef."

Bridget began to understand why that sandwich rescue had restored order when Mr. Chris had been mobbed by a flock of angry hens. Trying to get into the sync of things, Bridget observed the servers dipped their own soup, so she now got bowls and filled them with the cream of tomato that her customers had ordered.

Just when she felt pleased with herself, she obviously was not pleasing the hostess, Ida who had entered the kitchen, now yelled at her. "Pick up your starters. Pick up your starters." At Bridget's blank expression, Emily grabbed two plates of salad from the sandwich counter, whipped two pads of butter onto two small plates, and motioned Bridget to get the four plates in there, quick. "These starters go first." She paused a second. "Have they got water?"

"Not yet."

"For crying out loud."

Emily expertly placed all four plates on a tray and added two glasses of water, and napkins. "Get in there with them. Hopefully, they haven't walked out on you."

Bridget blinked helplessly at this formidable array. "What about the soup?"

"Get the soup, just get the soup."

Shaking her head in despair, she turned a pleading look on Emily who picked up the tray. She was gone before Bridget could recover from her feeling of inadequacy. She managed to dish the soup, allowing her time to calm herself. She picked up the bowls of soup and placed them on another tray and using her foot, kicked the 'Out' door open, just as she had seen Emily do. She walked slower, taking care not to spill any of the soup as she made her way to the customers' table.

Emily was calming the two women down, and from their glances Bridget knew it had been fully explained to them that she was a new girl, and that allowances had to be made for her. At once they began amusing themselves by calling her 'new girl'. Lest she show resentment, Bridget started for the kitchen as soon as she finished serving them, but it seemed impossible to get away from Ida. "Pick up something! Don't ever make a trip, in or out, without something in your hand."

Confused, Bridget stood there speechless. "You'll trot all day and you'll never get done! Get those dirty dishes over there, On No. 3. Pick up something!"

The afternoon dragged on. Bridget felt stupid, heavy, slow, and clumsy. Try as she would to 'pick up something', dirty dishes piled on her tables, and unserved orders in the kitchen, until she thought she would go insane from the confusion. Her trouble, she discovered, was that she had not the skill to carry more than two dishes at a time. After that first reprieve, Bridget learned that trays were reserved for use when necessary because the aisles were so narrow, they would lead to crashes, and this meant that at the tables for three or less, as was in her case, she had to master balancing the orders. But the trick of balancing while slipping through customers and tables was beyond her. She tried it once, but when she had to lift two hot fudge sundaes up above her head and bring them back down without allowing the cherry to fall, she almost faced disaster.

The climax came around three o'clock. The place was empty by then and the harried cashier came back to inform her she had lost a check. The subsequent refiguring showed that the check was equal to two hours pay, which meant that her two hours of wages was lost. She wanted to throw everything in the place at the cashier's head but did not. She said she was sorry, gathered up the last of her dirty dishes, and carried them into the kitchen.

When she entered the room, Mr. Chris and Emily were in a huddle, evidently talking about her. From their expressions as they started toward her, she sensed that the verdict was unfavorable, and she waited miserably for them to get it over with so she could get away from Ida, and the dish washers, and the smell, and the noise, and drearily wonder what she was going to do next. But as they passed Archie, he looked up and made a gesture such as an umpire makes in calling a man safe at the plate. They looked surprised, but that seemed to be the final decision. Mr. Chris said "hokay, hokay," and went into the dining room.

Emily came over to Bridget. "Well personally, Bridget, I don't think you're suited to the work at all, and Mr. Chris, he wasn't a bit impressed either, but the chef thinks you'll do, so against our better judgment we're going to give you a trial."

Bridget remembered the reconstructed club sandwich and the little nod she had received from Archie. She realized that it was indeed important to be in good with the Chef who seemed to even outrank the owner.

But by now her dislike of Emily was intense, and she made no effort to keep the acid out of her voice as she said, "Well please thank Archie for me and tell him I hope I won't disappoint him." She spoke loud enough for Archie to hear and was rewarded with a nod from him.

Emily ignored the comment. "Your hours are from eleven in the morning, a half hour earlier if you want breakfast, to three in the afternoon, and if you want lunch then, you can have it. We do not do a big dinner business here, so we only keep three girls on at night, but they take turns. You are on call twice a week from five to nine, same wages as in the daytime. Sundays we are closed. You will need white shoes. Ask for nurses' regulation at any of the stores or if you have a pair of nice white sneakers, use them." Pausing and looking at Bridget she asked, "Well what's the matter, Bridget, don't you want the job?"

"I'm a little tired, that's all."

"I don't' wonder, the way you trot back and forth."

Bridget said a personal thank you to Mr. Chris and to Archie before leaving. Exhausted, she wished she could just climb into her car, but that was not going to happen. On her way home, she made a call to the grandparents and asked if they could do her a favor. When she finally arrived home, the car was in the driveway.

She wanted to go thank them, but she was too exhausted and besides, if the car was here, the grandparents had most likely brought the children home from school. She was right. Her two sweet girls greeted her at the door and she barely noticed their grandfather as he walked out the door. Nor had she heard his wife drive up to give him a ride home.

She gave the girls milk and cookies and shooed them out to play. Then she changed her dress and put slippers on her aching feet. She was about to lie down when she heard a yoo-hoo, and knew Mrs. Steele had let herself in. Bridget sighed and went to join her. Immediately she could tell that Lucy was in a dark mood and she was about to hear all about it.

"Oh Bridget, Ashton didn't come home last night."

"Lucy, calm down. He probably ran into some…trucking emergency…"

"He phoned me around nine telling me he had a rush call from his boss and that it would take him too far and too late to get back home so he wouldn't be back until morning."

"So, did he arrive this morning?"

"He did. He showed up at ten, but yet…"

"No, but yet. You know it can happen in his line of work. It's not like he sits in an office all day."

Calming a little, Lucy responded, "You're right."

Now that she was calmed, Bridget asked, "Lucy can you lend me a couple dollars?"

"Sure, whatever you need."

"Maybe twenty if you have it?"

"Sure. No problem. She watched as Mrs. Steele left and while she was gone, Bridget made her some tea. When she came back, she sat down at the counter in front of the cup and reached across the island to hand Bridget a bill. "I didn't have any change so here's a fifty."

"Thanks. I'll pay it back."

"So why so tired my dear? Lots of orders?"

"I wish. No, I got a job."

Lucy removed the tea bag from her cup and placed it on the saucer. “You said you got a job. What kind of a job?”

“Oh, just a job.”

“So, what is it?”

“I'm a waitress at a place called, Hartalkar.

“Oh, that’s funny.”

“Why is it funny?”

“It’s called Hartalkar. Hartalkar is an Indian word that means people who go on strikes.”

Bridget, thinking how close that situation might have happened today said, “That is funny.”

“It was none of my business, but all the time you were answering those ads, and trying to get hired on as a saleswoman, or whatever it was I kept wondering to myself why you didn't try something like this.”

“Why, Lucy?”

“Suppose you did get a job as a salesperson. You would be paid by commission based on what you sold. Well, my dear, no one is buying anything right now. People eat, though, even now. You will have something coming in.”

All that Mrs. Boole had said, all that Miss Turner had said, all that her body had told her, after that trip to Pittsford, came sweeping over Bridget, and suddenly she hurried for the bathroom. The milk, the sandwich, the tea, all came up, while sobs racked her. Then Mrs. Steele was beside her, holding her hair away from her face and wiping her mouth. She filled a glass with water and handed it to her and without a whisper she led her to her bedroom.

Bridget collapsed in a paroxysm of hysteria, sobbing, shaking, writhing. Mrs. Steele massaged her shoulders, whispered soothing words and told her to let it all out. Bridget did just that. She cried until her tears dried up. Lucy handed her a Kleenex to wipe her eyes and blow her nose. After a long period of silence, Bridget spoke. “I can't do it, Lucy. I just can't do it.”

“Do what?”

“Wear a uniform. And take their tips. And face those awful people. They called me names. And one of them grabbed my leg. Ooh l can feel it yet.”

“What do they pay you?”

“Sixteen dollars an hour.”

“And tips extra?”

“Yes.”

“Baby, you're nuts. Those tips will bring in a couple of dollars a day, and you will be making… why, at least thirty dollars a day on just tips which is more money than you have seen since Bitmore Homes blew up. You must do it, for your own sake. Nobody pays any attention to that uniform stuff anymore. I bet you look cute in one. And besides, people have to do what they can do.”

“Lucy, stop. I'll go mad!”

At Mrs. Steele's look, Bridget pulled herself together, at least tried to make intelligible her violent outburst. “That's what they've been telling me, the employment people, everybody, that all I'm good for is putting on a uniform and waiting on other people, and…”

“And maybe they are right. Because maybe what they are trying to tell you is exactly what I am trying to tell you. You are in a spot. It is all right to be proud, and I love you for it. But you are starving to death, baby. Don't you suppose my heart's been heavy for you? Don't you know I would have sent roast beef in here, or ham, or whatever I had, every night, except that I knew you would hate me for it? You've just got to take this job.”

“I know it. I can't, and yet I've got to.”

“Then if you've got to, you've got to, so quit bawling,'

“Promise me one thing, Lucy.”

“Anything.”

“Don't tell anybody.”

“I wouldn't even tell Ashton.”

“I don't care about Ashton, or any of these people, what they think. It is on account of the children, and I do not want anybody at all to know it, for fear somebody will say something to them. They mustn't know it; and specially not Chloe.”

"That Chloe, if you ask me, has some funny ideas.”

“I respect her ideas.”

“I don't.”

“That’s because you don't understand her. She has something

in her that I thought I had, and now I find I haven't. Pride, or whatever it is. Nothing on earth could make Chloe do what I'm going to do."

"That pride, I wouldn't give a snap of my finger for it. You are quite right about her. Chloe wouldn't do it herself, but she's perfectly willing to let you do it and eat the cake."

"I want her to have it. Cake, not just bread."

CHAPTER 9

During the six weeks Bridget had been looking for work, she had seen quite a little of Greyson. He had dropped around one night, after the children had gone to bed, and was quite apologetic about what he had said, and penitently asserted he had made a sap of himself. He mentioned that after thinking about it, he probably was trying to distance himself by talking about Cameron and now he regretted it.

Bridget said there were no hard feelings, and brought him into the den, though she did not bother to light a fire or serve a drink. When he sat down beside her and put his arm around her, she got up and made one of her little speeches. She said she would be glad to see him any time. She wanted him as a friend. However, it must be distinctly understood that what was pass was past, not to be brought up again under any circumstances. If he wanted to see her on that basis, she would make him welcome. "I really want you to come by, but on those terms."

Greyson was silent as he contemplated his ability to be a friend to someone as contagious as this innocent woman. He knew that what had passed between them was in a moment of weakness. He had happened into her life right when it seemed to her to be falling apart. He knew that and had taken advantage of it. But now after getting to know her, he felt a little ashamed. Finally, he said, "Thank you Bridget. I really want to be your friend. I can let bygones be bygones."

"Great. I appreciate it."

Thereafter he dropped by rather often, arriving usually around nine, for she did not want the children to know quite how much she was seeing him. Once, when the children were spending a weekend at the Porters around the corner, he came on Saturday evening and took her out. She expressed a preference for a quiet place, not too fancy so they took a drive and ate in a roadside inn in Webster. But one night, when her affairs were beginning to get desperate, he happened to sit beside her on the sofa again, and she did not move. When he put his arm around her, in a casual, friendly kind of way, she did not resist, and when he pulled her head on his shoulder, she let it stay there. They sat a long time without speaking.

At first it was a gentle touch of her hair as he stroked her. It felt so comforting, and Bridget leaned closer into his body, feeling safe and protected. When Greyson sat forward, gently moving her head from his shoulder, Bridget started to panic, thinking he was about to leave and she…her body needed him.

Once he was forward on the sofa he turned and pulled her face toward him. He kissed her gently at first and when he felt her responding, the kiss was deepened. Bridget felt a tingling sensation in her pelvic and it moved closer to him. She did not feel his hand as it left her face and moved down across the front of her body, squeezing pass her waistband and down into her panties. But when his fingers entered her, she gasped her whole body reacting to his touch and there was no way she could have stopped.

Her body slid down on the sofa and she watched as Greyson lowered her pants and slid her panties off until they laid in a puddle next to the sofa. And then he entered her. It was spontaneous and wonderful as they worked their bodies together until they reached their climax.

When her breathing settled and she had time to think, she admitted to herself that she was thankful for those moments of relief, of forgetfulness. So much so that she did not worry that they had brought the past back to the present.

It had been wonderful, and she did not regret it then, or now as she sat hoping she would see Greyson that evening. It had been a cursed day and the thought of having to buy a uniform with money she had to borrow from a friend, angered her. She knew that if Greyson came, she would not have to think about the uniform she would have to buy in the morning, or the sentence she would begin serving at her new job.

"Okay lady return to reality. What you should be doing is studying the menu and practice filling out the order form. And try juggling more dishes so you do not spend all your time parading back and forth. Maybe then, stupid, you'll make yourself some money."

She was in the midst of this reprimand when the doorbell rang. She was a little surprised, for it was only a few minutes after seven. She went to the door, and with it still locked, she leaned into the peephole and saw instead of Greyson standing there, it was Cameron.

Surprised, she absently touched her hair and adjusted her sweater before opening the door.

"Oh. Why hello, stranger." She said in a somewhat surprised, somewhat breathless voice.

It had the right effect as Cameron frowned, puzzled by her reception. "Bridget, how are you?"

"Can't complain. How's yourself?"

"Okay. Just thought I would drop around for a little visit, and maybe pick up a couple of things I left in the desk, while I'm about it."

"Well come in."

Her attitude stunned him as he tried to decide if maybe he should play it safe and back out the door. He had seen enough murder mysteries to know that this scene matched one of those perfect setups. But it was too late. He had barely run the scenario through his head when suddenly there were such whoops from the back of the house that any further discussion of his reason for dropping by had to be postponed indefinitely. Both children came running, and Cameron swept them into his arms and began turning around with one clinging on each side. Then when he finally set them down, they dragged him to the measuring wall so that he could see how much they had grown. His verdict was "at least two inches, maybe three."

That ended in a fit of giggles from both of his daughters as he had seen them both the previous weekend. She knew time passed slower for the young, but also knew it was a game they played. They loved him and believed anything he said, just like she had years and years ago. Now she watched loving the closeness and trust that still existed between him and his daughters. Why if he had told them he had taken a trip to the moon, they would have believed that too.

When they finally settled down, Bridget led them to the den, and Cameron took a seat on the sofa. with both children snuggled up beside him. Bridget sat in the chair across from them and told him they had good report cards from school, and Chloe was doing splendidly with her piano practice. "Oh, yes, Izzy lost a tooth. It was a back molar, so it was not visible."

Cameron looked at his youngest daughter. "So, did the tooth fairy pay for that tooth?"

"She did, she did daddy. I got twenty-five cents for it."

That led to a parade of showing him their latest possessions which for Izzy was a butterfly wing she had found in the yard and, then she opened a larger box and held it out. Cameron looked inside, smiling at first, then looked up in horror.

"What is it?"

"Ah, you don't want to see, Bridget."

"Yes, I do."

Bridget reached out and took the box from Cameron and when she looked inside, she felt her stomach heave. Laying amongst tissue paper was a wing, covered with dead maggots. It was not a butterfly wing, but one of a bird. Bridget quickly handed the box back to Cameron and then turned to her daughter.

"Izzy, honey, how did you get that?"

"I found it in the yard like that."

Bridget at that moment breathed, unaware she was holding her breath and thinking that her daughter was running around ripping wings off butterflies and birds.

"Oh, Izzy, you can't keep that. It's nasty and probably has germs." She turned to Cameron. "Daddy will have to throw it away and you have to promise me not to pick up something like that again."

"Okay I won't. I'm sorry."

"It's okay baby. You didn't know better, but you do now." Bridget hugged her daughter and gave her a kiss. By the time Cameron returned, Izzy was settled and happy again and Cameron fought hard to contain himself, his eyes twinkling with laughter. But he just smiled and patiently sat as his daughters showed him the rest of their new possessions. They had dolls, brought back by Mrs. Steele from her trip with her husband, gold crowns they were to wear at the pageant that would mark the closing of school in a couple of weeks, some balls and perfume bottles they had obtained in trades with other children.

When the girls finished their presentations and went to put them away, Cameron asked Bridget about various friends and what they were up to and she answered in friendly fashion. But as this took the spotlight off the children, they quickly became bored. After a spell of ball bouncing, which Bridget stopped, and a spell of recitations from the school pageant, which ended in a quarrel over textual accuracy, Izzy began a stubborn campaign to show Daddy the new sand bucket her grandfather had given her. As the bucket was in the garage, and Bridget did not want to go out there, Isabella began to pout. Then Chloe, with an air of sophistication, said, "Aren't you terribly thirsty, Father? Mother, would you like me to open the Scotch?"

Bridget's head turned quickly to look at Chloe. At first, she was shocked, but that quickly turned to fury, something she had never felt toward her children. Sure, she got mad at them, but never had she felt this extreme fierceness. How did Chloe know about the bottle of Scotch that she kept well-hidden and why did she act as though she was allowed to pour drinks for anyone. She stared at her daughter trying to decipher that strange, sneered expression that she had never witnessed before.

As she tried to calm herself her mind turned to the fact that if she opened that bottle, that meant that Cameron would sit there, and sit there, and sit there, until every drop of it was gone, and there went her Scotch, and there went her evening. Maybe that was what it was about. Chloe not wanting her father to leave.

At Chloe's remark, Isabella forgot about the sand bucket, and began to shriek, “Yes, Daddy, we're going to have a drink, we're going to get drunk!”

When Cameron said, “I might be able to stand a drink, if coaxed,” Bridget knew the Scotch was doomed. She went to the kitchen, got it out of the cupboard, and opened it. She turned out ice cubes, set glasses on a tray, and found the seltzer. When she was nearly done, Chloe appeared. “Can I help you, Mother?”

“Chloe, how did you know about that bottle of Scotch. It was up on the top shelf.”

Chloe did not answer her question, instead said, “I didn't know there was any secret about it.”

“Well, it’s not a secret, but it’s a grown-up thing and hereafter, I'll do the inviting.”

“But, Mother, it's Father.”

“Don't stand there and look me in the eye and pretend you don't know what I'm talking about. You know you had no business saying what you did, and you knew it at the time, I could tell by the cheeky look on your face,”

“Very well, Mother. It shall be as you say.”

“And stop that silly way of talking.”

Again, Chloe did not answer her directly as she continued, “But I remind you, just the same, that there was none of this kind of stinginess when Father was doing the inviting. Things have indeed changed here, and not for the better, alas. One might think peasants had taken over the house.”

Bridget had to force herself to remain calm. “Do you know what a peasant is?”

“A peasant is a very ill-bred person.”

Not knowing what else to say, Bridget replied, “Sometimes, Chloe, I wonder if you have good sense.”

Bridget stood shaking her head at her eleven-year-old daughter that tried to be so grown. Chloe stalked out the kitchen, and Bridget grimly arranged the tray, wondering why Chloe could put her so easily on the defensive, and hurt her so, but she knew why. She had thrown their father out the house and as much as her world was turned upside down, so was that of her daughters.

Having a drink was a ritual in the household, one that had started when Cameron and she lived a better life and proceeded on its prescribed course tonight. First, he filled two stem glasses with seltzer water for the children, then he poured two smaller drinks for himself and Bridget, containing perhaps two thimbles full of liquor. He next added ice and then the seltzer while the children sat patiently waiting.

Since the drinks were all the same color and while Cameron prepared them, Chloe and Izzy were usually arguing or talking amongst themselves, so they did not notice the difference in theirs. Bridget figured they soon must tell them that they were drinking just seltzer water, or the authorities would come knocking at their door. She had a feeling she had not seen the last of Chloe's bouts of anger.

But for now, it was a ritual that she felt was necessary to keep. After the preliminaries were out of the way, it was enjoyed by each child differently. To Chloe, it was an opportunity to stick out her little finger, to quaff elegantly. Bridget knew she was imitating either Renée Zellweger, or Catherine Zeta Jones in the movie Chicago. She had not let her watch it, but she obviously had peeked at it when she and Cameron had viewed it.

Chloe pried her father with lofty questions about their current conditions and he replied seriously, and at some length, that while things had been less than perfect, he now saw definite signs of improvement.

But to Isabella, it was a chance to get drunk, as she called it, and this she did with the utmost enthusiasm. As soon as she got half of her fizz water down, she jumped up and began spinning around in the middle of the floor, laughing at the top of her lungs. Bridget caught her glass when this started, and held it for her, and she spun around until she was dizzy and fell, in a paroxysm of delight. Something always caught in Bridget's throat when this wild dance began. She felt in some vague way, that she ought to stop it, but the child was so delightful that she never could make herself do it. Eventually Chloe realized she was no longer the center of the stage and watching her sister, said, "Personally, I think it's a disgusting exhibition."

But Isabella was not done yet. She began to sing a song her father had taught her.

"I went to the animal fair,
The birds and the beasts were there.
The big baboon by the light of the moon
Was combing his auburn hair.
The monkey he got drunk.
And sat on the elephant's trunk,
The elephant sneezed and went down on his knees.
And what become of the monk?"

While she was singing, her father contrived to pretend to be an elephant. He walked on his hands and feet, not his knees. Stuck one arm out in front of his face like his trunk. Put his lips together and blew, making a squeaky elephant sound. Then, having concealed a bit of his drink in his mouth, spit water out.

Isabella began circling around, coming nearer and nearer with her recitation. When she was almost on him, and had tweaked his trunk two or three times, he gave a series of mighty sneezes, so that they completely prostrated him. When he opened his eyes, Isabella was nowhere to be seen. He then began searching the house for her. When he returned, pretending to be worried, Chloe tried to get his attention.

Chloe picked up her glass, stuck out her little finger, took a fastidious sip. "Well, Father, I don't really see why you should get so upset about it. It seems to me anybody could see she's right behind the sofa."

"That's enough Chloe. For that, you can go to bed." Bridget's eyes blazed as she spoke, and Chloe got up quickly. Cameron paid no attention. As he charged around the sofa and grabbed the ecstatically squealing Isabella in his arms, said it was time they both went to bed, and asked how would they like Daddy to tuck them in? As he raised the child high in the air, Bridget felt pains of regret because she realized at that moment, she could never love another man like she loved Cameron.

She stared at him, wanting to cry and shout out that she wanted him back, but pride came to the surface and she remained still. Bridget then turned her attention to her daughter. Oh, how much like Cameron was Chloe and she also feared for her love of her.

When he came back from tucking in their daughters and poured himself another drink, she was thinking about her position. She was working, he was not. He asked her again how she had been, and she said fine, but all the time her choler was rising, and she knew that before long she would explode. At that moment, the doorbell rang. Instinctively she knew who it was. She excused herself and went to answer it. Peeking through the keyhole she saw Greyson, standing staunchly and looking as handsome as ever. Bridget adjusted her face as she opened the door and Greyson smiling, stepped over the threshold, and started to pull her into his arms. Bridget quickly whispered, "Cameron's here."

She watched as his face froze for a moment, but then he quickly went into character. In a voice that would be heard all over the house, he bellowed, "Why, Bridget! Say I have not seen you in forever! Gee you are looking great! Say, is Cameron in?" He said it all without pause.

Bridget had to suppress a giggle before answering. "He's in the den." She said this aloud and mouthed silently, 'thank you.'

"I'll only be a minute, but I have to see him."

If Greyson elected to believe Cameron still lived here, Cameron evidently preferred to follow suit. He shook hands with a show of hospitality, offered a drink as though the liquor were his own, and asked how every little thing was; quite as though nothing had happened. Greyson said he had been trying to see him for a couple of months now, over something that had come up, and so help him God, this was the first chance he had had.

"So, tell me, what's come up?"

Greyson thought quickly on his feet. "It's about those three houses in block 14. Do you know if there was any verbal promise made at the time of the sale that the corporation would put a retaining wall in the rear?"

Cameron said, "Absolutely not," and launched into details as to how the lots were sold.

"I thought so, but it sounded reasonable since they back up to the school fields."

Cameron put fresh ice in their glass, and a little more liquor, and a squirt of seltzer, and handed Bridget her glass. She took a quick sip and through secret thoughts of her own she broke out in a ripple of unchecked laughter.

She had a charming laugh, a little like Isabella's, and it startled the two men to turn towards her. Bridget continued to laugh and though they had not a clue why, they laughed with her, as though there had never been a stock market crash, a breakup of the marriage, or a sour feeling over who got the job as the receiver.

Greyson, evidently a little nervous, and more than a little uncertain about his status, decided presently that he had to leave. Cameron walked him ceremoniously to the door where he turned and said, “Thanks, Bridget.”

Shortly thereafter, Cameron announced he had to go. Bridget could tell he was drunk and when he leaned in for a kiss, she slipped her hand in his pocket and took his keys. She closed the door but stood there beside it and in a few minutes the bell rang. She opened the door, and he was standing there, looking a little foolish. “Sorry to bother you, Bridget but my car key must have fallen out of my pocket. You mind my looking?”

“Why, not at all.”

He went back to the den, snapped on the light, and looked all over the den where he had been playing with Isabella. She watched him with pleased, interest.

Presently she said, Well come to think of it, perhaps I took that key.”

“You took it?”

“Yes.”

“Well, gimme it. I got to go home. I...”

She stood smiling as the dreadful truth dawned on him, and his face sagged numbly. “You think I’m too drunk to drive.”

Bridget nodded.

“Would you like me to give you a ride?”

“I’d appreciate that very much.”

“Are you staying at Mrs. Donahue? I say that because I think that is Mrs. Donahue’s car.”

Cameron stood with a sheepish grin wondering if she had planned this to find out where he was living. Drunk, but not that drunk he did not fall into the trap. “Prefer not to say where I'm staying. I am staying where I am staying. But if you drop me by Maggie’s, it is all right. Got to see her for a minute, so you can drop me there if it's convenient for you."

Her face distorted so much so that there were wrinkles around her eyes and mouth. Cameron did not like the idea he had caused that expression, but he remained silent. Bridget only said, "any where's convenient for me."

They went out together and got in the car and Bridget was glad it was dark so that the neighbors could not see them. "What is Maggie's address. I know she lives in East Irondequoit somewhere, but I'm not sure of her address."

"Cameron gave her the address." Ah, yes, Woodrow Avenue. I remember now. I think we rented something there…"

"Yes, Bridget, we did."

"Don't get so mad. I'm only making conversation." She was quiet, then started again. "Let me guess, three bedrooms, one bath…. Probably a little over a thousand square feet?"

Cameron did not respond. "Come on Cameron, you're a builder. You can quote stats from just looking at a place,"

"Bridget, pay attention. Your turn is just ahead."

He was right. She would have missed it if he had not alerted her. She turned and drove down the street and when she reached the address, she started to pull into the driveway, but thought better of it. Instead, she parked on the road in front, ignoring the surprised expression on Cameron's face, she got out and helped him out.

He was barely able to stand on his own and though this was as far as she wanted to go, she continued, supporting him up to the door. "Push the doorbell, Cameron."

He managed that and in seconds the door opened and Maggie Donahue, shamelessly took possession of her husband. Neither one of them spoke a word to each other.

"Good night, Cameron." Bridget had almost remained civil, but before she could stop herself, she added, "And I have a couple of old bras at the house, tell her. They're clean and fresh and she can have them any time she drops around."

"Kindly shut up."

"Sure, no problem." Bridget turned and went to the car as quickly as she could. The last thing she had wanted was to make Maggie feel superior. No, the last thing she wanted was for that woman to see her cry. She could not drive fast enough as she headed down the street and started back home, tears flowing, unchecked from her eyes.

When she pulled into the drive, she was still agitated and needed to get away. She just needed to blow off some steam before she walked back in that house. She knew it was not right, but she backed out the driveway and went to the corner and turned on List Avenue. Her first thought was to just drive around the side streets, for a while, but she knew that would not be enough.

She drove down List, turned on Wyndale and at the bottom of the hill, turned onto Oakview and continued, minding the speed limit as she crossed Titus. The street was empty of traffic and pedestrian, but she kept to the speed limit, not wanting to get a ticket. When she reached the entrance to the expressway, she eased onto the lane and once officially on the road, she gunned the engine, glad that her father-in-law had seen it upon himself to get the car fixed and was kind enough not to mention it to her.

Excitedly she watched the needle swing pass 40, 50 and then 60 mph where she eased off a little on the gas, topping out at 65 mph. She decided to go a little faster so moving into the passing lane, she watched the speedometer hit 75 mph. Bridget breathed a long, tremulous sigh. The car was pumping something into her veins, something of pride, of arrogance, of regained self-respect, that no talk, no liquor, no love, could possibly give. Once more she felt like herself, and began thinking about the job with cool detachment, instead of shame. Its problems, from balancing the dishes to picking up the starters, flitted through her mind, and she began to laugh through her tears. What a few hours ago had seemed formidable, now seemed doable.

She took the next exit off the expressway and headed back toward home. Once there, she drove into the garage and turned off the engine. Looking up, she said, “Thank you,” as she opened the car door and hurried, humming as she went up to the door. She felt good as she checked to make sure all the doors and windows were locked and then checked on the children. They were sleeping soundly, but she could not resist leaning over and kissed Izzy first and then lingered over Chloe.

As she kissed her oldest daughter, she stirred sleepily, and Bridget could not resist whispering. “Something wonderful happened tonight, and you were the cause of it all, and I take everything back that I said. Now go to sleep and don't think about it anymore."

Groggily Chloe replied, "I'm so glad, mother."

"Goodnight Chloe."

"Goodnight."

CHAPTER 10

Bridget's financial troubles had eased a little, for she quickly became the best waitress in the place and that earned her more tips. The trick of balancing dishes she learned by practice. She made the children laugh as she delivered their dinners and put extra plates that could not fit on the surface, on her arm. She then practiced arranging her fingers so she could carry more glasses. She did have several accidents, but she found that the china that Cameron's mother had bragged about and given them as a wedding gift was not very expensive since she could go to the dollar store and replace ones that she dropped.

The day came when Chloe tested her and when she bumped into her mother with her arms laden with food and nothing dropped, the girls applauded while Bridget stuck out her tongue and began parading around the island without dropping anything.

She learned fast that tips came from the regular customers, so she tried to do something special for them and in return they gave her larger tips. Tell them the sad story of your life and that tip went even higher. She learned that men were better tippers than women. So, to increase these tips even further, she thought up little schemes to find out their names, remembered all their little likes, dislikes, and quirks, and saw that Archie gave them exactly what they wanted.

Bridget had a talent for discreet flirtation but found that this did not pay. Serving a man food, apparently, was in itself an ancient intimacy; going beyond it made him uncomfortable and sounded a trivial note in what was essentially a solemn relationship. Simple friendliness, coupled with exact attention to his wants, seemed to please men most, and on that basis, she had frequent invitations to take a ride, have dinner, or see a show.

At first, she did not quite know what to do about them, but soon invented a refusal that was not a rebuff. She would say she wanted him to "keep on liking her," or jokingly that he "might feel differently if he saw her when she wasn't in uniform." This had the effect of arousing a good lively fear that perhaps she was not so hot in her street clothes, and at the same time of leaving enough pity for the poor working girl to keep him coming back, so she could serve his lunch.

Having someone accidently on purpose bump into her on purpose turned out, was practically a daily hazard, and this she found best not to notice. Even a 'bumper', if properly handled, could be nursed into a regular who left good tips, no doubt to prove he really had a heart of gold.

She held aloof from the restaurant itself, and the people she worked with. This was not due to any dislike or feeling of superiority she just did not have time for friendships. Instead, she studied the business and in her own mind, she was critical of the operation and had thoughts of ways it could be improved, but was afraid to get drawn into talk, for fear she would say what she thought, and lose her job. So, she confined her observations to share with Lucy and almost every night she blew off steam giving her an unrestrained account of the way things were done. Her special grievance was the pies. They were bought from the grocery store from the frozen section. "Can you imagine, Lucy, the frozen section!"

Lucy laughed. "Come on Bridget, I've been known to serve a frozen pie before."

"Yes, but you aren't selling it to a customer and are buying a more expensive brand. These pies have no inviting appearance, their sticky and tasteless and do not get me started on the filling… As for the crust, it is not digestible. And it is not only me who thinks this. One day I heard, Emily, crying to Ida that she was ashamed to serve a slice of pie that had been delivered that day. "I'm that ashamed to ask a customer to eat it! It's just awful, and we expect our customers to pay for it."

"Well, there's nothing you can do about it so don't get yourself all worked up over it."

The next day at work was no different as Bridget listened to Emily again complain about a comment from a customer on his pie. Mr. Chris who took all complaints with a martyr shrug, merely said, "Maybe the pie is lousy. If the customer does not want to eat it, see me and I'll approve a new check."

Bridget opened her mouth, to support Emily, but knew that was not the way to go. She knew, as well as they all did, that a new check would not make the pie any better. It would just decrease the sales and that would eventually bite them in the butt.

But at that moment it flashed through her mind perhaps the real remedy was to make a bid for the pie contract herself. This was a way to earn more money if she played her cards right. Bridget's whole attitude changed that day. Instead of avoiding personal contact with the employees, she began to show interest in them. She knew she had to get Ida sold on the idea, but also everybody else as well.

That afternoon she was rather more helpful to the other girls and later, at lunch, sat down with then and socialized. She was careful to let them do most of the talking, while she listened. Meanwhile, she reflected what she was to do about Ida.

She was working that evening, and after they closed noticed

Emily hurrying out with a glance at the clock. And when Ida joined them at the door she asked, “Which way are you going? Do you need a ride?”

Emily spoke first. “I wouldn’t turn down a ride, Bridget.”

Ida looked at Bridget. “You have a car?”

Choosing her words carefully, she replied. “I do. It’s not new, but it gets me where I’m going.” Then turning to look at them added, “Where to ladies?”

First Ida directed her to her home just about a block from work and then she drove Emily home, which was farther and happened to be just off the route she took to work. When Emily climbed out, she said, “I drive this way to work. Would you like me to pick you up on days we are working together?”

“Oh, that would be nice. Yes, thank you Bridget.”

From then on Emily had a ride, and Bridget had a better situation and more importantly she had Ida's ear, with no possible interruptions for a considerable time every day. They became bosom friends, and somehow the talk always got around to pies. Emily was bitter indeed at the product Mr. Chris offered his customers, and Bridget listened sympathetically. And then one night she innocently inquired, “What does he pay for those pies, Ida?”

“He gets some off brand-named frozen pies for somewhere around four dollars each.”

“Hmmm.”

“Why? Why are you asking?”

“I make pies and whatever he pays I'd be willing to meet the price and make him some that people would really want to eat. I'd make him some that would be a feature.”

“Could you do it? Honest?”

“Yes. Actually, I do it now and sell them all the time.”

“Then I'll find out what he’ll pay.”

CHAPTER 11

From then on pies became a feverish conspiracy between Bridget and Ida. They talked every chance they got and worked on the logistics of the plan. They had to figure it all out before presenting the idea to Mr. Chris. Unlike what she had been doing, selling cakes and pies to her neighbors, this was a whole different ball game, but Ida was there, helping her all the way.

First, they worked on developing a business plan focusing on the concept of profitability and organization of the business. Many afternoons they would sit in front of their computers at lunch scrolling through websites to find detailed research on the costs of pie production, and how the market worked. They had to convince the restaurant that they were not only offering a better product than the competitors, but a stable source for pies. Many of those arguments became the background for their presentation. Ida had convinced her that though it might not seem necessary, Mr. Hartalkar was quite a businessman and to get the project going, they had to act like businesswoman.

At the beginning Bridget thought it was too much and to be honest, a little scary. This was not one pie at a time business, but Ida kept her going. “Listen Bridget you know you excel in baking and you have a passion for pies. Selling pies offers an opportunity to express yourself and this opportunity offers you a way to make some good money.”

“Ida, I don’t know. What with the house, my daughters and baking for the neighborhood, when will I have time for enjoying life?”

“Okay, Bridget, you want to sit and worry about the gas bill and the mortgage. You want to wait until it all disappears, and you have nothing. Is that what you want?”

At those moments, Bridget thanked Ida who was becoming the one person she could count on. As they worked through the details, Ida kept reminding her that this pie business could soar. She has already experienced the income from selling to individuals, so the next step is to sell to restaurants, then bakeries and even retail outlets.

“Whoa, Ida, you’re scaring me. I am only one person.”

“I know, but if you don’t’ put the ribbon out there to reach, you won’t get anywhere.”

Bridget nodded her head and not dismissing the idea, said, “We need to work on a selection of pie types and flavors, based on popularity and market trends.” So, they went to work on watching and reading ads and keeping track of the types ordered by the customers.

Ida began working on ways to advertise the change of pastries at the restaurant, even figure a way to offer pies to take home. This would work by putting up fliers at the restaurant and later, a place to display the pies for sale.

The day finally came when they were ready. She knew that Ida believed in her, but would she believe in her product. So, one Sunday Bridget drove over to Ida's with a beautifully made apple pie and over coffee they talked about the final steps to their plan which included getting Mr. Chris on board and then producing a steady flow of pies. In their research they had figured how many slices of each type of pie would sell each day since this was a business that had a product shelf life, and their aim was to have fresh pies every day.

As Ida started in on her slice of apple pie, she took little nibbles at first, then a large fork full, smiling and nodding at the same time. “Bridget, this is good.” She chewed, laughed, and added. “No, this isn’t good, it’s spectacular!” She was impressed.

Emily was married, to a construction guy who ran a one-man business. Work had always been sporadic, but more so in recent months and Bridget suspected that a pie might lift both their spirits. She knocked on the door of their modest house and Emily answered.

“Bridget, what are you doing here?”

"Can I come in."

"Sure, sorry…" Bridget entered the front room, trying not to appear shocked by the disarray as Emily moved aside to let her in. It was the first time she had stepped inside the house and she had a feeling that Emily was not happy. Bridget knew the signs since she had gone through them herself.

"What is that wonderful smell, Bridget?"

Careful not to show her worry, Bridget smiled. "A cherry pie."

Emily looked wonderingly at Bridget. "I made it for you and your husband to enjoy this evening."

"Oh, how sweet of you. Please, come in and join us, please."

"No, I can't. I have to get back to the girls."

"How can I thank you, Bridget. This is a wonderful surprise."

Bridget did not hesitate. She began sharing every detail of her adventure and what it would mean to her and the customers if it panned out as planned. "What about Ida?"

"Ida's in." She then explained what Emily could do to help and when she finished, Emily could not contain herself as she clapped her hands. Emily was in.

As Bridget made her way back down the drive, she was smiling and when she climbed in her car, she felt her confidence grow. Seeing the way Emily was just surviving, encouraged her even more that this was the right thing to do. She did not want to just survive, she wanted to live and to do that, she had to make money. Sure, there would be sacrifices, but hopefully it would all turn around. With a new determination, she drove home.

The next day, during the luncheon rush, while Mr. Chris had stepped over to the bank to get more change, Emily stopped Bridget in the aisle, and said in a hoarse stage whisper, “He pays a straight five fifty for those pies and gets three dozen a week.”

Bridget stopped dead in her tracks and looked at Emily. “How…?”

“We’ll talk later.”

That night, Emily was full of information as Bridget drove her home. She had managed to make copies of the information on the pies they purchased, the cost and what income they produced for the restaurant. Bridget could not fathom the idea she could make three dozen pies a week until Emily reminded her, she did not have to deliver all three dozen at once. That settled her down and she felt that confidence again as they worked on when to approach Mr. Chris.

“You leave it to me, Bridget. Just leave it to me; You will not have to say one word. I have been thinking about it all along that we had to do something about those pies, and now it is happening. Just leave it all to me.”

The showdown came the following day, and the face-off was noisier than expected. As she caught snatches of the conversation, she heard Mr. Chris say there were over thirty bakeries in Rochester so why would someone buy pies at his restaurant over an actual bakery.

Emily was indeed ready as she retorted, “That’s like saying, why would people come here over going to a big named chain restaurant.”

That hit too close to the belt for Mr. Chris so he struck back saying business would be better if it was not for the shotty service.

“Well, for your information, Mr. Chris, you’ve been losing customers for years too, and didn't have sense enough to know it. And besides,” Emily went on, “here's a woman that makes wonderful homemade pies.”

“You have a point here, missy?”

“Yes, I do, Don’t you want more customers?”

Emily knew she was winning when Mr. Chris retorted, “Don’t bother me. I’m busy.”

A shy person would have backed off at this point, but that was not Emily. “Bridget can make any kind of pie you want and as many as you want in a standard order size.”

“How do you know their good.”

“I’ve tasted them. She made a cherry pie that my husband went wild over and an apple pie that Ida enjoyed immensely.”

“Don’t want apple, or cherry.”

“Why is that?”

“Well missy who thinks she knows everything. When you slice into fruit pies, the juices run down and right behind it comes the fruit. You end up wasting half a pie."

That quieted Emily as she tried to figure her next step. She went into the dining room and whispered excitedly. "I think you heard him. I think he would still go for apple, but what about pumpkin and lemon for the other choices?"

"I can make them, but…"

"We'll talk later, it's about time for the breakfast crowd."

The rest of the day was busy waiting on customers and by the end of the afternoon, things quieted. Bridget wanted to talk, but Emily figured that Mr. Chris was watching and if they put their heads together, he would be right over to pull them apart. Instead, they washed off the tables and chairs and checked the condiments before stopping for the day. They walked out together and once in Bridget's car, Emily opened up, sharing with Bridget what she figured was a well thought out plan. Bridget liked it.

The next day Bridget picked up Emily and they rode in talking all the way with the aroma of fresh baked pies filling their nostrils. At Emily's request, Bridget made just three pies: pumpkin, lemon, and apple. Just three, Emily cautioned and no more. They are samples, but you have to remember only one each.

Bridget did as told and when the newly hired waitress, Anna came in, Emily had another ally and pounced on her.

"What do you think of the pies here Anna?"

"You know what I think of them. Just what you do."

"Well, I want you to tell Mr. Chris that."

"What, get myself fired. No."

"He won't fire you and not just because he needs you. He will listen to you instead. You are going to serve pies to our customers, free."

"Come on Emily, that'll definitely get me fired."

"No, because they are three pies made by Bridget and Mr. Chris didn't pay for them. We are going to offer them to the customers first and have them pay, but if they say they don't want a slice, we'll give it to them free."

"So, what's the catch. It comes out of our pay."

Bridget joined them. "No, it comes out of no one's pay. We will just ask for their critique after they try it."

It was a busy day and several times they wanted to just get a handle on the regular orders, but faithfully they managed to sell every slice of the three pies and get good feedback. The next day Bridget provided three more.

"I know it's costing you, but we'll sell your pies for you."

So that is how they began, Anna helped Bridget with getting ratings on the free pies and those that the new customers were willing to pay for. Some of the regulars tried it and even offered to pay.

When Mr. Chris gave Ida a flyer to attach to the door, she added to it, pies. Lunch had barely started when Bridget managed to sell two slices of pie. Mr. Rand, one of her regular customers, came in early with another man, and when she handed him the menu to pick out his dessert, she asked innocently, "Would you care for a slice of pie, Mr. Rand? The lemon is particularly good today."

Mr. Rand looked at his companion. "That just shows how much principle she's got. The pies here stink, she knows they stink, and yet she says the lemon is particularly good today. Layoff the pies and go for something else because you don't want to leave here with a bad taste in your mouth."

It was becoming an exciting game as they calmly listened to the complaints about the former pies and jotted the customers' remarks down. Then with a smile of conspiracy they would reply, "We have a new variety of freshly baked pies today, Mr. Rand. If you do not like it, you don't have to pay for it."

Mr. Rand thought about it for a minute. "Well, is it any good?"

"You try a slice and tell me what you think. I think you'll like it."

The other man chose chocolate ice cream, and Bridget hurried to the kitchen to get the orders. As she came back with both desserts and the coffee, her heart gave a leap as she heard a customer say, "That pie looks good." When she set it in front of Mr. Rand the other man did not even let her put the ice cream down. "Say, I want some of that! Can I switch?"

"Why certainly!"

“I don’t know how it taste, but she's right. It seems better and that meringue looks two inches thick.”

By noon, the lemon pie was a few smears of filling in an empty plate, and by one o'clock, all three pies were gone. By three, Emily approached Mr. Chris with everybody standing around, to watch the result. She said just look how those pies went. She said the lemon was gone before she could even turn around, and one customer wanted a second slice, and she did not have it to give him. She said it was just terrible what the people said, when Bridget's pies ran out and she told them she would have to serve the regular pies.

To all this, Mr. Chris made no comment, merely hunching over his desk, and acting as though he was deaf. Emily plowed on, louder and louder. She said there was one lady, in a party of four, that wanted to know where they got such wonderful pies, and when she pointed out Bridget, the customer was amazed.

Mr. Chris twisted uneasily, kept his head down, and said not to bother him, he was busy. Then wanting to hold his own he put on an angry face and looking directly at Bridget spurted out. “So that's what you were up to. A chance to make more money?”

He jumped up and found Anna's finger not six inches from his nose, leveled at him as though it were a six shooter. Giving him no time to recover, she spoke, “So that's it. You figured it out or someone told you that Bridget was making those pies! You knew what we were doing all along and you let us carry out the charade. I should have known."

Emily stared at Mr. Chris and he returned the stare until he could not hold it in anymore. He burst into loud laughter and pointed a finger at Ida. "She told me when I asked her to put more pies on the counter and she said there wasn't any space left. I drilled her on why that was, and she had to spill the beans."

Emily looked over at Ida who turned and looked back. She mouthed, "Sorry," and Emily smiled to let her know it was okay.

At this point Emily went to get Bridget and the three of them sat down to negotiate the price but finally Mr. Chris agreed when Bridget said, "These pies aren't wimpy! They are deep and 9" wide to feed up to 12 folks! The flakey, buttery pie dough is rolled and formed by hand, and all the fillings are made from scratch. If it goes well, we can incorporate special orders for whole pies. That right now looks like I would need seven days in advance." Seeing the frown on Mr. Chris's face she quickly added, "That's for now. It will get better."

They had won and at the price range they had discussed. Emily and Anna went out for a celebratory drink with Bridget before she had to hurry home. She still had a half dozen pies to make before morning.

On the strength of her new contract, Bridget purchased a good cell phone to be used for the business and began to drum up more business from the neighborhood. Pies had to be fresh, so she had to sell them within a day after she made them and making a few extra pies were no more trouble.

A month later it was more than working. Shortly after expanding sales in the neighborhood and offering the pies at Hartalkar word got out and another restaurant contract came in for two pies a week. So, a little over a month of the time she had been hired as a waitress, she was working harder than she knew she could and still hold out until Sunday, when she could sleep. She was exhausted and knew she could not handle her household responsibilities along with full care of her children, so she hired a woman named Francine Brown who came highly recommended by friends. She cooked the children's lunch and helped with the wash. Francine was good at following directions and did everything asked of her. Once when she was baking pies, Francine joined her in the kitchen, fetching what she needed and explaining that she used to help her mother bake. "I loved it. So, if you need any help, let me know."

That is how it started and soon with Francine helping when she could, it was all falling in place.

Bridget could tell her children were proud of her starting her own business, but as for the waitressing, Bridget did not tell them.

That she kept secret. As the business flourished and Bridget made money to support them and have extras, she started to feel good about herself. Two months before, she barely had money to buy bread. Now she was making enough to pay for the necessities, plus her daughter's lessons and other school expenses.

People seemed to know her and when she walked down their street, she made sure she looked like a going concern. She wore top of the line sports suits and got a permanent. It felt good to be on top, but two things would bring her back to reality.

The first was the arrival in the mail of a bill for the mortgage. That she settled by asking Greyson for a loan, which he gladly gave her. She made sure he understood she planned to pay him back.

The second was the biggest surprise. She had purchased a couple back up uniforms once she had extra cash so that she did not have to worry about having to launder them every day. These she hid in the back of her closet. One day not long after that, she came home to find Francine in one of her uniforms.

Bridget stood there, her anger spreading through her. She had not bought uniforms for Francine. Francine was happy just putting on an apron over her street clothes and Bridget was fine with that. Now, seeing Francine in restaurant regalia, she began trembling with rage, but left the kitchen for fear of what she might say. But Francine caught the look and followed. "I told her you wouldn't like it, Mrs. Bitmore. I told her right off, but she hollered and carried on, so I put it on, just to keep her quiet."

"Who hollered and carried on?"

"Miss Chloe ma'am,"

"Miss Chloe?"

"She makes me call her that."

"And she told you to put that uniform on?"

"Yes, ma'am.'"

"Very well. It is quite all right, if that is how it happened, but can you take it off now. And hereafter, remember I am giving the orders around here, not Miss Chloe."

"Yes ma'am."

For the first time she saw the error of her ways. She had changed and acted highbrow and so Francine started calling her ma'am and her daughter was putting on airs. She would need to make changes. Before Francine left the kitchen, Bridget stopped her and watched as Francine, timidly turned back around.

"And Francine, don't call me ma'am. My name is Bridget."

That broke the ice and Bridget stood watching as Francine crossed the distance between them and Bridget gave Francine a hug. Francine hastily disappeared and returned with her street clothes and her apron and then they made her pies, and nothing more was said about it that afternoon, or at dinner.

Chloe seemed to not take notice of Francine's change of clothes. But after dinner, when Francine had gone home, Bridget summoned both children to the den, and talking mainly to Chloe, announced they were going to discuss the uniform.

Chloe was as clever as she was smart. "Certainly, Mother.

It's quite becoming to her, don't you think?"

"Never mind whether it's becoming or not. The first thing I want to know is this. Those uniforms were in the back of my closet. Now how did you happen to find them there?"

"Mother, I needed a scarf, and went to see if any of mine had been put with your things by mistake."

"In the closet?"

"I had looked everywhere else, and…"

"All your scarfs were in your own top drawer, and they still are, and you weren't looking for any scarf at all. Once more you were snooping into my things to see what you could find, weren't you?"

"Mother, how can you insinuate such…"

"Weren't you?"

"I was not, and I resent the question."

Chloe looked Bridget in the eye with haughty, offended dignity. Bridget waited a moment, and then went on. "And how did you happen to give one of those uniforms to Francine?"

"I merely assumed, Mother, that you had forgotten to tell her to wear them. Evidently, they had been bought for her. If she was going to take my things to the pool, I naturally wanted her decently dressed."

"To the pool? What things?"

"My swimming things, Mother."

Little Isabella laughed loudly, and Bridget stared bewildered. School being over, she had left money so the children could go down and swim in the pool at the high school which they could get to by just going out the back door and crossing the school fields. But that Francine was included in the excursion she had no idea. It quickly developed, however, that Chloe's notion of a swim in the pool was for herself and Isabella to go parading with Francine following two paces behind, all dressed up in a uniform, and carrying their swimming bags.

"I never heard of such goings on in my life."

"Well, Mother, it seems to me wholly proper."

"Does Francine go in swimming?"

"Certainly not!"

"What does she do?"

"She sits by the pool and waits, as she should."

"For Miss Chloe, I suppose?"

"She knows her place, I hope."

"Well hereafter, there'll be no more Miss Chloe. And if she goes with you to the pool, she goes in her own clothes, and she has a swim. If she hasn't a suit, I'll get her one."

Inwardly she was seething as she listened to her daughter. This was her own fault, she kept reminding herself and therefore she had to be forceful, but not angrily tell Chloe what to do.

"I want you to listen, and listen closely, Francine is not a maid. Francine is my friend that helps me with you and with the house." She paused searching for an example they could understand. "She is like Mrs. Steele next door. She is my neighbor who helps me, and she is my friend. Do you understand?

Is that clear enough for you?"

Bridget thought better of saying any more than that. She could have said that there was a time when a black child was not allowed to swim in pools with white children, but she didn't want to cause them any anguish so she remain still, waiting for Chloe to respond.

Chloe sat in the window seat, filing her nails with her head down so that Bridget could not see her face. "Mother, it shall be as you say."

Little Isabella, who had been listening to all this with vast delight, now rolled on the floor, screaming with laughter, and kicking her heels in the air. "She can't swim! She cannot swim, and she will get drowned! And Peter will have to pull her out! He's the lifeguard, and he's stuck on her!"

Bridget pressed her lips together to keep from laughing at this. Bridget began to understand Francine even going with the girls to the pool and hard as she fought, watching little Izzy, tears weld in her eyes and she burst out laughing despite herself.

It wasn't until Chloe elected to regard the inquest as closed by saying, "Really, Mother, it seems to me you made a great fuss over nothing. If you bought the uniforms for her, and certainly I cannot imagine who else you could have·purchased them for, so why shouldn't she wear them?" That is when Bridget knew it was not over.

Chloe had slightly overdone it. In a flash, from the innocent remark she could not imagine who else the uniforms could have been bought for, Bridget knew the truth, and that meant the whole thing had to be dealt with profoundly. For Chloe's purpose in giving Francine the uniform, might be more sinister than a desire to put on airs at the pool. It might be considerably more devious, and Bridget needed to address it now.

So, Bridget did not act at once. She sat looking at Chloe, the squint hardening in her eye; then she scooped up Isabella in her arms, and announced it was time to go to bed. She carried Izzy to her room and helped her undress and then she read to her as she always did. But all the time she was thinking of Chloe, who never allowed herself to be read to anymore, who was becoming a person she did not know or like.

Chloe who had followed them to the bedroom, sat down at the dresser while Bridget attended to Isabella. After Isabella was tucked in and given a good night kiss, Bridget turned toward her other daughter, and said, "You, follow me to the den, now."

Chloe got up angrily and threw down her brush. "Yee gods what now?"

When they got to the den, Bridget closed the door, sat down in the armchair, and motioned Chloe to stand in front of her. "Why did you really give Francine that uniform?"

"For heaven's sake, Mother, haven't I told you once? How do I have to tell you? I will not have you questioning me on this. Good night. I'm going to bed."

There was no holding back as Bridget jumped up and caught her by the arm. She swung Chloe around to face her. "You knew, when you gave it to Francine, that that was my uniform, didn't you?"

"Your uniform?"

Chloe's simulation of surprise was so cool, so calculated, so innocent, that Bridget waited before continuing, wanting her words to sting. "I've taken a job as a waitress in a restaurant."

"As a what?"

"As a waitress, as you very well know."

"Yee gods! Yee…"

Bridget clipped her on the cheek, but Chloe laughed audaciously, and it was too much for Bridget. Before she knew it, her hand came out and really smacked her daughter's cheek.

More from shock then force, Chloe fell to the floor and while she lay there, Bridget practically screamed at her. "Yes, I am a waitress. I do it so you and your sister can eat and have a place to live and clothes on your back. I have taken the only job I could get, and if you think I am going to listen to a lot of silly nonsense from you about it, you are mistaken. And if you think your nonsense is going to make me give up the job, you are mistaken about that, too. How you found out what I was I don't know."

"The uniform, stupid. You think I'm dumb?"

Bridget clipped her again and went on. "You may not realize but everything you have cost money. From Francine, to your food, and everything else that you have."

Chloe was defiant. She got up, her eyes hard, "Aren't things bad enough? Did you have to degrade us by…"

Anger thrummed through her veins making it hard to speak or allow herself to touch her daughter. She was so mad she had to fight the nausea that was swelling in her stomach. All she could do was watch as Chloe got up, staggered to the sofa, her face flushed and a vein throbbing in her neck. Her hands were clenched in fists and her lower lip pushed forward as she flung herself down. Then she gave a soft laugh and whispered in a voice filled with contempt rather than anger, “A waitress.”

Bridget could not hold back her tears as she started to cry. She rarely struck Chloe, telling Mrs. Steele that the child did not need it, and that she did not believe in beating children for every little thing. But this was not the real reason. The few times she had tried spanking she had gotten exactly nowhere. She could not break Chloe, no matter how much she spanked her. Chloe got victory out of these struggles sending her adversaries away in ignoble defeat. It always came back to the same thing. She was afraid of Chloe, of her snobbery, her contempt, her unbreakable spirit. And she was afraid of something that seemed always lurking under Chloe’s bland, phony stoniness; a cold, cruel, coarse desire to torture her mother to humiliate her above everything else, to hurt her. Bridget yearned for warm affection from this child, such as Cameron apparently commanded. But all she ever got was a stagy, affected counterfeit. This half loaf she had to accept, trying not to see it for what it really was.

She wept, then sat with a dismal feeling creeping over her, for she was as far from settling the main point as she had ever been.

Chloe had to be made to accept this job she had taken else her days would be dull misery, and in the end, she would have to give it up. But how? Presently, not conscious of having hatched any idea, she began to talk.

"You never give me credit for anything, do you?"

"Oh Mother, please let's not talk about it anymore. It is all right. You're working in a restaurant, and I'll try not to think about it." The calm with which she spoke scared Bridget and before she knew it, she heard herself speak.

"As a matter of fact, I felt exactly about it as you do, and I certainly would never have taken this job if it hadn't been that I…" Bridget swallowed her mind swinging as it searched for a reasonable explanation that would satisfy her daughter. "That I had decided to open a place of my own, and I had to learn the business. I had to know all about it and…"

Bridget watched as Chloe's body straightened and her eyes twinkled in anticipation. With interest she asked, "What kind of a place, Mother? You mean a…"

"Restaurant, of course."

Chloe blinked, and for a dreadful moment Bridget felt that this did not quite meet Chloe's social requirements either. Desperately she went on. "There's money in a restaurant, if it's run right, and…"

"You mean we'll be rich?"

"Many people have gotten rich that way, but..."

That did it. Even though a restaurant might not be quite the poshest thing that Chloe could imagine, riches spoke to the profoundest part of her nature. She ran over, put her arms around her mother, kissed her, nuzzled her neck, and insisted on being punished for the horrible way she had acted.

When Bridget had given her a faltering pat on the bottom, she climbed into the chair, and babbled happily to Bridget about the limousine they would have, and the grand piano, on which she could practice her music.

Bridget gladly promised all these things, but later, when Chloe was in bed and she was undressing, she wondered how long she could keep up the pretense, and whether she could find another job before her bluff was called. And then a hot, electric idea flashed through her mind. Why not have her own restaurant? She looked in the mirror, and saw a calculating, confident woman's face squinting back at her. Well, why not?

Her breath began to come just a little bit fast as she canvassed her qualifications. She could cook, she had such a gift for it as few ever have. She was learning the business; in fact, as far as pies went, she was in business already. She was young, healthy, and stronger than she looked. She had two children which was all she wanted, all she could be expected to bring into the world, so there need be no more of that. She was implacably determined to get ahead, somehow.

She put on her pajamas, turned out the light, but kept walking around the room, in the dark. Despite herself, the limousine, the chauffeur, and the grand piano began to gleam before her eyes, but as real this time, not imaginary. She started for bed, then hurried to the children's room. “Chloe?”

“Yes, Mother. I'm awake.”

She went over, knelt, put her arms around the child, held her passionately. “You have a gift my darling and no matter what I say, not what anybody says, don’t give up that pride, that way you have of looking at things. I wish I had it because it means you will never give up on yourself!”

“I can't help it, Mother. It's how I feel.”

Thinking about her day, Bridget said, “Something else happened tonight.”

“Tell me.”

“Nothing to tell. Only now I feel it, now I know it, that from now on things are going to get better for us. So, we will have what we want. Maybe we will not be rich, but we will have something, and it will all be on account of you. Every good thing that happens is on account of you, if Mother only had sense enough to know it.”

“Oh Mother, I love you. Truly I do.”

“Say it again .... Say it just once more.”

Chloe reached up and hugged her mother, whispering, “I love you Mother.”

CHAPTER 12

As the months rolled by, Bridget's attitude toward the restaurant changed, from critical disapproval to eager curiosity. Mr. Chris, while his cuisine might not excite her, had been in business many years, and it dawned on her now that his system was the 'tried and true' system that any restaurant must use if it is to run at all. She began to study it hard, noting the bookkeeping, the marketing, the method of' using up leftovers, particularly the tricks used by Archie, who did many things that annoyed her, but never used two motions where one would suffice, never wondered if a dish was done, but always knew, and at that moment picked it up.

Some of his principles she adopted at once in making her pies, for she was addicted to a deal of peeping into the oven, and giving them one more minute, just to make sure. Now she put them in by the timer and took them out by the timer, and saved herself much fretting, and made even better pies.

All the time her confidence was growing, her idea clarifying as to the kind of place she meant to have. But one thing vexed her constantly. Where was she going to get the money? During her free time, she surfed the internet and learned that the minimum equipment requirements for a restaurant set up were washing equipment, freezers and grills, prep tables, refrigerator, ice machines, and safety equipment. That was in just setting up the kitchen.

On another site online and from conversations with restaurant owners she learned that opening a restaurant requires a huge investment of time and money. But the challenges do not stop there—once open you must focus on improving processes, managing labor schedules, and controlling restaurant costs.

Not only do you have to manage many costs including, labor, equipment, and food—but you must do it while dealing with inevitable price increases. Whether it's food cost increases due to inflation or a labor cost rise due to rising minimum wage, cost increases, like taxes, are pretty much a guarantee in the restaurant industry.

She almost backed down but remembered Chloe's ambitious nature and continued.

It was a battle of figures as she spent her spare time working through it alone. It amazed her the extent of line items and their cost, even at the beginning of the business. There was security deposits that ranged from $2,000 to $12,000 if renting or loan down payment of 10% if buying a building. In either case there would be construction and renovation costs which she researched by visiting construction companies to get real costs if she built her own place, or if she found a suitable building, the cost to renovate.

She spent a lot of time on the State and County websites checking out licensing costs. There was the business registration fees of $1,200 plus renewals and in general, in the restaurant business, it would cost around $4,500 for the liquor license filing fee.

Her research continued, covering building permits, health permits, food handler's permit, zoning permits, and alcohol tax permits. These costs were minor, she thought as she put them on her budget line.

But it was not over yet. She checked into professional services like bookkeeping, accounting, and consulting. To that she had to consider marketing costs before launch like signage and advertising, beginning food inventory, wages, and salaries.

Bridget's head was spinning, and she found herself mentally and physically exhausted, but she plowed ahead. She had to learn how to remain ahead of the curve, learn what costs to focus on and how do control these costs to stay profitable,

To save this money, at her present income, was going to take a long time, and there was always the risk that she would lose her job, or that some shift in the pie situation would wipe her out completely and leave her exactly where she was in the spring. She had to get started, but on whose money she did not know. She thought about Greyson, and even about the Steeles, but she doubted if they were good for such a sum, and some instinct told her not to ask them.

For a short time, she flirted with the idea of getting it from Mr. Arnold, a retired butcher turned federal meat inspector. She knew him from the restaurant as he was one of her regular customers and always left her a nice tip. She worked on his romantic nature to the point where he suggested meeting her outside.

The more she thought about it, the better it felt, but then realized she should have her notes in order if she were to impress him enough to make a deal. So, one night, when Greyson had reached the stage of yawns, she turned on the light and sat down at the desk in front of her computer. "Greyson, want to help me with something?"

"Not particularly."

"I have to have it soon. Tomorrow, maybe."

"What is it?"

"I don't know what you'd call it, but I need an estimate of costs or something like that. I need it for a man that may back me in business, But I want it all typed, with the right words for what I mean so it looks businesslike."

"Greyson turned around and blinked. "What kind of

business?"

"Just a restaurant."

"Hey, wait a minute, wait a minute."

Greyson came over to her. Then he pulled up a chair and sat down. "Start all over again. And at the beginning. Not in the middle."

Bridget paused and looked at him. "Okay, you asked for it. You are to become bored out of your skull."

Bridget began at first haltingly, feeling suddenly self-conscious about it. She told him her plan of opening a small restaurant, where she would do the cooking herself, and on the menu would be just chicken. But once she got started, she could not stop. "They have steak places and fish places. And I thought since where I work practically every other order is for chicken, it seems to me as though I ought to have plenty of customers." She paused to catch her breath, not worrying what Greyson my think as she rattled on. "I did a lot of thinking and planning and watching and that's how I know what I need and how to go about it, but most of all I did a lot of thinking about what I liked and disliked about the restaurant business."

"I found that the problem was with the system. So many prices, so much to create that may not be ordered for days. It was too much to keep track of. So, I thought, why not simplify and then I would not have to fool with all those a la carte prices, or bookkeeping, or menus, or leftovers or anything like that.

Everybody gets a chicken and waffle dinner, or chicken and

vegetables, if they want, but, listen… all at the same price. And then I will have pies to take out and keep on getting all the wholesale pie business that I can, and, well, it looks like one would help the other. I mean, the pie business would help the restaurant and the restaurant would help the pies."

Greyson seemed to be listening, but she wondered if that was true when all he said was, "And who is this guy?"

Keeping her patience, Bridget said, "Just a customer that eats lunch at the restaurant just about every day. We talk and I have learned enough about him to know he has money. And if I could show him it was a good investment, he might be willing to take a chance on me."

Greyson took several turns around the room, looking at her as he went. She was so accustomed to think of him as someone to sleep with, she forgot how smart he was.

"You really think you can pull it off?"

"Why, don't you?"

"I'm asking you."

"It seems as though it ought to pay. I have worked it all out in my mind, researched through the internet and talked with people in the business and I am quite sure I have thought of everything. I can certainly cook. And I've studied the business from top to bottom with an eye on how to save money."

"What does that mean?"

"That's the main thing, Greyson, about this idea of mine. What costs in a restaurant is waste, and the extras, like printing menus, and the people you need for every little feature you put in. But this way, there would not be any waste. All the leftovers would go into gravy and soup, and there would not be any printing, or extras of any kind. I certainly think I can put it across."

"Then if you can, I might be able to put you in on a deal. One that would start you off with a bang. A deal that would leave you sitting so pretty you wouldn't even need a backer."

“Greyson! If you do not look out, I'll cry.”

“You do the crying later and listen to what I'm going to say to you. You know that model home we had? That dream house that Cameron built, so we could take the prospects in there and show them what their place was going to look like if they spent twice as much dough as any of them had?”

“Yes, of course.” She had special, rather romantic reasons for remembering the model home.

“Okay. They have to get rid of it.”

“Who?”

“The receivers for Bitmore Homes, Inc. The outfit that pays me to be their attorney, and messenger boy, and thief, and anything else they can think of. They must get rid of it, and if you will take it over and put this chicken business in it, it is yours. And believe me, Bridget, if that is not a natural for a restaurant, I never saw one. Why, that place even feels like a restaurant already. Right there under the trees, with the old colonial architecture that Cameron spent all that dough on is not that a place to enjoy a meal! Dump a little gravel on one side, free parking for everybody that comes in. All the rooms are oversized and you can pick and choose what you want to do with them. Every stick in the place complies with the fire law and the health law, even to the bathrooms and there is two of them, not just one. If you really mean this, I can get it for you for around $70,000 outright, or one thousand bucks a month."

"That's.... that is wonderful. I think I'm going to cry."

"I know what you've got and what you haven't got, and I'm telling you, if you want it, it's yours."

"How...?"

He leaned down close, looked melodramatically around, as though to make sure nobody could hear. Then, in a low voice, "They've got to establish losses."

"Who?"

"The receivers! On their federal income tax, the return due next March, they must show losses. If they do not, they are sunk. That's why it's yours at such a cheap price."

"Greyson, I'd still have to have money."

"Who says you would? That is the beauty of it. Once you take title to a piece of property around this town, that is all they want to know. You can get all the credit you want, more than you can use. You think, these supply houses are not feeling this Depression too? They cannot give the stuff away, and all they ask is do you own property, or not. They will deliver anything you want, and connect it up for you, too. You need a little cash, two, three hundred dollars, maybe, I can take care of that. All you've got to do is take over that property and get going, quick."

For the first time in her life, Bridget felt the hot excitement of a conspiratorial deal. She comprehended the credit aspect of it, once Greyson explained it, and she did not need to be told how perfect the place was for her purposes. In her mind's eye she could already see the neon sign, a neat blue one, without red or green in it.

BRIDGET BITMORE
Chicken - Waffles - Pies
Free Parking

But it all seemed too good to be true, and when she asked eager questions about it, Greyson explained. "There's no catch to it. They are in one hell of a hole on those properties, even if they sold some before things got bad, the federal rulings leave them worse off than they were before. Cameron insisted on quality on the structure and the equipment. He said, 'nothing but the best,' and so it was. In his defense, no one knew that the ground would drop out of the market and change the world."

Greyson stared around the room feeling comfortable and in charge. "Bridget, that house is the biggest pain in the ass we have, but all the Corporation is wanting to recapture is the $144,700 they paid Cameron for the lot, and the structure is priced at one hundred and two dollars per square foot.

If we let you have it for the price I quoted, we have a large loss that would make a major dent in the bottom line. Why our taxes will be reasonable."

"But with me?"

"Why not? No one else wants it. It is not a house the average joe can live in. All Cameron was building was an impressive showcase that served as a real estate office, but nobody wants a house with that layout and style. Got to be somebody that can use it for something else, and that means you."

"I know, but before I get too excited about it, you'd better be sure."

He broke off, sat down, and began cursing, first softly, then rising vehemence. Sensing something wrong, she asked, "What is it, Greyson?"

"Cameron."

"What's he got to do with it?"

"Original incorporator."

"Well?"

"He's an original incorporator and you're married to him, and there goes your restaurant and the best deal I have had a chance to put across since Bitmore Homes folded.

It was ten minutes before Bridget could get through her head the ramifications of community property, and the fact that Cameron, by merely being married to her, would be co-owner of the restaurant, and therefore subject to a ruling. He left presently, saying he would talk to his colleagues and look up the law.

Bridget went to bed frantic. Her first big chance would be lost on a legal technicality. She had a recurrence of her bitter fury against Cameron, and the way he seemed to thwart her at every turn. She suffered through the workday and was anxious when the next night Greyson was back, looking more cheerful. “Well, it's okay, but you'll have to get a divorce.”

“Is that the only way?”

“Well? Cameron left you, didn't he?”

“I wish there was some other way.”

“Why?”

“Because I don't know how Cameron’s going to act about it. You never can count on Cameron. If it were just his heart, that would be all right. But he has some twist in his head, and you never know what he is going to do. He might make trouble.”

“How?”

“He'd think of some way.”

“There's no way. If he will let you get a divorce on the ground of cruelty, do it nice and quiet. If he gets tough, you spring that Donahue woman on him, and he must give way, because on infidelity he cannot block it. You do not ask him. You tell him.”

“It takes a year, doesn't it?”

“You getting cold feet?”

“No, but if it's no use, why do it?”

“It takes a year before your decree becomes final. But as soon as it is entered, that ends the community property, and that's all you've got to worry about."

Bridget paused and gave it some thought before responding. "Well, I'll see him."

"Cut out that 'well' stuff. Look, Bridget, you might as well get this thing cleaned up. Because even if it were not for this State thing, you would hardly dare go into business, still married to Cameron. You do not know where he gets his money. For all you can tell, you would no sooner hang out a sign than you would have more judgments and attachments and garnishees slapped on you than you could count. You would be broke before you started. But soon as you shake Cameron, you're all right."

"I said I'd see him."

"If it is money that is worrying you, forget it. In court, I will represent you myself, and the rest of its nothing. But get going. The deal's hot, and you haven't got one day to lose."

CHAPTER 13

The following Sunday when the children were invited to dinner by the Porters, Bridget eagerly gave her okay. It was perfect. The Porter children who lived on the street were best friends with her girls and they spent a lot of time together and the Porters loved having them so she knew they would have fun while giving her some space.

Cameron was coming over. She had sent word to him that she wanted to see him, and this obviously was an arrangement that would insure his finding her alone. She started her pies early, in the hope she would be done before he got there, but she was up to her elbows in dough when he walked in the kitchen door. He asked how she had been, and she said fine, and she asked how he had been, and he said he could not complain. Then he sat down quite sociably and watched her work. It was some time before she could bring herself to broach the subject, and when she did broach it, she did so after considerable beating around the bush.

Finally, she came to the point, realizing that to hide anything from him would be a mistake. Cameron would find out some way, so she went for honesty.

She told about the model home, and the legal points involved, and quoted Greyson in places that became difficult. Then, gulping a little, she said, “So, it looks as though we’ve got to get a divorce, Cameron.”

He received this statement with a very grave face and waited a long time before he spoke. Then he said, “That's something I'll have to think about.”

“Have you any particular objections?”

“I've got plenty of objections. For one thing, I belong to a church that's got some pretty strict rules on this matter.”

“Oh!”

She could not keep the acid out of her voice as she spoke. That he should bring up his perfunctory connection with the Episcopal church struck her as farfetched, particularly as her understanding was that what his church objected to was not divorce itself, but remarriage of divorced persons. But before she could make the point, he went on, “And I'd have to know more about this deal of Greyson Hobbs'. A whole lot more.”

“What have you got to do with that?”

“You're my wife, aren't you?”

She turned away quickly, thrust her hands into the dough, tried to remember that arguing with Cameron was like arguing with a child. Presently she heard him saying, “I probably know ten times as much about federal taxes as Greyson Hobbs does, and all I can say is it sounds to me like a lot of hooey. It comes down to a straight question of collusion, Is there any, or isn't there? In all cases involving collusion, the burden of proof is on the government, and in this case, there cannot be any proof, because I can testify, any time they call me, that there wasn't any.”

“Cameron, don't you see that it isn't a question of proving anything to a court, one way or another? It is whether they let me have the property or they don't. And if I do not get a divorce, they won't.”

Bridget stood thinking. “And what am I going to tell Greyson?”

“Just refer him to me.”

Cameron patted his thighs, stood up, and seemed to regard the discussion as closed. She worked furiously at the dough, tried to keep quiet, then wheeled on him. “Cameron, I want a divorce.”

“Bridget, I heard all you said.”

“What's more, I'm going to get one.”

“Not unless I say the word.”

She had enough. “Okay. What about Margaret Donahue?”

“What about Greyson Hobbs?” He retorted.

She had reached her boiling point and she picked up the dough she had been kneading and threw it at him.

Cameron was taken by surprise, frozen solid in place so that the dough hit him square in the face. They watched in slow motion as the dough, like a flying saucer floated and grew until it reached its target. There it spread over his face, hung there like a veil for a moment, then stretched downward until it landed in a big blob on the floor, leaving remnants of itself on the target.

It took Cameron a while to recover, but when he did, he started talking. "So, you thought I wouldn't find out about you and Greyson. Well, my dear, I have friends and they knew what was going on."

As he talked, he walked behind the island and leaned over the sink, pulling pieces of dough off his face, his mouth going a mile a minute. "Thought you could pull the wool over my eyes? Well think again."

When he stopped talking, all her anger released itself as she yelled viciously at how he was not making a living for his family and now that she wanted to provide for her children he wanted to stand in her way. "What kind of man does that Cameron, tell me, what kind of man blocks any hope of survival for his family?"

Cameron was not about to let her get the upper hand as he tried to get back to the subject of Greyson. Bridget's heart was pounding and her eyes tearing as she tried desperately to make this man see what must be done. Finally, she gave it to him from both barrels. "It's not just me you hurt, but what about Maggie Donahue."

"What about Maggie?"

“I have friends too and they talk. They tell me about you and what they see. She’s married and she’s a home wrecker.”

She had carried it too far and she knew it when Cameron said that he would fix it so she would never get a divorce, not in this state she would not. As she screamed once more that she would have a divorce, she did not care what he did, he said they would see about that, and left.

Later Bridget sat talking with Lucy who listened as she sipped her tea, not saying a word. “Well, aren’t you going to say anything?”

Lucy shook her head, twirled her teabag then looked at Bridget. “It's the funniest thing, baby. Here you lived with Cameron; how long was it? Ten or twelve years, and still, you don't understand him, do you?”

“He's got a rebellious streak in him.”

“No, he hasn't. Once you understand Cameron, you know he is not rebellious at all. Cameron’s like Chloe. Unless he can do things in a grand way, he is not living, that's all.”

“What's grand about the way he acted?”

“Open your eyes. Look at it, for once, the way he looks at it. He does not care about the church, or the law, or Greyson. He just put all that in to sound big. What is griping his soul is that he cannot do anything for his kids. If he must stand up in court and admit he cannot pay a cent to support his kids, he'd rather die.”

"It's the truth. He's not doing anything for them now."

"Oh, but now is just a trifling detail, a temporary condition that he doesn't count. When he puts over a deal…"

"That'll be never."

"Will you just let me talk for a while. It is his fear of being a deadbeat dad and I am telling you that is what is stopping him. But he cannot hold out forever. For one thing there is the Donahue woman. She will not like it, when she finds out you asked for a divorce and he would not give it to you. She is going to wonder if he really loves her... though how anybody could love her is beyond me. And all the time he has it staring him in the face that the harder he makes it for you, the harder he is making it for the kids. And Cameron, he loves those kids, too. Bridget, Cameron's on the end of the plank, and there's nowhere for him to go but off."

"Yes, but when?"

"When he gets the pie."

"What pie?"

"The pie you're going to send him. It is going to be a very special pie. It does not appeal to his stomach, except incidentally. It appeals to his higher nature, and in Cameron, that means his vanity. You're going to tell him that it's a pie you've been fooling around with and you want his opinion on its commercial possibilities."

"Why would I do that, Lucy. Tell me why."

"Because it'll help you get what you want."

Bridget thought for a moment and then she understood. "I

don't really mind making Cameron a pie."

"Then get at it."

So, Bridget made him a pie, a deep-dish creation, that went above the average chocolate cream pie. It was a makeover with the addition of hazelnut, a silken richness with the sweet hazelnut liqueur and fresh nuts that gave it a certain brightness that would make anyone sit up and take notice. It was about as commercial as a hand whittled clothespin, but she wrote a carefully worded note and at the end asked his opinion, and a P.S., saying she had put his initials on it to see if she could still do monograms. She sent it by Francine, and sure enough around the middle of the week there came another invitation to the children, for Sunday dinner at the grandparents.

Bridget worked frantically to take care of her pie orders and get them out early. When she finished, she prepared a cold lunch for two, knowing Cameron had arranged that Sunday dinner so that they could talk. When Cameron arrived, Bridget had a cocktail waiting and the cat and mouse game began.

Cameron began by saying the pie was exceptional. He told Bridget that there was a great need for homemade pastries since people no longer had the time to bake from scratch. All this was what Bridget had known for some time, but did not mention that, instead she thanked him for his opinion. A pause settled between them making Bridget feel fidgety, wanting to guide the conversation, but remained quiet following Lucy's instructions. Finally, he said, "Well Bridget, I told you I'd think that matter over, and I have."

"Well?"

"Of course, any way you look at it, it's unpleasant."

"It certainly is for me."

"It's just one of those things that two people hate to think about. But we really have nothing to do with it."

"I don't know what you mean, Cameron."

"I mean, whether it's unpleasant for us, is not important. It is what is best for our kids that counts, and that is what we must think about. And talk about."

"Did I ever have any other reason? It is for them that I want to take advantage of this opportunity. If I can make a go of it, I can give them what I want them to have, and what you ought to want them to have, too."

"I want to do my share."

"Nobody's asking you to do anything. I know that when you are able, you will be glad to help out."

"Bridget, there's one thing I can do, and if you're set on this, I want to do it. I can see that you have' a place to sleep, and that the kids have, and that nobody can take it away from you. I want to give you the house."

Bridget was flabbergasted. This she had not expected at all. The house had long ceased to be a possession, as far as she was concerned. It was a place that she lived in, and that crushed her beneath interest, taxes, and upkeep. That Cameron, with a straight face, should offer it to her like a prize was astonishing. And then she remembered what Lucy had said, and knew she was in the presence of a man and his pride. She got up suddenly, went over, and put her arms around him. “You don't have to do that.”

“Bridget, I want to.”

“If you want to, there is only one thing I can do, and, that is, take it. But you do not have to. I want you to know that.”

“All right, but you've got to take it.”

“I'm sorry I said what I did about Mrs. Donahue.”

“I've been hating myself for what I said about Greyson. Christ, I know there'd never be anything between you and him.”

“But…” she began, knowing there was more.

“We keep saying things that we don't mean.”

“I know. I hate this just as much as you do. But it must be. For our children.”

“Yeah, for their sake.”

They talked low and close for a long time, and then got to laughing over the way he looked when she hit him with the dough. Then they got to discussing another angle they could use to simplify it all.

“That would work Cameron, but I’m not going to outright lie in court.”

“I know, so…”

“I guess you'll have to hit me, Cameron.”

“You talk like Chloe. She's always wanting to be hit.”

“I'm glad there's a little of me in her.”

He doubled his fist, brushed her chin with it. Then they both burst into shaking, uncontrollable sobs. This was not what either one of them had expected to happen to their life. They both could not help wondering what had gone wrong, even though it stared them in the face.

The next thing she knew, she was in court, raising her hand, swearing to tell the truth, the whole truth, and nothing but the truth, so help her God, and giving her name, address, and occupation, which she described as ‘homemaker’.

Then she was answering questions put to her by a Greyson she had never seen before, a solemn, sympathetic, man who gently urged her to tell an elderly judge the story of Cameron’s unendurable cruelties, his silences, during which he would not speak to her for days on end; his absences from home, his striking her during an argument over money.

Then she was sitting beside Greyson, and Lucy Steele was up there, corroborating everything she said, with just the right shade of repressed indignation. When Mrs. Steele got to the blow, and Greyson asked her sternly if she had seen it, she closed her eyes and whispered, “I did.”

Then Bridget and Lucy were out in the corridor where Greyson presently joined them. “Okay. Decree's entered.”

“Why so soon?”

That is how it goes when you got a properly prepared case. No trouble about a divorce if it is handled right. The law says, cruelty, and that is what you got to prove, but that is all you got to prove. That sock in the jaw was worth two hours of argument."

He drove them home, and Bridget made drinks, and Cameron came in, to sign papers. She was glad, somehow, that since the real estate deal started, Greyson had been curiously silent about romance. It permitted her to sit beside Cameron without any sense of deceit, and really feel friendly toward him. The first chance she got, she whispered in his ear, "I told them the property settlement had been reached out of court. The reporters, I mean. Was that all right?"

"Perfectly."

That this elegant announcement should come out in the papers, she knew, meant a great deal to him. She patted his hand, and he patted back. Greyson left, and then Cameron, after a wistful look at his glass, decided he had to go too. But something caught in Bridget's throat as he went down the walk his shoulders thrown bravely back. Mrs. Steele looked at her sharply. "Now what is it?"

"I don't know. I feel as though I picked his bones. First his kids, and then his car, and now the house, and everything he's got."

“Will you kindly tell me what good the house would do him? On the first call for interest, he would lose it, wouldn't he?”

“But he looked so pitiful.”

“Baby, they all do. That's what gets us.”

CHAPTER 14

It was a hot morning in October, her last at the restaurant. The previous two weeks had been a mad scramble in which it had seemed she would never find time for all she had to do. First, she had to get the deed to the property handled, then it was off to getting contractors in to ready the location and finally visits to the restaurant equipment store, to order the dishwasher, freezers and grills, prep tables, refrigerator and ice machines, and safety equipment. Her precious credit entitled her to get everything she needed.

To help herself, Bridget made calls on restaurant proprietors, to get her pie orders to the point where they would really help on expenses and found time to dash to the model home, where painters were transforming it. Secret worry about money and work sent her to bed at night almost too exhausted to sleep.

But now it was almost over. The equipment was in and the

particularly gigantic range made her heart thump when she looked at it. The painters were done, and she had three new pie contracts signed. The load of debt she would have to carry, the interest, taxes, and installments involved, frightened her, and at the same time excited her. If she could make it through the first year or two, she told herself, then she would have something to be proud of.

So, at the restaurant she sat with the girls at breakfast, listening to Emily instruct the new girl, Shirley, who was to take her place. Her mind was so tied up with the major changes being made in her life that she felt only physically there. Every now and then she picked up on the conversation. At one point when Emily shared with Shirley the secret of getting larger tips, Bridget smiled. At another point when she told her to not forget the starters, Bridget remembered her first day.

Emily was so busy training Shirley that she took no notice of Ida trying to get her attention. Bridget seeing this, excused herself and went over to see what Ida wanted.

"Tell Emily I have to seat this customer at her station."

"I don't mind taking care of it for her." Then she added with a smile, "I'll make sure she gets the tip." Ida smiled back.

Bridget turned to see Emily getting up and said, "Sit down. I'll take care of the customer for you."

Bridget put on a sincere smile, realizing this would be the last time she waited on a customer in this restaurant. The next one she waited on would be at her own place. She felt good as she went to take the customer's order. As she stood silently giving him time to make up his mind, she wondered whether his bald spot was brown by nature, or from sunburn. It was a tiny bald spot, with black hair all around it, but it was a bald spot just the same.

While he continued to study the menu, she decided that it had to be sunburn. From there her eyes traveled over the rest of the customer. She determined from a side glance he might be Italian or maybe Latin. Having watched him walk over to the station, she knew he was tall and had a lanky built. He also was wearing a pair of jeans that fit his body nicely.

At that moment he looked up and Bridget shifted her weight, looked into brown eyes above a neatly clipped moustache and prepared herself to take his order.

“What in the hell am I looking at this for? Why does anybody ever look at a menu for breakfast? You know exactly what you're going to have, and yet you keep looking at it.”

“To find out the prices, of course.”

She had no intention of making a joke, but his eyes were friendly, and it slipped out. “Did you hear the one about the blind man?”

“No, do tell.”

“A blind man walks into a restaurant and sits down. The waiter, who is also the owner, walks up to the blind man and hands him a menu and he says, I'm sorry, sir, but I am blind and can't read the menu. Just bring me a dirty fork from a previous customer. I'll smell it and order from there."

The man was silent. His head was down so she couldn’t read

his face and started to apologize. 'I'm so sorry. This is a clean…"

He snapped his fingers as though this were the answer to something that had worried him all his life and said, "That's it, of course, the prices." Then they both laughed, and he got down to business. "Okay you ready?"

"Shoot."

"Orange juice, oatmeal, bacon and eggs, fried on one side and not too much, dry toast, and large coffee. You got it?"

She recited it back to him, with his own intonations, and they laughed again. "And if you could step on it slightly? I want to go to Charlotte for a little swimming before the sun goes down."

"Ah, that's nice. I wish I could go to Charlotte."

"What's stopping you. Come on."

"You better look out; I might say yes."

When she came back with his orange juice, he grinned and said, "Well? I meant it."

"I told you I might take you up on it so be careful."

Bridget went back to the kitchen and returned with the rest of his order. His eyes met hers before she reached the table, and she could not repress a little smile as she approached. As she set down the plate she asked, "Well, what are you grinning about?"

"And what are you grinning about?"

The man thought about it a moment and then said, "I never do this, but I'm going to come right out and say it. I like you."

"Thanks. I like you too."

"You know what a highly original thing for you would be to

do.

"What's that?"

"Say yes, to my offer to come with me."

A wild, excited feeling swept over her. It suddenly occurred to her that for the moment she was free as a bird. Her pies were all made and delivered, the children were with the Porters at the beach, the painters would be done by noon so there was nothing to detain her at all. It was as though for just a little while she was unlisted in God's big index, and as she turned away, for the first time in a long time she felt free. She stopped and turned back around.

"Give me a minute," she said as she went to the kitchen, and beckoned to Ida.

"Ida, I think I make the new girl nervous. Emily is handling her like she handled me, and I came out all right. Right?"

"Yes, you did."

"So, why don't I just quietly leave now?"

Ida looked over toward Mr. Chris, who was doing his morning accounts. "Well, he'd just love to save a buck."

"Of course, he would."

"All right, Bridget, you run along, and I wish you all kinds of luck with your restaurant, and I'll be out the very first chance I get."

Bridget turned to leave, and Ida called her back. "Bridget, don't forget your last check!"

"I'll pick it up next week."

“That's right, when you come with the pies.”

“Yes, when I come with the pies.”

If put into words, the rest of her movements were quick, breathless, and eager. Bridget felt like a young girl again as she reached into her pocket and pulled out a piece of paper. She leaned on the table and quickly wrote down her address and handed it to him.

“Oh, I thought we could leave together.”

“No, I need to take my car home.”

“Okay, I’ll follow you, then.”

“No, take this and give me a few minutes and I’ll meet you there. I have some errands to do, but I’ll hurry.”

He wanted to get started and she knew it, but she needed to see that the model home was locked after the painters got out, only she did not go into that.

“Let’s rendezvous at twelve fifteen.”

“See you then.”

The man put a tip on the table and Emily went over to collect it while Bridget hurried to her locker, changed, and on her way out said goodbye to these people who had taken a chance on her.

Bridget went to the model home and found that it was locked. Next, she raced over to Target and bought beach items feeling happy she had money to pay for them. Then she hurried to her car and started home. It was fourteen minutes to twelve, by the car clock, when she pulled up the drive. While she waited for the garage door to open, out of habit she glanced toward Lucy’s and seeing the shades were closed, she figured the Steeles must have gone away for the weekend.

She pulled the car into the garage and hurried inside with her bundles. Bridget rushed toward her bedroom as she whipped off her dress and hurriedly grabbed a pair of shorts and a top from her dresser. She wasted no time putting on her clothes and taking the new beach bag, stuffed her purchases in it, along with a floppy hat. She then went over to her dresser and grabbed a comb and dropped that into the bag as she made her way into the bathroom to get a clean towel and soap. She stood thinking, then closed the bag, got out a light coat and hurried out the door.

Bridget could feel her heart beating faster and took a deep breath. This was so unlike her to just go out with a stranger. No, it was not like her at all, but she felt he was a nice person and she had nothing to be afraid of. Her thoughts were interrupted when a blue Corvette pulled into the driveway.

“Get in... Say, you look great.”

Bridget climbed in glad she was not wearing a dress as her body sank down to the seat. She fastened her seat belt and they backed out of her driveway, heading toward Charlotte. It was then she realized she did not even know his name.

“By the way, my name is Bridget.”

“Bridget is a nice name. Does Bridget have a last name?”

“Yes, it’s Bitmore.”

He was quiet for a moment, then asked. “Bitmore, like in Bitmore Homes?”

“Yes, I was married to Cameron Bitmore, but we’re divorced now.”

He said, “Hmm.”

“Hmm, what?”

Jokingly he said, they were the worst homes ever built, as all the roofs leaked. Bridget said that that was not the problem. The problem was how the treasury leaked, and they both laughed gaily.

“So, are you going to tell me your name?”

“My name is Nicholas…friends call me Nick.”

“So, Nicholas, do you have a last name.”

“Lombardi.”

“You can call me Nick.”

“If I ever get to know you well enough to call you by your first name, I'll call you that.”

“Is that a promise, Mrs. Bitmore?”

“It is, Mr. Lombardi,”

She was happy. She was sure he had given her his real name and not a phony one. She knew some men did that so that later they could not be reached. She settled back, lost a slightly uneasy feeling she had had, of being just a pickup.

Once the Corvette was on the expressway, Nick stepped on the gas, passing every car on the road until coming to their exit. At that point Nick got off and looking around, Bridget realized they were not at Charlotte Beach. She started to say something, but instead began working out a plan in her head.

How could she have been so stupid to climb into a car with a stranger. She was being kidnapped and would probably be raped and left by the side of the road if she were lucky. It was just like everything in her life. It starts out great and then ends in disaster.

As she stared around, she realized they were at Lake Ontario, but not at the park. Instead, he took a little road off to the right that was unpaved. When they stopped, the first thing she saw was a little shingled cabin. That is where he parked.

Nick jumped out of the car and leaned in. "I'm sorry, should have asked you if you want to change here. I always do, but if you prefer a bathhouse, there is one around on the other side."

Not knowing what else to say she replied, "I think this is fine."

He took her bag, and they went clumping around a boardwalk to the front. He unlocked the door, and they stepped into the hottest, stuffiest room that Bridget had ever been in.

"Woosh!"

He strode around, throwing up windows, going out back and opening doors, letting air circulate in a place that evidently had not been opened for a while. While he was doing this, she looked around. It was the living room of a rough mountain cabin, with a rough board floor through whose chinks she could see the earth beneath. Two or three rugs were scattered around, and the furniture was oak, with leather seats. However, there was a stone fireplace, and a masculine look to everything, but she half liked it.

"Are you hungry? We can get lunch at the tavern, or would

you rather swim first?"

"Hungry? You just had breakfast!"

"Then we'll swim."

He picked up her bag and led the way to a small back room whose only furnishings were a cotton rug, a chair, and an iron bed, made up neatly with blankets. "If you can manage here, I'll use the front room, and see you in a few minutes."

"I won't be long."

Both spoke with elaborate casualness, but she was no sooner alone than she dropped the bag on the bed and zipped it open even more quickly than she had zipped it shut. She was terrified he would reappear before she had finished dressing. Yet the possible consequences, as such, were not what frightened her. The heat, and now the breeze that was blowing in, filled her with a heavy, languorous, feeling that made her want to dawdle. But as he left her, she had caught a whiff of her hair and it reeked of Archie's bacon grease.

Bridget knew this was always the case, especially when she was too tired to take the time to wash it. Usually when Greyson came, she would pull it back in a ponytail, but as to whether Greyson noticed this, or liked it, or did not like it, she cared no more than she cared whether he dropped by or did not drop by. But that this man should notice she did care.

She slipped feverishly out of her clothes put them on a chair, slipped quickly into her suit. She put on the rubber shoes and grabbed the soap. Near her was a door that seemed to lead to some sort of small corridor. She opened it and peeked around the door.

She could see it led to the back of the little house and she observed a privacy lattice placed along the back side of a walkway, up near the entrance. Cautiously she stepped out, telling herself she should wait, but not wanting to have him smell her hair she walked to the end of the lattice and peered around the yard until see saw a jetty, just steps away from her. She paused, trying to think sanely, but instead, her feet took off and clutching the soap tightly in her hand, she dove in.

The minute she broke the surface Bridget felt her heart rate soar. By the time her body glided over the stony bottom her breathing was erratic, and it took a minute or two to calm down. Then she pushed and swam up to the surface.

She saw no one around so quickly took the soap and rubbed it against her wet hair. Then using her free hand, worked up a lather. Sure, she had gotten the smell out, she ducked underwater and holding her breath, rinsed the soap out of her hair. When she came up again, he was standing there, so she let the soap flutter to the bottom.

"You were certainly in one hell of a hurry."

"I was hot."

"You forgot your cap."

"Yes, I did."

"You look like a drowned rat."

Ignoring his last remark Bridget wiped the water from her face and said, “Well, are you just going to stand there and watch me, or swim.”

Before she finished her sentence, Nick dove in and she enjoyed watching the shock on his face as he returned to the surface. “Wow. It is freezing cold. Why didn’t you warn me?”

Bridget tilted her head to the side and with her lips pressed close and her eyebrows raised, he got the message.

That began a pretend battle of splashing and swimming around each other and when they tired, a challenge began.

Nick said, in a someway superior attitude, “Did you know the water you see in a lake is not always the same?” Not waiting for a response, he continued. “In fact, water is always on the move through the water cycle, being constantly recycled, sustaining life and creating dramatic weather worldwide.”

Not wanting to be outdone, Bridget asked, ““Did you know that ‘Water Music’ is a suite of short pieces for a small orchestra composed by German born English composer George Frederic Handel, known particularly for its highly spirited movements in dance form?” And like Nick she did not wait for a response as she added, “Most of the pieces were originally intended for outdoor performance, and the work premiered on a barge on the River Thames, where it provided entertainment for a royal cruise hosted by King George I of Great Britain on July 17, 1717.”

She could see that Nick was indeed impressed and was about to ask how she knew that when she started shivering uncontrollably. The sun was going down and Bridget headed for the jetty and Nick followed. Catching up with her Bridget felt his hands move under her body and he lifted her up. She did not stop him and admittedly felt comfortable in his arms as he carried her out of the water.

The minute they were out of the water, she was not sure it was her body shivering or his as the cool evening air hit them, and Nick moved swiftly across the lawn until he reached the welcoming heat of the cabin. He did not put her down, but instead continued with her in his arms until he reached the bedroom.

She was helpless, not wanting him to stop as she kicked the beach bag off the bed and just like their word battle for superiority, they continued the need to outdo each other.

It was like nothing she had experienced before as they caressed each other into ecstasy and when their bodies became as one, she thought she would faint and die. It was so wonderful and though she knew the spontaneousness of it made it exciting, there was more to it than just that. Unbeknownst to her, Nick was amazed by her and could not remember ever being so overcome by lust and desire. He had never ever dreamed of such a transport.

They laid there quietly as the last of the daylight disappeared over the horizon. Bridget was the first to break the silence. "I'm hungry."

"Me too. I hate having to say it, but we need to get dressed."

Bridget gathered her things and went into the bathroom to dress. When she returned to the bedroom, he was waiting for her.

She had thought it would be weird after what they had experienced together, but it was not, not at all. Nick drove them to a local tavern by the lake for a light dinner and they talked comfortably. When Nick paid the check, they left and climbed into his car. Bridget started to ask him if he could put up the top, but he was already on it.

They arrived at the cabin to find that the fire had gone out and the cabin was dark and cold. She watched while Nick built a fire until he asked her to get a bottle of wine out of the fridge in the kitchen.

Still wrapped in her coat, she found the wine and in the sparse offerings in the cabinets, were two wine glasses that she carried back with her. Nick had finished with the fire and took the wine bottle. She watched as he opened a pocketknife that had a simple cork bottle opener attached and with the ease of experience, had the wine opened and poured.

They sat by the fire talking in the way one has of not saying anything too personal or important, even though they felt comfortable with each other. Of course, Bridget wanted to know about the cabin and the house behind it but did not mention it. When Nick said he was hungry again, Bridget agreed and said, "I saw a Wegmans on our way to the tavern, why not go there and get something and I'll cook."

At first Nick was against having her cook, but she said, "Look, you buy the food and I'll cook it and we can call it even. Otherwise, I'll have to pay since you bought the first meal."

Nick laughed and Bridget joined in. He put an extra log on the fire, and they hurried out, hoping to get back before the fire died and they did. While Bridget found what she needed in the kitchen, she carried the steaks and potatoes into the living room. When the wood had burned down and was giving off a red glow, Bridget put the steaks on the grate and using tongs she found in the kitchen, watched the steaks closely, turning them over for their final searing before putting them on plates that Nick supplied, along with two forks. She pierced the foil around the potatoes with her fork to check if they were done. They were. She had cut them into small chunks and seasoned them well.

The two worked at ripping off pieces of steak since they did not have steak knives and finishing off the potatoes as though they had not eaten in days. When they were done Nick helped her clean up, then he asked if she was ready to go home.

Bridget knew that she must go home, but it was hard to say the words. Finally, she looked at him and said, "Yes."

He could sense her words were not coming from her heart and just like her he also was not ready for her to leave. So, he picked her up and carried her into the bedroom. The heat from the fireplace did not warm the room, but neither one of them cared as they shivered from the cold and climbed under the blankets together. Feeling the heat of their bodies as they clung together under the covers, they again made love. Afterwards, they talked.

They really talked. Bridget learned that he was thirty-three years old, that he had attended the University of Rochester, that he lived in Charlotte, that his family lived there too, or at any rate his mother and sister, who, seemed to be all the family he had. When she asked him what he did, he said, "Oh I don't know. Do not get me wrong. I am not some poor smuck. I own a Fruit export company and I am part owner of an estate that is supported by a quarterly salary I draw."

"So, you don't work at all?"

"Don't say it like that. I like it better when it's said that I don't have to."

"Don't you want to do something?"

"Why should I?"

He seemed quite nettled, and she stopped talking about it, but she found it disturbing. But she detected there was something about this man's loafing that was different from Cameron's. Cameron at least had plans, grandiose dreams that he thought would come true. But Nick's loafing was not a weakness, it was a way of life, and it had the same effect on her that Chloe's nonsense had, her mind rejected it, and yet her heart, somehow, was impressed by it.

The offhand dismissal of the subject put her on the defensive too. Most of the men she knew were quite gabby about their work and took the mandate of accomplishment seriously. Their talk might be tiresome, but it was what she accepted and believed in. This bland assumption that the whole subject was a bore, not worth discussing, was beyond her comprehension. However, her uneasiness vanished when at daybreak she felt cold, and pushed her bottom against him. When he took her in his arms, she wriggled into his belly quite possessively, and drifted off to sleep with a sigh of deep content.

The next morning, they ate and swam and snoozed, and when Bridget opened her eyes after one of these naps, she could hardly believe it was late afternoon and time to go home. But still they dawdled, with Nick arguing they should stay another day, and make a weekend of it.

The Monday pies, however, were on her mind, and she knew she had to get at them. It was six o' clock when they drove over to the tavern for an early dinner, and seven before they got started. But the big Corvette went even faster than it had come up, and it was barely nine as they approached Irondequoit. “Want to see something, Nick?”

“What is it?”

"I'll show you.”

He kept following her directions and then stopped when she told him to. “You wait here. I won't be a minute.”

She got out her key and ran to the door, her feet crunching on the gravel that had been dumped for the free parking. Inside, she groped her way to the switchbox, and threw on the neon sign. Then she ran out to observe its effect. He was already under it, peering, blinking. It was, indeed, a handsome work of art, made exactly as she had pictured it, except that it had a blazing red arrow through its middle. Nick looked first at the sign, then at Bridget. “Well, what the hell? Is this yours?”

“Don't you see whose name is on it?”

“Wait a minute. The last I knew; you were a waitress.”

“But not anymore. Yesterday was my last day. I quit early to run off with you. From now on, I'm a businessperson.”

“Why didn't you tell me?”

“I didn't get any chance, that I noticed.”

At this tribute to his prowess as a lover, he grinned, and she pulled him inside, to see the rest of the building. She switched on the lights and took him through, lifting the painters' cloths to show him, the new maple tables, pointing out the smart tile floor covering, explaining it was required by the Department of Health. She took him to the kitchen and pointed out the range. He kept asking questions, and she poured out the whole story, excitedly flattered that a man of means was totally impressed by her small business.

Presently he asked when she was going to open.

“Thursday.”

“Next Thursday?”

“At six o'clock.”

“Am I invited?”

“Of course, you are.”

She switched off the lights, and for a moment they were

standing there in the dark with the smell of fresh paint all around them. Then she went into his arms. “Kiss me, Nick.” At that moment she knew he was impressed by her and it felt good.

“Why didn't you tell me about all this?”

“I don't know. I was going to, but I was afraid you might just think it was funny.”

He thought about it, then said. "I will be here Thursday. With bells.”

“Please. It won't be the same without you.”

He took her home, walked her to the door, and waited while she unlocked it. As she was waving goodbye, she heard her name called. Automatically she looked toward the Steeles, but their house was still dark.

As she peered through the darkness, she sees a woman running across lawns, as best a woman in her sixties can, yelling her name and obviously upset. Her loud, accusing voice is waking the other neighbors as one after the other pop out of their homes to witness the commotion.

Bridget kept her eyes on the woman and can soon see it is Mrs. Floyd, who lived two doors away.

By the time she reaches Bridget, she is breathless and limping. Bridget waits as Mrs. Floyd leans over trying to catch her breath and looks down and sees the reason she was limping. Mrs. Floyd either lost a shoe or forgot to put it on.

Finally, she straightens. “Mrs. Bitmore!”

There was a sharpness to her voice that annoyed Bridget but her quick prescience from the approach tells her that something was wrong. Then, in a tone of virtuous indignation that the whole street could hear, Mrs. Floyd cut loose. “Where in the world have you been? They've been trying to reach you ever since last night, and no one knew where you were.”

Bridget choked back an impulse to tell her it was none of her business where she had been, and managed to inquire civilly, “Who are they and what did they want with me, Mrs. Floyd?”

“It's your daughter.”

That took her breath away and her mind immediately went to Chloe. Anxious now, Bridget asked, “What’s wrong with Chloe…what has she done?”

“It’s not Chloe. It is your daughter Isabella. She's sick and they've taken her to a hospital, and…”

“Which hospital?”

“I don't know which hospital, but…”

Bridget dashed into the house and into the den, snapping on lights as she went. As she picked up the phone a horrible feeling came over her that God had had her number, after all.

CHAPTER 15

As Lily Bitmore made her dozenth remark about Bridget's disappearance over the weekend, Bridget's temper flared.

It had been indeed, a trying hour trying to reach the family and find out what hospital they had taken her precious Izzy. She calmed herself, knowing that there were only three choices, but the three were situated in different areas of the city and suburbs. She called her mother-in-law's cell, no answer. She next called her father-in-law's cell. Again, no answer. Remaining as calm as she could, she called Cameron's cell. Still no answer.

"What's wrong with these people..." Then she remembered you could not use cell phones in a hospital. "Now what..." Even as she asked herself, she knew. She called the closest hospital to her. It was not like the old days when a person picked up the phone and asked if they could help and then transferred you when they located the person you were trying to reach. No, it was not like that at all. Instead, she was greeted by a robotic voice that asked her to press a number from the list of numbers they recited to her. Time was flying along with her patience draining, but determinedly she held on, making the choice of the emergency room, and then holding until a human voice finally asked if they could help. "Yes, can you check to see if Isabella Bitmore is there?"

"And who are you?"

"I'm Bridget Bitmore, her mother. I had a message saying she was taken to the hospital but not which hospital."

A few minutes passed and she was finally told, they had no Isabella Bitmore shown as being admitted. She thanked them and went on to the next hospital, relaying the same information and ending with the same results. Last, she called Rochester General Hospital and at the end of the conversations she was told her daughter was there.

She let out a sigh and started toward the door, realizing then that Mrs. Floyd had followed her into the house.

Now that she had finished on the phone, Mrs. Floyd had more to say. "I can't believe you. You're just recently divorced and already you are running off with some man and leaving other people to take care of your children."

Bridget ignored her, thinking she needed to call Mrs. Steele. Lucy answered on the second ring, obviously up even though there were no lights on.

"Lucy, Isabella is at Rochester General Hospital. I don't

know what happened, but I am on my way there."

There was a slight pause before Lucy spoke. "Yes, I know."

Bridget could hear disgust in her voice and decided not to ask what was wrong as she said goodbye and hung up.

As soon as she ended that conversation, Mrs. Floyd thought it right to degrade her again, but Bridget would not have it. "Shut up Mrs. Floyd and go home."

Mrs. Floyd, taken by surprise managed to get her body moving as she huffed out the door. Bridget could only imagine what she would tell the other neighbors, but she did not care. The only thing she cared about now was getting to Isabella.

Bridget hurried to the garage and climbed into her car, telling herself to calm down, but knowing she would not, or could not obey that voice as she remembered to press the garage door opener and wait before backing out into the street, not looking either way to see if anything was coming.

At the corner she made a right and headed down List Avenue, to Wyndale where she swung around the corner, ignoring the stop sign. The car practically drove itself down the hill to Oakview where she turned right again and headed up the hill to the light, which was already changing to green.

"Thank god," she whispered as she hurried through the intersection where the road changed its name to Portland; the street where the hospital was located. She lucked out again when she reached Ridge Road East and the light changed to green as she approached. Soon she was pulling into the emergency parking lot.

She had barely gotten out of her car when she was informed, she could not park there, and she told the security guard her daughter had been brought into emergency. The guard walked her to the front desk where she was told that Isabella Bitmore had been admitted and gave her the room number.

Hurriedly, she went back to her car and pulled around to park in the main parking lot. It was hard controlling herself as she drove around the ramp to find an open parking space, but when she did, she expertly pulled the car into it and hurried inside. There she made her way to the bank of elevators. She pushed the 'up' button and then scanned the elevator lights to hurry to the one that would arrive first. There she stood and rushed inside as soon as the doors open.

She was alone in the elevator which hopefully meant there would be no stops before she reached her floor. She pressed the button and stayed by the floor indicator menu, watching as the door closed.

Bridget prayed hard as the elevator ascended and when it stopped, she stepped out feeling a little less frantic as she followed the directions on the card she had been given in emergency. Easily she maneuvered through the long corridors until she was headed in the direction of her daughter's room.

Unaware she had been holding her breath, she released it now and when she looked up, she saw them.

Cameron came to her rescue. Bridget gave him a wan smile and asked, “Can you take me to Izzy right now?”

“Sure, Bridge, sure.” They walked to one of the curtained rooms and he stepped aside to let her enter first. There on the bed, looking small and helpless, her curls spraying across the white pillow was her baby, hooked up to monitors and unaware of her presence so she moved in close, touched her cheek and whispered, “I’m here baby. Mommy’s here.”

“Come on Bridget. She’s asleep and we should let her sleep.” Bridget let Cameron guide her out of the room and back to the waiting area.

She sat with Cameron, Chloe, and her in-laws at the end of the hospital corridor, waiting for the doctor, listening to Cameron explain what had happened.

“Isabella seemed fine on Friday. She was her old active self. But by Friday evening she complained of abdominal pain. At first, we were not going to go to the beach and see if she got better, but Chloe was being her usual self, complaining and then Isabella said she felt much better, so to the beach we went.”

“I can’t believe…”

“No, wait, Bridget. She did seem fine. That is until we ate lunch and she started vomiting. Before we could get home, she had an accident…”

“What kind of accident?”

“She had diarrhea and it was all over the back seat. When father parked the car and carried her inside, he thought he saw blood in the watery diarrhea."

"So…"

"Well, she started running a fever, so we called Dr. Crawford and he had advised taking her to the hospital."

Mrs. Bitmore had interrupted Cameron and corrected him. From the look he gave his mother, Bridget knew she was in for a taunt. She braced herself.

"The doctor didn't say any such thing. He had ordered we take her home and we had taken her home. But when we got there the house was all locked up and it appeared nobody was there. We called the land line and there was no answer and so we called your cell and still there was no answer. So, we called Dr. Crawford back." Lily Bitmore paused for effect. "It was then that he ordered we take her to the hospital, because there was no other place to take her."

Bridget's head snapped up and her mouth started to open but in time she stopped herself from asking what was the matter with them. They could have taken her to their house. This was not the time or place to start a confrontation, so she swallowed the words back before giving them life.

Cameron took up the story again stating soothingly there was nothing serious the matter, just a bad cold and not the flu as Bridget had been told.

Bridget's mother-in-law took the floor again, making more insinuations, until Bridget said, "I don t know that it's any of your business where I was, or anybody else's, Mom."

Mrs. Bitmore turned white, and sat bolt upright, but kept quiet. Bridget could read her and knew she was thinking her upbringing primitive and like she felt so many years ago, she wondered what her son had seen in this black woman who proved constantly she had no breeding. Oh, she had known her mother-in-law had problems accepting her, but that did not matter now because she loved her grandchildren and would do anything for them. That is why the handling of this situation was so out of character. But then it came to her. Obviously, Cameron had informed his parents of their marital situation and had probably said she had thrown him out without explaining the circumstances.

Finally, Bridget, trying to keep the peace said, "I was at the beach if you must know. When some friends invited me up to their cottage by the lake, I did not see why I was the one person on earth that had to stay home. Of course, I should have. That is what you," she continued turning to face Lily, "would have done since married woman are not to have a life outside the home. Right, Mrs. Bitmore?" Not waiting for a reply, she added, "But I didn't know at the time that I had a set of in laws that couldn't even find a place for a sick child that had been left in their care. I'll certainly know better next time."

"I think Mother's perfectly right." Up to now, Chloe had been coldly neutral, but when she heard about the cottage by the lake, she knew exactly whose side benefitted her. Even though Bridget could read the reasoning in Chloe's eyes, she thanked her.

Cameron looked unhappy and said nothing. Mr. Bitmore had a solemn rebuke, "Bridget, everybody did the best they could, and I don't see any need for personal remarks."

"Who started these personal remarks?"

Nobody had an answer for this, and for a time there was silence. Bridget had little appetite for the squabble, for deep down in her heart she had a premonition that Isabella was sick. After what seemed an interminable period Dr. Crawford joined them in the waiting room.

All eyes turned in his direction. He was a tall, stooped man who had been the family doctor ever since Chloe was born. "Bridget," he said. She stood and went over to him. "Come with me."

Out of the corner of her eye she saw Mr. Bitmore grab his wife's arm and motioned her to be still.

Bridget followed him down the corridor to Isabella's room. "Wait here, Bridget."

She was barely in the room, but she stood quietly while he went over to Isabella's bedside and took her temperature and flashed a light into her eyes before guiding the nurse over to the far corner of the room. They spoke in a whisper and Bridget tried to hear what they were saying. But she could not.

Worry was written all over Bridget's face when Dr. Crawford turned and walked back to stand in front of her. "We get a lot of these cases, especially at this time of year, parents bringing in their children who suddenly shoot up a temperature, start running at the nose, refuse everything you give them to eat, and. you would think they were seriously ill. Then the next day they are out running around. Though I do not mind telling you I am glad you brought her in. Even in a case of a cold, you can't be too careful."

"Thank you, doctor. Can I see her?"

Dr. Crawford smiled. "She's sleeping, but of course, you can see her."

Bridget went to her daughter's bedside. Her curls splayed across the pillow and her eyes remained closed even as she whispered, "Mommy's here, Izzy. Mommy's here." She looked so small and helpless, and Bridget had all she could do not to snatch her up into her arms. Dr. Crawford crossed over to Bridget and said, "I think we need to let her get some rest, Mother." Bridget nodded.

Bridget was feeling much better when she returned to the waiting room where she was greeted by a sea of concerned faces. She did not take the time to sit but instead stood near the doorway of the waiting room and told them that Isabella had a cold and would be fine. They wanted to keep her overnight, so she was going to take Chloe home. With that, they left together.

Chloe was glad to be alone with her mother and her mother rewarded her with details about the people who had stopped by Saturday and invited her up to the lake. Bridget felt a tinge, lying to her daughter, but she told herself it was a way of thanking her for being on her side. She named no names but made them quite rich and high toned. When asked about the house, Bridget embellished on that as well and her reward was Chloe looking at her with admiration and it was just what Bridget needed. Later in her bedroom she undressed and had turned out the light when she remembered her pies. It was three o' clock before she finally was able to turn in.

All the next day Isabella was on her mind and she had an unreasoning, hysterical sense of being deprived of something her whole nature craved; the right to sit with her child, to be near Izzy when she needed her. And yet the best she could manage was a few minutes in the morning, and an hour after dinner. She had all but fallen apart from exhaustion and worry when she stopped by that morning to see Izzy and the nurse had said the doctor thought it best to keep Isabella for another day. "I thought she was okay."

The nurse padded her shoulder. "She is Mrs. Bitmore. Isabella is doing fine, but Dr Crawford thought it wouldn't hurt to keep her an extra day for observation."

"Well, can I see her?"

"Yes, of course."

Bridget's heart had contracted when she saw Isabella, all her bubbling animation, gone. When she spoke to her, she was not sure she heard her as she made no sound or showed any recognition. She hated to leave her, but she could not stay. She had to go deliver pies, to payoff painters, to check on announcements, to negotiate a contract for chickens, and then to make more pies. It was dinner time before she got another respite, and she was too exhausted to even eat. She fidgeted impatiently while Francine fed Chloe, then Bridget loaded Chloe in the car, and they went back to the hospital together.

It was much the same as before. Isabella slept, unaware of them and Chloe became bored and impatient, so they checked with the nurse who informed them that the doctor was gone for the evening. Bridget was told that the doctor would speak to her in the morning so after a few moments with Isabella, they returned home. Once back home, she tucked Chloe in bed and then sat in the den drinking a glass of wine. She asked God to take care of her child and though exhausted, when she finally turned in for the night, she could not sleep.

Bridget called the hospital at eight the next morning, and after getting a favorable report, stayed on the phone, crowding her business into the next two hours. Around ten, she loaded her pies into the car, made the rounds of delivery, and arrived at the hospital around eleven. She was surprised to find Dr. Crawford already there, whispering in the corridor with a big hairy man in what looked like an undershirt. His bare arms were covered with tattoo marks.

As everyone said, it is a matter of opinion. But Bridget was not into it even though she knew that tattoos today were a trend in modern society. Before that it was a sign of low cast individuals, military men, or worse, criminals. But today, they were increasingly commonplace. Teachers, college instructors, EMT's, police officers, management, human resources: all had comrades who were inked. Yet Bridget had to ask herself why people chose to get tattoos. She had read somewhere that the primary motivation had to do with personal reasons such as to mark significant experiences like the memory of a loved one and at that thought Bridget felt the tears coming and changed her focus on the undershirt…that had not made a comeuppance yet and hopefully it never would.

Sensing her presence, Dr. Crawford excused himself and went over to Bridget. "Now I don't want you to get alarmed, but Isabella should be more active, but she is drowsy and complaining of a headache." He paused, rubbing his chin. She also has severe diarrhea."

We checked her temperature and found it had gone up. It's a hundred and four now, and I don't like it."

"You mean she might have an infection of some kind?"

"I don't know, and there's no way to tell. I have taken a culture and sent it to the lab. Whatever is going on with Isabella, we want to find it quickly so we can treat it."

"I agree. She is not herself. Something is wrong…" Bridget could not finish as she gulped down sobs and turned from the doctor.

“Bridget, it’s all right to cry. I understand how you’re feeling, cry now but put on a happy face for your child.”

Bridget, her hands shaking with fear, went into Isabella’s room. She had that same terrible feeling in her bowels that she had had that day on the boulevard when she did not know where she was or how to get where she was going, but she managed to plaster a smile on her face for Isabella. The child's eyes were dull, her face hot, her whimpering a constant accompaniment to her rapid breathing. A nurse was by her bedside and did not look up as she continued spooning ice into the fluttering little mouth. “This happened after I talked to you, Mrs. Bitmore. She had a nice night, temperature constant and we thought she would be all right in a few hours. Then just like that her temperature went up.”

Isabella began to fret, and the nurse turned her attention to her talking soothingly telling her, her mother was here. “Bridget spoke to her youngest child. “It's Mamma, darling.”

“Mamma!”

Isabella's voice was so weak, and Bridget again felt the urge to gather her into her arms, but she merely took one of the little hands and patted it. Then Dr. Crawford came in, and other doctors, in white smocks, and two nurses. They worked together taking her vitals and recording the readings on the monitors. When they were done with that, Dr. Crawford turned to Bridget. “Bridget, do you mind waiting in the hall. We’ll come and get you when we’re done.”

With a slight nod, Bridget left the room and stood in the hallway, wondering what to do. She started walking up and down, quietly, slowly. Somehow, by a supreme effort of will, she made time pass without breaking down entirely.

Then two nurses came out of the room, followed by one of the doctors who paused and said, “You can go in now.”

Bridget went in Izzy’s room. The same nurse, the one who had spoken to her before, was at the head of the bed, taking Izzy’s temperature while around her small arm, was a blood pressure cuff. Bridget stood hesitantly wondering where to stand so that she did not get in the way, but so she could see her daughter. Dr. Crawford was bent over, peering intently at Isabella. The nurse said, “Her temperature's down, doctor.”

“Good. What is it?”

“A hundred and one.”

“That's good. What’s her pulse?”

“Down too. It’s ninety-six.”

Dr. Crawford turned to face Bridget. “That's wonderful news, Bridget.”

At his direction, they walked out to the corridor where Dr. Crawford filled her in on the test they had done and told her soon they should know the results of the cultures and be able to take it from there.

Somewhere on the floor a buzzer sounded, then sounded

again, sharply, persistently. It seemed to Bridget that Dr. Crawford turned rather quickly, that their saunter was no longer a saunter. Bridget started to tremble when she saw an orderly hurry pass them headed in the direction of Isabella's room. She grabbed the doctor's arm. "Not now Bridget. Please stay out of the way."

The doctor rushed ahead, and Bridget moved forward at a much slower pace, wanting to join him, but suddenly afraid to enter the room. She stood at the door entrance, off to the side, out of the way, and felt her heart pounding inside her chest. Something was wrong with Isabella and there was nothing she could do.

The staff worked. "What's happening, please tell me what is happening."

It was not until no one answered did she realize she had asked the question in her head, afraid to interrupt whatever they were doing to Izzy. Without stopping what he was doing, Dr. Crawford ordered, "Nurse, get Dr. Collins,"

"Yes sir."

From the ice that was forming around her heart, Bridget knew it was serious. She leaned back against the wall in the room that was now filled with hospital personnel.

The nurse returned, followed by Dr. Collins, a short, heavy man who bent over Isabella and studied her as though he was looking through a magnifying glass. Without moving his face from hers he said, "I don't know what this is, Dr. Crawford."

"I know. At first she had all the symptoms of a cold or the

flu."

"I know."

Dr. Collins snapped orders in a curt, clipped voice. "Get oxygen, adrenalin, ice."

He turned to Dr. Crawford. So, fill me in on all her symptoms."

"Well, when she refused to eat, she said her mouth tasted funny and the nurse said her breath smelt garlicky. Beyond that it's just what you see on her chart." He paused and remembering, said, "Oh yes, she was sweating excessively."

"Ah ha. Anything else?"

"She wasn't eating or drinking much."

Dr. Collins knew Dr. Crawford well and found him to be a good and thorough doctor, but even the best of them could benefit from a consultation.

"Any rash?"

"Not sure. Her skin was so spotty from a high fever. I can't be sure."

As he spoke, Dr. Crawford was checking Isabella and found a small rash just above her hip.

"Nurse, check her temperature again."

Several seconds passed. "It's a hundred and four."

From her vantage point Bridget could see Isabella's teeth stopped chattering and her face was flush. "Her temperature's rising, Dr. Collins."

"Take off all the covers." Dr. Collins ordered and whispered something to the nurse.

Two nurses stripped off the blankets and one disappeared. When she returned, she was wheeling something on a cart pass Bridget and over to Isabella's bed side.

"Dr. Collins?" Dr. Crawford had a surprised expression as he saw what Dr. Collins had ordered. "Oh, yes, Dr. Crawford, while some hospitals use water blankets, wraps or ice packs, I like to use the noninvasive Arctic Sun Temperature Management System, which involves putting gel pads on the patient's body to monitor and maintain core temperature in a therapeutic range—between 32 degrees and 38.5 degrees Celsius. I find it manages the temperature more efficiently and provides greater skin protection."

"I heard about that. Febrile children treated with tepid water sponging plus antipyretic drugs are more uncomfortable than those treated with antipyretic drugs alone, although they exhibit slightly more rapid reductions in temperature."

"That's right. When febrile, seriously ill patients are externally cooled and are sedated or paralyzed with drugs that suppress shivering, they may have a more rapid reduction of fever and reduced energy expenditure than if treated with antipyretic drugs alone."

Silence filled the room as everyone seemed to stand motionless. The only sound to be heard was Isabella's labored breathing. Then the nurse monitoring the pulse said, "A hundred and twelve…A hundred and twenty-four, and thirty-two .... "

Presently Isabella was panting like a little dog, and her whimpering had a pitiful note in it that made Bridget want to cry out against the injustice that one so small, so helpless, should have to bear such agony. But she stood perfectly still, not distracting by so much as a movement the attention of those on whom Isabella's life depended.

Another nurse rushed pass Bridget and entered the room. "Doctor, I have the test results."

The child's struggle went on and on, and then suddenly Bridget tightened. The breathing stopped for a second, then resumed in three or four short, harrowing gasps, then stopped altogether. Dr. Collins motioned quickly, and two nurses stepped forward. They had scarcely begun their rapid lifting and lowering of Isabella's arms before Dr. Crawford had the mask of the oxygen apparatus over her face. Dr. Collins filled the neck of a vial, snapped it off quickly filling a syringe, he lifted the covers and jabbed it into Isabella's rump. The first nurse had Isabella's wrist, and Bridget saw her catch Dr. Collins's eye and glumly shake her head. The artificial respiration went steadily on. After a minute or two, Dr. Collins refilled his syringe and again jabbed it into Isabella's rump. Another minute went by, and Bridget saw glances exchanged between nurses. This time as Dr. Collins refilled his syringe, she stood up. She knew the truth, and she also knew that one more jab into the lifeless little bottom would be more than she could stand.

“Stop! Please stop.” She moved into the room and stared down at the lifeless body of her youngest daughter. She lifted the mask of the oxygen apparatus, bent down, kissed Isabella on the mouth, and moved away.

The activity in the room was like a cartoon sketch with people moving quickly about the spinning room and she felt her body go limb.

She was sitting in the hall again, and Dr. Crawford was passing something under her nose that made her pull back, irritably. The cruel suddenness of it had left her numb, as though she had no capacity to feel. Dr. Crawford dropped down beside her, took off his glasses and massaged his forehead.

“I’m so sorry Bridget. So sorry.”

Choking back her tears she asked, “So, what happened?”

There was a pause and then finally Dr. Crawford said. “I’m going to be honest with you, we don’t know. It could have been a combination of a lot of things. Dr. Collins is one of the best and he is not sure, but we will find out. It will just take some time.”

“Don’t blame yourself. If I had not been so caught up in my new business venture, I might have noticed it sooner. She hopped, skipped, and jumped through life, full of energy and humor. Now as I sit here, I remember Izzy saying more than once she felt icky…. her words and wanted to go to bed. I knew it was unusual given how much she loved staying up late. She said staying up late made her feel special…” Bridget’s throat closed and she swallowed hard before she could continue. “If anyone should have known it was me."

Bridget stared straight ahead of her, as Dr. Crawford realized what was happening and spoke. "We've got to stop it. I loved her like she was mine. And there is only one thing I can say. I did everything I could. And you too, Bridget. We both did everything that could have been done."

They sat for a few minutes, both swallowing, both locking their teeth behind twitching lips. Then, in a different tone, he asked, "Do you want to make some calls here, or rather wait until you get home?"

"Here if you don't mind. I'm not ready to face the family."

"Come with me." He took her to his office on the same floor, Bridget dropped down on the chair behind the doctor's desk watching as he walked out, closing the door behind him.

She had witnessed her child cling to life. She had been given the survival speech. And now she knew what it was like to make that end-of-life choice. As she sat there, trying to force air in her lungs, just so she could breathe, the feeling of having to stay on this earth now without Isabella felt impossible. She wanted to die. She wanted to go where her child was so that she could take care of her. It was her job to raise her daughter and she had not finished it. For God's sake, she was only six years old!

It took reminding herself that she had a job to do. It was up to her to inform the family, so pulling herself together as best she could and feeling as though someone else was in her body and that she would never be the same person again, she pulled out her cell and turned it on. She watched as it came to life, building the logo on the screen and then finally waiting for her instructions. She pressed the phone image and when it came up, she pressed, contacts.

Bridget was thankful she did not have to try and recall the number as she dragged her finger up through the listing until she found the one, she was looking for. She pressed on the name Mrs. Donahue.

She heard the phone ring and wondered what she was doing at that moment with Cameron and the thought sent a rage through her body she could not contain. She stood and began walking around the doctor's office. When the connection was made, she heard a sleepy voice say, "Hello. This is Maggie."

She remained quiet, trying to calm herself before saying, "I want to speak to Cameron."

"Bridget?"

"Don't you say my name…don't you… Put Cameron on."

"Sorry, Mrs. Bitmore. Cameron isn't here."

Bridget knew she should leave a message to have him call her. That would be the nice thing to do, but she was not feeling nice and through clenched teeth said, "Mrs. Donahue. Will you tell Cameron that Isabella passed a few minutes ago? I am at the hospital. I wanted him to know, right away."

There was silence, and the sound of someone clearing their throat and then, "Mrs. Bitmore, I'll tell him. I will tell him just as soon as I can find him. And Mrs. Bitmore I am so sorry… if there is anything, anything at all I can do…"

"No, thank you." Her words came out sharp and cutting as if the blame laid on this woman's shoulders.

There was an unpleasant silence and then Mrs. Donahue said, "I'll tell him."

Without thanking her, Bridget hung up the phone.

The connection ended, Bridget dropped back down in the chair in the unfamiliar surroundings of the doctor's office and put her head down on her arms. She cried as if her heart would break as she relived standing beside Izzy's bed as she lay motionless, her brown curls spread out on the white pillowcase and her long lashes resting on her cheeks. Suddenly it was too much, and Bridget got up from the desk, hurried over to the door and started running down the hallway until she was at Isabella's room.

Not caring whether she was alone or not, she went to Isabella's bedside and lifted the white sheet off her face so that she could stare at her once more. All the tubes had been removed and it was only Isabella laying there, looking peaceful and she reached down and pulled her baby up into her arms, not wanting to let her go.

She stayed at the hospital, in this room feeling close to Izzy. Her child who was such an easy going, loving child was gone. She would never hear her infectious laughter or see her beautiful smile again. Bridget started sobbing and did not try to stop. Her world was broken. The one person who gave meaning to life and kept everyone sane was gone. Who would do that now?

Not able to stall much longer, Bridget got up and walked to the elevator. In the parking lot she climbed into her car and sat behind the wheel, and like a new driver, tried to remember what she needed to do to make the car go. Finally, she got the car started.

She drove home mechanically; dreading the stop signals, for sitting there, waiting for the light to change, she would have time to think, and when her mind went back to what had happened her throat would clench, and the street would blur so that she could barely keep the car on the road.

When she finally pulled into her driveway, she was surprised to see Cameron's car. He must have been watching for her because as soon as she turned off the engine, he was beside the driver side door.

She had wanted to scream at him and lay every ounce of blame on his shoulders but seeing his face and knowing how much he loved Izzy, all she could do was cry.

Cameron helped her out of the car and into the house where he sat her down in the den. She could hear Francine, somewhere in the house trying to quiet Chloe. Bridget allowed herself to lean back against the sofa and shut out the loud sobs coming from the kitchen.

Francine must have told her that Bridget was home. In a flurry, a figure dropped down on her knees and laid her head in Bridget's lap sobbing uncontrollably.

That motion brought Bridget back and she heard her daughter saying through her tears. "I owed her a dollar! Oh, Mother, I cheated her out of it, and I meant to pay it back, but I owed her a dollar!"

Soothingly, Bridget explained that if she really meant to pay it back, that made it all right, and presently Chloe was quiet. Then she began to fidget. Bridget kissed her and said, "Would you like to go over to your grandparents darling? You could practice your piano lessons, or play, or whatever you want to do."

"Oh Mother, do you think it would be right?"

"Isabella wouldn't mind." Chloe trotted out of the room and Cameron looked a little shocked.

"She's a child, Cameron. They do not feel things the way we feel them. It's better that she is not here while arrangements are being made."

Cameron nodded. A match in the fireplace caught his attention, and he stooped to pick it up. In the process he bumped his head. If he had been hit with an axe he could not have collapsed more completely. Instinctively, Bridget knew poking the fireplace had brought it all back, the game he used to play with Isabella, all the gay nonsense between them were flashbacks. She knew because she had them too.

This time Bridget led him to the sofa, took him in her arms

then together, in the darkened room, they mourned their child. When he could speak, he babbled of Isabella's sweet, perfect character. He said if ever a kid deserved to be in heaven she did, and that is where she was all right. “Goddam it, that's where she is.”

Bridget knew this was his solace from pain. Too realistic, too literal minded, to be stirred much by the idea of heaven, she nevertheless craved relief from this aching void inside of her, but without success.

Cameron pulled himself together and called his parents and five minutes after he hung up, they arrived at the door to pick up Chloe. Chloe gave her a kiss and then hurried out of the house. Mr. Bitmore stepped inside and said hesitantly, “Do you mind if I stay?”

“No, come in Dad, we can use your help.”

Nerves on end, the three reacted to the sound of the phone ringing and Cameron recovered first and answered it. She listened as in a stern voice he said they were in mourning and Mrs. Bitmore could not possibly talk business today. Bridget barely listened. The restaurant seemed remote, an unreal, part of a world that no longer concerned her.

Around three thirty, Mr. Pendleton arrived. He was a roly poly little man, and after seven seconds of purring condolences, he got to the point. Everything in connection with the body had been taken care of. In addition, notices had been prepared to be placed in tomorrow’s papers.

Mr. Pendleton, an expert at managing the lowest point in a person's life, informed Bridget, and Cameron the next step for them was to make funeral arrangements; especially where they would like the body sent.

Bridget sniffed, but managed to control the tears as she nodded. She was grateful to Cameron when he patted her hand and said he would attend to all that. "Fact of the matter, Pop is better at this." Cameron paused and gave Bridget's hand a squeeze. "He and mom want to handle this for us if it is okay with you. They wanted to come over when I came, but I told them to wait a little while."

"Thanks, I appreciate that."

So, the two men talked to Mr. Pendleton, while Bridget half listened at first, but when they discussed the fact that she was a little girl, maybe they wanted to consider a private funeral service in the home. That is when Bridget broke down again.

Cameron excused himself and came to her side, holding her until she stopped shaking. He whispered in her ear, "I don't want to deal with a lot of people showing up so I'm thinking privately at home is best, but only if you agree. Bridget nodded and Cameron held her a moment longer before going back to discuss the arrangements.

"Mr. Bitmore, I would suggest the funeral be held three days from now and if it works out for the funeral home it would be best held at noon."

"Fine, Cameron said.

"Do you need someone to help choose a cemetery?"

"No," he replied absently. He turned and looked at Bridget as he said, "She will be buried at the Irondequoit Cemetery located on Culver Road in the Bitmore family plot." Bridget nodded her approval as she always knew they would all be buried there. That plot had been acquired on the death of the uncle who left Cameron the farm. From there the two men agreed the services would be conducted at the house, by the Reverend, Dr. Barthwell, whom Mr. Pendleton said he knew very well, and would call at once. Dr. Barthwell was Cameron's reverend, and for a miserable moment Bridget felt ashamed that she could claim no reverend as her own.

As a child she had gone to the Methodist Sunday school, but then her mother had begun to shop around, and in her exploration, she became interested in astrology. She believed astrologers could predict the future by understanding the positions of the planets and Sun and Moon in the birth chart of an individual. In fact, it was her mother's astrologers who had named Chloe and Isabella.

The Astrologer told them the Biblical baby's name Chloe is Greek in origin and its meaning is greenery. In Greek mythology, Chloe is another name of Demeter, the pagan goddess of fertility and agriculture. Chloe, to Bridget it fit; especially, the 'greenery'. No one loved money more than Chloe.

As for Isabella. Her name was derived from the name Isabel, a biblical name from the Hebrew Elisheva, meaning 'God is perfection' or 'God is my oath'. Some shorten the meaning to ‘belle’ which means beautiful. That was exactly what Isabella was, beautiful inside and out.

Cameron’s cell rang and instantly Bridget thought it was Mrs. Donahue, but it was not. She could tell by the conversation he was talking to his mother. When he hung up, he said, “Mr. Pendleton, can we get you some coffee.” She knew he wanted to continue the arrangements at a distance so they would not upset her. When Mr. Pendleton nodded, the two Bitmores walked with him to the kitchen.

They settled on a white enameled casket, with silver handles and satin lining, which would be furnished complete, with two limousines and the bearers of his choosing.

Mr. Pendleton explained when the body would be delivered and that they would handle the set up necessary. As they were walking him to the door, Mr. Pendelton paused. “Oh, I almost forgot. The burial clothes.”

Hearing this, Bridget looked up and with a faint smile, she went with Cameron back to the children's room. They decided on the white dress Isabella had worn at the school pageant, and they packed it in her little satchel. When Bridget added the gilt crown and fairy wand she looked up and said, “She loved them so…” Cameron dissolved in tears. They stood holding each other, consoling each other. “She's in heaven, she's got to be.”

"Of course, she is, Cameron."

With the satchel in hand, Mr. Pendleton left.

CHAPTER 16

The next day Mrs. Steele came over and joined them in the den. She slipped in without a greeting, sat down beside Bridget, and began patting her hand, then gathered her into her arms like a little child.

When she released Bridget, she looked over at Cameron and asked, "You want a drink, Cameron?"

"Not right now, Lucy."

"It's right there, and I'm right here."

"Thanks, I'd rather not,"

She turned to Bridget, "What can I do to help?"

"There's a couple of things, Lucy."

Bridget slowly got up and with Lucy holding her arm, took her to the bedroom where she wrote a number on a piece of paper. "Will you call my mother for me, and tell her? Say I'm all right, and the funeral is three days from today at noon and will be held here." Then looking at Lucy sternly, added, "and be nice to her."

"But Bridge…" Lucy took one look at her friend's face and changed her tone. "I will. I will. Anything else?"

"I don't have a black dress."

"I'll get one for you. Size five?"

"No, size seven."

"Shoes?"

"I have them, but gloves. Size six."

"I'll have everything. And…" Lucy paused unable to bring herself to say it aloud.

"What is it, Lucy?"

"They'll be dropping in now."

Bridget looked at her, a quizzical expression on her face.

"People, I mean. They want to offer their condolences." She paused before adding, "Bridget, I know it is a burden, but they don't so I took the liberty of putting some things together."

Lucy left and a short while later she returned and took charge. By then, quite a few people had dropped in. Along with Chloe and the Bitmores there were neighbors, Mrs. Floyd, Mrs. Harbaugh, Mrs. Reece, and there was Greyson. To Bridget's surprise, Mr. Arnold, the butcher, who had seen the notice on the internet stopped by as well.

Francine's contribution was tea and sandwiches, which she had just begun to pass when Mrs. Steele came in carrying a gigantic set of lilies. With a wave of the hand, she dismissed the florist driver, and finding the card, read, “Mr. and Mrs. Otto Hildegarde… oh, aren't they beautiful, just beautiful!” Then, to everybody in the room, “You know, the couple Bridget visited over the weekend, up at the lake. Lovely people. I'm simply crazy about them.”

Then Bridget knew that there had indeed been talk, serious talk. But she also knew, from the look, that went around, that now it was squelched by Lucy’s quick thinking. She felt warm gratitude toward her friend for dealing copiously with something she would have been helpless to deal with herself. Cameron took the lilies and placed them on the island.

There was a basket of gladioluses from Hartalkar’s Restaurant where she had worked her first job. But the one that made her swallow hardest was a mat of white gardenias, to which was attached a blue bird card, with all their names; the people who had become part of her family. Even Chris, the owner had signed it.

It was all happening around her.

When Dr. Barthwell arrived, the Bitmores and Bridget’s mom, Anne Spears were there. Her mother informed her that her sister Eleanor and her husband Maxwell Temple would be arriving soon and that they planned to stay at the hotel in Irondequoit.

Bridget had expected her mother to raise Cain which is why she had not wanted to call her herself. She loved her, but she could be such a nuisance, wanting to be in the midst of everything but Bridget was shocked when she heard Lily Bitmore arguing with Dr. Barthwell.

She tried to correct him on several points of ritual. The trouble was that Lily Bitmore, who had been originally a Methodist, and only joined the Episcopal Church after marrying Mr. Bitmore, was somewhat confused as to the service that was to be used the following day. Mr. Bitmore told her, she had the burial service, the communion service, the psalms, and perhaps even the wedding service, so thoroughly mixed up that it was rather difficult to disentangle them. Lily said she did not care, she wanted the twenty third psalm, it was only right they should have it.

There was no use telling her there would be no praying for the child's soul. Mr. Bitmore sharply reminded her that the burial service had nothing to do with a soul. The whole point was that the soul had already gone, and the burial was nothing but the commitment of a body. As Cameron listened unhappily, Mr. Bitmore kept calling on Dr. Barthwell, as a sort of referee. That gentleman listening with bowed head, presently said, "As the child wasn't baptized, certain changes will have to be made in the service anyway. Small omissions, but I am required to make them. Now in that case, there is no reason the twenty third Psalm, and the little passage in the communion service that Mrs. Bitmore evidently has in mind, and whatever else we want, cannot be included. At the end of the service, special prayers can be, and often are, offered, and I will be glad to include these passages, that is, if the mother feels the need of them too."

He looked at Bridget, who nodded. At first, she had resented Lily's taking charge in this high-handed way, and felt mean remarks rising within her. Now she went to the children's room and packed Chloe's things, so the Bitmores could have her back in the morning, properly dressed. When she came out with the little suitcase, the Bitmores decided it was time to go. Dr. Barthwell, however, stayed a few minutes longer. Taking Bridget's hand, he said, "'I have often thought the burial service could be a little more intimate, a little more satisfying to the emotions, than it is. It is quite true, as Mr. Bitmore said, that it is the commitment of a body, not the consecration of a soul. Just the same, most people find it hard to make the distinction, and to them, what they see is not a body. It is a person, no longer alive, but still the same person, loved and terribly mourned. I hope I can arrange a service that will be satisfactory to everyone."

Right up until the day of the funeral, people kept coming and flowers kept arriving. Lucy dropped off the outfit and stayed with her, helping Bridget greet the many people offering their condolences. For such a young child, Isabella had touched many lives.

CHAPTER 17

The day of the funeral arrived, and Bridget felt relieved that soon it would all be over, at least this part of the journey. She was talking with a guest when a hush fell over the room, and she turned to see Mr. Pendleton's assistants carrying Isabella in the door. Under Cameron's direction, they set up trusses near the window, arranged the casket, and stepped back to permit the guests to pass by.

Bridget could not look. But then Mrs. Steele caught her arm, and she had to look. In the setting sun, a rainbow was shimmering over the spray, framing Isabella's head. This gripped Cameron's heart tightly and he broke down. Mr. Bitmore was immediately at his son's side and helped him to a chair while guests tiptoed silently past the casket.

Bridget stared at her daughter laying there against the satin, her eyes closed, and her hair artfully arranged. There was something unreal about Isabella's appearance. The flushed cheeks, the animation of life, was gone. All that remained was a waxy pallor that suggested nothing of Isabella was left.

Then the Bitmores arrived, with Chloe in tow and Dr. Barthwell followed. Conversations filled every corner of the home and Bridget was exhausted, just trying to focus and listen when spoken to. And then finally the room was quiet.

After Dr. Barthwell left, Cameron and Bridget were able to talk a little more naturally. She still had to make pies, and he kept her company in the kitchen, and even helped her where he could, merely wanting to be friendly.

When the pies were made, they sat drinking coffee in the kitchen, neither one wanting to return to the front of the house where Isabella laid.

"You don't have to worry about me, Cameron. If Mrs. Donahue is waiting up for you, why don't you run along?"

"She's not waiting up."

"You sure?"

"Yeah, I'm sure."

He changed the subject. "Bridget, can I tell you something? About what really happened Saturday?"

"Certainly."

"Mom, she was just scared, that was all. Mom was never any good in a spot like that. And me, maybe I take after her, because I was scared too. That is why, when Doc Crawford began talking hospital, I fell for it so quick. But Elizabeth, or as you like to call her, Mrs. Donahue, she was not scared. We had to stop there, on our way to the hospital, because I was still in my beach shorts, and I had to put on some pants. And Elizabeth, she raised hell about taking Isabella to the hospital. She wanted to bring her right in, without delay. That is what I wanted too, only my parents were against it. I should have stood up against them." He paused and with a choking sound added, "Now, I know it was a good thing they didn't listen to us…"

"If that's what happened, it does her credit."

"She's a good friend."

"If that is what she did, I want you to thank her for me. It was better that she was brought to the hospital, but if she had been put in Mrs. Donahue's care, I wouldn't have had any objection at all."

"She's as broken up as if it was her own child."

The two of them sat lost in their own thoughts and the next thing Bridget knew, it was daylight. She woke with one arm asleep, and her head on Cameron's shoulder. As it all came back to her, she saw they were sitting on the bench at the bottom of their daughter's bed.

"Cameron, sorry I must have been asleep."

"You slept three or four hours."

"Did you sleep?"

"I'm all right."

They rose slowly, and then as if of one mind, started arranging the flowers. Bridget got a dust cloth and began moving about the house, cleaning, dusting, putting things in order. Presently she got breakfast, and they ate it in the kitchen. With everything in order, Cameron left to get dressed.

Around ten, Mrs. Steele came over, with the black dress and gloves, and took the pies for delivery. She was followed by the Porters from across the street who arrived with Cameron, in a dark suit and Chloe, in white. Then Francine arrived in a dress of garnet silk. Before she put on her apron to help, Bridget saw the Temples drive up with her mother, and sent Francine out to let them in. When Bridget heard them in the den, she sent Chloe to say she would be there in a minute. Then she tried on the dress, noted with relief that it was a fair fit and quickly finished dressing. Carrying the black gloves, she went to the den.

Her mother, a small, worried looking woman, got up and kissed her, as did her sister Eleanor Temple. Eleanor was several years older than Bridget and had a house wifey look. Neither of them had the least trace of the resolute squint that was the most noticeable thing about Bridget's mother's face, nor did they share her voluptuous figure.

Maxwell Temple got up and shook hands, awkwardly and self-consciously. He was a big, raw boned man, with a heavy coat of sunburn and a hint of the sea in his large blue eyes. Then Bridget saw her nephew William, a boy of twelve, in what was evidently his first time wearing a suit. She shook hands with him, then remembered she should kiss him, which she did to his acute embarrassment. He sat down and resumed his unwinking stare at Chloe.

To Chloe, the Temples were the scum of the earth, and William was even scummier than his parents, if that was possible. Under his stare she became haughtily indifferent, crossing one bored leg over the other, and fingering the tiny cross which hung from a gold chain around her neck.

Dr. Barthwell arrived and without hesitation, asked everyone to be seated. He began the service. His first words were, "I am the resurrection and the life, saith the Lord; he that believeth in me, though he were dead, yet shall he live; and whosoever liveth and believeth in me, shall never die. "

It was not the words, it was the voice, that crumpled Bridget as though something had struck her. Sitting there with Cameron and Chloe, she had expected something different, something warm, something soothing, particularly after Dr. Barthwell's remarks earlier. And then this flat, faraway whine, with a dreadful note of cold finality in it, began intoning the service. Not naturally religious, she bowed her head as if from some ancient instinct and began shuddering from the oppression that closed over her.

But it was Chloe who offered the purest sendoff of all as she walked slowly over to the piano, and without a word, sat down and began playing. She clearly sang the words of Psalms 23.

The Lord is my shepherd; I shall not want.

He maketh me to lie down in green pastures: he leadeth me beside the still waters.

He restoreth my soul: he leadeth me in the paths of righteousness for his name's sake.

Yea, though I walk through the valley of the shadow of death, I will fear no evil: for thou art with me; thy rod and thy staff they comfort me.

Thou preparest a table before me in the presence of mine enemies: thou anointest my head with oil; my cup runneth over.

Surely goodness and mercy shall follow me all the days of my life: and I will dwell in the house of the Lord forever.

A hush fell over the room for some time before Dr. Barthwell presented his final reading in a gentle, deeply feeling voice he recited, Matthew 19, verses 13 through 15.

Then some children were brought to Him so that He would lay His hands on them and pray; and the disciples rebuked them.

But Jesus said, “Leave the children alone, and do not forbid them to come to Me; for the kingdom of heaven belongs to such as these.”

After laying His hands on them, He departed from there.

It was time to go to the cemetery. Cameron took her arm and Chloe her hand, and they went slowly through the living room and into the limo that would take them to the gravesite where she would say her last goodbyes to her child.

Tears streamed from her eyes as they drove the short distance to the cemetery and once there, Bridget was like a zombie, following the lead of Cameron while seeing and feeling nothing. When she finally pulled herself together, she stared at Dr. Barthwell who looked old and frail in his white robes. In a moment, however, he dropped his voice, adopted a softer, more sympathetic tone, and she found herself enthralled by what was spoken.

The moment had come for the special prayers made necessary by Bridget's mother and for intimate solace. They murmured on, and her lips began to twitch as she realized they were mainly for her benefit, to ease her pain. But it made her feel worse. She should have taken command but instead had left it to others. Then, after an interminable time, she heard,

"O God, whose mercies cannot be numbered; Accept our prayers on behalf of the soul of Isabella, thy servant departed, and grant her an entrance into the land of light and joy, in the fellowship of the saints; through Jesus Christ Our Lord. Amen."

Those words soothed her as Chloe's voice had and she seemed less troubled as she floated through the rest of the day allowing her soul to seek its own place of comfort. She managed to stay on her feet and have the appropriate expression in response to those who lingered at the house.

The long, dark hours of the night came, and she was left alone. Nighttime loneliness crept over her making Bridget feel sad and scared. There was no one to console, no one to be brave in front of, no one to face but herself. The Porters, left in the afternoon, taking Cameron with them, and the Temples shortly after, taking her mother, hoping to reach Washington before dark. Then, after an early dinner, she had Francine take Chloe to a movie.

Bridget found herself in a house from which all flowers, all chairs, all wire racks had been removed. Desolation swept over her. She tramped around, then changed into her smock and began making pies.

When Francine returned with Chloe it was around eleven and she took Francine home. From the garage until entering the house again, she held tight to Chloe's hand, not wanting to let her go. Chloe had a glass of milk and talked gaily about the movie. It was 'Dolittle', and Bridget winced at the circumstantial account of how after his wife's death, Dr. John Dolittle decided to hide from the world with his beloved animals only he must take a journey to a mysterious island to find a healing tree, which is the only medicine that can help the dying Queen Victoria in Buckingham Palace. To Bridget it was too sad a movie and the beauty of the message was lost on her.

When Chloe went to bed, Bridget helped her undress, and could not bring herself to leave. Shyly she asked, "Would you like to sleep with me tonight, darling?"

"Yes Mother, of course!"

Bridget was pretending to herself that she was doing Chloe a kindness, but Chloe was not one to let such an opportunity past her by as she immediately began to give comfort, in large, doses. "Why you poor, dear Mother! I'm here for you."

She so wanted to resent it, but it was soothing to the gaping wound in her heart.

They went to her bedroom, and Bridget hurried into the bathroom to change into her pajamas and get ready for bed, afraid to take her eyes off her daughter for too long. When she returned to the bedroom she climbed into the bed and pulled Chloe into her arms. She cuddled her daughter close and though she fought to silence her heart, it was not possible.

She loved Chloe, but it was Izzy her heart cried for and forgive her, if she had to lose one of her daughters, she wished it had been Chloe.

CHAPTER 18

There was something unnatural, a little unhealthy, about the way she inhaled Chloe's smell as she dedicated the rest of her life to this child who had been spared. She promised herself that she would find a way to give this child everything including her attention.

She meant it, but as much as she wanted to it was not easy, especially following her resolve on the day the restaurant was to open. All the advertisements were out and if she did not open that day, it would be the death of her dream.

She was up at daybreak carrying out this resolution, setting out pie plates, flour, utensils, cans of supplies, all sorts of things, for removal to the model home turned restaurant. There was a great deal of stuff, and she packed it carefully into the car, but it still required several trips.

Finally, on her last trip there, she was greeted by the staff who were waiting for her. She had hired a waitress named Celine and a man, to do double service as dish washer and vegetable peeler. His name was Waldo. Both had been engaged the previous week, on the recommendation of Ida. Ida Castle had developed a good eye for hard working people since she had been the hostess at the restaurant where Bridget had worked.

Celine, in her mid-twenties with green eyes that twinkled when she smiled had the appearance of being flighty, but her friend Emily had agreed with Ida. Celine would prove to be a good and dependable waitress.

Waldo was skinny and handsome in a way and addicted to wearing a red and black check shirt along with his well-worn jeans. Since it was impossible to be sure that he had more than one change of clothes, he had incurred the enmity of Archie, but once he was in his kitchen garb, he was all right.

Bridget entered the restaurant and managed a smile before letting her mind go to what needed to be done. She took a deep breath and crossing her fingers addressed them. “Thank you for being part of this adventure with me. I have big hopes for us and as such, well, it is just us to start, and there is a lot to do. I know it’s not why you were hired, but if we want to open this place, I will need you to help me put it in order.”

Celine stepped forward, her ponytail bouncing. “Whatever you need, Miss Bridget. I am ready to start.”

“No problem,” Waldo added.

“Okay, here’s what I need.” They were to give the place a

thorough cleaning, and as soon as the front room was done, they were to hang the blinds that lay in a pile on the floor. She showed how the fixtures worked, and on Waldo's assurance that he was a virtuoso with the screwdriver, she drove back to the house, picked up her pies, and made the rounds of delivery.

Bridget had to admit she was worried, but she had to trust them if she was going to get the place open. She wished she could have helped, but for now the pies were the income she could depend on. When all the deliveries were made to the businesses, she hurried back to the restaurant.

She wasted no time climbing out of her car and rushing to the restaurant door. There she stood, took a deep breath, and pushed it open. She stepped over the threshold and froze, slacked jaw, unable to move and her gaze fixed on the vision before her.

Waldo had indeed done a great job with the blinds and the fixtures were almost done. When she walked in, he was hanging the last of them.

Celine had placed the tables and chairs, around the room, so that what had been a dreary pile of wood and metal, in one corner was now the bones for seating customers. It was beginning to take shape.

“This is wonderful. I can’t thank you enough for your help.”

Bridget still had things to do, but when the laundry service delivered her napkins and tablecloths, she could not resist setting a table to see how it looked. To her, it was beautiful. The red and white check of the linen combined pleasantly with the maple, and with Celine wearing her brick red uniform, it would be impressive.

She allowed herself a few minutes to drink in the picture with her eyes. Then, after praising her small staff until Celine was blushing and Waldo shifted from one foot to the other, she was careful to explain that she had to finish the deliveries, but she would appreciate them tackling the kitchen when they finished. With her face glowing with pleasure, she left again to resume her errands. She still had to deliver pies to customer homes and there were a few other errands on her list.

Bridget felt relaxed as she began running the remaining errands. Her first stop was the bank to deposit checks. From there she went to Wegmans for vegetables, eggs, bacon, butter, and miscellaneous grocery items.

She next went to pick up the chicken she had ordered from a local farm whose owners had been long time neighbors to the Bitmores. Mr. Houston smiled at her as she walked up the lane. "I'm so glad you chose our chickens. I packaged it in the quantities you requested, and I guarantee the quality."

"Thanks Mr. Houston. I appreciate it."

He helped her load the chicken in the car, told her to make sure she got it to the freezer immediately and she assured him she would.

Back at the restaurant, she was impressed to find the kitchen in order and Celine mopping the floor. Waldo had washed the new dishes and set them in piles waiting for her instructions. They had done a wonderful job in a short period of time and she let them know how much she appreciated it.

Knowing Chloe was in school, Bridget called Francine. In the meantime, she talked with Celine, getting to know her better, then went to the kitchen and helped Waldo put away the dishes and tried holding a casual conversation, but he was not a talker.

When Francine arrived, she asked Waldo to join them in the front where, at Bridget's request, Francine was spreading out a lunch she had prepared for them. Bridget picked up a half a sandwich, gave Francine a wink and hurried into the kitchen.

Bridget settled into what she really loved, cooking. She got out the chickens, went over them carefully for pinfeathers, found Mr. Houston's plucking a great deal better than most markets tended to do and that pleased her even more. Then she took a small cleaver and sectioned them up. It would have been much easier to have it all prepared, but she had not been sure exactly how she wanted them cut. Besides, she was more than capable to handle that herself.

As she worked, she decided she was going to serve half a fried chicken, with vegetables or waffle, but she hated the half chicken that was served in most places. It came on the table in one loathsome piece, and she wondered how people could possibly eat it. She was going to do it differently.

First, she cut off the necks, then cut the chickens in half. Then she took off the wings and the legs. The legs she separated into second joints and drumsticks, and then she trimmed the breasts so there was only a sliver of breastbone backing them, without any wishbone or rib. Then, remembering Archie's system for such things, she packed breasts, drumsticks, second joints, and wings into four different pans, and placed them in the fridge so she could pick up a portion with one motion.

The necks and bones she pitched into a pot, for soup. The giblets she cut up and put in a pan, for gravy.

She was making the cream of tomato soup when Waldo entered the kitchen. “Need a hand?”

“Yes, thank you. Can you cut up the vegetables?” Bridget had pulled them out and put them on the cutting board when she put the chicken in the fridge.

Around four, Greyson came in giving his approval to the layout. His main activity, since she had seen him, had been to send out the announcements, and for this he had drafted his secretary. She had utilized all the old Bitmore Home lists, so that every person who had bought a home, or had even thought of buying a home, had been covered. Bridget listened, pleased that all this had been so well attended to, but he kept hanging around, and she wished he would go, so she could work. Then she noticed him looking at the showcase. This was the most expensive piece of furniture she had, and the only one that had been made to order. The base and back were of maple, but the sides, top, and shelves were of glass. It was to display the pies she hoped to sell to the "take out" trade, and presently, looking rather self-conscious, Greyson asked, "Well, how did you like that little surprise I fixed up for you?"

"What surprise?"

"Didn't you see it?"

"No…"

"Tell you what," he said, leading her out of the room, "Stay here in the kitchen, then, and wait." She started to object, but he pushed lightly on her shoulders. "Stay here."

"Yes, sir."

Mystified, she stayed and more mystified, she waited, and Greyson appeared a moment later, picked up two of her pies and left the kitchen. He repeated the action twice more; caution her to not peek and keep still.

"Okay, follow me."

Bridget, puzzled, walked with him to the front of the restaurant. She could see him arranging the pies in the showcase. Then she could see him fumbling with something against the wall. Suddenly the showcase lighted up, and she gave a little cry, and placing her hands on her cheeks, she covered her mouth in surprise.

Greyson beamed. "Well, how do you like it?"

"Why Greyson, what a wonderful surprise. It's beautiful!"

"Something I did for you while...well, the last few days. I slipped in here at night and worked on it." He proudly pointed out the tiny reflectors that screwed into the maple, almost invisibly, to shoot the light downward, on the pies; the bulbs, no bigger than her finger, the wiring, cunningly tacked to the back in such manner as to leave the panels free to slide.

"That's just amazing, but I thought we were about tightening our belts."

"You know how much that little job cost?"

"I haven't any idea."

"Well, let's see now, the string of twinkly lights were in a box from when I use to decorate my own Christmas tree. I had to dust and clean them and then I had your electrician put in the switch while doing the wiring so that was no extra costs. Finally, a few staples to hold the wires and what looks like a million costs only time and I had plenty of that."

"I just can't tell you how much I appreciate it."

"Took me maybe an hour. But it ought to sell pies." Then, with a crooked smile added, "And get me a free dinner."

"You can count on it."

Time was passing inexorably fast, and she hurried back to work as soon as he left, though in a pleasant glow realizing that everybody was giving her their all. The vegetables, started before Greyson came, were now ready, and they scooped them up. She put them in pots and filled them with water. Waldo, making several trips waved her on while he got the pans on the burners and turned on the flame.

"Waldo, can you turn on the waffle grill?"

"Already done, Miss Bridget."

Smiling, Bridget made waffle batter and carried it over to the grill, lying beside it the dipper that held exactly one waffle. She made pie crust and stuck it in the fridge while she prepared a batch of biscuits.

Her ice cream arrived, and Waldo and Celine brought it back. Chocolate, strawberry, and vanilla, just as she ordered. She went back to the biscuits and Waldo and Celine prepared the containers before putting them in the glass domed freezer. Waldo got out the scoops and putting them on top of the ice cream; he explained the process to Celine.

Bridget was happily impressed. When she had first worked at the restaurant, she was appalled at how much there was to remember from day one. There were innate skills plus lessons to be learned in the restaurant business from waitressing to managing and she had learned them all the hard way.

But she did learn. From learning the menu, multitasking, anticipating customer requests and following the rules, when it came to handling someone's food you had to work quickly and know how to handle different personality types. Sometimes she wished that Chloe would give it a try. If anyone needed a lesson in self-sacrificing, she did.

Still diligently working she heard Celine say, "Thanks Waldo, I read the manual too." That made Bridget smile even more. The most important lesson she took with her was one of her own. What she had done was written a manual that covered every aspects of the job, the running of the restaurants, et cetera. This way the job was learned by absorption and not hit and miss.

When Celine finished what she was doing, she went over to Waldo, who said defensively, "I just meant if you need help, you can always just ask me. That's all I meant."

"And, my friend, I'll help if you need it." That put a smile on both their faces and Celine returned to making sure the dining room was in order and suddenly she heard Celine singing. Bridget had to choke back a laugh as the words to the song floated in the air. She sang to a tune Bridget was not familiar with but was sure those were not the original words.

"Dip it and carefully place it on top, like a crown. And do not forget the starter salads, soup, water and coffee…"

At five thirty Bridget looked around, pleased that all the prep work was done, and the kitchen was ready. She checked out front and Celine seeing her, smiled as she turned around, arms out from her sides. It was flawless. The lighting just so and each table properly dressed. Not a chair was out of place.

"Thank you, Celine. It's perfect."

Celine smiled and Waldo, walking past her said, "Come on

Celine, it's time to get ourselves ready." They walked through the dining room and to the kitchen where they parted ways.

Bridget was in the kitchen when Waldo entered.

"Waldo, it's..." She paused. Waldo had changed. He was wearing a fresh pair of blue jeans, neatly pressed with a white open collared shirt. He had arranged his hair and Bridget could not help saying. "My, you clean up well."

When Celine returned, Bridget praised her before excusing herself to change. As she dressed, she recounted everything. She was confident, she had thought of everything construction wise. Out front there was a bathroom for men and one for women, elegantly identified with shadow figures. Just behind the kitchen where there were three bedrooms originally planned, she had one split into two full bathrooms, marked appropriately. The other was her office and the big walk-in closet was an overflow pantry. In the private employee bathroom there was lockers, of which only two were now being used. Celine had marked hers and so had Bridget. Inside there was a backup outfit in case of an emergency change requirement and room for whatever else they wish to place in there.

Bridget was proud of her choice in outfits for herself, Celine, and Francine. They all were wearing brick red dresses with different styles, but with the same fancy white aprons. On their feet were comfortable, but classy brick leather-colored shoes. Bridget, because of being conscious of her legs, wore her dress longer than the other two.

The atmosphere was electrified as they anxiously waited to begin. There was no doubt in her mind that she had the best employees a person could hope for and having them work with her had not only given them a chance to know each other, but to feel as though they had a personal stake in the restaurant.

Before opening the doors, she assembled Waldo, Francine, and Celine for final instructions, paying most attention to Celine. “I'm not expecting many people, because it's our first night and I haven't had a chance yet to build up my trade. But if you should be rushed, remember, get their orders. I've got to know whether they're having vegetables or waffles before I can start and don’t hesitate to ask when you need help.”

“I'll keep biscuits out all the time, and you pick them up yourself.” Bridget paused. “Oh yes, keep the biscuits separate and cover them with napkins to keep them warm. I’ve made a lot of them so start with one for each person at the table and if they want more, give them more.”

“You’ve made plenty, Miss Bridget?”

“Yes, why?”

Celine surveyed the place with a practiced eye, counting tables. There were eight tables for two, around the wall, and four tables for four, in the middle. Bridget saw the look, and went on, “You'll be able to take care of them if you get their orders. There is plenty of room here. You are using a tray, and that will help.

Any time you need her, Francine is willing to help serve or bus tables."

"No, that's not it," Celine said. "You said you made lots of biscuits so why not give each person two. Most people will want two."

Bridget paused, considering, and then said, "Good thinking Celine. Two it is."

Bridget took one last look around and went back to the kitchen, lit the oven, and checked the waffle irons. She was using a gas waffle iron, instead of the usual electric waffle iron, because that is the old-fashioned kind of round waffle that people really like best. She went to the switch box, put on the lights. The last switch worked the outside sign, and when it was on, she went out to look. There it was, as beautiful as ever, casting a bluish light over the trees. 'Bridget's House of Chicken N' Waffles'. Beneath the large fancy lettering it said simply, 'Sweet, Delicious, Fresh, Hot, Waffles'. She drew in a deep breath and went back inside. At last, she was open, at last she had her own business.

There ensued a long wait as Bridget sat nervously at one of the tables for two. Celine, Francine, and Waldo stood in a corner whispering. Then they started to giggle, and a horrible pain shot through Bridget. It was the first time it had occurred to her that she could open a restaurant, and then have nobody show up. She stood abruptly and went to the kitchen where she kept touching the waffle irons, to make sure they were hot and just when she was feeling the most despondent, outside, a car door slammed. She looked up. Through the far window she saw a car in the parking lot and watched as four people got out and headed toward the restaurant door.

She let out a breath of air and visibly allowed her shoulders to drop down, not aware how she had tensed her body. She whispered, "It's happening…it's really happening."

She had a moment of complacency as she reached for the chicken, now she would reap her reward for all her observing, thinking, and planning.

She had had the free parking located in the rear, so she could see exactly how many customers she had, even before they came in; she had simplified her menu, so she could start the chicken without waiting for the waitress to report; she had placed her fridge, range, materials, and utensils so she could work with the minimum of effort and now was the first test.

Feeling as though she were starting a well-tuned machine, she took out four each of breasts, second joints, drumsticks, and wings, rolled them in the flour box beside the range, gave them a squirt from the olive oil bottle that stood beside the flour. She shoved them in the oven, for the brief baking that preceded frying in butter. Not yet closing the oven door, she shoved a pan of biscuits in, beside them. Celine appeared.

"Four at No. 9, soup right and left, two and two, one waffle."

To most, it was like a foreign language but to Bridget it was music to her ears. She smiled and sweetly corrected Celine on not calling the soup since she would dip it herself. She turned toward Waldo, who smiling said, "Go ahead, I've got this."

Bridget went out to greet her first guests. They were strangers to her, a man, woman, and two children, but she made them a little speech, saying they were her first guests, and she hoped they liked her place and would keep coming back. She added that if they liked the food and service to tell their friends.

Celine entered the dining room with the starters, the soup, crackers, butter, napkins, water, and salad. Salad, for some reason, is served first in Rochester. Bridget's eye checked the tray, finding it in order. Two more people came in. She vaguely remembered them as Bitmore Homes buyers of six or seven years ago, but her waitress training came at once to her aid. Their names were on her tongue before she barely saw their faces, "Why how do you do, Mrs. Sawyer, and Mr. Sawyer! I'm so glad you were able to come!"

They seemed pleased that they were recognized, and Celine seated them at a table near the window. As soon as Celine came over to get their orders, she went back to the kitchen, to start more chicken.

The first order went out smoothly, with Francine bussing the dirty dishes to Waldo, who went to work at once. But then Celine appeared, looking worried.

"Two at No. 3, but one of them is a kid that won't have soup. Says she wants tomato juice with a piece of lemon and some celery salt. I told her we don't serve it, but she says she's got to have it and what do I do now?"

It was no trouble to guess who that was. "Don't worry Celine. I'll handle it."

She found Cameron with Chloe, at one of the tables for two. Cameron was in a light suit, meticulously groomed and wearing a black band on one arm. Chloe was in a fancy ruffled dress and wearing one of Bridget's floppy hats. Both looked up with a smile, Chloe exclaiming how pretty Bridget's dress was, Cameron nodding approvingly at the restaurant. "By God, this looks amazing. Perfect location with plenty of parking. This place is not only fancy, but sturdy."

He stamped his foot. "And it's built sturdy. I saw to that. I bet there was no trouble with the Department of Health when they inspected the building."

"They passed it without even looking."

"How about the restrooms?"

"They passed them too. Of course, we had to cut a door through, so both opened into the old secretary's office. We made that into a kind of lounge. It is against the law for a bathroom to open into the kitchen, you know. But that, and the painting, and the gravel, and the swing doors, were about all we had to do. It cost money though."

"I bet it did."

"Would you like to look around?"

"Thanks Bridget. I'd love it."

She took them both through every inch of the facility, and felt proud when Cameron admired everything profusely, but she was not quite so proud when Chloe said, “Well Mother I think you've done very well, considering everything.” She did not need an explanation and was thankful as they returned to the dining room and she heard another car door slam.

She excused herself from her family and turned to greet her new customer, It was Greyson, and he was quite excited. “Say, you're going to have a mob. You hear me, a mob. That is the thing to remember with direct mail advertising. It is not what you send. It is where you send it. I got that stuff of yours right to the people that know you, and they are coming. I bumped into six different people that told me they would be here; and that is just six I happened to bump into. I’ll say it again, a mob.”

Greyson pulled over a chair and sat down with Cameron and Chloe. He had no sooner seated himself when Cameron asked him if he had attended to the transfer of beneficiary on the fire insurance. Greyson said he figured he would wait till the place burned down. Cameron said okay, he was just asking.

When Bridget looked up, Emily was standing in the door. Emily had been her friend at Hartalkar’s Restaurant. She went over and kissed her and listened while she volubly explained that her husband had wanted to come, but got a call on a job, and simply had to investigate it. Bridget took her to the table that now had only one chair, the other having been borrowed by Greyson. Emily looked around, taking things in. “Bridget, it's just grand.

And the space you got. You can get two more fours in easy, just by shifting those twos a little bit. And you can use trays, big as you want. You got no idea how that will help. It will save you at least one girl. At least."

It was high time for Bridget to get back to the kitchen, but she lingered, patting Emily's hand, basking in her approval before finally returning to the kitchen.

The well-oiled machine was in high gear now, humming smoothly, pulling its load. So far, Bridget had found a few seconds for each new arrival, and particularly for each new departure, to give a little reminder of the homemade pies she had for sale, and wouldn't they like to take home one? But now she was working a bit feverishly, frying chickens, turning waffles. When she heard a car, door slam she did not have a chance to look out and count customers. Then she heard another door slam. Then Celine appeared. "Two fours just came in, Miss Bridget. I got room for one but what do I do with the other? I can move two twos together, but not till Miss Emily leaves."

"No! Let her alone."

"But what'll I do?"

"Seat four, ask the others to wait."

Despite herself, her voice was shrill. She went out, asked the second party of four if they minded waiting. She said she was a little rushed now, but it would only be for a few minutes. One of the men nodded, but she hurried away, ashamed that she had not foreseen this happening on her opening day. With Francine and Celine helping they brought chairs from her office for the customers to sit on while they waited. When she got to the kitchen all hell was breaking loose as tension began to rise. Celine was practically screaming at Waldo. When she heard Bridget, she turned and spoke. “He's washing plates, and the soup bowls are all out, and if he won’t let me have them, I can't serve my starters!

“Soup bowls. I need soup bowls!”

Celine screamed this at Waldo, but as Bridget shushed her down, Francine came in, exhausted by the unaccustomed work, and dumped more soup bowls in the pile, which went down with a crash, three breaking. Bridget made a futile dive to save them and heard another car door slam. And suddenly she knew that her machine was stalled, that her kitchen was swamped that she had completely lost track of her orders, that not even a starter was moving. For one dreadful moment she saw her opening turning into a fiasco, everything she had hoped for slipping away from her in one nightmare of an evening. Then beside her was Ida, whipping off her hat, tucking it with her handbag next to the counter and going over to the peg beside Waldo where he hung an extra apron.

“Okay, Bridget, it's these dishes that's causing it all. Now she is no good out there now, none whatever, so let her wipe while he washes, and that will help. We’ll load the dishwasher as we go so the next load will be out and ready.”

As Bridget nodded at Francine and handed her a towel, Ida's quick eye spotted dessert dishes, and she set them out on a tray. Then, to Celine, "Call your soup."

Ida was pleased as peach when she heard Celine recite, "I want a right and left for two, three and one, chicken and tomato for four, and they have been waiting for..."

Ida did not wait to hear how long they had been waiting. She dipped soup into the dessert dishes, dealt out spoons with one hand. and crackers with the other, and hurried out with the tray, leaving butter, salad, and water to Celine. In a minute she was back. "Okay, Bridget, I got your family to take a walk outside. They were all through eating anyway. Then I put two at my table, and that took care of four. Then as soon as I take care of the check for that first party of four, that will take care of four more, and..."

The voice, continued, and Bridget responded to it with a tingle that started in her heart and spread out through the rest of her. Her nerve came back, her hands recovered their skill, as things began moving again. She was pouring a waffle when Mrs. Steele appeared at the door and came tiptoeing over to her. "Anything I can do, baby?"

"Oh, Lucy. I don't think so, it's getting under control..."

"Oh yes there is." Ida seized Mrs. Steele by the arm as she usually seized the members of her command. "You can take off that hat and get out there and sell pies. Don't bother them while they're eating but stay near the showcase and when they get through see what you can do."

"I'll be doing my best."

"Containers are in the drawer under the case. You will have to unfold them and then tie them up and put the carrying handles on. If you have any trouble, just call for me or ask Bridget."

"What's the price, Bridget?"

"Six dollars each." Mrs. Steele laid her hat beside Ida's and went out. Soon Bridget saw her opening the cash register. Surprisingly, Lucy was busily filling orders for pies. When she had a lull, she slipped off her apron and went out. Nobody was standing now, but every seat was filled, and she felt as she had felt at the funeral, when she walked through the living room and saw all those half-remembered faces. These were people she had not seen in years, people reached by Greyson's clever system of mailing. She spoke to them, asked if everything was all right, received their congratulations.

It should have been expected, but Bridget was not prepared for words of sympathy about Isabella. She had compartmentalized her feelings as well as her life and having them clash through put her into a tailspin. She quickly hurried through the kitchen and into the bathroom. She stood there, looking around and feeling as if her heart would explode. What was she doing? Her daughter had died, and she was relishing in the glory of her restaurant. How could she be so cold and unfeeling. Just when she was about to make the biggest mistake of her life, Lucy appeared.

"I heard. I know what you are thinking, and I am telling you right now that Isabella died through no fault of your own and your death is not in God's plan. Now, are you going to hang in here and feel sorry for yourself or are you going to make Isabella and the rest of us proud."

It was exactly what she needed to hear. Lucy left and Bridget checked her face, then returned to her post. It was well after eight when she heard another car door slam.

Cameron, his friend Greyson, and Chloe had adjourned to the bench in the parking area. But now, as a foot crunched on the gravel, the conversation stopped, and then Chloe burst in the back door. "Mother! Guess who just came in!"

"Who was it, darling?"

"Nick Lombardi!"

Bridget's heart skipped a beat. The unexpected appearance of the man she had slept with, the man she had barely known and let sweep her away when she should have been with her baby girl was her just punishment. She had lied to the family when they had asked where she had been and now, they were about to find out the truth. Cautiously she studied Chloe. But Chloe's shining eyes did not suggest knowledge of her mother having any relationship with this man and so, like a fool she piled on one more lie. "And who is this Nick Lombardi?"

"Oh, Mother, don't you know?"

"I guess not."

"He's a golf pro and he lives in Manhattan, and he's rich, and good looking, and all the girls just wait for his picture to come out in the paper. He's boss!"

It. was the first she had known that Nick was anybody. To her he was a nice customer whom she had a brief affair. Chloe began dancing up and down, and Cameron came in, followed by Greyson, who looked as though he had just beheld God. “Sa a a y! If that guy's here, Bridget, you are in! Why there is not a restaurant in New York that would not pay him to eat there. Isn't that so, Cameron?”

“He's very well known.”

“Known? Hell, he's hot.”

Celine came in, from the dining room. “Wow!”

Chloe went to the door, peeped out, and disappeared while Greyson began speculating as to how Nick knew about the opening. He was not on any list, and it seemed unlikely he had seen the Irondequoit papers.

Cameron, with some irritation, said that Bridget's reputation as a cook had spread everywhere, and that seemed sufficient reason, at least to him, without doing any fancy sleuthing about it. Greyson not seeing this as a compliment to his job of advertising, instead said, “I think I will ask him how…” He stopped in midsentence, standing there with his mouth open while those in the room watched in awe.

Bridget felt herself being turned slowly around. Nick was there, looking down at her gravely, intently. “Why didn't you tell me about your little girl?”

She was caught in a lie, but even more embarrassing was when she thought she had been found out, her first instinct was to deny. She had been tempted but knew now that extending the lie with even more dishonesty only made things worse. Now, with all eyes on her Bridget replied sadly. “I don't know. I just couldn't.”

“I thought we had something special, and I didn't hear about it until your daughter just now told me.”

Bridget felt that cold fist around her heart at the mention of Chloe. Chloe was at the bottom of any embarrassing moments and why should she not be now. Bridget, not wanting to discuss this matter further, changed the subject. “She seems to be quite an admirer of yours.”

“She's the most delightful little girl I've met in a long time, but never mind about her. I'd like you to know that if I’d had any idea about what you were going through, you'd have heard from me.”

As though to corroborate this declaration, he produced flowers from behind his back. She gave him a quizzical look, then stared at the two orchids. They were beautiful. “Thank you, Nick. That was thoughtful.”

Bridget needed a minute to decide what to say to her family. “Wait a minute. I’ll put these in some water.” Hurriedly, Bridget went to the kitchen and found a pitcher that she filled with water and stuck the flowers in it. Then just as quickly she returned to the dining room. Just as quickly she decided she would not say anything until absolutely necessary.

Anxiously wanting an explanation, when she turned back around the men had followed her to the kitchen. So, she introduced Nick to Cameron and Greyson and was relieved when

Emily came over, demanding that the kitchen be cleared. Nick leaned in and gave her a little peck on the cheek to which Cameron and Greyson reacted by eyeing her a little queerly.

By nine o'clock there were only two customers left, and as they were eating the last of the chickens, Bridget went to the switchboard and cut off the sign. Then she counted her cash. She had hoped for thirty people and had ordered extra chickens to be safe. Now, she was thankful for her foresight. Truly, as Greyson had promised, there had been a mob.

She went to the cash register and was told that all the receipts and cash were accounted for. Bridget smiled. "I can't believe we were able to pull it off. How did we do?"

Celine held up a hand full of receipts and Ida opened the register and retrieved the cash. Breathless, Bridget reached out and took the cash that Ida had put into neat bundles. "Wow!" She fingered the bills. "Wow! I can't believe it."

"Believe it. There is several thousand dollars here for one night's work. I think you covered your expenses and more."

She hugged Ida and put the bills in the bank bag and stuck it on the shelf under the register. Then, having little to do until Celine, Waldo, and Francine finished, she went in the back and changed her clothes. When she returned her eyes went to the orchids. She leaned over them thinking about her time with Nick and then whispered, "Why not," as she gently pulled off a blossom and pinned it to her dress.

Emily was finishing, but Cameron, Greyson, Nick, Chloe, and

Mrs. Steele were sitting sociably at one of the tables for four. Cameron and Nick were discussing golf, a subject that Cameron seemed impressively familiar with. Chloe had curled herself into the crook of her father's arm and was relishing the fact she was in the presence of a celebrity. Bridget pulled up a chair and sat down beside Mrs. Steele, who at once began whispering, at first, in Bridget's ear. Bridget blurted out, "No, what are you thinking. No, we can't."

Staring into the faces around her she said, "It would be nice to relax a bit…"

It was Nick who got it. His face lit up and he bellowed "Yes!"

Suddenly they all got it and echoed, "Yes, Bridget. Yes."

Mrs. Steele went out to her car. When she came back, she had Scotch and a bottle of club soda. "Oh, I don't have a liquor license. I could get in trouble for this."

"Relax Bridget. We are not going to tell. Besides, you aren't serving it." Bridget had Celine bring glasses, ice, and an opener, and Mrs. Steele poured the scotch, then passed the soda around for everyone to add what they wanted. Celine brought a bucket of ice and sat it in the middle of the table while Bridget went over to lock the door.

Cameron filled a glass with club soda and ice and handed it to Chloe who wrinkled her nose. Then raising to his feet, Cameron raised his glass to Bridget. "To the best woman that any guy was crazy enough to let get away from him."

"You ought to know, you cluck." Mrs. Steele was quite

positive about it and everybody laughed and raised a glass to Bridget.

She did not know whether to raise her glass or not, but finally did. Then Ida was standing beside her, taking in the conviviality with a twisted grin that seemed strange and pathetic on her plain face. Bridget jumped up, quickly made her a drink, and said, "Now I'm going to propose a toast." Raising her glass, she intoned, "To the best friends anyone could have."

After a few sips of their drinks, Greyson stood and looking around at each of them said barely above a whisper, "To Isabella. I know you're smiling down on us."

In reverent response came, "To Isabella!".

Each person at the table was wrapped in silence. Isabella had left an amazing impression on all their hearts. Cameron kept wiping at his eyes, as did Greyson, and Bridget found a Kleenex and quietly blew her nose. What they needed was an interruption and an interruption came when Celine joined them.

Celine was flustered, and first giggled, then looked as though she was going to cry, and paid no attention when Bridget introduced her around. Then she plopped down in a chair and began, "Bridget I don't know whether to laugh or cry. You got no idea how they went for that chicken. And how amazed they were at the waffles. Why, they said, they never got such fluffy waffles in a long time, and they had no idea anybody knew how to make them anymore. It is a hit, Bridget. It's going to do just grand, and I hope I will have a job for a long time." Bridget sipped her drink, feeling trembly and self-conscious. She was beyond being simply happy.

She could have sat there forever, but she had Chloe to think of, and Celine to think of too, for after such help, she had to give her a lift home. So, she reminded Cameron that Chloe had to go to school. She got up and the others followed. Bridget went to the kitchen to shut down and gather her things, waiting until Waldo and Celine were ready before turning out the lights.

Back in the front room Bridget got the cash bag and looked around to make sure everything was in order. In the midst her gaze fell upon a small figure, barely more than a shadow, that was skipping about with her curls flying and smiling broadly. Bridget's breath choked in her throat as she whispered, "Izzy," is that you baby?" And just as quickly as it had appeared, it vanished.

It was the first time she had felt Izzy so close or thought she had seen her. Bridget was no longer grief stricken or confused about how to move forward.

Unaware she had been crying, Bridget wiped her tears, smiling now as she stepped outside. She locked the door, fondly holding the handle for a moment before joining the others.

On the lawn, the party gathered around Mrs. Steele's car, and Bridget suspected the Scotch was being finished somewhat informally, but she did not wait to make sure. Calling to Cameron not to keep Chloe up late, she loaded Celine into her car, and slowly backed out of the parking lot and headed down Titus Avenue.

After dropping off Celine, Bridget allowed herself to feel the exhaustion that took over her body. She could not remember ever being this tired, but it was a good feeling. When she pulled up to her house, she was surprised to find the blue Corvette outside.

Bridget climbed out of her car and cautiously went up to the front door. She opened it slowly. Inside the house was dark, but she could see a flicker of light from the den, so she headed in that direction. She found Nick and Chloe in the dark except for the fire they had lit for themselves, and evidently getting on famously. To Bridget, Nick explained, "We had a date."

"Oh, you did."

"Yes, we made a date that I was to take her home, so I did. Of course, we had to take Pop home first."

"Or at least, to the..." But before Chloe could finish her languid qualification, she and Nick burst into howls of laughter, and when she could get her breath she gasped, "Oh Mother! We saw Mrs. Donahue! Through the window! And...they flopped!"

Bridget was not sure what they were talking about, but then she caught on and felt she ought to be shocked, but the next thing she knew she had joined in, and then the three of them laughed until their stomachs ached, and tears ran down their faces, as though Mrs. Donahue and her liberated bosom were the funniest things in the world.

It was a long time before Bridget could bring herself to send Chloe to bed. She wanted to keep her there, to warm herself in this sunny, carefree friendliness that had never been there before.

When the time finally came, she took Chloe in herself, and helped her undress, and put her in bed, and held her tight for a moment, still ecstatic at the miracle that had happened. Then Chloe whispered, “Oh Mother, isn't he just wonderful!”

“He's terribly nice.”

“How did you meet him?”

Bridget mumbled something about Nick's having come into Hartalkar’s restaurant once or twice, then asked, “And how did you meet him?”

“Oh Mother, I didn't! I mean, I did not say anything to him. He spoke to me. He said I looked so much like you he knew who I was. Did you tell him about me?”

“Yes, of course.”

“Then he asked for Isabella, and when I told him about her, he turned perfectly pale, and jumped up, and, said he didn’t know.”

"Yes, I know.”

There was a sweet pause and then Chloe spoke. “And Mother, those orchids!”

"Would you like them?”

“Oh, yes, Mother.”

“All right, you can wear one to school. Now goodnight my sweet daughter.”

“Good night mother.”

Bridget left the bedroom and returned to the den to find Nick staring into the fire. Hearing her enter, he turned, smiled, and sat down on the couch. Bridget sat down beside him and was about to say how exhausted she was when he leaned over and kissed her deeply. She melted into his arms. In a husky voice he said, "I've been looking at you in that dress all night and all I wanted to do was undress you."

"Oh, is that so."

"Yes, woman, take it off."

"Oh, Nick, I'm exhausted. I wouldn't be much fun."

"I'm not looking for fun."

He carried her to the bedroom and kicked the door closed behind them. He undressed her and silenced her requests to take a shower or at least brush her teeth. Soon he had them both naked and under the covers where he worked his body into a frizzy before finally entering her. All the time Bridget was thinking this was a wonderful way to climax the evening, but her mind and body were far away thinking of Cameron, Greyson, Lucy, Ida and yes, Nick. She moaned more for the joy of seeing the sign and the restaurant up and running and making so much money in one day. But most of all she felt the joy of seeing Isabella again. It was the stamp of approval.

When Nick finally got her attention back, she felt her body release at the same time with his and she smiled, thinking lastly of her beautiful daughter Chloe.

CHAPTER 19

From that one night her life changed. Some months after that first opening of the restaurant Nick became a part of her life, though overall not quite so satisfactory a part as it had seemed, in that first week or two, that he might be. For one thing, she had discovered that a large part of his appeal for her was physical, and this she found disturbing. So far, her sex experiences had been limited, and of a routine, tepid sort, even in the early days with Cameron. This hot, wanton excitement that Nick aroused in her seemed somehow shameful; also, she was afraid it might really take possession of her, and interfere with her work, which was becoming her life. For despite mishaps, blunders, and catastrophes that sometimes reduced her to bitter tears, the little restaurant continued to prosper.

Whether she had any real business ability it would be hard to say, but her common sense, plus an industry that never seemed to flag, did well enough. She saw early that the wholesale pie business was the key to everything else, and tenaciously kept at the job of building it up, until it became self-sufficient and covered all expenses, even above the wages due Jackson, the baker that she hired.

Bridget was able to see light at the end of the tunnel where her original investment was concerned and that eased her mind plenty. That Nick could throw her out of step with this precious venture was a possibility that distinctly frightened her.

And for another thing, she felt increasingly the sense of inferiority that he had aroused in her, that first night at the lake. Somehow, by his easy flippancy, he made her accomplishments seem small and of no consequence. It especially hurt when he had Chloe siding with him. And even though he sometimes brought his friends there, and introduced them, and asked her to sit down, she felt uneasy.

Once, unexpectedly, he had pointed the car toward Cobbs Hill, and said he wanted her to see his home. She was nervous at the idea of meeting his mother, but when they got there it turned out that both mother and sister were away, and the help was off for the night.

At once she hated the mansion which indeed it was, hated the feeling she had been smuggled in the back door, almost hated him. There was no sex that night, as Nick professed to be puzzled, as well as hurt, by her conduct.

She had a growing suspicion that to him she was a servant, an amusing servant girl, with pretty legs and a flattering response in bed, but not his equal in any sense of the word.

Yet she never declined his invitations, never put on the brakes that her instinct was demanding, never raised the hatchet that she knew one day would have to fall. For there was always this delicious thing that he had brought into her life, this intimacy with Chloe that had come when he came, that would go, she was afraid, when he went.

Nick seemed devoted to Chloe., He took her everywhere, to golf tournaments, to horse shows, to his mother's, granting her all the social equality that he withheld from Bridget, so that the child lived in a utopia. Bridget lived in a version of utopia too, a paradise of more modest design, one slightly spoiled by wounded pride. She was aware that Chloe's love came at a cost and was fake, but she hoped that she could nurture her feelings by meeting her demands.

So, without complaint the expensive gear that her utopia required, Bridget purchased riding, swimming, golf, and golf outfits.

If Bridget knew nobody in Cobbs Hill, she had the consolation that Chloe knew everybody, and had her picture on the society pages so often that she became quite blasé about it. And so long as this went on, Bridget knew she would put up with Nick, with his irritating point of view, his amused condescension, his omissions that cut her so badly. She still believed that when we give love, we get love back, but sometimes it is just an illusion of what we gave them.

If one thing in life is certain, it is that taxes will never stay static. Eventful changes in Bridget's life as well as frequent adjustments by legislation were cause for increasing the bottom line and that is when she began to show interest in politics and asked Nick to help her understand her options. Nick played along for a bit, then bored with the topic changed the subject.

"Can I tell you something?"

"Sure, what is it?"

"It's about Chloe."

"What's she up to now?"

"Music…" He paused in reflection. "Well, I know it's none of my business, but what the hell. She's good and loves her music and…"

"Nick, she takes lessons."

"She takes lessons from some cheap little ivory thumper in Irondequoit, and she has a complaint." He paused wondering if he should go further with this and then decided. "She doesn't think she's getting anywhere." Trying to make light of it, he flashed one of his endearing smiles, his white teeth highlighted by his brown skin. "Well, it's none of my affair…"

"No, go on."

"I think she's got something."

"I always said she had talent."

“Saying she has talent and doing the right thing about it are two different things. If you do not mind my saying so, I think you know more about pies than you do about music. I think she ought to be taught by somebody that can really take charge of her.”

“Who, for instance?”

“Well, there's a fellow in Cobbs Hill that could do wonders with her. You may have heard of him, Hosea Taylor, Jr., quite well known, on the concert circuit, but now leads a quiet life, taking in a few pupils he sees as promising and in his spare time being the organist at my church. I am sure I can get him interested in her. If he takes her on, she'll reach her full potential.”

Feeling a little put out now, Bridget asked; “When did you learn so much about music?”

“I don't know a thing about it. But my mother does. She has been a patroness of the Philharmonic for years and she knows all about it. She says the kid really has talent.”

Not wanting to be petty, but unable to help it Bridget said, “Of course I never met your mother.”

This slightly waspish remark Nick let pass without comment, and it was some minutes before he went on. “And another thing that makes me think she's got it is the way she works at it.” He was aware of what she was thinking so said it himself. “All right, all I know is golf, but when I see a guy who is out there every day swinging the golf club when there's nobody else around, I think to myself, maybe one day he'll be a golf pro.”

Less offensive Bridget nodded her head. “I see what you’re

saying."

"It's the same way with her. As far as I know, she never misses a day on that old piano at her grandfather's, and even when she comes over to Mother's she does her two hours of exercises every morning, before she will even talk about golf, or riding, or whatever Mother has in mind for her. She's dedicated and you don't even have to be a musician to figure that out."

Bells were going off and despite her almost religious conviction that Chloe had talent, Bridget was reading between the lines. She knew Chloe too well to fall in one of Chloe's traps. Chloe's earnest practicing at Nick's mother's, Mrs. Lombardi, might mean a consuming passion for music, and it might mean a consuming passion for letting the whole household know she was around. And as for Mr. Taylor, Jr., he might have been a celebrated pianist once, but the fact that he was now organist at one of Cobbs Hill's swanky churches cast a certain familiar color over his nomination as teacher. Overall, Bridget was sure she detected one of Chloe's schemes. And in addition to that, she resented what was evidently becoming a small conspiracy to tell her what she should do about her child, and the implication that what she was already doing, by Cobbs Hill standards, was not anywhere near good enough.

After that conversation with Nick, it was some time before she said something about the incident to Chloe. But as it was her nature, the more she allowed it to gnaw at her conscious, the more she began to fear that perhaps she was denying the child something she really ought to have. And then one night Chloe broke into a violent denunciation of Miss Waldorf, the lady to whom Bridget had been paying fifty dollars a lesson for Chloe. She knew her daughter and something about the outburst did not have the usual phony sound to it.

She had done her homework in choosing Miss Waldorf though and knew that she was one of the few female pianists to compete in this largely male world of music, Clara Waldorf was a superstar of her day. Her talents far outshone those of her composer husband Robert. She wrote her own music as well. One critic had professed: "The appearance of this artist can be regarded as epoch-making… In her creative hands, the most ordinary passage, the most routine motive acquires a significant meaning, a color, which only those with the most consummate artistry can give."

At first, she hesitated, but finally troubled and without any explaining on her part, Bridget asked suddenly if Mr. Taylor, Jr., of Cobbs Hill, would be better. Of course, she had not taken Nick's word for it. She had headed to the internet knowing that she would have to decide for the change whether she agreed or not. The most favorable report she found that stuck with her because it fit Chloe was, "If I belong to a tradition it is a tradition that makes the masterpiece tell the performer what he should do and not the performer telling the piece what it should be like." Not familiar with this world she did know that the fact he could turn his hand to music from any period and was particularly respected for his interpretations of Haydn, Mozart, Beethoven, Schubert, Brahms, and Liszt would be the credentials most acceptable.

Now as she stood in front of her daughter, she felt confident as she announced her decision to consider Mr. Taylor, Jr. as her new music teacher.

Chloe's reaction was as if she really did not know what to do with herself, so she just jump up and down, and spun around until she collapsed on the sofa. She had never seen Chloe so happy. "Calm down darling. You're going to have a heart attack."

"I can't calm down. This could be the best thing to ever happen in my life."

The very next day Bridget made a call to Mr. Taylor, Jr.'s studio. As she waited patiently on the line, Chloe fidgeted and tried to hear the conversation. When she waved her away and told her to get a pad and pencil, Chloe magically produced both and handed them to Bridget. Then standing over her mother's hand, she watched as she wrote down the details. Even though it was not necessary, she disconnected the call and said, "It's all set. You have an audition with Mr. Taylor."

"Ah, that's 'virtuoso' Taylor, Mother, or maybe he prefers 'professor'." Chloe paused, her forehead wrinkling in concentration. "I think we should call him 'professor'." And in her mind, that was it.

On the day of the engagement with the music professor, Bridget rushed through her work so she could dash home and take Chloe to the audition. For the occasion, she laid out a flowery dress and low-heeled pumps, but when Chloe got home from school, and saw the pile on the bed, she threw up her hands in horror. "Mother! I cannot be dressed up! Ooh! It would be so country!"

Bridget knew the voice of society when she heard it, so she sighed, put the things away, and waited while Chloe tossed out her own idea of suitable garb which included a maroon sweater, plaid skirt, and flat heeled shoes. She looked away when Chloe started to dress.

A year and a half had indeed made some changes in Chloe's appearance. She was still no more than medium height, but her haughty carriage made her seem taller. The hips were as slim as ever but had taken on some touch of voluptuousness. The legs were Bridget's, to the last graceful contour. But the most noticeable change was her full breast that had appeared almost overnight on her high, arching chest. They would have been large, even for a woman and for a child of thirteen they were positively startling.

Bridget had purchased a child's bra when Nick had told her Chloe needed one. Embarrassed he had said, "For Christ's sake get her a grown-up bra." Bridget had been shocked, and furious. But not Chloe, she had laughed gaily, and picked out bras in every color and style that met her fancy. Plus, the fact that she paraded around as she tried on each one, did embarrass Bridget as she watched her daughter swaying her hips and moving about like some proud, pedigreed show dog.

Mr. Taylor, Jr. lived just off the Cobbs Hill traffic circle, in a house that looked usual enough from the outside, but which, inside, turned out to be one gigantic studio, with all the first floor and most of the second given over to it. It startled Bridget, not only by its size, but by its incredible bareness. There was nothing in it but a big piano, long shelves of music, a wooden wall seat across one end, and a bronze bust, in one corner, labelled Mozart. Mr. Taylor, Jr. himself was a squat man of about sixty, with bandy legs, thick chest, and the longest fingers she had ever seen. He walked haughtily, with white hair wildly flaring out at all angles.

He was quite friendly, and chatted with Bridget until she was off guard, and grew gabby. When she mentioned the restaurant, Chloe tossed her head impatiently, but Mr. Taylor said, “Ah!” in a flattering way, remembered he had heard of it, copied down the address, and promised to come in. Then, rather casually, he got around to Chloe, had a look at the music she had brought, and said they might as well get the horrible part over.

Chloe looked a little set back on her heels, but he waved her to the piano and told her to play something; anything, so long as it was short. Chloe marched grandly over, sat down on the bench, twisted her hands in a professional way, and meditated. Mr. Taylor, Jr. sat down on the wall seat, near Bridget. Then Chloe launched into a piece known to Bridget as Rachmaninoff Prelude.

It was the first time, in recent months, that Bridget had heard Chloe play, and she was delighted with the effect. The musical part she was not quite sure about, except that it made a fine noisy clatter. But there could be no mistaking the authoritative way in which Chloe kept lifting her right hand high in the air, or the style with which she crossed her left hand over it. The piece kept mounting to a rousing noisy climax, and then inexplicably it faltered. Chloe struck a petulant chord. “I always want to play it that way.”

“I'll tell Mr. Rachmaninoff when I see him,”

Mr. Taylor’s voice rang of sarcasm while his brows knitted above his eyes that stared crazily during the pause in her playing. None of this was lost on Chloe.

He made no comment, but got up, found a piece of music, and put it in front of her. “Let's try the sight reading.”

Chloe rattled through this piece like a human piano, while Mr. Taylor, Jr. alternately screwed up his face as though he were in great pain and stared hard at her. When silence mercifully stole into the room, he walked over to the shelves again, got out a violin case, set it beside Bridget, opened it, and began to resin the bow. “Let us try the accompanying. What's your name again?”

“Miss Bitmore.”

“What?”

"Chloe."

"Have you ever been accompanied, Chloe?"

"Just a little."

"Just a little, what?"

"Yes, I have."

"I might warn you, Chloe, that with young pupils I mix quite a little general instruction, in with the musical. Now if you do not want a clip on the ear, you'll call me Sir."

"Yes Sir."

Bridget wanted to kick up her heels and laugh at a Chloe who was suddenly meek and humble. However, she pretended not to be listening, and stared at Mr. Taylor, Jr.'s violin as though it was the most interesting piece she had ever seen. He picked up the violin and turned to Chloe. "This isn't my instrument, but there must be something for you to accompany, so it'll have to do. Sound your A." Chloe tapped a note, he tuned the violin, and set a piece of music on the piano. "All right a little briskly. Don't drag it."

Chloe looked blankly at the music. "Why, you've given me the violin part."

"Ah, so I have."

He looked on the shelves for a moment, then shook his head.

"Well, the piano part is around somewhere, but I don't seem to see it now. All right, keep the violin part in front of you and give me a little accompaniment of your own. Let's see, you have four measures before I come in. Count the last one aloud."

"Sir, I wouldn't even know how to…"

"Begin."

After a desperate look at the music, Chloe played a long, faltering figure that ended somewhere up in the high notes. Then, thumping a heavy bass, she counted, "One, two, three, four and…"

Even Bridget could detect that the violin was certainly not Mr. Taylor's instrument. As he accompanied her, he spoke out, "The timbre is homogeneous in all registers with only the very lowest and highest notes exhibiting any different qualities."

Just as obvious was Chloe's unfamiliarity with this type of instruction, but she struggled on.

The music filled the room. "Okay, the low notes should sound rather dull, dry and hollow which gives them a melancholy character. Next that middle register is mellow, light, wafting, bright and rich."

Bridget could see the change in Chloe as she struggled to match his words. "Now the higher notes should possess great brilliance and sound penetrating and shrill. These are the notes that are ideally suited for playing melody lines along with the violins and are therefore found precisely fulfilling this task in practically every orchestral work."

This went on for some time, but little by little, Bridget thought, it was getting smoother. Once, when Mr. Taylor, Jr. stopped, Chloe repeated the last part of the air he had been playing, so that when he came in again it joined up quite neatly. When they finished, Mr. Taylor, Jr. put the violin away and resumed staring at Chloe. Then spoke. "Where did you study harmony?"

“I never studied harmony, Sir.”

“Hmmm.”

He walked around a few moments, said “Well” in a reflective way, and began to talk. “The technique is simply God awful. You have a tone that is unpleasant to the ear, but that may respond to whatever we do about it. And the conceit is almost unbelievable. That certainly will respond. It's responded a little already, hasn't it?”

“Yes Sir.”

“But play that bit in the Rachmaninoff again, the way you said you always wanted to play it.”

Rather weakly, Chloe obeyed. He was beside her on the bench now and dropped his long fingers on the keys as he played after her. A tingle went through Bridget at the way it seemed to reach down into the vitals of the piano, and find sounds that were rich, dark, and exciting. She noted that it no longer seemed heavy but became a thing of infinite grace. He studied the keys a moment, then said, “And suppose you did play it that way. You'd be in a little trouble, don't you think?”

He played another chord or two. “Where would you go from there?”

Chloe played a few more chords, and he carefully played them after her. Then he nodded. “Yes, it could have been written that way. I really think Mr. Rachmaninoff's way is better. I find a slight touch of banality in yours, don't you?”

“What's banality, Sir?”

"I mean it sounds corny. Cheap. Play it an octave higher and put a couple of trills in it."

Chloe played it an octave higher, and it was easy to see she was embarrassed. "Yes Sir, I guess you're right."

"It's not that I'm right, Chloe, it's that it makes musical sense."

This seemed so incredible to him that he sat in silence for some little time before he went on, "I have plenty of pupils with talent in their fingers, very few with anything in their heads. Your fingers, Chloe, I am not so sure about. There is something about the way you do it that is not exactly right, but never mind about that. We will see what can be done. But your head that is different. Your sight reading is remarkable, the sure sign of a musician. And that trick I played on you, making you improvise an accompaniment to the little violin of course, you did not really do it well, but the amazing thing was that you could do it at all. I do not know what made me think you could, unless it was that idiotic bit you pulled in the Rachmaninoff.

"So…" He turned now to Bridget. "I want her over here twice a week. I am giving her one lesson in piano and my rate is eighty dollars an hour, the lesson is a half hour, so it will cost you forty dollars, I am giving her another lesson in the theory of music, and that lesson will be free. I cannot be sure what will come of it, and it is not fair to make you pay for my experiments. But she will learn something, and at the very least get some of the conceit knocked out of her."

So, saying, he took a good healthy breath. Then he added, "I suppose nothing will come of it if we're really honest about it. Many are called, in this business, but few are chosen, and hardly any find out how good you must be before you are any good at all. But we'll see ...." Then as if he had no feelings whatsoever, he turned and said, "God, Chloe, but your playing stinks. I ought to charge a hundred dollars an hour, just to listen to you."

Chloe started to cry, as Bridget stared in astonishment. Not three times in her life had she seen this cold child cry, and yet there she was, with two streams squirting out of her eyes and cascading down on the maroon sweater, where they made glistening silver drops. Mr. Taylor, Jr. airily waved his hand. "Let her bawl. It's nothing to what she'll be doing before I get through with her."

So, Chloe bawled, and she was still bawling when they got in the car and started home. Bridget kept patting her hand. Then, in explosive jerks, Chloe started to talk. "Oh, Mother I was so afraid he wouldn't take me. And then he wanted me. He said I had something in my head. Mother, in my head!"

Then Bridget knew that an awakening had taken place in Chloe, that it was not in the least phony, and that what had awakened was precisely what she herself had mutely believed in all these years. It was as though a light had gone off and radiated her soul.

So, Nick was vindicated, but when Bridget snuggled up to him one night in the den, and wanted to talk about Chloe's audition with Mr. Taylor, the result left a great deal to be desired. When she tried to break through his habit of treating everything with offhand remarks, saying was not it wonderful, and how did he ever think up something like that, she sensed his disinterest and changed the subject.

Only Bridget needed to talk about it, so she called Cameron. He came the next afternoon, to the restaurant. She had Celine serve lunch and told him about the audition. Cameron listened patiently after explaining Chloe had told him about it and his mother had mentioned it as well, but now he got it all, in complete detail. Bridget told about the studio, the Rachmaninoff prelude, the sight reading, and the accompaniment to the violin selection. He listened gravely, except for the laugh he let out over the "Sir" episode. When Bridget had finished, he sat quietly, taking it all in and then solemnly, announced, "She's some kid. We made some great kid. She's going to make us proud; I just know it."

Bridget sighed happily. This was the reaction she wanted.

He went on, reminding her that she had always said Chloe was artistic, gallantly conceding that he himself had had his doubts. Not that he did not appreciate Chloe, he added hastily, hell No. It was only that he did not know of any musical talent on Bridget's side or his, and he always understood this kind of thing ran in families.

As was Cameron's way, he dealt with the positive first and once he had reveled in it, he dealt with the negative. Since she had known him, every discussion was handled this way. If they talked about the past, he would take any negative connotation and polish it with possibilities in the future. If there was one thing that she still loved about him, it had to be his approach to the good and the bad in life.

Now, having polished off the past, he looked at the future. The fingers, he assured Bridget, were nothing to worry about. Because suppose she did not become a great pianist? From all he had heard that market was shot anyway. But if it were like this guy said, and she had talent in her head, and began to write music, that was where the real dough was, and it did not make a bit of difference whether you could play the piano or not. To emphasize he said, "Look at that character, Charlie Harper."

Bridget's head snapped up and gave him a puzzled look. "Who?"

"You know, the character in 'Two And A Half Men'.

"You've got to be kidding…"

"I know, I know he's not real, but I'm making a point here. It was not that he could play the piano that made him famous, but that he could compose those jingles. It was those jingles that put a million bucks in his bank, and more was always coming in along with opportunities in other areas of entertainment."

"Like what?"

"Like doing videos and concerts of a sort." He paused, "I'm not saying she will be a jingle writer; I'm just making a point that there are many avenues in music to take and I believe the sideways is Chloe's way."

Bridget was understanding what Cameron was saying and the more she listened to him, the better she felt. No one knew Chloe like Cameron did. He knew her and understood her even better than she. So, when he said she need not worry about Chloe now, Bridget believed him.

Having Chloe turn into a Charlie Harper, with or without a million dollars in the bank, was not exactly what Bridget had in mind for her. In her imagination she could see Chloe already, wearing a pale green dress to set off her coppery hair, seated at a big piano before a thousand people, grandly crossing her right hand over her left, haughtily bowing to thunderous applause, but no matter. The spirit was what counted. Cameron spun her dreams for her, while she closed her eyes and breathed deeply, and Celine poured him more coffee. It was the middle of the afternoon before Bridget returned to earth, and said suddenly, "Cameron, can I ask a favor?"

"Anything, Bridget."

"It's not why I asked you here. I just wanted to tell you about Chloe. I knew you'd want to hear every facet."

"I think I know why you asked me but tell me anyway."

"I want that piano, at your Mom's."

"Nothing to it. They'll be extremely glad to give it to Chloe."

"No, wait a minute. I do not want it as a gift, nothing like that at all. I just want to borrow it until I can get Chloe a piano that…"

He interrupted her. "It's all right. They'll see it as a contribution to Chloe's success."

"No but wait a minute. I am going to get her a piano. From speaking to people and searching the internet I found the Steinway grands to be highly praised. They're the gold standard of musical instruments and they say over 19 out of 20 concert pianists choose the Steinway grand piano."

Yes, but a grand piano?" It's way too big for any room in the house."

"Yes, I know, so that's why I am talking about a baby grand."

Cameron, nodded. He had heard Chloe play his mother's piano and knew to his daughter it was the instrument she wanted.

Bridget was ready for this discussion and went to get her tablet. When she returned, she sat beside Cameron and opened it, revealing how much thought she had given to the matter.

"So, I decided on the Model 0."

Cameron looked at the details on the size and said, "Ah, 5 feet, 10 ¾ inches." He stared off into the distance and then smiled at Bridget. "Big enough to satisfy those who demand a full, rich sound, yet sized to fit in almost all homes." No problem it will fit in the house.

"I know. I may need to move a few things, but it will fit."

"Great…ah…Bridget?"

“Don’t say it. Twenty-three to twenty-six thousand dollars. But they will allow me to pay in installments. I just do not dare take on any more debt. What I am going to do, I am going to open a special account, down at the bank, and keep putting money in and I know by next Christmas, I mean a year from now, I can manage it. But just now…”

“I wish I could contribute a little.”

“I know you do, but I’m not asking you to.”

Quickly she put her hand over his and patted it. “You've done plenty. Maybe you have forgotten how you gave me the house outright, and lots before then. You have done your share. Now it is my turn. I do not mind about that, but I do want them to know, Mom and Mr. Bitmore that is, that I am not trying to get anything from them. I just want to borrow the piano, so Chloe can practice at home, and…”

“Bridget.”

“Yes?”

“Will you just kindly shut up?”

“All right.”

“Everything's under control. Just leave it to me.”

It was a bright day for Bridget and Chloe when the movers arrived with the grand piano in tow. Chloe took charge of the movers, ordering them around, threatening them if they even put one scratch or dent in her glorious piano and finally settled down once it was placed in the dining room. Bridget had chosen to put it there since she no longer entertained large groups or had fancy dinner parties, so it was a room aching for a new life. At Chloe's insistence, she gave her a free hand in furnishing the room and a meager budget to do it in.

The dining room had a coffer ceiling that had never been played up, but now as Chloe prepared the room, she began by calling on friends to help her hang a gorgeous light fixture that would be positioned over the piano and because it was to be placed just off center of the room, Bridget was worried about the placement of the light. But it worked. Over against the front wall she had another friend help her create two bookshelves on either side of the window where she would put her books and music. For the window area that was now a little alcove, she had the same friend build a seat with storage in the base and she added a cushion and some pillows. Cameron helped install two sconces on either side of the bookcases for extra lighting. Chloe was ecstatic when Francine offered her two deep chairs that she had been given by her grandmother but were too big for her place. They were white and in great shape, so Chloe added a couple accent pillows for color. Finally, she purchased some floor carpet samples that were the same style and sat down and cleverly took a top sheet to use as the backing and glued the pieces together.

Watching her daughter find a way to create the room she

wanted with such a small amount of money, made Bridget proud. She was sure that this would keep their new relationship in tack and that was worth everything to Bridget.

So, with the grand piano settled in its new home, Bridget started her contribution and on January 2, she went to the bank and deposited $250, after carefully figuring that $250 a week, at the end of two years would equal the highest cost grand piano. And if her business kept improving, she might be able to increase that amount.

CHAPTER 20

Bridget had been so busy with the restaurant business she had not noticed that Nick was acting differently. He seemed moody and preoccupied, with little of the flippancy that was normally part of his character. It was at a bar one night, she took notice. When the check came, he looked at it with dismay and embarrassment, "I am sorry, I didn't bring enough money with me. Do you mind."

She started to ask him about his credit cards, but just said, "Sure, no problem."

Then another night when she wanted to go to a fancy restaurant, he instead said they should go to her restaurant for dinner. She tried to take it as a compliment, but he knew after working there all day, going out meant somewhere different.

At that moment she knew something was wrong, but she hesitated to ask. It was Chloe who let the cat out of the bag. Walking home from the restaurant one night, she suddenly asked

Bridget, “Heard the news?”

“What news, darling?”

“Some internet stock going belly up!”

"Bridget knew nothing about the stock market, except she did not have the funds, nor the stamina to throw money in it. A ‘win some, lose some’, was not part of her repertoire so she had those with the knowledge handle her investments. She recalled Cameron saying that the stock market is brutal. You can make all the decisions and still have a bad outcome. Some people say all you will ever get is an eight percent return at the end of your investing life. That she felt was nothing to get excited about.

As they walked, Chloe said, “Nick always told me the stupidest reason to buy a stock is because it’s going up and then he turned around and did just that.”

They were at the house and once inside, Bridget, out of curiosity wanted to hear more. “Chloe let’s sit in the den. I’ll make a fire and you can tell me all about it.”

“Not much to tell, Mother.”

“Tell me anyway.”

So, Chloe continued. “Well, Mother, I really don't know a great deal about it, except that it's all over Cobbs Hill, and you hardly hear anything else. They had invested heavily in some internet stock, the Lombardis; that is his mother, and the Simpsons, that is his sister. They lost a fortune.” Chloe paused, “No, that’s putting it lightly. They lost three fortunes.”

“When did that happen?”

“Three or four months ago. Nick had a lot of money tied up in his company that was on the verge of bankruptcy, so his parents kicked in to save it.”

“Wait a minute, Chloe, I didn’t know he had a company.”

Chloe looked at her mother with a puzzled expression on her face. “How could you not know. His every move was in the paper. His parents are… correct that… were rich, but he wanted to earn his own way, so he started a catalog selling golf equipment that not only sold the equipment, but a book he had written on how to become the best golfer, ever. It was, of course, a high-end store that invested a lot of money in frills that ate into the profits until finally it was on the verge of bankruptcy. So, when he heard about this stock, he decided to take a chance, and encouraged others to do the same. The end game was that he lost the store, His parents, on his praise of the stock, had over invested their funds and suffered a major lost as well so there was no money to help him out of his financial situation. Anyway, there is a big sign on the lawn, 'For Sale, Owner Must Sacrifice’ and Nick's showing the prospective buyers around.”

“You mean their house?”

“I mean their palatial residence in Cobbs Hill behind the iron fence and brick wall.” Chloe got up and returned with two glasses of tea. “A buyer had better show up pretty soon, or Nick will be living in the ghetto. It certainly looks as though he’ll have to go to work.”

Bridget was taken aback, unable to process it all. Nick’s

family was rich, and Nick had earned a lot during his pro golf career. Where had all the money gone. She pondered that as she looked at her daughter. Chloe showed no sympathy. This family had taken an interest in her and shown her around as if she were their own daughter. Now, as she stared at Chloe, she saw only indifference, nothing more.

Bridget continued to see Nick, but one thing was clear, Nick wanted no sympathy from her. For a time, she ate with him, drank with him, and slept with him under the pretense that she knew nothing whatever. But presently the thing became so public, what with pieces in the paper about the sale of his beach house in Charlotte and the disappearance of his corvette in favor of a battered little Chevrolet, Nick figured he owed her an explanation.

He began to talk about it. But he always acted as though this were some casual thing that would be settled shortly, a nuisance while it lasted, but of no real importance. Never once did he let Bridget sympathize with a hug or words of encouragement that it would get better. She felt sorry for him. And she also felt snubbed and rebuffed. Even with all she had accomplished, she felt that he did not accept her as his social equal, though from what Chloe had shared, should have proved she was.

And then one night she came home to find him with Chloe,

waiting for her. They were in the den, having a furious argument about a golf tournament, which continued after she sat down. It seemed that a major company was organizing a new golf tournament and Nick had been invited to make the trip and provide feedback. Chloe was urging him to go.

"They are rookies at this, and you have an opportunity to help make the tournament great."

"I've got too much to do."

"Such as what?"

"This and that."

"Right. Nick, you must go. If you do not, they are sunk. It will be embarrassing. And they will be another no name tournament. Plus…" She started to say the obvious but stopped herself.

Chloe did not understand how someone could be rich and then poor the next day. That was beyond her, but Nick's situation tore at Bridget's heart that he should want to go, and not be able to, and it kept bothering her long after Chloe had gone to bed. When Nick got up to go, she pulled him down beside her, and asked, "Do you need money?"

"Oh Lord no!"

His voice, look, and gesture were those of a man pained beyond expression at an insinuation utterly grotesque. But Bridget, nearly two years in the restaurant business, was not fooled. She said "'I think you do."

"Bridget, you leave me without any idea of what to say to you. I have run into a little bad luck, that is true. My mother has, we all have. But it is nothing. I can still hold up my end of it if that's what you're talking about."

"I want you to go and assist in setting up the tournament, Nick."

"I'm not interested."

"Wait a minute."

She found her handbag, took out her check book and wrote out a check. She handed it to Nick. Nick did not even look at the check, but instead looked into her eyes. He could see she really was trying to help and that the more he refused, the more determined she would get. Finally, he took the check. "I'll pay it back."

"I know you will."

'It's a loan and I will pay you back."

"Fine."

Bridget had started up something that began to get out of control.

With the warm June weather, her business took a sharp drop. For the first time, she had to skip an installment on Chloe's piano. The next week, when he changed his mind about going to a bar that he liked, she offered to treat, and they went. Before she knew it, it was becoming a habit to keep Nick able to enjoy the life he was used to.

Her business continued light, and when the summer had gone, she had managed to make only three payments on the piano, despite hard scrimping. She was appalled at the amount of money Nick was costing her and fought off a rising irritation about it. She told herself it was not his fault, that he was merely going through what thousands of others had already gone through and were still going through. She told herself it was her duty to be helping somebody, and that it might as well be somebody that meant something to her. She also reminded herself she had practically forced the arrangement on him.

It was no use. The piano had become an obsession with her by now, and the possibility that it was slipping away from her caused a baffled, frustrated sensation. that almost smothered her. Eventually Bridget found herself taking advantage of Nick. She started with small matters such as taking Chloe to Mr. Taylor's for her lessons, but it grew to no longer asking, but telling him to pick up supplies for the restaurant. She knew just as Nick had changed, she had too. Now she ordered him around, told him when to show up; even at times what to eat.

In so many ways she began to despise him for taking her money, and on his side, he did little to make things better. Nick, alas, was like Cameron. A catastrophic change had taken place in his life, and he was wholly unable to adjust himself to it. In some way, indeed, he was worse off than Cameron, for Cameron lived with his dreams, and at least they kept him mellow. But Nick was an amateur cynic, and cynics are too cynical to dream. He had been born to a way of life that included taste, manners, and a jaunty aloofness from money, as though it were beneath a gentleman's notice. As for his golf pro image, that was dying a slow death as he constantly canceled tournaments and advertising opportunities. He said it was because they wanted to get the 'dirt' on him, and he was not going to give them a chance.

But what he did not realize was that all these things rested squarely on money, it was the possession of money that enabled him to be aloof from it. For the rest, his days were dedicated to play, play on which the internet cast a certain agreeable importance, but play, nevertheless. Now, with the money gone, he was unable to give up the old way of life or find a new one.

He became a jumble of sorry fictions, an attitude with nothing behind it but pretense. He retained something that he thought of as his pride, but it had no meaning, and exhibited itself mainly in mounting bitterness toward Bridget. He criticized her constantly. Even Chloe was having a hard time wanting this new Nick around. The gay little trio was not quite so gay.

And then one night in the den, Nick said the wrong thing back to Bridget when she relented and gave him money. "Your paid gigolo thanks you."

Bridget was livid, all thought and feeling left her body as she spat out, "I don't think that was very nice."

"It's true, isn't it?"

Ignoring him she asked, “Is that the only reason you come here?”

“Not at all. Come what may, swing high, swing low, for better or for worse, you’re still the best piece of ass I ever had, or ever could imagine.”

He said this with a nervous, rasping little laugh, and Bridget felt the rage bringing her blood to a boil. Her face felt hot, and she became aware of a throbbing silence that had fallen between them and for the first time, Bridget felt the difference between their races. Sheer pride demanded that she say something, and yet for a time she could not. Then, in a low, shaking voice, she said, “Nick, go home.”

“What's the matter?”

“I think you know.”

“Well, by all that's holy, I don’t know!”

“I told you to go.”

Instead of going, he shook his head as though she were incredibly obtuse and launched into a dissertation on the relations between the sexes. “Let me tell you something. Women are always seeking an emotional connection with a man, especially if you had sex within a few days or weeks of meeting?”

Bridget started to interrupt.

“No, let me finish. “You know, men love sex, and a lot of them would rather just “hook up” than commit. No surprise there, right? You convince yourself that you are okay with his casual boundaries. You try to be casual with his late night booty calls, except that…after a while…you are not okay with it. But eventually it comes to asking yourself does he actually feel anything for you in return, or is he still happy to continue your casual arrangement?"

Bridget starts to interrupt again, the anger she felt inside, showing on her face, but Nick ignores it.

"So, my dear if you are going to deny this fact that men are often more interested in physical attraction than an emotional attraction, you're being naive. As long as a woman gets what she wants it does not bother her that men think about and want sex. A lot. The women who get ahead are those who understand men's heads, both of them and can differentiate between physical attraction and emotional attraction. But all that leads to a different type of relationship when the dependency switches hands."

Nick took an irritably deep breath. "So what I am saying is that I paid you a compliment and what you really objected to was my language, wasn't it? If I had said it flowery, so it sounded poetic, you would have felt differently, wouldn't you?

Bridget gave him an incredulous stare. Then, gathering herself with an effort, she rose to one of her rare moments of eloquence. "If you said that and intended it as a compliment, it might have been one, I don t know. Almost anything can be considered a compliment in some light. But when you tell me that, and it is the only thing you must tell me about our relationship, then it is not a compliment. It is an insult and one of the worst things ever said to me.

"Oh, so you want me to fawn all over you."

"No, I want you to go."

Hot tears started to her eyes, but she winked them back. He shook his head, got up, then turned to her as though he had to explain something to a child.

"Were not talking about things. We are talking about words; I am not a poet. I do not even want to be a poet. To me, that is just funny. I say something to you my own way, and wham you go moral on me. Well, what do I do now? It's a pure question of narrow-mindedness, and…" He did not get a chance to finish.

"That's not true."

She felt dizzy with hatred for this man. Her face muscles tightened, and the glittering tears made her eyes look hard, cold, and feline. She stood perfectly still, her legs feeling stiff, and looked at him, where he stood facing her on the other side of the room. After a long pause. she went on, in a passionate, trembling voice. "Since you have known me, that is what I have been to you, a piece of ass. You have taken me to mountain cabins and bars. You have never introduced me to your friends, except for a few men you have brought over to dinner sometimes. I have never been even introduced to your mother, or your sister, or any member of your family. You are ashamed of me, and now that you are in my debt, you had to say what you just said to me, to get even. It is not a surprise to me. I've known it all along."

Bridget paused to catch her breath. “Now you can go.”

“None of that is true.”

“Every word of it is true.”

“So far as my friends go…”

“They mean nothing to me.”

Ignoring what she said Nick responded. “It hadn't occurred to me you'd care to meet any of them. Most of them are dull, but if meeting them means anything to you, that is easily fixed. As far as my mother goes…”

“She means nothing to me either.”

Again, he ignores her interruption. “So far as my mother goes, I cannot do anything about her now, because she is away, and so is my sister. But you may have forgotten that with this restaurant of yours you keep somewhat peculiar hours. To have arranged a meeting would have been idiotically complicated, so I did the best I could. I took your daughter over there, and if you knew anything about social conventions at all, you would know that I was dealing in my own way with what otherwise would have been a situation. Certainly, my mother took an honest interest in Chloe just as I would have expected, a little more interest than you seemed to be taking, I sometimes thought.”

“I want you to stop talking before you say something, I will never forgive you for saying.”

In her heart, Bridget knew that Nick was being as dishonest

about Chloe as he was being about the rest of it. Obviously, he liked Chloe, and found her an amusing exhibit to drag around, no doubt because she was precisely the kind of snob that he was himself, and that most of his friends were. And, by doing so much for the child, he could neatly sidestep the necessity of doing anything about the mother. But to argue about it would jeopardize the enchanted life that Chloe now led, so Bridget veered off in a new direction. "Nick, why don't you tell the truth? You look down on me because I work and..."

"Are you crazy?"

"No. You look down on everybody that works, as you practically admitted to me the first night, I was with you. All right, I work. It is not at all elegant work, but it is the only work I can do. I cook food and sell it. But one thing you'd better get through your head eventually." Putting all the venom she felt in her voice she continued. "You'll have to go to work and maybe then, that part of your aversion will lessen."

"Of course, I'm going to work!"

"Ha ha. When?"

"As soon as I get the damned house sold, and this mess straightened out that we've got ourselves into. Until that's over, work, for me, is out of the question. But as soon as it's over..." His voice trailed off.

"Nick, you make me laugh. I used to be married to a man who owned a real estate business, and there is no use trying to kid me about houses, and how to get rid of them. There is nothing about that place that cannot be put in the hands of an agent and handled like any other. No, it is not that. You'd rather live there, so you can have an address on Cobb's Hill, and cook your own eggs in the morning, and drive over to the club in the afternoon, and have your dinner here with Chloe, and take your spending money from me than work. That is all, isn't it?"

"Sure,"

His face broke into a sunny smile, he came over, roughly pushed her into a little heap, took her in his arms. "I don't know anybody I'd rather take money from than you. Your paid gigolo is damned well satisfied."

She pushed his arms away, trying to repulse him. But she was taken by surprise, and her struggles had no steam in them. Try as she would, she could not resist the physical effect he had on her, and when she finally yielded, the next hour was more wanton, more shamefully exciting, than any she remembered. And yet, for the first time, she felt an undertone of disgust. She did not forget that not once had the money been mentioned, not once had he offered to give it back.

Yet, they parted amicably, he apologizes for the offending remark, she tells him to forget what she had said, as she was upset, and did not mean it. But both meant it, and neither of them forgot.

CHAPTER 21

"What are you doing about getting your liquor license?"

Bridget was taken by surprise. "I haven't given it much thought. I just have too much on my plate right now."

"You can take a minute to get the process going."

"Quite frankly, the restaurant has gotten over the hump and is doing great again so I don't see how it matters whether I can serve drinks or not."

"It matters."

Mrs. Steele, having coffee with Bridget just before closing time began to talk very rapidly. She explained that being able to offer drinks before, during or after a meal was what made a restaurant successful.

"I thought good food and a brilliant idea made a restaurant successful?

"It does, Bridget, but even if people scrambled here for the best chicken and waffles, they have ever had, it gets old. But you know what does not? Being able to socialize with a glass of wine or something stronger. That never gets old. You think you have a nice clientele here, don't you? And you think they will stick by you, because they like you, and like your chicken." Lucy paused to take a breath, "You're an idiot if you think that. It will get old and when they find out you're not going to serve them that drink, they're going to start going elsewhere."

Bridget was listening and knew Lucy had always been supportive and given her good advice, but it was not like her to bear down hard on any issue, unless of course she thought it was for the best. As she sat quietly staring at her friend, she sensed more in this conversation. Lucy's tone of voice sounded angry, and her words were harsh. Finally, she said calmly, "What is it Lucy?"

"Stop overthinking. I've told you if you keep doing that, you'll get grey hairs."

"Come on Lucy, what are you really getting at?"

Mrs. Steele was trying to compose herself. She was shocked at how she had allowed her worry to transfer into hurting her friend. There was a sickening silence between them as each woman tried to figure out how to direct the conversation.

Finally, Mrs. Steele spoke. "First, let me say, I'm sorry Bridget." Silence followed and Bridget remained still, waiting. "Bridget, my husband, Ashton's business is going through a hard patch and we, like everyone else, need to review our options.

What I thought was I could work here. I could manage a bar within your restaurant. I could make the mixed drinks and help with stocking the bar. I could do this. What I do not know, I would learn…"

"I don't know, Lucy…"

"How's this? You put in the booze, and I'll take charge of it for you, for a straight ten percent of what I take in, plus tips, if, as, and when there are any."

"You? A bartender?"

"Why not? I'll be a damned good one."

This struck Bridget so funny that she laughed until her stomach hurt. But Mrs. Steele did not laugh. She was in dead earnest, and for the next few days nagged Bridget relentlessly. Bridget still regarded the whole idea as absurd, but on her trips downtown in connection with the pie business, she began to hear things. She had to talk to somebody, and on such matters she had not much confidence in Cameron, and none in Nick. On a sudden inspiration she called up Greyson. She saw him quite a lot, in connection with their real estate relations, but their previous connection had by tacit consent been completely erased, as if it had never existed. The results of that put them on a comfortable platform of business as usual, which is what worked best. So, Bridget did not hesitate to make the call to Greyson and invite him over to discuss a matter she wished to have his opinion.

Greyson listened while Bridget explained her quandary, then nodded. "Well, I don't know what you're hemming and hawing about. Of course, you'll sell liquor."

"Why? I've done quite well without adding a new headache."

"Because there's a lot of money in it."

He looked at her with his familiar stare that she always found vague and shrewd. It was like he felt she could not be that naïve. Only it had not occurred to her that this could be a money maker.

He went on, a little annoyed at her stupidity, "What the hell? Every drink you sell will be about eighty per cent profit, even at what you must pay for your liquor. And it will pull in more people for the dinner trade. If Lucy Steele wants to take it over, then okay. If you think she does not know enough about bartending, you are even a bigger fool. Who gave you advice and helped you learn about serving drinks and mixing them?" He paused for effect, "Yes, it was Lucy. What she doesn't know she can learn from the internet."

"You're right. You are right, Greyson."

"Of course, I'm right. That is why you contacted me. You should get going on it and get going on it fast." Greyson paused, smiled, and added, "And be sure you put on your sign, Cocktails."

"I'll need my liquor license first."

"That's where I come in. I'll take care of that for you."

The next time Mrs. Steele approached the subject, she found Bridget in a different frame of mind. She nodded approval of what Greyson had said about the sign, then became coldly businesslike about other obligatory preparations. “I'll need a bar, but there's no room for one until you make alterations, so I'll have to get along with a makeshift one.” Then Lucy’s face lit up. “What about your bar cart? “

“I don’t have a bar cart, Lucy.”

“Yes, you do. That wood thing you have in your kitchen that you use to wheel out pastries on. It has wheels and under the top are those rings that you use to hang things on…they would hold four bottles of wine easily.” Lucy continued to think and then added. “Let’s see you can use that lower metal framed area for liquor and a couple tracks added to one side can be used to hold glasses.” She looked at Bridget. “If I remember correctly, the top is removal and is a tray?”

“Yes.”

“Great. That will come in handy.”

Lucy Steele went on. “Then I want a couple of leather seats, near the door, with a low table between them. Between trips to the tables, I will be running my own little soiree over there, and I'll sell plenty of drinks to people waiting to be seated for dinner.” She was doing well now. “Then I'll want a special person to bus the table assigned to me alone. Your kid Waldo has a friend that will do, by the name of Emmett, something.” She paused in concentration. “Yes, Emmett Cann. He won't be available for general work, because he'll have to wash glasses for me all the time, and wash them the way I want them washed, and bring beer from the fridge when I call for it, and ice and whatever wine we sell, and he'll have all he can do, just helping me."

Bridget started to speak, but Lucy beat her to it. "Then I will need a full set of cocktail, highball, and wine glasses; not too many to start, but we'll have to have the right glasses for the right drinks." Again she paused for a breath. "Then, let's see. You will need pads of special bar checks, to run separate from the others. It's the only way we can keep it all straight."

"Wow, Lucy and I was worried how we could get it off the ground. You've razed it and finalized it in one swoop."

"Yes, well, I have been giving it a lot of thought. I do not start something unless I think it through from top to bottom because I know what can happen if you do not. I'm sure I've missed something, but that's about all I can think of now."

"How much are we talking?"

"That we need to discuss."

Changing the subject, Lucy said, "Let's see, unless you plan on some fancy party, between the two of us we have glasses to spare so that won't be an extra expense."

Bridget was caught up now and added, "Lucy, you know that small table I have in front of the window in the den. It has four chairs, but I only keep two there. Will that do for the table?"

Again, Lucy's face lit up. "You know, that would be perfect."

"So now it's the liquor, stirrers, lemons, olives, cherries…" Lucy counted off on her fingers. I think to start we should have a full base of liquor, wine, and beers. I will make a list out for you. I would say we should spend about five hundred to start."

"Wow!"

Mrs. Steele looked at her friend with a slight frown on her face, then remembered that Bridget was all about income; outgo scared the pants off her, so she added gently, "Now Bridget. Look at it this way. You know how much it costs for a bottle of wine, a can of beer or a standard bottle of hard liquor and we are not talking top shelf here. Now, think of it this way. One can of beer equals what they call, two standard drinks. A bottle of wine equals five standard drinks and a bottle of hard liquor, straight is about sixteen standard drinks."

Bridget's wheels were turning, and it suddenly came clear. She could make a boat load of money from the bar.

"Okay, we'll do it, but Lucy you will need to know how to make all those drinks…"

"Stop worrying baby I'll handle it all. I will purchase what we need. All you need to do is get me the startup money."

Bridget smiled wanly as she tried not to think about the money. "I'm with you on this Lucy but give me a day to give it more thought."

"Sure, no problem."

That night she laid awake for hours, her mind darting from one thing to another, trying to figure where she could get the five hundred dollars. Every penny she earned was accounted for and she had that little reserve of two or three hundred dollars, but she dared not dip into it. Experience had taught her that emergencies arose constantly, and they usually demanded cash.

It was a long time before she allowed herself to accept the only way, she could get the money. She would have to rob the special account for Chloe's piano. It now amounted to over a couple thousand dollars, and the moment she thought of it she tried not to think of it. There had to be another way. There just had to be. But she knew this was what she had to do; knew that this would mean Chloe could not have her piano by next Christmas.

Then once more rage began to suffocate her not at Mrs. Steele, or any of the circumstances that made this new outlay necessary, but at Nick, for. the money he had cost her, those endless thirties and fifty dollars which now, if she had them, would see her through. She worked herself into such a state that presently she had to get up, put on a kimono, and make herself a cup of tea, so she could quiet down.

CHAPTER 22

Christmas morning Bridget woke up with one of her rare hangovers. It had indeed been a busy night at the restaurant, for the bar, opening promptly on December 6, had outdone all that had been expected of it. Not only had it taken in large sums itself, but it had drawn a bigger dinner trade, and an even bigger liquor trade. Mrs. Steele, in gabardine slacks of the same brick red as the waitress' uniforms, white silk jacket with brass buttons and red ribbon around her hair, seemed to catch the diners' fancy, and certainly she was expert enough to please the most fastidious. Tips went up, and when the kitchen celebration finally got going, it was exceedingly festive.

Jackson, the baker, was supposed to be off at night, but he showed up anyway, and got the party started with a bang by making a pass at Astrid. Astrid was a Swedish girl Bridget had hired mainly for her bubbly personality and good looks, and then found out was a great waitress too.

Then, just to be impartial, Jackson made a pass at Celine, Emma, and Audrey. Emma and Audrey had been hired on the day after the opening, just to forestall the possibility of another jam up. The ensuing squeals were enjoyed by Waldo and Emmett, who sat apart, not quite a part of things, yet not quite out of them. They sat near Mrs. Ottoman; an assistant cook Bridget was training.

Jefferson did emphatically not enjoy them, being a seventeen-year-old who drove the little secondhand delivery truck Bridget had bought, and painted cream, with "Bridget Bitmore, Pies," lettered on it in bold red script. He concentrated on ice cream and cake, and eyed Jackson's efforts with stony disapproval, to the great delight of Celine, who kept screaming that he was learning 'the 'facts of life'.

Bridget had sat down with them, and put out wine and whiskey, and taken two or three drinks herself. Her heart hurt from thoughts of Isabella. She missed her so much, especially at the holidays which she believed had something to do with the fact Izzy had still believed in Santa Claus and the Easter Bunny, probably Cupid as well. Each morning she still said, 'hello' and each night she said 'goodnight' to her sweet baby girl.

What with the liquor, and the thanks she received for the one-hundred-dollar bonus she had given each of them, she began to feel so friendly that she weakened in her resolve to give Nick nothing whatever for Christmas. First, she took his orchids out of the icebox and pinned them on, to a loud chorus of applause. Then she had another drink, went over to the cash box, and smooched four $100 bills. These she put in a little envelope and wrote on it, "Merry Christmas, Nick." Then, hearing from Mrs. Steele that he had arrived, she went into the dining room, weaving slightly, and elaborately took him outside. Under the trees she slipped the envelope into his pocket and thanked him for the orchids, which she said were beautiful. Then she invited him to smell them.

Laughing a little, obviously delighted at her condition, he reminded her that orchids had no smell. "Smell em anyway." So, he smelled, and reported that the orchids still had no smell, but that she smelled fine. She nodded, satisfied, and kissed him. Then she took him inside, where Cameron, Greyson, Mrs. Steele, and Chloe were sitting at a table, having a little celebration of their own.

And yet the evening had had an unpleasant finish. Nick and Chloe began whispering together, and went into laughter at some joke of their own. Bridget heard the words 'mistress' and 'low lives' and concluded, probably correctly, that they were laughing at the party in the kitchen.

Infuriated, Bridget launched into a long, boozy harangue on how anybody who worked for a living was as good as anybody else. Greyson tried to shush her down and Mrs. Steele tried to shush her too, but it was no use. She went on to the bitter end.

This had the effect of bringing down the curtain, front and rear.

Now, as she got up and recalled it all, she felt embarrassed by her actions. She had given Francine the day off, so she went to the kitchen, made herself coffee, and drank it black. Then, hearing Chloe's water running, she knew she had to hurry. She went to her bedroom, got a pile of packages out of' the closet, and took them to the living room. Quickly she arranged a neat display around the base of the tree that had already been set up and decorated. Then she took out her own offering and looked at it. It was a wristwatch, She had put off buying it until the last moment, hoping the profits from the bar would permit her to order the piano anyway. But the unforeseen had again intervened. The liquor had run more than expected and other purchases had come up. So, at the last-minute Bridget had dashed downtown and bought this watch for Chloe. She listened close and heard its tiny tick, but it did not sound much like a grand piano. Glumly she wrapped it, wrote a little card, tucked it under the ribbon. Then she set it beside the package from Cameron.

She had hardly straightened up to survey the general effect when there came a tap on the door, and Chloe, in her most syrupy Christmas voice, asked "May I come in?"

Bridget smiled as she opened the door. Suddenly Chloe was smothering her with kisses, saying, "I wish you a Merry Christmas my darling, darling Mother!" Then, just as suddenly, the kisses stopped and so did the greetings.

Chloe surveyed the room and her eyes fell on the old Bitmore piano. There they stopped transfixed, her lips pressed tightly together, and Bridget realized that Chloe knew.

Someone had told her about the grand piano she would be getting at Christmas. Was it Cameron, Nick, the cashier at the bank who was friendly with Greyson? They all eventually knew, but it had not mattered. What mattered was one of them had told Chloe and now she had expected to see it there, as a fine surprise, this Christmas morning.

Bridget licked her lips, opened her mouth to make explanations, but at the cold look on Chloe's face, she could not. Nervously she said something about there being a great many presents, and hadn't Chloe better make a list, so she would be sure who sent what? Chloe still made no reply but stooped down and began pulling ribbons. When she got to the wristwatch, she examined it with casual interest and laid it aside without comment.

Bridget was not in the mood for Chloe's indifference and before she said something to ruin the day, she went back to her bedroom. There she laid down on the bed and tried to control herself. And like more than once before, she whispered, "Isabella, it shouldn't have been you. It should have been Chloe if it had to be either of you to die." The idea made her tremble, afraid she would be punished for thinking this way, but she was unable to stop.

She heard the doorbell and heard Cameron's voice. Bridget checked her face and patted her hair in place. She entered the living room in time to hear Chloe ecstatically thank him for the riding boots he had given her, and she call him her darling, darling father. Cameron accepted her praise and the hug she gave him and told her the boots could be exchanged if they were not the right fit. Chloe then proceeded to try them on. “They are perfect, father,” said Chloe. “I’m not going to take them off all day. I might even sleep in them,” she laughed, giving Bridget a cold stare.

The three of them headed to the kitchen for the flowers they were going to put on Isabella's grave, but when Chloe turned and headed back to the front room, Cameron quickly pulled Bridget back and with a jerking thumb toward the living room he asked, “What's the matter with her, she knows we’re leaving through the garage door, here? She sick?”

“It's about the piano. What with the bar and one thing and another I could not get it this Christmas? But obviously somebody told her about it, and she’s angry.”

“Not me.”

“I didn't think so.”

“What did you give her?”

“A wristwatch. It was a nice watch, a little one, the kind they're all wearing, and you'd think she'd at least…”

But the trembling had reached Bridget's mouth by now, and she could not finish. Cameron put his arm around her, patted her back lightly, waiting for the trembling to subside. Then he asked, “Is she coming with us?”

“I don't know.”

Cameron called out to Chloe, but she did not answer him. So, they went out the back door and climbed into the car. Bridget was in the driver's seat and backed the car out, closing the garage door as they continued down the driveway. Cameron asked her to stop, and she did. He reached over and lightly tapped the horn. After a few seconds, he tapped it again. There was no response from the house.

"Okay let's go."

Bridget could hear the disappointment in his voice as she eased into the street, and they drove to the cemetery. Once there Bridget threaded her way slowly along the drive, so as not to disturb the hundreds of others who were out there visiting their loved ones. When they came to the Bitmore plot she parked the car and together they got up and walked to their daughter's grave.

"Every time I come; I feel close to Izzy."

"I know, but she's not down there Bridget, she's in heaven. Coming here is just a ritual for the living, is all."

"I know, yet each time I leave it is still just as painful as the day she left us."

"Hmm, and it always will be."

They stood for a long time just looking at the grave before Cameron spoke again. "Coming here makes me open up more to the reality that she is gone from this earth, and it is helping me to heal."

Bridget nodded. Then as she lowered to her knees and

Cameron followed suit, she read the stone aloud, "Isabella Marie Bitmore, In our hearts forever…" Bridget paused and turned to Cameron with a quizzical expression on her face, "Where's…the rest of the date".

"Now, Bridget, don't make anything of it." The little marker that had been placed, there by Cameron's parents a short time before only had the years on it. It was a plain white stone, with the name, and under it the dates of the brief little life. Cameron mumbled, "They wanted to put a quotation on it, 'Suffer the little children,' whatever it is, but I remembered you like things plain."

"Yes, but…"

Look at the grandparent's stones. Bridget did. They only had the years carved into them. "Now, tell me why you want the world to see the exact date of the best thing that happened and the ending date that it all went away?"

Bridget had never thought of it. There was no reason. Finally, she said, "I like it just like it is."

Figuring Bridget could use a little humor, Cameron turned to her and said, "And another thing they wanted to put on Isabella's stone was, 'Erected by her loving grandparents Lily and Spencer Bitmore', but I told them. "Hey, keep your shirt on. You'll get your names in this marble orchard soon enough."

This struck Bridget as funny, and she started to laugh, but somewhere down the drive a child began to giggle causing a great lump to rise in her throat and Cameron quickly got up and started pacing. She stood up, turned, and saw him behind her walking back and forth. Slowly she leaned over the grave and arranged the flowers in the vase, whispering to her beloved child. “I miss you Izzy. Mommy misses you.” She kissed the palm of her hand and placed it on the stone then paused for one last look before turning and taking a hold of Cameron’s arm. As in life, Izzy drew them closer together and she felt Cameron lace his fingers through hers and squeeze.

When Bridget got home, she found Chloe exactly where she had been earlier; in the chair near the Christmas tree, the boots still on, staring malevolently at the Bitmore upright. Bridget sat down and opened a package Cameron had brought with him when he came, a jar of preserved strawberries from Mrs. Donahue. For a few moments, except for the crackle of paper, there was silence. Then, in her clearest, most affected drawl, Chloe said, “Christ, but I hate this dump.”

“Is there anything in particular that you object to?”

“Oh, no, Mother, not at all, not at all and I do hope you don't begin changing things around, just to please me. No, there is nothing. I just hate every lousy, stinking part of it, and if it were to burn down tomorrow, I wouldn't shed a furtive tear.” With a smug expression on her face she added, “Oh, yes, for the layman that’s from Artist, Mario Lanza (Alfred Arnold Cocozza) song, Una furtiva lagrima.”

Chloe pulled out a pack of cigarettes, lit one, and threw the match on the floor. Bridget's face tightened. "You'll put out that cigarette and pick up that match."

"I will like hell."

Bridget got up and felt the frustration of the whole bloody time spent in the presence of this child move her body as she crossed the room and slapped Chloe hard on the cheek.

She did not feel her hand withdraw or remember anything at all except the feel of her head swiveling on her neck and a ringing in her ears. She felt her body drop down on the sofa and her mind desperately tried to catch up until it registered that Chloe had slapped her back. To add insult to insult Chloe blew smoke into Bridget's face.

Still not done with her punishment Chloe went on, in her cool, insolent tone, "Irondequoit, Rochester, Land where the waters meet. A high class, positively restricted development for discriminating people that run filling stations, and furniture factories, and markets, and pie wagons. The garden spot of the world in the pig's eye. The armpit of America!"

Coming to her senses, Bridget angrily asked, "Where did you hear that?"

She was sure that was not a line out of some piano concerto and not something that Chloe was capable of phrasing on her own. In response, Chloe came over and leaned down close. What she said, threw Bridget off her guard once more. "Why you poor goddam sap... Did you think Nick wanted to marry you?"

There was no holding back. All her anger and frustration boiled in her veins as she looked at this thankless stranger that she had given birth to. There was something more going on and she was not sure what it was, but that just infuriated her even more. "If I were willing, yes."

"Oh! Ye gods and little fishes hear my cynical laughter. That is from 'Ye gods and little fishes', by James Alexander Henshall. Pardon you for your ignorance." She took a deep breath as she spatted out, "Stupid, don't you know what he sees in you?"

This was no longer a battle between a mother and a daughter, and she let all the hate and frustration out. "You think it's probably exactly in tune to what you think of me."

"No, not entirely. He likes your legs."

"He told you that?"

"Why certainly."

Chloe's manner showed that she relished Bridget's consternation. "Of course, he told me. We are particularly good friends, and I hope I have a mature point of view on these matters. Really, he speaks very nicely about your legs. He has a theory about them. He says an apron is the greatest provocation ever invented by woman for the torture of man, and that the best legs are found in kitchens, not in bars. And he calls himself an optimist."

"Why is that?"

Chloe gave Bridget an annoyed look. “A pessimist is a man who thinks all women are bad. An optimist is a man who hopes they are; that’s what Chauncey Mitchell Depew said.”

Again seeing the puzzled expression on her mother’s face, she said, “You are stupid. Chauncey Mitchell Depew! was a Republican politician. He served two terms as United States Senator from New York and was somehow connected to Cornelius Vanderbilt.” She paused. “I think that’s right. Anyway, that’s pretty close.”

Chloe went on at some length, snapping her cigarette and when it went out lighting another one and throwing the match on the floor. But now her taunts were senseless grabs at straws trying to hurt her. But her words had already done the damage. Bridget was stunned at learning she had been a fool. She had put up with Nick because she thought he brought Chloe closer to her, but all the time he had been belittling her, even poking fun at their intimate relations. Was it always his goal to set the child against her? As Chloe rattled on, Bridget paid close attention and she heard Chloe saying, “After all, Mother, even now Nick's shoes are custom made.”

“They ought to be. They cost me enough.”

Bridget snapped this out bitterly, and for a second wished she had not. But the cigarette, suddenly still in midair, told her it was news to Chloe, quite horrible news, and without further regret Bridget rammed home her advantage, “You didn't know that did you?”

Chloe stared incredulously. Sure, she knew the bottom had fallen out of his world, but she figured he had found a way to crawl back to the top. This shook her so she decided to make it a joke. "You buy his shoes? Yee gods and little…"

But Bridget did not allow her to finish. "His shoes and his shirts and his drinks and everything else he's had in the last few months, including his golf dues. And you need not call on your gods and little fishes anymore or mention any more lines from the operas. If you want to see some dates I have them all written down, with an exact amount beside each one."

"So, Miss Bitmore, you made a slight mistake. It is not my legs that he likes me for, it is my money. It may interest you to know that that is why he is such a good friend of yours. He does not haul you over to your music lesson because he wants to. In fact, he often complains about it. He does it because he must. And surprising though it be to you, he will marry me, or not marry me, or do anything I say, so his proud, gentlemanly belly can have something to eat."

Bridget got up, somewhat haughtily, "So you see, what he sees in me is about what you see, isn't it? And unfortunately, you are in exactly the position he is in, too. You must do what I say. The hand that holds the money cracks the whip. And I say there will be no more money for you, not one cent, until you take back everything you have said, and apologize for it."

Chloe's answer was to abandon the grand manner, and become a yelling, devilish adolescent of fourteen. Coldly, Bridget listened to her curses, and watched as she launched a kick at the Bitmore piano.

"And that is the piano you are going to practice on, until I get ready, in my own good time, to buy you another.

Chloe screamed at the top of her lungs, then leaned over the piano and began pounding the keys and swinging her hips sensuously. Picking up her coat, she stalked out of the house. Bridget went to the window and watched as she headed up the street.

As far as Nick was concerned, their relationship was at an end, but she did not do anything about it at once. She received him as usual when he dropped in at the restaurant that night, and the next two or three nights. She even submitted to his embraces, deriving a curious satisfaction from the knowledge that his access to the absolute best legs was rapidly drawing to a close. Stoppage of the spending money brought Chloe to her senses, as no beating had ever done, and when it did, Bridget forgave her quite honestly, in a teary little scene two or three days after Christmas.

It was almost automatic with her by now to acquit Chloe of wrongdoing, no matter how flagrant the offense. In her mind, the blame was all Nick's, and presently she knew exactly how she would deal with him, and when. It would be at the New Year's party he had invited her to, a week or so before.

She remembered the conversation. Nick had said, "If it's

okay, I thought I'd ask Norbett and Jennifer Irving who I play golf with. I think you might like them. We could meet at my house around ten, have a drink, then go to the Woodcliff Hotel."

The Woodcliff Hotel & Spa was in the scenic hills of Fairport New York and was considered one of the ultimate luxuries.

Nick continued. "They'd planned a great New Year's Party."

This had obviously been an effort to kill two birds with one stone, to give some plausibility to what he had said about her hours, and at the same time introduce her to some of his friends. He could tell she had taken it as evidence of a change of heart and accepted. Indeed, she had more than accepted. She had consulted anxiously with Mrs. Steele over what she should wear and gone into Macy's and picked out an evening gown. Then she had gone into a veritable agony over the question of a coat. She did not have a fur coat, and the prospect of making her debut in nothing but her battered blue wool coat haunted her horribly. But Mrs. Steele, as usual, stepped into the breach. She knew a lady, it seemed, with a brocade coat. "It's a beautiful thing, Baby, ashy rose, all crusted with gold, just what you want with your hair. It is really a Chinese mandarin's coat, but it has been altered, and you could not put a price on it. There is nothing like it on sale anywhere. It'll be the snappiest thing in the room, even at the Woodcliff."

"But will it be warm enough?"

"It's not like you're planning an evening under the stars. You will be going from home, to car, to hotel. It'll be warm enough for that."

So, Bridget got the coat, and when the dress arrived, she could not wait to try them both on. When she did the effect took her breath away. She felt sexy but also in control and confident the outfit would send the same message to those around her.

The dusty blue of the dress with the rose-colored coat over it, she had to admire. She bought gold stockings and gold shoes, and her doubt of fitting in changed to smug complacency. All this against her brown skin spoke of elegance and not commonplaceness.

This had all been arranged before Christmas, and her choice of the New Year's party as the occasion for the break with Nick may possibly have been prompted by a matter-of-fact determination not to let such a costume go to waste, as well as a vivid recollection of the four hundred dollars she had contributed to the expense of the evening. However, no such motive obtruded on her own virtuous consciousness. It was merely, she told herself, that a resolve had to be made, and New Year's morning was a good time to make it. As she rehearsed the scene mentally, it became clear in its details, and she knew exactly how she would play it. At the Woodcliff, she would be gay, and rattle her rattle, and blow her horn. Back at Nick's house, she would watch the Irvings take their departure, and then, at his invitation to come in, she would decline, and climb into her car. Then, at his surprised look, she would make a little speech. She would say nothing of Chloe, or money, or legs. She would merely remark that all things had to end some time, and it looked as though he and she had reached that point. It had been very pleasant, she had enjoyed his company, every minute of it, she wished him the best in the world, and she certainly hoped he would regard her as his friend. At this point she saw herself putting out a graceful hand, and in case he merely stood there looking at it, she would smile graciously and drive off.

The whole thing, perhaps, was a little stuffy, and certainly it was sing songy as she kept adding to it. But it was her valedictory, and no doubt her privilege to deliver it any way she chose.

On December 31st, the weather took a turn for the worse with winter storm warnings in effect for Monroe, Orleans, Wayne, Genesee, Wyoming, Livingston, Ontario, and Yates counties from 7 PM until 1 PM. It was being reported that a major storm that had already brought heavy snow, freezing temperatures, and a wintry mix across the Midwest into Texas, and now across the Ohio River Valley would continue making its approach towards Western New York that night. Before the morning was over, quite a bit of snow was falling. By midafternoon, tall tales interrupted the broadcasts, of heavy snowfall and people being stuck on the road. The worst of it was outside the Irondequoit area where nearly two feet of snow fell, and parts of the Rochester area was in shut down mode while crews struggled to clear streets and haul away snow. But in Irondequoit, except for a light blanket of snow nothing ominous met the eye, and Bridget viewed the snowstorm as an annoyance, a damper on business, but nothing to get excited about.

Around five o'clock, when it did not let up, she stopped Mrs. Ottoman from sectioning more chickens, on the possibility that nobody would be there to eat them, and they could wait until the next day. When Celine, Emma, and Audrey called in to say the roads were bad Bridget told them to stay home and be safe. It worried her a little, but she was sure they could handle the restaurant and when Astrid came, she set her to cleaning the kitchen counters.

Around six, Nick called up to know if she wanted to cancel their plans for the evening. Laughing, she asked, “Now, why would I want to cancel?”

“Have you been listening to the weather reports?”

“Do you mean you're getting cold feet?”

“No, not at all. Just being the perfect host and giving you one last chance to back out if you want to.”

“Why, this little snow is nothing.”

“Then I'll be expecting you.”

“Around ten.”

By seven thirty not one customer had showed up, and Mrs. Steele abruptly suggested that they close, and begin getting Bridget dressed, if she was still fool enough to go to the damned party. Bridget agreed, and started her preparations to lock up. Then she,

Mrs. Steele, Mrs. Ottoman, Waldo, Emmett, and Astrid all burst out laughing at the discovery that there were no preparations; no dishes to wash, no bottles to put out, no cash to count. Bridget simply cut the lights and locked the door, and as the others went scuttling off into the night, she and Mrs. Steele climbed into her car and drove down Bitmore Drive. It was a little windswept, a little rough from the snow that had piled up, but not that bad.

She was surprised to find Francine and Chloe there. Francine had been afraid to start home, and timidly asked Bridget if she could spend the night. Chloe, due long ago at the Taylors for dinner, a party, and an overnight visit, said Mrs. Taylor had called to say the party had been postponed. At this, Mrs. Steele looked sharply at Bridget, and Bridget went calmly to her room and began taking off her uniform.

Not wasting a minute, Bridget headed to her bathroom and showered. She washed the restaurant smell out of her hair and then stepped out to dry herself. Over at the dressing table she applied her lotion and perfumed her body before getting out the hair dryer. While she dried her hair, she managed to work with one hand, pulling out her curling iron and plugging it in and by the time her hair was dry, it was ready for use.

She had to look perfect, Bridget thought as she curled and tried to control her hair into a cascade of curls by using hair spray. Once satisfied, she put on more makeup than she had ever worn since her wedding day and then came the coup de grâce. She picked her best undergarments and then slipped into her gown.

Her hair fluffed out softly; her dress adjusted to the last fold and her face fashioned quite close to the look of the day, she was ready. She stepped out of the room. “What do you think ladies.” Francine was entranced, and even Chloe admitted that “you really look quite nice, Mother.”

She stepped back into her room and stood before the full-length mirror for a final critical inspection. In a few minutes, Mrs. Steele who had disappeared for a final look at the weather, returned and sat on Bridget’s bed, looking moodily at her friend. “Well, I hate to say it after taking all that trouble to get dressed, you shouldn’t go to that party.”

“Why, for heaven's sake?”

“Because it's bad out there. You call that idiot up and tell him you're not coming.”

“Can’t do that.”

“Oh, he'll understand. He'll be relieved.”

“I never had his landline number.”

“Call his cell.”

“Can’t do that since it was shut off for nonpayment.”

“Well, he should understand if he has windows to look out.”

“I'm going.”

“Baby, you can't.”

“I said I'm going.”

Irritated, Mrs. Steele ordered Chloe to get the trench coat she wore to school, and her boots. Bridget protested, but when Chloe appeared with the things, Mrs. Steele went to work. She pinned

Bridget's dress up, so it was a sort of sash around her hips, with a foot of white slip showing. Then she put on the boots, Over the gold shoes. Then she put on the evening coat and pulled the trench coat over it. She next found a kerchief and bound it tightly around Bridget's head.

Bridget suddenly transformed into something that looked like a refugee as she sweetly said goodbye to them all.

She exited through the kitchen door and stepped into the garage, where she checked to be sure her snow brush and other necessities were in the car. Satisfied, she climbed in and pressed the garage door opener, ignoring what she saw behind her as she started the engine and turned on the wipers. When she was settled, she waved gaily to the three anxious faces at the door and then slowly backed out of the garage and onto the street.

She turned onto Portland Avenue and finding it mostly clear, she smiled confidently. She thought it funny that people should get so excited over a little light snow, especially in Rochester.

On the expressway, the traffic was moving until suddenly it started slowing down. She could not see ahead but decided to take the next exit. She did just that and turned on her GPS to guide her. Her confidence was building again when at a light, a police officer knocked on her car window. She lowered it slightly. He asked, "Are you heading to Cobbs Hill?"

"Yes."

"You can't get through. Not without taking a detour."

"Well? Which way do I go?"

He took off his hat, swooshed the snow off the top of the plastic covering and gave her intricate directions as to how she was to drive to the area. He informed her she might be turned back since they were already getting hit by the storm.

"But believe me, lady, unless you really have to get there tonight, it'll be a whole lot better to turn back."

Bridget, use to driving in the snow, felt comfortable; especially on the familiar roads she had traveled quite frequently. She came to an area where all traffic both ways had to work with one lane. Once through that mess she did not run into any more problems. The roads had been plowed and traffic was moving well.

She could see lights in Nick's house and parked in the driveway that looked freshly plowed. Nick popped out of the door, in a dinner coat, and stared as though he could hardly believe his eyes. Then he yelled something at her, popped in the house again, and emerged, carrying a big doorman's umbrella with one hand. The umbrella he opened for her, and they hurried up to the house.

"God, I figured you would not show after taking a look outside, but here you are, huh."

Bridget smiled sweetly. "You put the lights on and got all dressed up. If you do not look out, I'll begin wondering who you were expecting."

"All that was before I turned on the tv and heard what it's really like out there. How in the hell did you get here anyway? For the last hour it has been nothing but a story of bridges closed, roads blocked, whole areas under snow and yet here you are."

"Don't believe everything you hear."

Inside, Bridget was shocked. The whole place was under gray, ghostly cloths that covered rugs, furniture, even paintings. She shivered as she investigated the great dark drawing room, and he laughed. "Pretty gloomy, hey? Not quite so bad upstairs." He led the way up the big staircase, snapping on lights and then snapping them off when she had passed, through several big bedrooms, all under cloths as the drawing room was, to a long narrow hall, at the end of which was the tiny apartment where he lived. "This is my humble abode. How do you like it?"

"Why it's quite nice.

"Really servants' quarters, but I moved into them because it seemed cozier, somehow."

The furnishings had the small, battered, hand me down look of servants' quarters, but the area was friendly. Bridget sat down and slipped off the boots. Then she took off the kerchief and trench coat and unpinned her dress. His face lit up as she emerged like a butterfly from her very drab cocoon, and he turned her around, examining every detail of her costume. Then he kissed her. For a moment he had the old sunny look, and she had to concentrate hard to remember her grievances. Then he said such grandeur deserved a drink. She was afraid that with a drink she would not remember any grievances at all and asked if they had not better wait until the Irvings arrived.

"Who?"

“Isn't that their name?”

“Good God, they can't get here.”

“Why not?”

“They live in Canadice and it's three feet deep in snow. Haven't you heard there is a storm going on? I think you were hiding two blocks up the street, and just pretended to drive over from Irondequoit.”

Lying slightly, she replied, “I didn't see much of a storm.”

Following behind him as he led her to the bedroom, she was in for a shock. It was a tiny cubicle, with one window and a cot made up as a bed. He had put her trench coat there and on what appeared to be a side table sat a cocktail service, consisting of a great silver shaker, a big L on its side, and beautiful crystal glasses. But not seven feet away, in the smallest, old-fashion bathroom she had ever seen, sat a small refrigerator. She walked in and moving off to the side she watched as he opened the door and pulled out an old-fashion ice tray and popped out a few ice cubes to put in the ice bucket. Bridget noted there was an egg carton, bacon, and milk in the fridge.

When Nick started back to the bedroom, she was right behind him and saw on a table, near the door of the bathroom a little two burner hotplate and a can of coffee. Wishing she had not come; she went back and resumed her seat by the fire.

He served the drinks presently, and she had two. When he reached for the shaker to pour her a third, she stopped him. “If I'm going to drive, I think I've had enough.”

“Drive? Where to?”

“Why isn't the Woodcliff where we're going?”

“Bridget we're not going anywhere.”

“Well, we certainly are.”

“Listen.”

He stepped over and snapped on a small television that he had hooked up to Roku. The two extravagance he could not do without was his television and internet. An excited announcer was telling of bridges closed between Irondequoit and Henrietta, of a wrecked automobile on the expressway, of the fear that a whole family had been stranded in their car, stuck in a snowbank. She tossed her head petulantly. "Well, my goodness, the Woodcliff's not in Henrietta. It’s in Fairport.”

“Wherever it is, and however we go to get to it, we must take the expressway and by last report it is a raging snowstorm, with half the lanes closed and three feet of snow coming down too fast to plow. We are not going. The New Year's party is here.”

He filled her glass, and she began to sulk. Despite the liquor, the main idea of the evening was still clear in her mind, and this turn of events was badly interfering with it. When he put his arm around her, she did not respond. Amiably, he said she was a very problematical drunk. On two drinks she would argue with Jesus Christ, on three she would agree with Judas Iscariot. Now would she kindly tilt over number three, so she would be in a frame of mind to welcome the New Year the way it deserved? When she did not touch the drink, he asked for her key, so he could put her car in the garage. When she made no move to give it to him, he went downstairs.

Bridget realized the room was quite cold and she shivered as she watched the snow falling outside the window and heard the wind as it roared, setting the snow swirling as it fell.

She began to think it was all his fault and by the time he returned, he took one look at her face and spoke. "Well, I guess one more drink didn't help your attitude. I suppose there is nothing to do but go to bed. I pulled a tarp over your car, so it will probably be all right. I have green pajamas and red. Which do you prefer?"

"I'm not going to bed."

"You're not very amusing here."

"I'm going home."

"Then good night. But in case you change your mind, I will put out the green pajamas, and…"

"I haven't gone yet."

"Of course, you haven't."

Bridget swallowed and readied herself for the attack. "Why did you tell her that?"

What with the liquor, the snow, and his manner, her grievances had heavy compression behind them now, and she exploded with a snarl that left her without the least recollection of all the stuffy little things she had intended to say. He looked at her in astonishment. “Tell whom what? If you don't mind my asking.”

“You know perfectly well what I'm talking about. How could you say such things to my child? And who gave you the right to talk about my legs anyhow?”

“Everybody else does. Why not me?”

“What?”

“Oh come, come, come. Your legs are the passion of your life. They all but get a cheer when you drove that food truck, and if you do not want them talked about, you ought to wear your skirts longer or your slacks looser. But you do want them talked about, and looked at, and generally envied, so why this hollering fit? And after all, they are damned good looking.”

“We're talking about my child.”

“Oh, for God's sake, what do you mean, child? If she is a child, she's forgotten more about such things than you'll ever know.”

“That’s an awful thing to say…”

“You ought to keep up with the times. I do not know how it was in the past. Maybe sweet young things were kept in the dark until they were in their twenties, but now with the internet and television they know all there is to know before they have even been told about Santa Claus. Anyway, she knows we do it. Do you think she does not know we see each other and make love together? Hell, she even asks me how many times.”

“And you tell her?”

“Sure. She greatly admires my capacity and yours. Yours she

simply cannot get over. She would say, "Who'd think the poor mope had it in her?' "

As Nick mimicked Chloe, Bridget knew this was nothing he had invented, as a sort of counter offensive. Her rage mounted still higher. Bridget said, "I see," then said it over again, three or four times.

Finally, she went over to him and asked, "And how about the best legs being found in kitchens, not in the fancy hotel rooms?"

"What in the hell are you talking about?"

"You know what I'm talking about."

Nick stared at her, touched his brow, as though in a great effort of recollection. Then, snapping his fingers briskly, he said, "Oh, I knew there was something familiar about that. Yes, I did give a little dissertation along those lines one afternoon. We passed a girl she had on a uniform of some sort, and an apron, quite a pretty little thing, especially around the ankles. I admit, I said that. Nothing original, I assure you. I had almost forgotten it ... How does that concern us?"

He was plausible, circumstantial, casual, but a little flicker around the eyes betrayed him. Bridget did not answer his question. She came in closer, and there was something snakelike about her as she said, "That's a lie. You were not talking about any girl you saw on the street. You were talking about me."

Nick shrugged and Bridget backed over to a chair and sat down. Then she began to talk slowly, but with rising stridency. She said he had deliberately tried to set Chloe against her, to hold her up to ridicule, to make the child think of her as an inferior, somebody to be ashamed of. "I see it all now. I always thought it was funny she never invited any of these people she met here in Cobbs Hill to come see her occasionally. Not that I do not give her the opportunity. Not that I do not remind her that you cannot accept invitations all the time without giving any in return. Not that I did not do my part. But No. Because you were filling her up with all this foolishness, she has been ashamed to ask these people over. She actually believes Irondequoit is not good enough for them. She thinks I am not good enough. She…"

"Oh, for God's sake shut up."

Nick's eyes were black now and had little hard points of light in them. "In the first place, what invitations did she accept? My mother's, right here in this house. Well, we went all over that once, and we are not going over it again. Oh, yes, and to the Smiths. And so far, as I know the only invitation Roman and Alicia ever got out of you was an invitation to go over and buy their dinner in that restaurant, and they did go over."

"So, what. Are you saying my restaurant is below their standard? Besides, no check was ever presented to them."

"Okay, so no check evens it out."

"She's a kid Nick and should be hanging with girls her own age."

"And right there's where I suggest you get better acquainted with your own daughter. She is a strange child. Girls her own age do not interest her. She likes being around older women."

“If they're rich.”

“Anyway, she's damned nice to them. And it is unusual as hell.

“And you can't blame them for liking it. And liking her. But her socializing with women old enough to be her mother is not the type of friends she can reciprocate with her own, say, dinner party. What are you trying to do, make me laugh?”

In some elusive, quicksilver way that she could not get her finger on, Bridget felt Nick getting the upper hand in the discussion and like Chloe, she abandoned logic and began to scream.

“You've set her against me. I do not care a bit for your fine talk. You've set her against me.”

Nick stared sullenly a few moments without speaking. Then he looked up. “Ah, so this is why you came. Stupid of me not to have thought of it sooner.”

“I came because I was invited.”

“On a night like this?”

“It's as good a time as any other.”

“What a nice little pal you turned out to be.”

“I admit I had something to say, too.”

He looked with a little self-pitying smile into the fire, evidently decided to keep his intentions to himself, then changed his mind. “I was going to say you'd make a fine wife for somebody if you got your head out of your ass.”

She had been feeling outpointed, but at this, all her self-righteousness returned. Leaning forward, she stared at him. “Nick, you can still say that after what I've said to you? Just to have somebody take care of you, you would ask me to marry you? Haven't you any more self-respect than that?”

“Ah, but that's not what I was going to say.”

“Nick don't make it any worse than it is. If I got excited about it, you were going to let it stay said. If I did not, you were going to pretend that was what you were going to say. Gee, Nick, but you're some man, aren't you?”

“Now suppose you listen to what I am going to say.”

“It doesn’t matter. I'm going home.”

She got up, but he leaped at her, seized her by both arms, and flung her back in her chair. The little glittering points of light in his eyes were dancing now, and his face was drawn and hard. “Do you know why Chloe never invites anybody to that house of yours? Do you know why nobody, except that string bean that lives next door, ever comes over?”

"Yes, I do. It’s because you set her against me.”

“Because you are a goddam pain in the ass, and you are afraid to have people get close to you.”

Looking into his contorted face, she suddenly had the same paralyzed, shrunken feeling she had had the morning Miss Turner told her off, and sent her over to the housekeeper's job, because there was nothing else, she could do. And she kept shrinking, as Nick went on, pouring a torrent of bitter, passionate invectives at her.

"It's not her. It is not me. It is you. Doesn't that strike you as funny? That Chloe has a hundred friends, here, there, everywhere she goes, and that you haven't any? No, I am wrong you have one. That bartender. And that is all. Nobody ever gets invited to your house, nobody."

"What are you talking about? How can I give parties, or invite people, with a living to make? Why you…"

"Living, my eye! That is the alibi, not the reason."

He walked around, panting, ·then turned on her again. "I like a fool, like a damned idiot, I once thought maybe I'd been mistaken, that you were a lady. That was when you handed me the money that night, and I took it. And then I took more. And then what? Could you go through with it? The very thing that you yourself started. A lady would have cut her heart out before she let me know the money meant anything. But you, had to make a chauffeur out of me, didn't you? To get your money's worth. A lackey, a poodle dog. You had to rub it in. Well, no more. I have taken my last dime off you, and God willing, before my sun goes down, I will pay you back. I guess that is one reason I love Chloe. She is so different from you. She would not ask for payback. No, that's one thing she wouldn't do, and neither should I."

"Except from me."

White with rage, she opened her evening bag, took out a crisp ten-dollar bill, threw it at his feet. He took the fire tongs, picked it up, dropped it on the fire. When the flame flared up, he took out a handkerchief and mopped his face.

For a time, nothing was said by either of them, and when their panting had died down, Bridget began to feel ashamed, defeated, and miserable. She had said it all, had goaded him to say it all too, those things that she knew he felt, and that left her crumpled and unable to answer. Yet nothing had been settled, there he was and there she was. As she looked at him, she saw for the first time that he was tired, worn, and haggard, with just a touch of middle age dragging at what she had always thought of as a youthful face. Then a gush of terrible affection for him swept over her, compounded of pity, contempt, and something motherly. She wanted to cry, and suddenly stood and reached out to touch his arm.

He made no move, but he did not repulse her touch either, and when she leaned back, she felt better. Then again, she heard the snow, and for the first time was afraid of it. She drew the coat around her. Then she picked up her drink number three, drank half of it and set it down again. Without looking at her, he filled her glass. They sat a long time, neither of them looking at the other.

Then abruptly, as though he had solved a difficult problem, he banged his fist on the arm of his chair, and said, "Damn it, what this needs is the crime of rape!"

He came over, put one arm around her, slipped the other under her legs, and carried her over to the bed. A little moaning laugh escaped her as he dumped her down on the cot. She felt weak and drugged. In a moment, the brocaded coat was off and sliding to the floor.

She thought of her dress, and did not care, she wanted him to rip it off her, to tear it away in shreds, if he had to, so he got her out of it. But he was not ripping it off. He was fumbling with the zipper, and for a moment her fingers were over his, trying to help. Then something stirred inside of her, an unhappy recollection of what she had come for, of what had been piling up between them these last few months. She fought it off, tried to make it sink, under the overwhelming blend of liquor, man, and snow. It would not sink.

If she had lifted a mountain, it could not have been harder than it was to put both palms on Nick's chest and push him away, squirm off the bed, and lurch to her feet. She grabbed both coats as she ran into the other room. He was after her, trying to drag her back, but she fought him off as she snatched up the boots and dashed into the dark hall.

Somehow, she got through the ghostly rooms, down the stairs, and to the front door. It was locked. She twisted the big brass key, and at last was on the porch, in the cold wet air. She pulled on both coats and stepped into the boots. Then suddenly the light came on, and he was beside her, reaching for her, trying to pull her back. She dashed out into the snow, yanked the cloth off the car, let it fall where it may and jumped in. As she snapped on the lights and started the motor, she could see him under the light, gesticulating at her, expostulating her. There was nothing of passion in his face now. He was angrily telling her not to be a fool, not to go out in that storm.

She started out. On side streets the roads were barely passable now and she literally crawled, barely able to see even an inch in front of her as the snow came down in sheets. She pulled over to where she thought was the curb, found the snow brush and got out to try removing some of the snow before climbing back in. Then, cautiously, feeling a throb of fear every time the car slid on the icy snow she continued. As she turned at the traffic circle, she caught the lights of another car, behind and she felt less alone.

There were no traffic lights or streetlights working now so the way was black and wildly unfamiliar in its current snow-covered condition. She got over the bridge without trouble, but when she came to the detour, she was afraid, and waited until the other car caught up a little. Then she went on, noting with relief that the other car turned into the detour too. She had no trouble for a mile or so, and then she came to a large accumulation of snow that she feared her car could not make it through.

All resolution having deserted her, she stopped and waited, to see what the other car was going to do. It stopped, and she watched. A door slammed, and she strained her eyes to see. Then Nick's face was at the window, not six inches from her own. Snow was pouring off his cap and his ski coat that was buttoned to his ears. Furiously he pointed at the snow. “Look at that! It never occurred to you there would be something like that, did it? Damn it, the trouble you're putting me to!”

For a moment or two, as he savagely ordered her to lock the car, get out, and come back with him, she had a happy, contented feeling, as though he were her father, she a little girl that would be taken care of, anyway. Then once more her fixed resolve rose in her. She shifted into reverse and backed up. She backed up to the intersection and turned.

When she had followed the new road a few feet, she saw it led down into a parkway, covered with trees, blocking the road from some of the snowfall. She proceeded by inches, rolling and braking, then rolling on again. Then ahead of her she saw that the way had been plowed and there was barely any snow covering it. She increased her speed. It was the lunge of the car that told her the road was now a sheet of ice. When she stepped on the brake the car slid sideways and she lost control. The car slid off the side of the road. She looked out the windshield and thought she saw water. She screamed, thinking she was in the lake or a pool of some sort.

She was alone in a pool that extended as far as she could see. She screamed again. The wind was driving the snow against the car, so she rolled down the window, knowing she had only herself to depend on. Outside, she could see she was okay. The car was okay. She could do this. Carefully she stepped on the gas and eased the car back onto the curb of the road, hoping no one was coming. When she finally managed to get out of the ditch, she put on the hand break and sat there trying to decide her next move.

In what seemed minutes her breath had misted the glass so she could see nothing. Then the door beside her was jerked open, and once more Nick was standing there. He braced his right arm against the door jamb. "All right, now open the door further so that I can get a good hold on you and hang on tight. I think we can make it back."

Bridget did not hesitate as she tightened the scarf over her head and zipped the rubber boots over her shoes. She had two layers of coats and a dress to protect her body and leaning over, she opened the glove compartment and saw she did have her gloves in there and a light that Harbor Freight gave away free with any purchase and until now she had not used it. She tucked it safely in her pocket. Then, shivering, she motioned to Nick to move his hand. When he did, she pulled the door shut and locked it. Then she slipped out the opposite door, locking it. A yelp came out of her as she stepped out and the snow came up to her knee and the wind almost swept her off her feet. But she held on to the door handle and steadied herself. Above her was a high bank; evidently with some sort of sidewalk on top of it. Paying no attention to Nick and his barely audible shouts, she scrambled up, and then slipped, slid, and staggered heading home through the worst storm in the annals of the Rochester weather bureau, or of any weather bureau.

She passed many cars stalled as hers was stalled, some deserted, some full of people, who mostly were either on their way or returning from some New Year's celebration. She slogged on, keeping to the side of the highway though nothing was moving in the lanes. She had her small light shining and the rail to hang onto when the snow was so heavy, she could barely move a leg forward.

Suddenly a plow passed by, stopped, and waited for her to catch up.

"Lady, what are you doing?"

"My car was stuck, and this was the only choice I had?"

"Climb in."

Without hesitation she worked her way around the front of the cab and when she reached the other side the door was opened. She used the handrail and swung up into the cab.

"Where can I take you."

Bridget gave her the address and soon they were making their way, him plowing and she trying to get warm. She was in a hysteria of weakness, cold, and pain when they finally reached Bitmore Drive, and half ran, half limped, the rest of the way to the house.

Chloe and Francine, like two frightened kittens, had not slept very well that night, and when lights began to snap on in the house, and a sobbing staggering apparition appeared at their door, they screamed in terror. When they realized it was Bridget, they dutifully followed her to her room, but it was seconds before they got readjusted to the point of helping her out of her clothes and getting her into bed. But suddenly Francine recovered from her fright, and was soon running around frantically, getting Bridget what she needed, especially whiskey, coffee, and her heating pad. Chloe sat on the bed, rubbing Bridget's hands, spooning the scalding coffee into her mouth, pushing the covers close around her. Presently she shook her head. “But Mother, I simply can't understand it. Why didn't you stay with him? After all, it wouldn't have been much of a novelty.”

“Never mind that,” she said through chattering teeth. “I learned something tonight. Tomorrow you get your piano.”

At Chloe's squeal of delight, at the warm arms around her neck, the sticky kisses that started at her eyes and ended at her throat, Bridget relaxed, and soaked up this moment of happiness. She knew Chloe’s ways and accepted them, but a lot of the change in her she blamed on Nick. She told herself that Chloe was a child in a woman’s body; that was true, but she was a child. Her child. If she wanted her to change, it was her job to find a way to do it. That is what mothers were for.

The last think Bridget saw was her daughter’s face and the arrival of the new day before she fell into a deep sleep.

CHAPTER 23

For some time after that, Bridget was too busy to pay much attention to Chloe. Relieved of Nick, she began to have money, above installments on the piano and everything, else. Despite hard times, her business flourished and each day she realized what Lucy had told her; the bar would be indeed profitable. Soon she was able to pay off the mortgage on the property and the balances on her equipment. Now the place was hers, and she took a step she had been considering for some time. The pies put a dreadful strain on her kitchen, so she built an annex, out back of the parking space, to house them as a separate unit. There was some little trouble about it, on account of the zoning regulations. But when she submitted acceptable exterior plans, which made it look like a rather large private garage and agreed to display no advertising except the neon sign she was already using, the difficulty was smoothed out.

Of course, the construction met with less favorable acceptance as trucks drove down the street delivering materials and workers swung hammers and ran their saws. More than once she caught the eye of a disgruntled neighbor, but soon it was done with only the move in of the furnishings to be completed. Unlike opening the restaurant, all the legal, staffing and customer aspects were in place so that she only had to concentrate on a good floor plan to make it run smoothly. When she was satisfied with the results, she sat down with Jackson to go over what they would be offering now that they had adequate space to work.

Jackson had grand ideas and knowing he could accomplish them, Bridget went along. From the day the shop opened, it became the talk of the county and soon Jackson needed an assistant, and then another. Bridget purchased a new delivery truck, outfitted properly for pastry deliveries and she bought herself a new car.

Her car had never quite recovered from the battering it took in the storm, and so she needed a new one. This time she gave as much consideration to her image as she did to the restaurant and bakery, purchasing a sleek maroon Land Rover Sport that cost $113,900 but she could afford it and felt safe in it. It was the first time that Chloe approved of her choice and actually kissed the car when the dealer delivered it.

Ida had become as close to Bridget as Lucy and so she was

more than just a friend. Bridget listened to her ideas for the business. Upon seeing the bakery annex, she grew thoughtful, and then one night started a campaign to get Bridget to open a branch in Pittsford, with herself as manager.

"Bridget, I know what I'm talking about. That town is just crying for a place that will put out a real line of ready desserts. Think of the entertaining they do over there. Them giving parties of some sort every night, and the dessert nothing but a headache to try and find; especially when they want them warm. And look how easy you can give them what they want; why you are making all that stuff right now. And look at the prices you will get. And look at the sidelines you got. Look at the fountain trade. Look at the sandwich trade. And I can do it all with four girls, a fountain man, a short order cook, and a dishwasher. Even you admitted that the pie truck did amazing in that area."

Ida barely took a breath as she tried to lay out her plan to Bridget who, not wanting to assume risk when she had a certainty, was in no hurry about it. But she drove over to Pittsford and made inquiries and began to suspect that Ida was right. Then, snooping around one afternoon, she ran into a vacant property that she knew would be right for the location. When she found out she could get a lease for an absurdly small rental fee, she made up her mind.

There followed another hectic month of furniture, fixtures, and alterations. She wanted the place done in apple red, but Ida obstinately held out for light green walls and soft, upholstered booths where people would find it comfortable to sit. Bridget gave in, but on the day of the opening she almost fainted. Without consulting her, Ida had gone beyond the bakery items and ordered a lot of preserves, cakes, health breads, and other things she knew nothing about. Ida however said she herself knew all about them, at any rate, all that was necessary to know. By the end of the month, Bridget was not only convinced, but completely flabbergasted. Ida's idea and Bridget's chosen location proved a winning combination.

"Bridget, we're in. In the first place I got a lunch trade that is almost like the Brown Derby. People that do not want planked whitefish and special hamburgers. They want those little sandwiches I got, and the fruit salads, and you just ought to hear the comments. And I hardly get them cleared out before I got a college trade, wonderful, refined kids that want a soda or a malt before they start playing golf on the conveniently located golf course. And when they go my tea trade starts, and on top of that I get a little dinner trade, people that want to eat light before they catch a preview or something at the local theater. And then on top of that I got a late trade, people that just want a cup of chocolate and a place to talk. From twelve noon until twelve midnight, I got business. And the takeout trade from those people, it's enough to take your breath away."

The receipts bore her out. Ida had more than earned her salary and both she and Bridget could not be happier.

But it was not all smooth sailing. Mrs. Steele, when she heard what Bridget was up to, flew into a rage, and wanted to know why

Ida had been singled out to manage the Pittsford branch, instead of herself. Bridget tried to explain that it was all Ida's idea, that some people are suited to one thing, some to another, but got nowhere. Mrs. Steele continued to be bitter, and though Bridget tried to remind Lucy that she had the idea for the bar, and she had backed her did not help.

Bridget grew worried. She had come to depend on her tall, thin, friend and bartender as she depended on nobody else, not only for shrewd business advice but also for some sort of emotional support that her nature demanded. Losing her would be a calamity, and she began to seriously consider what could be done.

At that time there was significant talk about the revival of Charlotte Beach with the addition of a resort along the coast, a few miles from the boardwalk. Bridget began to wonder if it would be a good place for still another branch, with Mrs. Steele in charge. She drove down several times and looked it over. Except for one place, she found no restaurants that impressed her, and unquestionably the resort was coming, not only for summer trippers, but for year-round residents as well. Again, it was the lease that decided her. She found a large house, with considerable land around it, on a bluff, overlooking the lake. With an expert eye, she noted what would have to be done to it, noted that the grounds would be expensive to keep up. But when the terms were quoted to her, they were so low that she knew she could make a good profit if she got any business at all. They were so low that for a brief time she was suspicious, but the agent said the explanation was simple enough. It had been a private home, but it could not be rented for that, as it was entirely too big for most of the people who came down from the city just to get a tan. Furthermore, the beach in front of it was studded with rocks and was therefore unsuitable for swimming. For all ordinary purposes it was simply a turkey, and if she could use it, it was hers at the rate quoted.

Bridget inspected the view, the house, the grounds, and felt a little tingle inside. Abruptly, she put the paperwork in motion. When the deal was through Bridget, one night held Mrs. Steele after closing time for a little talk. But she barely got started when Mrs. Steele broke in, “Oh shut up, will you for God's sake shut up?”

“But aren't you interested?”

“Does a duck like water? Listen, it is halfway between home and your place isn't it? Right on the main line, and Ashton still has his trucks. It is the first honest to God's chance he has had to get started again. Do you want me bawling right on your shoulder?”

“What's the matter?”

“It's him. Okay, I am working, and he must find something to do with himself, at night. So, he finds it. He says he is going to play pool, and he does come home with chalk all over him, I will say that for him. But he is a liar. It is a frazzle haired blond-haired person that works in one of those antique furniture factories. Nothing serious maybe, but he sees her. It is what I have been so jittery about if you have noticed. And now, if I can just get him out of here, and in business again so he can hold his head up… well, maybe that will be that. Go on, tell me some more."

So once again Bridget was in a flurry of alterations, purchases of inventory, and arguments about policy. She wanted a duplicate of the Irondequoit place, which would specialize in chicken, waffles, and pies, and operate a small bar as a sideline. Mrs. Steele, however, had other ideas. "Do they come all the way to the ocean just to get chicken? Not if I know them. They want a shore dinner too, like fish, lobster, and crab and that is what we are giving them. And that is where we make the dough. Do not forget, fish is cheap. But we must have a little variety, so we give them steak, right from our own built in charcoal broiler."

When Bridget protested that she knew nothing about steaks, or fish, or lobster, or crab, and would be helpless to do the marketing, Mrs. Steele replied she could learn. It was not until she sent for Mr. Arnold, the federal meat inspector who had been romantic about her in her waitress days, that her alarm eased a little. He came to the Irondequoit restaurant one night and confirmed her suspicions that there were about a hundred different ways to lose money on steaks. But when he talked with Mrs. Steele he was impressed. He told Bridget she was "smart," and probably knew what she was talking about. It depended mainly, he said, on the chef, and to Bridget's surprise he recommended Archie, of Mr.

Chris's establishment. Archie, he assured her, had been wasted for years in a second-class place, but “he's still the best steak man in town, bar none. Any bum can cook fish and make money on it, so do not worry about that. But on steaks, you must have somebody that knows his stuff. You can't go wrong on Archie.”

So, Bridget stole Archie off Mr. Chris, and under his dour supervision installed the built-in charcoal broiler. Presently, after signs had been put up along the road, tweets sent out and Facebook advertising, the place opened. It was never the snug little gold mine that Ida's place was, for Mrs. Steele was careless of expenses, and tended to slight the kitchen in favor of the bar. But her talent at making a sort of club out of whatever she touched drew big business. The ingenuity with which she worked out the arrangements drew Bridget's reluctant admiration. The big living room of the house was converted into a maple paneled bar, with dim lights. The rooms behind it were joined together in a cluster of small dining rooms, each with a pleasant air of intimacy about it. One of them opened on a veranda that ran around the house, and out there were tables for outdoor drinkers, bathing suiters, and the overflow trade. But the most surprising thing to Bridget was the flower garden. She had never suspected Mrs. Steele of any such weakness, but within a few weeks the whole brow of the bluff was planted with bushes, and here, it appeared, was where Mrs. Steele spent her mornings, spading, pruning, and puttering with a Japanese gardener. The expense, what with the water and the gardener, was high, but Mrs. Steele shrugged it off. “We're running a high-class place, Baby, and we've got to have something. For some reason I do not understand, a guy with an 'old fashioned' on the table likes to listen to the bumble bees."

But when the flowers began to bloom, Bridget paid without protest, because she liked them. At twilight, just before the dinner rush, she would stroll among them, smelling them and feeling proud and happy. On one of these strolls Lucy joined her, and then led her a block or two down the main road that ran through the town. Then she stopped and pointed, and across the street Bridget saw the sign,

STEELE'S LONG & SHORT DISTANCE HAULING DAY & NIGHT SERVICE

Mrs. Steele looked at it intently. "First he started getting the deliveries for the restaurant and then he was able to pick up other customers. He is on call all the time, too. All he needed was a chance. Next week he's getting a new truck, streamlined." She paused and turned to Bridget. "You see, I love that guy and want everyone to know he's mine. That is why I insist on being known as Mrs. Steele. I only let a select few people call me just Lucy." She touched Bridget's shoulder, "You understand, don't you?"

"Believe it or not, I do. So, is everything all right upstairs?"

Bridget referred to the terms of Mrs. Steele's employment. She settled on a lower pay and percentage in arranging for free quarters in the upper part of the house, with light, heat, water, food, laundry, and everything furnished. Bridget had allowed her a free hand in decorating once she had taken care of any structural problems. Lucy had done a great job.

Mrs. Steele nodded. "Everything's fine. Ashton loves those big rooms, and the sea, and the steaks, and well, believe it or not he even likes the flowers. We are living again, that is all I can say. We are living and enjoying life again."

Bridget never cooked anything herself now or put on a uniform. At Irondequoit, Mrs. Ottoman had been promoted to cook, with an assistant named Bella; Mrs. Steele's place was taken by a man bartender, named Jake. On nights when Bridget was at Pittsford or Charlotte, Astrid acted as hostess. Bridget worked from sun up, when her marketing started, and until long after dark. She worked hard and long. Just to get a minute she finally relieved herself of every detail she could assign to others.

The results were that she started to gain weight and the fat loosen, clumping up, and shifting downward, so features that were formerly round sank, and skin that was smooth and tight now was loose and sagged. Meanwhile other parts of her face gained fat, particularly the lower half, so that she saw the semblance of a bagginess around her chin and neck. She no longer looked or felt youthful. In fact, she was beginning to look matronly.

Not only her body changed, but her mindset did too. She engaged a driver named Theo who was the older brother of

Jefferson, who drove the SUV. To make it worthwhile for him, when she did not need him to drive, he handled the parking at the restaurant.

When Chloe first saw Theo, she did not kiss him, as she had kissed the car. She gave her mother a long, thoughtful look, full of something almost describable as respect.

And despite mounting expenses, the driver, the girl Bridget engaged to keep the books, the money kept rolling in. Bridget paid for the piano, paid off the mortgages Cameron had plastered on the house; she renovated, repainted, kept buying new equipment for all her establishments, and still it piled up. She began to buy expensive clothes and a pair of spanx to make her look thinner. She bought Chloe a little car, a Toyota CH R, in silver. She had seen the commercial of the woman running down the steps to climb into the car and she went crazy. Her payment came when Chloe not only hugged her but said it made her feel like a princess. For Chloe that was the highest praise possible.

On Greyson's advice, she incorporated the business. She chose Ida and Mrs. Steele as her two directors, in addition to herself. That was the first new expense suggested and then Greyson presented another. He told her she needed some major insurance. Bridget had purchased coverage on the sites, but now Greyson told her, "Think about someone getting hit by a car in the parking lot, or people getting salmonella poisoning at one of the establishments or the pie truck running over someone. All these are things that could happen, and they could take you for every red cent." After that Bridget had agreed to update her insurance. It was horribly expensive, but worth it, to be safe.

Through all the work, however, the endless driving, the worry, the feeling there were not enough hours in the day for all she had to do, one luxury she permitted herself. No matter how the day broke, she was home at three o'clock in the afternoon, for what she called her 'rest'. It was a rest, to be sure, but that was not the main idea. When Chloe turned sixteen, she persuaded Charlotte to let her quit high school, so she could devote her whole time to music. In the morning' she did harmony, and what she called 'paperwork'. In the afternoon she practiced. For hours she practiced exercises, but at three. she played operatic pieces, and it was then that Bridget arrived. Tiptoeing in the back way, she would slip into the hall, and for a moment stand looking into the living room, where Chloe was seated at the satiny black grand.

It was a picture that never failed to thrill her, the beautiful instrument that she had worked for and paid for, the no less beautiful child she had brought into the world; a picture moreover, that she could really call her own. Then, after a soft "I'm home, darling," she would tiptoe to her bedroom, lie down, and listen. She did not know the names of many of the pieces, but she had her favorites, and Chloe usually played one. There was one piece, something by Chopin, that she liked best of all, she said, "because it reminds me that there are others who have problems even worse than my own." Chloe, somewhat ironically, replied, "Well Mother, there's a reason for that," and she played it often when Bridget was home. Later she explained that the song "Memory" was composed by Andrew Lloyd Webber and the lyrics written by Trevor Nunn based on a poem by T. S. Eliot.

"Ah," is all Bridget said in reply. With the hours she kept she did not socialize or watch television and definitely didn't get out to a show.

"Well, if I like something, I want to know all there is to know about it," Chloe retorted.

Taking that as a hint, Bridget asked her to tell exactly what it was about.

A dreamy expression appeared on her daughter's face as she told her how the song had been written in 1981 and specifically for the musical Cats, where it is sung primarily by the character Grizabella as a melancholic remembrance of her glamorous past and as a plea for acceptance.

She concluded saying, "Memory is the climax of the musical and by far its best-known song, not only in the musical, but beyond."

It was easy for Bridget to see just how into her music, Chloe was. When she spoke of it, she seemed to transport to another dimension; just like the way she played sent Bridget beyond the walls of her existence.

Bridget was delighted at the way the child was coming along. She had balked at the idea of her quitting school, but they compromised on her being home schooled. This arrangement she told herself, was what made everything worthwhile.

One afternoon the concert was interrupted by a phone call. Chloe answered, and from the tone of her voice, Bridget knew something was wrong. Chloe came in and sat on the bed, but to Bridget's “What is it darling?” returned no answer at first. Then, after a few moments of gloomy silence, she managed, “Hosea’s had a heart attack.”

“Oh, my darling, I’m so sorry. “I know he meant more to you than just your music teacher…” She corrected herself, “Professor.”

“He knew it was coming on. He had two or three little ones. This one caught him on the street, while he was walking home. Mrs. Taylor is almost in hysterics about it.”

“You have to go over there. At once.”

“No, I can’t. Mrs. Taylor said he was connected to a heart monitor and having tests done and it would be better to come later.”

“Is there something I could do? I mean, if there are any special foods he likes, I can send anything that's wanted, hot, all ready to serve.”

“I can find out.”

Bridget watched as Chloe got up to leave, knowing not to stop her. Chloe had moved into the Steele house after Lucy and her husband had moved in above the restaurant. Until they decided what they wanted to do with the house, Bridget paid them rent. Just before she left, she heard her say, “God, but I'm going to miss that damned he bear.”

“Well, my goodness, he's not gone yet.” Bridget said sharply. She had the true Rochester tradition of optimism in such matters; to her it was almost blasphemous not to hope for the best. But Chloe got up heavily and spoke quietly. “Mother, it's bad. I know from the way he has been acting lately that he knew it would be bad when it came. I can tell from the way his wife was wailing over the phone that it is bad. And what I'm going to do I don't know.”

Special foods, it turned out; were needed desperately, on the chance that the stricken man could be tempted to eat, and in that way build up his strength. So daily, after being discharged from the hospital, for a week; Jefferson delivered a big hamper, full of chicken cooked by Bridget herself, tiny sandwiches prepared by Ida, cracked crab nested in ice by Archie, sherries selected by Mrs. Steele. Bridget Bitmore, Inc., joined hands to show what it could do.

Then one day Bridget and Chloe took the hamper over in person, together with a great bunch of red roses. When they arrived at the house, the morning paper was still on the grass, a market circular was stuffed under the door. They rang, and there was no answer. Chloe looked at Bridget, and Jefferson carried the things back to the car. That afternoon, a long, incoherent text arrived for Bridget. It was from Mrs. Taylor, Jr. It told of a wild ride to the hospital and asked if Bridget could check the house since they left in such a hurry. Bridget texted her back that she would.

Three days later, while Bridget was helping Ida get ready for the Pittsford luncheon rush, Chloe's car pulled up at the curb. Chloe got out, looking unkempt and sad. When Bridget unlocked the door for her, she handed her the paper without speaking, went to a booth, and sat down.

Bridget stared at the unfamiliar picture of Mr. Taylor, Jr., taken before his hair turned white, read the notice of his death with a blank, lost feeling. Then, noting where the funeral was to be held, she went to the phone and ordered flowers and dictated a long message to Mrs. Taylor, Jr., full of heartfelt sympathy. Still under some dazed compulsion to do something, she stood there, trying to think what.

She went over and sat down with Chloe. After a while Chloe asked one of the girls to bring her coffee. Bridget watched as Chloe hugged the cup, staring off in the distance and finally asked, “Would you like to shop for something to wear to the funeral?”

There was silence. Finally, Chloe looked at her and no matter how she tried, she could not read her expression. She started to ask again, but Chloe broke the silence and said, “What else can we do?"

"Would you like to ride to Charlotte with me, darling?"

"All right."

CHAPTER 24

For the rest of that day, Chloe tagged along with Bridget, silent about Mr. Taylor, Jr., but obviously in need of her mother's presence as she apparently did not want to be alone. The next day she hung around the house, and when Bridget came home at three, the piano was silent. The day after that, when she still moped, Bridget thought it time to jog her up a bit. Finding her in the den, she said, "Now darling, I know he was a fine man, and that you were very fond of him, but you did all you could do, and after all, these things happen, and…"

"Mother."

Chloe spoke quietly, as one would speak to a child. "It isn't that I was fond of him. Not that I did not love the shaggy brute. To me he will always be the one that taught me music, and…"

"Of course, but darling you need to keep learning and there are other teachers."

"Yes, about seven hundred fakes and advertisers in Rochester, and I don't know one from another, and besides…"

Chloe broke off, having evidently intended to say something, and then changed her mind. Bridget felt something coming and waited. But Chloe obviously decided she was not going to say it, and Bridget asked, "Can't you make inquiries?"

"There's one man here, just one, that Mr. Taylor, Jr. had some respect for. His name is Hammond, Joshua Hammond. He is a conductor. He conducts a lot of the musicals at Eastman School of Music. I do not know if he takes piano pupils or not, but he might. Bridget listened. She still felt that Chloe was holding back something, so she asked, "Has it anything to do with money? You know I don't begrudge anything for your instruction, and…"

Without hesitation Chloe replied, "Then let's call him up."

Mr. Hammond's studio was in downtown Rochester, in a building with several resident signs beside the door, and as Bridget and Chloe walked up to the second floor, a bedlam of noises assailed their ears. There were voices singing, pianists playing dizzy scales, and violinists sawing briskly in double stops. They continued and knocked on a door that was answered by a woman with an Italian accent. She left them in a windowless anteroom and went into the studio. At once there were sounds from within. A baritone would sing a Phrase, then stop. Then there would be muddled talk. Then he would sing the same phrase again, and there would be more talk. This went on and on, until Bridget became annoyed. Chloe, however, seemed mildly interested. "It's the end of the Pagliacci Prologue, and he can't hit the G on pitch. Well, there is nothing to do about him. Hammond might just as well save his time."

"To say nothing of my time."

"Mother, this is a studio. So, we sit."

Presently the baritone, a stocky, red faced boy, popped through the door and left sheepishly, and the woman came out and motioned them in. Bridget entered a studio that was rather different from Mr. Taylor, Jr.'s. It was almost as large, but nothing like as austere. One great black piano stood near the windows, and the furniture matched it, in size as well as elegance. Almost covering the walls were hundreds of photographs, all of celebrities so big that even Bridget had heard of some of them, and all inscribed personally to Mr. Hammond. The gentleman himself, clad in a gray suit received them with a flourish that reminded Bridget of something she had seen on TV where a duke waved off a pair of servants. She tried to ignore the comparison and stared at the tall, thin man of perhaps fifty, with a bony face and somber eyes for some time before realizing he was waiting for her to speak.

Bridget began explaining what they had come for, then bowed as he waved them to seats. Before taking her seat, Chloe explained she had studied with Mr. Taylor, Jr.

His attitude became slightly less formal as he struck a tragic pose, and said, "Poor Hosea. Ah poor...poor Hosea." Then he paid tribute to the man and said he was a great artist, not merely a pianist.

With a somber smile he permitted himself to reminisce. "When I first met Hosea, it was in 1975. We made a tour of Italy together. He played Rachmaninoff and I played Tchaikovsky. He was challenged one night as he was not feeling well and try as he might, he either hit the wrong keys or his fingers skated over them too lightly. We finished our last concert, in Torino and after the concert, we went to a little cafe, had a last drink, and said our goodbyes. Later I learned that Hosea had a box of Kleenex and he put it on the side of the grand and it had fallen in. That was what ruined his concerto."

Mr. Hammond's smile had broadened into a grin, and his black eyes sparkled so brightly they almost glared. Bridget, whether because of the anecdote itself, or the recent death of its subject, was not amused, but she smiled a little, to be polite. But Chloe obviously thought this was the funniest thing she had ever heard in her life, and egged Mr. Hammond on to more stories, but he looked at his watch and said he would now listen to her play.

Chloe who sat down at the piano was a quite different Chloe from the one who had so airily entertained Mr. Taylor, Jr. three years ago. She was genuinely nervous, and it occurred to Bridget that her encouragement to Mr. Hammond's storytelling might have been a stall for time. She thought a moment, then with grim face launched into a piece known to Bridget as the Brahms Rhapsody. Bridget did not like it much. It went entirely too fast for her taste, except for a slow part in the middle, that sounded a little like a hymn. However, she sat back comfortably, waiting for the praise that Mr. Hammond would surely bestow.

Mr. Hammond wandered over to the window and stood looking down at the street. When Chloe got to the slow part, he half turned around, as though to say something, then did not. All during the slow part he stared down at the street. When Chloe crashed into the fast part again, he walked over and closed the piano, elaborately giving Chloe time to get her hands out of the way. In the bellowing silence that followed, he went to the far corner of the studio and sat down, a ghastly smile on his face, as though he had been prepared for burial by an undertaker who specialized in pleasant expressions.

It was an appreciable interval before it dawned on Bridget what he had done, and why. Then she looked toward the piano to suggest that Chloe play one of her slower pieces. But Chloe was no longer there. She was at the door, pulling on her gloves, and before Bridget could say anything, she dived out the door. Bridget jumped up, followed, and in the hall called to her. But Chloe was running down the stairs and did not look up. The next thing Bridget knew, Jefferson was driving them home, and Chloe was sitting with writhing face and clenched hands, staring horribly at the floor.

All the way home Bridget fumed at the way Mr. Hammond

had treated them. She said she had never seen anything like that in her life. If he did not like the way Chloe had played the piece, he could have said so like a gentleman, instead of acting like that. And the very idea, having an appointment with two ladies for four o'clock, keeping them waiting until a quarter to five, and then, when they had barely got in the door, telling them a story about Kleenex. If that was the only man in Rochester that Mr. Taylor, Jr. had any respect for, she certainly had her opinion of Mr. Taylor, Jr.'s taste. A lot of this expressed Bridget's very real irritation, but some of it was to console Chloe, by taking her side after an outrageous episode. Chloe said nothing, and when they got home, she jumped out of the car and ran in the house.

Bridget followed, but when she got to Chloe's room, it was locked. She knocked, then knocked again, sharply. Then she commanded Chloe to open the door. Nothing happened, and inside there was silence. Francine appeared, and asked in a frightened way what the trouble was. Paying no attention to Francine, Bridget ran out to the kitchen, grabbed a chair, and ran outside. A sudden paralyzing fear had come over her as to what Chloe might be doing in there. Putting the chair near the house, she, stood on it and raised the screen. Then she pulled herself up and then dragged her body over the sill until she dropped down on the floor.

Chloe was lying on the bed, staring at the ceiling in the same unseeing way she had stared at the floor of the car. Her eyebrows were slanting and there was a deep crease forming on her forehead as she continued her intense gaze. Her hands were clenching and unclenching, and Bridget got the feeling she wanted to hit something and hit it hard.

Bridget, who had expected worse, first felt relieved, then cross. Unlocking the door, she said, "Well my goodness, you don't have to scare everybody to death."

Surprisingly, Chloe spoke. "Mother, if you say my goodness one more time I shall scream. I shall scream until the glass in the window shatters!" Chloe spoke through clenched lips in a low whisper, then closed her eyes. Stiffening, and stretching out her arms as though she were a figure on a crucifix, she began to talk to herself, in a bitter voice, between clenched teeth. "You can kill yourself right now you can drive a knife through your heart so you're dead and can forget you ever tried to play the piano. You can forget there was such a thing as a piano…you can..."

"Stop it Chloe. My g… No one said it is over. I love the way you play." Then seeing the look on her daughter's face added, "Well for heaven's sake, the piano isn't the only thing on earth. You could maybe write music." Pausing, Bridget tried to remember what Cameron had said that day, about Irving Berlin, but just then Chloe opened her eyes. "You damned, silly looking cluck, are you trying to drive me insane? Yes, I could write music. I can write you a motet, or a sonata, or a waltz or a cornet solo, with variation…anything at all, anything you want, And not one note of it will be worth the match it would take to burn it. You think I am hot stuff, don't you? You, lying there every day, dreaming about acceptance. Well, I am not. I am an Irondequoit

Prodigy. I know all there is to know about music, and there is one like me in every Irondequoit on earth, every one-horse conservatory, every tank town university. We can read anything, play anything, arrange anything, and we are just no good bastards. Like you. God, now I know where I get it from. Isn't that funny? You start out a Prodigy, then find out you're just a goddam bastard."

"'Well, if that is the case Chloe, it certainly does seem peculiar that he would not have known it. Mr. Taylor, Jr., I mean. And told you so. Instead of egging you on."

"Do you think he didn't know it? And did not tell me? He told me every time he saw me my tunes stunk, my playing stunk, everything I did stunk but he liked me. And he knew how I felt about it. Christ, that was something, after living with you all my life. So, we went on with it, and he thought perhaps time would change reality. In this racket you have got it, or you don't… and will you wipe that stupid look off your face and stop acting as if it was somebody's fault?"

"It certainly would seem, after all that work…"

"Can't you understand anything at all? They do not pay off on work, they payoff on talent! I am just no good! I'M NOT GOD DAM GOOD AND THERE'S NOTHING THAT CAN BE DONE ABOUT IT!"

When a shoe whizzed past her head, Bridget knew she was fighting a lost cause. She left the room, called her driver, picked up her purse, and was soon headed to Pittsford. She felt no resentment at this tirade. She understood at last that something catastrophic had happened to Chloe, and that it was completely beyond her power to understand. But that would not stop her from trying, in her own way, to think what she could do about it.

CHAPTER 25

In a day or so, feeling that Chloe was the victim of some sort of injustice, Bridget decided that the Messrs. Taylor, Jr., and Hammond were not the only teachers; that battles are not won by quitting, but by fighting hard; that Chloe should go on with her music, whether the great masters liked it or not. She presented several ideas to Chloe, but she cut her off mid-sentence. But Bridget kept trying. Chloe was talented and she had to help her see it. That is when she thought of another angle.

There was a celebrated dancer who often dined at the Charlotte Restaurant. Bridget asked Lucy to let her know the next time he stopped in and when he did, she made a point of talking to him. She told him all about Chloe and her talent. She even showed him a picture of her and when she finished, he told her not to worry. He said it took a lot of rethreading the needle to find what worked best and with Chloe's looks and good instruction, things might still be possible.

Bridget could not wait to tell Chloe. But at this Chloe merely yawned. But Bridget did not give up. She tried talking with several people and traced down all kinds of contacts in the hopes of helping her child. But even when she met with success, or what she saw that way, Chloe was not interested.

So, her hands tied, Bridget decided that Chloe should enter one of the local schools and prepare herself for college. Chloe scoffed at the idea.

Yet Chloe continued to mope in her room, until Bridget became thoroughly alarmed, and decided that whatever the future held, for the present something had to be done. So, one day she suggested that Chloe call up some of her friends and give them a little party. Accepting Chloe's opinion of the house, she said, "If you don't want to ask them here, why not out at Charlotte? You can have a whole room to yourself. I can have Lucy fix up a special table, there's an orchestra we can get, and afterwards you can dance or do anything you want."

"No, Mother. Thanks."

Bridget might have persisted on this, if it had not been for Francine, who heard what she was discussing with Chloe. In the kitchen she said to Bridget, "She isn't going to see any of those people. Not those Cobbs Hill people."

"Why not?"

Francine hesitated and then said, "I thought you knew."

"Knew what?"

"Well, Chloe had it out with Mr. Taylor, Jr.'s wife and she told everybody."

"Told them what, Francine?"

Francine took a deep breath. "She told them that Chloe had seduced her husband and that they had an affair. She said that Chloe caused his heart attack and it served them both right.

Bridget plopped down on a chair, shocked, unable to think straight. She suddenly thought of her daughter and how much she resembled Cameron. Even that day with dark circles under her eyes she was beautiful with those blue eyes and thick eyelashes. She had full lips and now a full sexual body and her famous sexual carriage now had come into play. But what shook up Bridget, now was exactly what all this meant…this child was no longer a child, At seventeen she was a woman, and an uncommonly wise one at that.

The days that follow revealed more changes. Bridget tried to like the clothes Chloe wanted, but could not. She harped on her choices, but Chloe put on the charm and called her darling Mother, and kissed her, and begged to be allowed to keep them so she gave in.

Thereafter, she hardly saw Chloe. In the morning, when she went out, Chloe was still asleep, and at night, when she came in, Chloe was not home yet, and usually did not arrive until two or three in the morning. Chloe tended to spend the night at home instead of the rental next door which of course Bridget paid for. But admittedly, she liked having her daughter stay with her.

One night, when Chloe's car drove up and she heard it bang against something, she ran to the window and watched as Chloe tried several times to get the car into the garage. Once she made it in, Bridget rushed back to her room and waited.

Soon she heard Chloe's heavy footsteps as she made her way to her room. Bridget knew that Chloe was drunk, But when she went to Chloe's door, it was locked, and there was no answer to her knock.

Then one afternoon, when she came home for her rest, Chloe's car was there, and so was a dreadful girl, named Elaine. Her place of residence, it turned out, was Pittsford, her occupation actress, though when Bridget asked what plays she had acted in, the answer was merely, "character parts." She was tall, pretty, and cheap, and Bridget instinctively disliked her. But as this was the first girl Chloe had ever chosen as a friend, she tried to be nice to her.

Then Bridget began to hear things. Francine cornered her one night, and began a long, whispered harangue. "Bridget, it may be none of my business, but it's time you knew what was going on with Chloe. She has been in here a dozen times, with that awful girl she goes around with, and not only here but at the Irondequoit Lounge down the street, and at other places. And all they are up to is picking up men. And the men they pick up! They are driving all around in that car of Chloe's, and sometimes they have one man with them, sometimes five. Five, Bridget. That day there was three inside, and the girls were all over them, while two more waited outside. And at this sleazy dive bar downtown they drink a lot and are getting a reputation for..." Francine, seeing Bridget's expression, didn't finish.

Bridget felt she had to get answers before it got any worse. She held off the talk, telling herself she wanted to research the matter before making any accusations, but she realized she was afraid of what she might find. Finally, she braved up. She began by trying to get Chloe's phone and check her Instagram and Snapchat accounts, but that took some doing since Chloe always had her cell with her. Until she could manage that she began checking out her laptop and computer.

She viewed her accounts on Facebook, twitter, Pinterest Tumblr, and some she had never heard of like Flickr and Reddit. She watched videos on YouTube, and finally the opportunity came when Chloe was in the shower and Bridget saw her phone lying on the floor next to her bed.

Without taking a moment to think she hurried in, grabbed the phone, and sat on the edge of her bed. Knowing she would not have much time she pressed the Instagram app, then the Snapchat app. Then seeing the high count on her text message app, she click and read. What she had seen and heard on social media did not compare to what she read in her daughter's text messages.

Bridget had thought the worse and nothing could be as bad as what she had conjured in her mind so one Sunday morning she started the conversation by asking Chloe when she was going to get on with her life and Chloe's responds got her to the question she really wanted answered. "What are you doing, Chloe?"

It turned out not to be the right time as Chloe was in the mood to hurt. She talked harshly and vulgarly about what she was doing and who she was seeing. Her tone was enough to keep Bridget quiet as she looked at this stranger before her.

"After all, Mother, it was you that said I couldn't lie around here all the time. And just because that prissy Francine… oh well, let's not get on that subject. Suffice it to say there is nothing to be alarmed at, Mother. I may go into acting is all." She paused for effect. "And Elaine…well she may be a drug user…" Seeing her mother's expression, added, …" not a drug addict, but she knows directors. Lots of them. All of them. And I'm sure you know how directors give a test."

Bridget tried conscientiously to keep her mouth shut, reminding herself whatever she said would only make matters worse. There was no handling Chloe. It was she who told her to think about another career. But she remained profoundly miserable, almost physically sick with what she pictured her daughter was doing.

One afternoon, at the Irondequoit restaurant, Bridget was checking inventory with Mrs. Ottoman when Celine came into the kitchen and said a Mrs. Witmore was there to see her. Then, lowered her voice, Celine added excitedly. “I think it's that famous director's wife.”

Bridget quickly washed her hands, dried them, and checking herself in the reflection on the side of the fridge, she padded her hair, and headed to the dining area.

A sudden coldness hit at her core and for a moment she could not move. Celine had said Mrs. Witmore but the name had not registered until now. This was the Mrs. Witmore to whom she had applied, years before, for the job as housekeeper. The lady turned, then came over beaming, with outstretched hand and alarming graciousness. “Mrs. Bitmore? I have been looking forward so much to meeting you. I'm Mrs. Witmore, Mrs. John Witmore and I'm sure we're going to work out our little problem splendidly.”

Bridget was taken aback as she led Mrs. Witmore to a table. She speculated wildly as to what this woman wanted. She had a panicky fear that it had something to do with that visit years before. If that were the case and Chloe heard she had once actually applied for a servant's job, she would never let her forget it.

As she faced her visitor, she suddenly made up her mind that whatever this was about, she was going to deny everything; deny that she had ever seen Mrs. Witmore before, or been to her house, or even considered a position as housekeeper. She had no sooner made this decision than she saw Mrs. Witmore eyeing her sharply.

"But haven't we met before, Mrs. Bitmore."

Bridget felt relieved. The woman did not remember her.

"Possibly in one of my restaurants."

"But I don't go to, ah, this type of restaurant, Mrs. Bitmore."

"I have a branch in Pittsford. You may have dropped in for a cup of chocolate some time, many people do. You probably saw me there."

Mrs. Witmore nodded her head, "No doubt that's it."

As Mrs. Witmore continued to stare, Celine appeared and began dusting tables. It seemed to Bridget that Celine's ears looked bigger than usual, so she called her over, and asked Mrs. Witmore if she could offer her something. When Mrs. Witmore declined, she pointedly told Celine she could let the tables go until later.

Mrs. Witmore settled into her coat like a hen occupying a nest, and gushed, "I've come to talk about our children, Mrs. Bitmore; our babies, I'm almost tempted to say, because that's the way I really feel about them."

"Ours?"

"Your little one, Chloe. She is such a lovely girl, Mrs. Bitmore. I do not know when I have taken a child to my heart as I have Chloe. And my boy."

Bridget, nervous and frightened, stared for a moment and said, "Mrs. Witmore, I haven't any idea what you're talking about."

"Oh come, come, Mrs. Bitmore."

"Seriously, I don't know."

Bridget's tone was sharp, and Mrs. Witmore looked at her steadily, her lips smiling, her eyes not believing. Then she broke into a high, shrill laugh. "Oh of course you don't! How stupid of me, Mrs. Bitmore. I should have explained that my boy, my baby, is Richard Witmore."

As Bridget still stared, Mrs. Witmore saw at last that this might not be pretense. Her manner changing, she leaned forward and asked eagerly, "You mean Chloe hasn't told you anything?"

"Not a word."

"Ah!"

Mrs. Witmore was excited now, obviously aware of her advantage in being able to give Bridget her own version of this situation, whatever it was, first. She folded her hands and shot appraising glances at Bridget for some time before proceeding. Then, "Shall I begin at the beginning, Mrs. Bitmore?"

"Please."

"They met it seems only yesterday, actually it was several months ago, at my house. My husband, no doubt you have heard of him, he is a director, and he was considering Chloe for a part. And as he so often does with these kids, when we have a little party going on, he asked her over. That is Chloe and her little friend Elaine, another lovely child, Mrs. Bitmore. My husband has known her for years."

"Yes, I've met Elaine," surprised at how Mrs. Witmore considered her.

"So, it was at my own house, Mrs. Bitmore, that Chloe and

Richard first met, and it was simply love at first sight. It must have been first sight. That boy of mine, Mrs. Bitmore is so sincere, so…"

Bridget interrupted and then blurted out, "What are you trying to say?"

Mrs. Witmore swallowed, put on a fake smile, and explained, "They have committed themselves to each other."

"You mean they're engaged?"

"I was coming to that. No, I would not say they were engaged. In fact, I know that Richard had no such thing in mind. But Chloe has somehow got that idea. Of course, I understand it. Any girl wants to get married, but I can assure you, Richard had no such thing in mind. I want to make that perfectly clear."

Mrs. Witmore's voice was becoming a little high, a little strident, and she wiggled a stiff forefinger at Bridget as she went on. "And I'm quite sure you'll agree with me, Mrs. Bitmore, that any discussion of marriage between them would be most undesirable."

"Why?"

As far as Bridget was concerned, marriage for Chloe would be a catastrophe, but at Mrs. Witmore's manner she bristled with hot bias.

Mrs. Witmore snapped, "Because they're nothing but children! Chloe can't be over nineteen."

"She's seventeen."

"And my boy is twenty. That is too young. Mrs. Bitmore, it

is entirely too young. Furthermore, they move in two different worlds."

"What different worlds?"

Bridget's eyes blazed, and Mrs. Witmore hastily backed off.

"That is not quite what I mean, Mrs. Bitmore, of course. Let us say different communities. They have different backgrounds, different ideals, different friends. And of course, Richard has always been used to a great deal of money."

"Do you think Chloe hasn't?"

"I'm sure she has everything you can give her."

"You may find she's been used to just as much as your boy has, and more. I'm not exactly on relief, I can tell you."

"But you did not let me finish, Mrs. Bitmore. If Chloe's accustomed to wealth and position, so much the more reason that this should not for a second be considered. I want to make this perfectly clear, if Richard gets married, he'll be completely on his own, and it will certainly be hard for two young people, both born with silver spoons in their mouths, to live on what he can earn."

Having made this clear, Mrs. Witmore tried to compose herself, and Bridget tried to calm down. She said this was the first she had heard of it, and she would have to talk with Chloe before she could say what she thought. But as Mrs. Witmore politely agreed that this was an excellent idea, Bridget began to have a suspicion that the whole truth had not been told. Suddenly and sharply, she asked, "Why should Chloe feel this way about it, and your boy not?"

“Mrs. Bitmore, I'm not a mind reader.”

Mrs. Witmore spoke angrily, the color appearing in her cheeks. Then she added, “But let me tell you one thing. If you, or that girl, or anybody, employ any more tricks, trying to blackmail my boy into…”

“Trying to what?”

Bridget's voice cracked like a whip, and for a few moments Mrs. Witmore did not speak. Apparently, she knew she had said too much, and was trying to be discreet. Her effort was unsuccessful. When her nostrils had dilated and closed several times, she exploded. “You may as well understand here and now, Mrs. Bitmore, that I shall prevent this marriage. I shall prevent it in any way that I can, and by legal means, if necessary.” The way she said “necessary” had a very ominous sound to it.

By now the reality behind this visit was beginning to dawn on Bridget, and she became calm, cold, calculating. Looking up, she saw Celine at her dusting again, her ears bigger than ever. Calling her, she told her to straighten the chairs at the next table, and as she approached, turned pleasantly to Mrs. Witmore. I beg your pardon. For the moment I wasn't listening.”

Mrs. Witmore’s voice rose to a scream. “I say if there are any more threats, any more officers at my door, any more of these tricks she's been playing, I shall have her arrested, I shall have her prosecuted for blackmail, I shall not hesitate for one moment, for I've quite reached the limit of my patience!”

Mrs. Witmore, stood, trying to catch her breath and then with one more piercing look at Bridget, swept out the door.

Bridget looked at Celine. “Did you hear what she said?”

“I wasn't listening, Mrs. Bridget.”

Bridget scowled at her. “I repeat, did you hear what she said.”

Celine studied Bridget for a cue. Then replied, “She said Chloe was trying to blackmail her boy into marrying her and if she kept it up, she'd have the law on her.”

“Remember that, in case I need you.”

“Yes Miss Bridget.”

That night Bridget did not go to Cobbs Hill or to Pittsford. She stayed home, traipsing around, tortured by the fear that Celine had probably told everybody in the restaurant by now, what dreadful mess Chloe had gotten herself into.

At eleven that evening Bridget finished closing the restaurant and went home. She went to her room and lay down, pulling a blanket over her but not taking off her clothes. Around one, when Chloe's car zipped up the drive, she took no chances on a locked door, but jumped up and met Chloe in the kitchen.

“Mother! ... My. How you startled me!”

"I am sorry, darling. But I must talk to you. Something has happened.”

“Well at least let me take off my coat.”

Bridget went to the den, relieved that she had smelled no liquor. In a minute or two Chloe came in, sat down, and yawned. “Personally, I find pictures a bore, don't you? At least Christian Bale pictures. Still, I suppose it is not his fault, for it is not how he acts but what parts he plays. And I suppose he has nothing to do with how dreadfully long they are."

"Stop it Chloe. We need to talk."

"What is it?"

In a low, timid voice, she said, "A Mrs. Witmore was in to see me today. A Mrs. Victoria Witmore."

"Oh, really?"

"She says you're engaged to marry her son, or have some idea you want to marry him, or something."

"She's quite talkative. What else?"

"She opposes it."

Despite her effort to remain calm, Bridget blurted out, "What was she talking about? What does it all mean?"

Chloe reflects a few minutes, then said, in a polished voice, "Well, it would be going too far to say it was my idea that Richard and I get married. After the big rush they gave me, with father breaking his neck to get me a screen test and Mrs. Whitmore having me over morning, noon and night, and Sonny Boy phoning me, and emailing me, and texting me that if I did not marry him, he would end his young life. I think you might say it was a conspiracy. Certainly, I said nothing about it, or even thought about it, until it seemed advisable."

"What do you mean, advisable?"

"Well Mother, he was certainly sweet, or seemed so at any rate, and they were most encouraging, and I hadn't exactly been happy since my music teacher, Mr. Taylor, Jr. died. And Elaine did have a nice little apartment. And I was certainly most indiscreet. And then, after the big whoop de do, their whole attitude changed, alas. And here I am, holding the bag. One might almost say I was a bit of a fool."

If there was any pain, any tragic overtone, to this recital, it was not audible to the ordinary ear. Bridget, however, was not interested in such subtleties. She had reached a point where she had to know one stark, basic fact. Sitting beside Chloe, clutching her hand, she said, "I have to ask you something and you need to be honest. Are you pregnant?"

"Yes Mother, I'm afraid I am."

For a second the rage was so overwhelming that Bridget was afraid she would vomit. But then Chloe looked at her in a pretty, contrite way, as one who had sinned but is sure of forgiveness and dropped her head on Bridget's shoulder. Bridget fought to keep her guard up against Chloe's tactics, but failed. She gathered Chloe in her arms and held her tight, as she cried. "Why didn't you tell me?"

"I was afraid."

"Of me? Of Mother?"

"No, no! Of the suffering it would bring you. Darling Mother, don't you know I can't bear to see you unhappy?"

Bridget closed her mind to this blatant lie because she did not want to not believe it. Then, remembering, she asked, "What did she mean about officers?"

"You mean police?"

"Yes, Chloe," she said impatiently. "I mean police. She said they came to her home."

"My, that is funny."

Chloe sat up and laughed in a silvery, ironical way. "From what I have learned of the young man since this happened, I would say that any girl perhaps the count is in the thousands for that matter, could have sent officers to his door. He has a very inclusive taste." Seeing the expression on her mother's face she added, "Well, that's really funny when you stop to think about it, isn't it?"

Bridget was at a lost. How do you discuss a problem with someone who does not see it as a problem and especially when your knowledge came second hand. "Is that it, Mother?"

"Yes, Chloe, unless you have something more to say, that's it."

"Well, goodnight."

Bridget watched as Chloe left the room. She heard her close her door and heard her lock it. Bridget went to her room, feeling as though her life was being torn apart from the inside out and she could do no more than watch it happen.

In the morning, she went to the Irondequoit restaurant and called Cameron. Dispensing with Jefferson, she went down to

Mrs. Donahue's corner and picked him up. Then, driving toward the hills, she started to talk. She put in everything that seemed relevant, beginning with Mr. Taylor, Jr. and emphasizing Chloe's forebodings about it. When she got to Mr. Hammond, the music conductor, Cameron's face darkened, and he exclaimed at the cruelty of the man to treat a young girl that way.

Taking a breather, she began again telling him about Elaine, the drinking, and Ida's harrowing tales, followed by the visit from Mrs. Witmore. From there she articulated her discussion with Chloe before she finally broke down completely, blurting out, "Cameron! She is going to have a baby! She's in a family way!"

Cameron's grip tightened on her arm. "Hold it! Stop this goddam car. I got to get some place where I can move around."

She slowed down and pulled into the parking area on Lake Shore Boulevard. She had barely parked the car when he got out, began pacing beside the car and cursing profusely. He said goddam it, he was going to kill that son of a bitch if it was the last thing he did on earth. He said he was going to kill him if they hung him for it and his soul rotted in hell. With still more frightful oaths, he went into full particulars as to where he was going to buy the gun, the way he would lay for the boy, what he would say when he had him face to face and how he would let him have it. Bridget watched him striding up and down, and a fierce, glowing pride in him began to warm her. He demonstrated what she felt and could not do or say. Even his curses gave her a queer, morbid satisfaction. But after a while she said, "Get in."

He climbed in beside her, held his face in his hands, and for a moment she thought he was going to weep. When he did not, she started the car and said, "I know you would kill him, Cameron. I know you would, and I glory in you for it. I love you for it." She took his hand, and gripped it, and tears came to her eyes, for he eased her pain, by his ferocity. "But that wouldn't do Chloe any good. If he is dead, that's not getting her anywhere."

After a bit Cameron responded, "You are right."

"What are we going to do?"

Gagging over her words, Bridget presently broached the subject of an abortion. It was something she hated the thought of because it went counter to every instinct in her whole nature. Cameron cut her off with a gesture. "Bridget, I don't know about that. It is killing a child and we know how it feels when a child dies. We lost one and that is enough. By God, she is not going to have any operation, not to make it easy for a dirty little rat that took advantage of her and now wants to walk away scot free."

Cameron now turned toward Bridget, his eyes flashing. "He's going to marry her, that's what he's going to do. After he has given her child a name, then he can do as he pleases. He can leave her afterwards with my blessings because I will not have him as any relation to me. He can go to hell, for all I care, but before he does, he will march up beside her and say, 'I do.' I'll see to that."

"Yes, you are right. It's the best thing to do, Cameron."

Bridget drove along, and presently had a hollow feeling they were right back where they started. It was all very well to say the boy had to marry Chloe, but how could they make him do it? Suddenly she burst out, “Cameron, I'm going to get a lawyer.”

“It's just what I've been thinking.”

“You and I, we can't do a thing. Precious time is going by, and something must be done. And the first thing is to get that lawyer.”

“Okay, that is what I’ll do.”

When Bridget got home, Chloe was just getting up. Closing the door, she addressed the tousled girl in the green kimono. “I told your father. We had a talk. He agrees that we need a lawyer. I'm going to call up my friend Greyson Hobbs.”

“Mother, I think that's an excellent idea. In fact, I've already called him up.”

“You what?”

Chloe spoke sleepily, and a little impatiently. “Mother, can't you see that I'm trying to arrange things myself, without putting you to all kinds of trouble about it? I have been trying to spare you. I want to make things easy for you.”

Bridget blinked, tried to adjust herself to this astounding revelation. Could it be that Chloe was changing?

CHAPTER 26

Greyson arrived around three. Bridget brought him to the privacy of the den, then went and sent Francine on an errand that would take her all afternoon. When she got back to the den, Chloe was there looking beautiful and innocent in a simple little blue frock Bridget had bought for her first recital, back in poor, but simpler days. Greyson sat on the sofa looking through an ancient photo album, containing the last printed out pictures since now they were taken and stored in the cloud. He seemed amused as he slowly turned the pages. Sensing her presents, Greyson looked up and said, “Things certainly have changed.” Then casually added, “Let’s get down to business.”

He began by saying he had done a little inquiring around, and the situation was about what he figured it was. “The kid comes into dough on his twenty first birthday, that's the main thing. How much I do not exactly know, but it is well up in seven figures he is going to inherit. There is no way the mother, or the stepfather, or any of them can juggle the books to keep him out of it, and once he dies, whoever is married to him at the time cuts in for her share of the community property. That is what this is all about, and it is all that it is about. That is why they are breaking their necks to head it off. It has nothing to do with their being too young, or loving each other, or not loving each other, or the different ways they have been raised, or any of the stuff that mother has been dishing out. It's nothing but a game."

Greyson stopped talking then and Bridget drew a deep breath and spoke slowly, raising her voice a little, "Greyson, I'm not interested in whether he inherits, or how much he inherits, or anything of that kind. So long as I am here, I do not think Chloe will be in need financially. But a situation has been created. It is a terrible situation for Chloe, and the only thing that boy can do about it is marry her. If he is a decent boy, he will do the right thing on his own initiative, regardless of what his family says. If he is not, he'll have to be made to grow up and act like a man." Bridget looked for acceptance of her idea from the two and not seeing any, continued.

"Greyson, that woman had a great deal to say that I haven't told Chloe, but that I have witnesses to substantiate about law, and what she'll do. I will go just as far as she will. If it is the only way, I want that boy arrested and you can tell him he can be glad it is only the police he has to face, instead of Cameron."

"Arresting him may be a little tough."

“Haven't we got laws?”

“He's skipped town.”

Greyson shot a glance at Chloe, who considered a few moments before saying to him, “I think you'd better tell her.”

“Tell me what? What’s going on?”

“You see, Bridget, it just so happens we already thought of that. Two, three days, maybe a week ago, I took Chloe over to the Sheriff's office and had her swear out a warrant for Richard. No statutory rape, nothing unpleasant like that. Just a little morals charge, and the same afternoon, couple of the boys went over to serve it. He was not there. And so far…”

“So that's what she meant by officers!”

Chloe stirred uneasily under Bridget's accusing eyes. “Well Mother, if you're talking about what I said last night, I didn't know at that time that any officers had actually been there.”

Bridget turned on Greyson. “It does seem to me that on a thing of this kind, a matter as serious as this, I should have been the first one you would have talked to about it. Why the very idea, of legal steps being taken without my knowing anything whatever about it!”

“Now just hold your horses a minute.”

Greyson's eyes became very cold, and he got up and marched up and down in front of Bridget before he went on. “One thing you might consider, I've got a little thing called legal ethics to consider. Sure, I would have been willing to talk to you. We have talked plenty before, haven't we? But when my client makes an express stipulation that I not talk to you, why…"

When Bridget turned, Chloe was ready. "Mother, it's about time you got it through your head that after all, I and not you, am the main person in this situation, as you call it. I am not proud of it. I readily admit it is my own fault, and that I have been very foolish. But when I act on that assumption, when I try to relieve you of responsibility, when I try to save you unhappiness, it does seem to me you could give me credit for some decent motives, instead of going off the handle in this idiotic way."

"Idiotic way! I never in all my life I…"

"Now, Mother, nobody was asking any help from you, and as Greyson has taken my case as a great favor to me, I think the least you can do is let him tell us what to do, as I imagine he knows much more about such things than you do."

Bridget was furious. Her daughter was trying to keep her out of this matter as if it were none of her business. Even though she knew that was what Chloe did, it still hurt.

Greyson resumed in the casual way he had begun, "Well, as far as his doing anything goes, I'd say the next move was up to them. Way I look at it, we have taken round one. When we got the warrant, that showed we were serious.

"So, what will the warrant do."

"Well, the arrest warrant grants the law enforcement officers the right and ability to arrest Richard as committing a crime."

"Okay..."

"It's a step, Bridget. The arrest warrant was acquired in a

court of law by presenting the judge with probable cause for arresting him. To even get a warrant issued, we had to prove probable cause. We proved that. And we needed at least two pieces of evidence to present to the judge before requesting an arrest warrant. So that proves that we have a case, and that Richard is considered under arrest."

"So how can they arrest him if he's gone?"

"Yes, that can be a problem, but the warrant allows them to arrest him wherever they find him. This means he can be arrested at work, at home, or anywhere."

"It's a wide, wide world out there Greyson."

"Fleeing from justice is an overall bad idea. He will be considered a fugitive, and there are no legal benefits for trying to escape criminal prosecution. Of course, that has not stopped criminals from trying to hide from law enforcement. But for criminals who have fled to other states, the state seeking extradition must file the proper documents, show that you have been charged with a crime in that state, and show that you are a fugitive. It's a cat and mouse game and I'm willing to play it out."

"So what charge are you issuing this warrant?"

"Moral charge for indecent liberties with a child. On a morals charge, all the jury wants to know is the age of the girl. After that it is open and shut. When they made the move to get him under cover quick, that shows they knew what they are up against. And what they are up against is tough. So long as that warrant is out against him, he dare not come back to the state of New York, he cannot go back to college, or even use his right name, Course there's a couple of other things we might do, like suing the mother, but then we are in the news, and that is not so good. I'd say leave it like it is."

"But Greyson!"

Bridget's voice was a despairing wail. "Greyson! Time is going on. Days are passing and think about Chloe's condition I… we cannot wait. We have to act now."

"I think we can leave it to Greyson." Chloe's cool tone ended the discussion, but all that day and all that night Bridget fretted, and by next morning she had worked herself into a rage. When Jefferson reported, at noon, she had him drive her over to Mrs. Witmore's to "have it out with her." But as they drove up the drive, she saw the house man that had let her in, that morning long ago, talking to the driver of a delivery truck. She knew perfectly well he would remember her, and she called shrilly to Jefferson. to drive on, she had changed her mind. As the car rolled around the loop in front of the house, she leaned far back, so she would not be seen.

She had Jefferson drive her to Ida's, and telephoned Cameron and then dropping off Jefferson in Irondequoit, she again picked up Cameron at Mrs. Donahue's corner and headed up to the lake.

Cameron listened intently, his face changing colors and somehow remaining quiet until she had finished. When she did, he began shaking his head. "Bridget, I wish you'd told me you had Greyson Hobbs in mind. I am telling you, I do not like the guy, and I do not like the way he does business. Telling him to step on the gas is like, well, think about it, he has been liquidating Bitmore Homes for eight years now, hasn't he? And they're not liquidated yet."

Cameron reached over and touched Bridget's hand. "Bridget, he's not trying to get Chloe married. He's just running up a bill."

They drove in silence, each deep in their own thoughts until suddenly Cameron almost yelled. "To hell with him! What we want is to find that boy, isn't it? Isn't that right?"

"Yes…."

"We don't need a Greyson Hobbs for that. What we need is a private detective."

Bridget swung the car over to the shoulder and turned so she was looking directly at Cameron. They had the same interest, the same needs; and because of that, his thinking was more in line with hers. At last, she knew they were getting somewhere.

"Oh, Cameron, you're right."

Excitedly they talked about it, and then Cameron told her to get him to a computer. She drove to the Charlotte Branch Library on Lake Avenue, and Cameron hopped out before the car fully came to a stop.

"Wait here."

"But…"

"Wait here."

She watched as he hurried inside and she waited, turning on the car radio to keep her company. In less than fifteen minutes he was back, a slip of paper in his hands. “Here's three, with phone numbers and addresses. What say we go first to this SPI Agency? I've heard of it, for one thing, and it's right in downtown Rochester, not too far away.”

Bridget reached out and Cameron handed her the printout. “Read it to me, Cameron.”

“Welcome to The SPI Agency.” He turned to look at Bridget. “SPI stands for Special Private Intelligence Agency,” Bridget smiled, and he continued. “A professional organization that is dedicated to serve, process and investigate our clients request utilizing the most professional, effective, and efficient methods available in today’s marketplace. If you are looking for a company that is experienced to serve your civil documents, expeditiously process your legal records and…”

Cameron paused and looked at Bridget, “And this is the part we are most interested in…”

He began again. “and can investigate and locate your hard-to-find missing persons, then you have found the right company. The agents at The SPI Agency are exceptionally professional, extremely knowledgeable, and well equipped to handle all your company’s business needs. So, what are you waiting for?”

Cameron said in a soft, hush, “I do like a business that is upfront with what they do.” He smirked. Do you see the phone number there?”

“Yes.”

“Should we give them a call and let them know we’re

coming."

"That's exactly what I was thinking..." She turned slightly and asked, "Do you have your cell?"

"What do you think?"

"I think you do, but it probably needs to be charged."

Cameron nodded.

"Okay, plug it in and dig in my purse. Mine is in there somewhere."

"Why didn't you say something before..."

"I tried to stop you and tell you we could look it up on my cell, but you moved to fast."

Cameron nodded. It took a while, but eventually he found it and Cameron entered the number. While they waited, Cameron checked the hours of operation. "Great. They opened at seven in the morning and close at five in the evening."

The phone was picked up before the end of the second ring and Cameron immediately focused his attention. He explained why he was calling and answered the receptionist questions. Before he disconnected the call, they had an appointment in fifteen minutes.

"What do you think? I know we wanted to get in as quickly as possible, but maybe they don't have many clients...maybe they're not good..."

"Stop it. You have a way of worrying over nothing. Can't you just think of it as luck?"

"But it was so easy... Sorry. They're in Suite 503."

Cameron checked out the building on her phone and found that it was what was called the Executive Office building. The thumbprint picture on the site showed a tall grand building made of red brick and had white corner bricks outlining its edges. It said there were eight stories to the building. He scrolled down and found a better picture of the building.

"Look, this is what we're looking for. It was built in 1910 but renovated in 1960. Hopefully, they mean the structure and not the décor." He chuckled and Bridget joined in.

Cameron continued checking out the area since neither one of them was familiar with downtown. "Okay, it says that the building is on the corner of West Main Street and North Fitzhugh Street."

"Good, that helps."

"To occupy his time, he told Bridget that in the building was Espresso Express, Fence City Of Rochester, Jaco Wine And Spirits, Johnsons Sales, Laenan Servicing Corp, Lyell Equipment Corp, Mullrich Restaurant, Nanker Phelge Enterprises … "

Bridget started giggling.

"What are you laughing about?"

"The companies in the building. We can eat, drink and get us a private investigator."

"Cute, Bridget. Cute."

"Stop. That's it."

Bridget, with Cameron's help looked for a place to park and once they parked the car, hurried into the building, and took the elevator to the fifth floor. At the door of the agency, Bridget took a deep breath and together they walked in.

The receptionist walked them back to the office and once inside, she said. "This is Mr. Burma. He will be helping you."

"Hello, you are Mr. & Mrs. Bitmore?"

"Ah…," Cameron began, "yes."

"Have a seat. I'm Nestor Burma, at your service."

That would have sounded phony, but not coming from this serious faced man.

The SPI Detective Agency had a rather small office in the building and at first, Bridget was afraid that they should look for a bigger agency, but once meeting Nestor Burma she was impressed. He had one of those faces. His eyes seemed to see right through you and his mouth, though his lips were close, seemed to be smiling just the same. He had on a collared, light blue shirt with a dark blue tie that was loose around his neck. His suit looked well-tailored and neat. As Bridget glanced about, she saw a hat hanging on the coat rack behind him and it looked well-worn with its old fashion brim and finger pressed crease in the front. If ever there was a stereotype gumshoe, he was it.

He listened attentively as Cameron presented a concise description of the issue and refrained from asking any embarrassing questions. Cameron made sure to let Mr. Burma know about the Witmores.

"In case you do not know the family, let me fill you in on what we're up against. They own the big stone mansion in Pittsford that is constantly photographed. The woman who lives there is married to Richard Witmore Senior. We are talking about him, not the brother Robert. The fortune started with their father, Marvin, who founded a wine business in 1945. That small business grew into Witmore Brands, which generates over $7 billion in annual revenue. The company is known for its many acquisitions and investments which the new generation dumped into the movie industry…"

Bridget stared at Cameron in awe. Even she did not know all that or bothered to look the family up. She was impressed.

"Yes, I know of them." Then he tilted back in his chair and said he saw no difficulty. He got jobs of this sort all the time, and on most of them was able to show results.

"Good. So, what is our next move?"

"Since time seems to be of the essence, I'd have to have two fifty before I start. After that it will be one hundred and twenty-five dollars a day."

Bridget could not control her amazement and seeing the expression on her face he asked, "Have you ever worked with a private investigator before?"

"No"

"People are often misguided by movies and television shows they watch depicting private detectives as mysterious, gun toting spies that wreak havoc in the night. However, contrary to popular belief, licensed private investigators are unable to perform many things that are portrayed. Let me give it to you straight."

Cameron and Bridget nodded as he explained what he could

do and talked of his success. When he mentioned canvassing areas, Bridget was a little hesitant.

Seeing this, Nestor said, "Oh, don't worry, Mrs. Bitmore, this is all strictly confidential, and nobody'll know anything. But if we are to get the job done, we need to work through our connections.

Cameron countered. "I suggest we pay half the advance now, the other half when the boy is found, along with any additional expense." But Mr. Burma shook his head. "Like any business, each job requires an investment, and we are talking about money I'll have to payout before I can start. There are fees involved and they get paid up front. It is all part of getting this guy. Of course, other places may do it cheaper, and you're perfectly welcome to go where you please. But, as I always say, the cheaper the slower in this business; and the riskier."

Bridget wrote the check. On the way home, both of them applauded themselves handsomely for what they had done, and agreed it should be between themselves, with nothing said to Greyson or Chloe until they had something to "lay on the line," as Cameron put it.

So, for several days Bridget was ducking out when she had a call from Mr. Burma. When she was in ear shot of others, she spoke in guarded tones. Then one afternoon he told her to come in. Bridget did not hesitate as she let everyone know what to do in her absence and to call if they ran into any problems. She then contacted Cameron and as to the usual arrangement picked him up outside.

Bridget and Cameron, drove, silently at first and then Bridget asked. “What do you think he wants to see us about?”

“I think he’s found him?”

“This soon?”

“Let’s hope so.”

They parked the car and quickly headed in the building, arriving just in time to catch the elevator to the fifth floor. In the office, Mr. Burma was all smiles.

“We had a little luck. Of course, it was not really luck. In this business, you cannot be too thorough. We found out that when your man left town, he was driving a rental car, and we found out from where. With its GPS location feature, you can track the location of the car in real-time to know where exactly it is at a particular time. So, we know where he is and since no one else does, he won’t be spooked.”

“Wow, that’s great.”

“So now what.”

“We have the warrant, so I give the information to the police and they pull him in.”

“But…”

Mr. Burma looked up. “But what? Are you getting cold feet? If so, it’s a little late now.”

“No, How much do we owe?”

Mr. Burma picked up a sheet of paper off his desk and handed it to Cameron. “Here's the itemized bill.”

Cameron reached out and took the bill and looked it over. He handed it to Bridget who did the same. She took out her checkbook and asked, “Who do I make it out to?”

“To the company, SPI Detective Agency. The office manager is putting all the information in a folder. It will have the address where he is hiding out as well as a cell phone number, which you probably do not want to call.

Bridget turned to Cameron and smiled. He was not sure what that smile meant, but it worried him.

“If you do not have a lawyer, it’s time to get one. I think you are going to need a good one. That family will be getting the best they can find.”

Bridget thanked him and handed him the check. His office manager came into the room, handed Mr. Burma a thick manila envelope, which he in turned handed over to Bridget.

“Thank you, Mr. Burma. Do you mind if we call the police?”

Cameron was taken aback at first but remained silent.

“No, not at all. I am glad I could help. By the way, the young man is using is real name. Didn’t even use a fake one.”

Driving back toward Irondequoit they were quiet. Cameron was going through the folder and pulled out a photo. He turned it so that Bridget could see it. “This rich playboy is what we will have as a son in law. Can you believe it!”

Silence returned until they were almost at the corner where Bridget would drop Cameron off. Finally, they discussed what was to be done, and stuck with the conclusion, that they had to go through with it. When Bridget pulled the car over to let him out, she said despondently, "Listen, Cameron, I need to tell Greyson and Chloe." Cameron nodded glumly then climbed out the car.

Back home, Bridget went to the kitchen and told Francine she needed her to run an errand. She gave her instructions and then when she knew she was alone in the house, she made the call to Greyson. She told him what she had done, and the information they had. She then read him the address furnished by Mr. Burma. "Wait Bridget. I need to get a pen. Hold on."

While she stared at the cell waiting for his return, she drummed her fingers against her cheek as if hearing a tune in her head and she was keeping time. Finally, he was back on the line and she slowly repeated the address.

"That's great. I know where that is."

"So, are you going to call the police, or should I?"

"No, not right now. I think I should talk to him first, but I'll do that if it gets difficult."

"No, Greyson, call the sheriff and take someone with you."

"No, I have to be sure first that he's there. Nothing to worry about."

"Greyson, he is there. Mr. Burma is a reputable private

investigator. I want that boy arrested."

"Bridget, why don't you let me handle it."

Furious, Bridget disconnected the call and jumped up, her eyes blazing, her hair slightly askew. When she turned to dash out, Chloe was at the door. At once she launched into a denunciation of Greyson.

"That man's not even trying to do anything. I have told him where that boy is. I had a detective find out and still he does nothing. Well, that is the last he will hear from me! I'm going over to the sheriff's office myself!"

Quivering with her high, virtuous resolve, Bridget charged for the door. She collided with Chloe, who seemed to have moved to block her path. Then her wrist was caught in a grip like steel, and slowly, mercilessly, she was forced back, until she plunged down on the sofa. "You'll do nothing of the kind."

"Let go of me! What are you pushing me for? What do you mean I'll do nothing of the kind?"

"If you go to the sheriff's office, they'll bring Sam Witmore back. And if they bring him back, he will want to marry me, and that does not happen to suit me. It may interest you to know that he has been back. He sneaked into town, twice, and a beautiful time I had of it, getting him to be a nice boy and stay where his Mamma put him. He is quite crazy about me. I saw to that. But as for matrimony, I beg to be excused. I'd much rather have the money."

Bridget stared at the cold, beautiful creature who now sat down opposite her, and who was yawning, as though the whole subject were a bit of a bore. The events of the last few days began ticking themselves off in her mind, particularly the strange relationship that had sprung up between Chloe and Greyson. It was like a movie being played in reverse until finally she got the picture. She raised her head and pushed her lower jaw forward as she squinted. Through clenched teeth she said, "Now I know what that woman meant by blackmail. You are just trying to shake her down, shake the whole family down, for money. You're not pregnant, at all." With each syllable her voice rose higher.

"Mother, at this stage it's a matter of opinion, and in my opinion, I am."

Chloe's eyes glinted as she spoke, and Bridget wanted to back down, to avoid one of those scenes from which she always emerged beaten, humiliated, and hurt. But something was swelling within her, something that began in the sick anger of a few nights before, something that felt as though it might presently choke her. Her voice shook as she spoke. "How could you do such a thing? If you had loved the boy, I would not have a word to say, not one word to blame you. To love is a woman's right, and when you do, I hope you give everything you have. But just to pretend you loved him, to lead him on, to get money out of him how could you do it?"

"Merely following in my mother's footsteps."

Bridget flew up from her seat and yelled, "What did you say?"

"Oh, stop being so tiresome. There is the date of your wedding and there is the date of my birth. Figure it out for yourself. The only difference is that you were a little younger at that time than I am now; a month or two anyway. I suppose it runs in families."

"How could you… Why do you think I married your father?"

"I rather imagine he married you. If you mean why you got yourself pregnant, I suppose you did it for the same reason I did… for the money."

"What money?"

"Mother, in another minute I'll be getting annoyed. Of course, he has no money now, but at the time he was quite rich, and I am sure you knew it. When the money was gone you kicked him out. And when you divorced him, and he was so down and out that Ms. Donahue had to keep him, you quite generously stripped him of the only thing he had left, meaning this lovely, incomparable, palatial hovel that we live in."

"That was his idea, not mine. He wanted to do his share, to contribute something for you and Izzy. And it was all covered with mortgages, that he could not even have paid the interest on, let alone the payments."

"At any rate, you took it."

By now, Bridget had sensed that Chloe's boredom was pure affectation. She was enjoying the unhappiness she inflicted and had probably rehearsed her main points in advance. This, ordinarily, would have been enough to make Bridget backdown, seek a reconciliation, but this feeling within kept goading her. After trying to keep quiet, she lashed out, “But why? Why will you tell me that? Don't I give you everything that money can buy? Is there one single thing I ever denied you? If there was something you wanted, could not you have come to me for it, instead of resorting to blackmail. Because that woman was right. That is all it is! Blackmail! Blackmail! Blackmail!”

In the silence that followed, Bridget felt first frightened, then coldly brave, as the feeling within drove her on. Chloe reflected, and asked, “Are you sure you want to know.”

“I dare you to tell me!”

“Well, since you ask, with enough money, I can get away from you; you poor, half-witted idiot. From you, and your pie wagon, and your chickens, and your waffles, and your kitchens, and everything that smells of grease. And from this cabin, that you blackmailed out of my father with your threats about Ms. Donahue, and its neat little two car garage, and its lousy furniture, and from Irondequoit women that wear uniforms. I want to get away from every rotten, stinking thing that even reminds me of the place or you.”

Bridget could not even be shocked by Chloe’s outburst because she had heard it all before. Keeping her voice as calm as possible she only said, “I see.”

Bridget sat back down, but then got up again. “Well, it's a good thing I found out what you were up to, when I did. Because I can tell you right now, if you had gone through with this, or even tried to go through with it, you'd have been out of here a little sooner than you expected."

She headed for the door, but Chloe was there first. Bridget laughed, and tore up the card Mr. Burma had given her. She had a feeling that Chloe had lied and did not know where the Witmore boy was and by God, she would not find out from her. "Oh, you needn't worry that I'll go to the sheriff's office now. It'll be a long time before they find out from me where the boy is hiding, or you do either."

Again, she started for the door, but Chloe did not move. Bridget backed off and turned back around to sit. If Chloe thought she would break, she was mistaken. Bridget sat motionless, her face hard, cold, and implacable. After a long time, the silence was shattered by the phone, Chloe jumped for it. After four or five brief, cryptic mono syllables, she hung up, turned to Bridget with a malicious smile. "That was Greyson. You may be interested to know that they're ready to settle."

"Are you?"

"I'm meeting them at his office."

"Then get out." She stared at this stranger she had brought into the world and added, "Get out now."

To her astonishment, Chloe uttered, "I'll decide that. And I'll decide when."

"You'll get your things out of this house right now or you'll find them in the middle of Bitmore Drive when you come back."

Chloe screamed curses at Bridget, but presently she got it through her head that this time, for some reason, was different from all other times. Bridget watched her daughter stomp down the hall and enter her bedroom. Soon she came out with a half-closed suitcase, parts of clothes dangling out the sides. She continued her trail carrying out her things, and half packing them in her luggage.

"Oh yes, and don't think you can stay at the rental either. That is off limit to you, too."

Chloe made no response and after that Bridget sat quite still, and when she heard Chloe drive off, she was consumed by a fury so cold that it almost seemed as though she felt nothing at all. It did not occur to her that she was acting less like a mother than like a lover who has unexpectedly discovered an act of betrayal and avenged it.

CHAPTER 27

It was over a year after she had thrown her daughter out that Cameron called up to invite her to the stage play. For her, it had been a dismal time. She had found out soon enough where Chloe was staying. It was in the swanky new built apartment building at 260 E Broad St. From checking the listings along with information from Cameron, she had a 2-bedroom apartment that was running her three thousand a month.

Every fiber of her being had wanted to pay a visit there, to take back what she had said, to reestablish things as they had been, or try to. But when this thought entered her mind, or rather shot through her heart like a hot arrow, she set her mind as if it had been cast in iron, and not once did she even drive past Chloe's building.

She was at a crossroads wanting to cut all ties with this evil child, but unable to stop loving her. She was her flesh and blood and her only living offspring and she could not stop loving her any more than she could say she did not love Cameron.

She discovered wine helped, and in the boozy dreams of her daily rest, she pictured Chloe as worsening, as finally going through all her money and starving until she had to come back, penitent, and tearful, for forgiveness. This view of the future was somewhat obscured by the circumstance that Bridget did not know exactly how much Chloe had obtained from the Witmores, and thus could not calculate, with any degree of accuracy, when destitution was likely to strike.

But Cameron contributed a thought that assisted drama, if not truth. Cameron, having tried unsuccessfully to stand on his rights as a father to bluff information out of Greyson, and having threatened even to hold up the settlement unless full data were furnished, had learned only that his consent was not needed for a settlement. All the Witmores wanted was a release from Chloe, a signed letter denying promises, intimidation, or pregnancy. That episode had left him with a lower opinion of Greyson's honesty than he had had before, if that were possible, and he hatched the theory that Greyson would have every damned cent of that settlement before the year was out. He told Bridget that it did not make a bit of difference what they paid, or what he got, or what she got. On this theory Bridget eagerly seized, and pictured Chloe, as horribly bruised in spirit, creeping to the strong, silent mother who could cope with Greyson or anybody else.

When the scene materialized almost daily before her eyes, with a hundred little variations and embellishments, she always experienced the same brief ecstasy as she lifted the weeping Chloe into her arms, patted her, inhaled the fragrance of the soft, coppery hair, and bestowed love, understanding, and forgiveness. One slight incongruity she overlooked, Chloe in real life, rarely wept.

At Cameron's mention of a show, it took her a moment or two to collect her wits. “What show?”

“Why, Chloe’s.”

“I don’t understand. You mean she's playing the piano on television?”

“No, singing, the way I understand it.”

“Chloe? Singing?”

“Maybe I better come over.”

By the time he got there, she was a tremble with excitement. She found the station and read the description that appeared on the info. Sure, enough there was Chloe's name, with the news that the popular singer will be heard tonight at eight thirty, on the Irish comedian Graham Norton show along with several ‘A’ list celebrities. There would be live music, lots of jokes and fun from Graham and the celebrities themselves.

Together they looked at the picture and commented on how lovely Chloe looked. When Bridget wanted to know how long this had been going on, meaning the singing, Cameron said quickly you could not prove it by him, as though to disclaim participation in secrets that had been withheld from Bridget. Then he added that the way he got it, Chloe had been on television quite a lot already, on the little afternoon programs that nobody paid any attention to, and that was how she had gotten this chance on a big national hook up. She started making videos of herself singing on YouTube, Instagram singing some throwback songs like 'Story Of Me'. Britney Spears, "I'm Not A Girl, Not Yet A Woman' and others.

While Cameron talked, Bridget got the wine she had been sipping, poured two more glasses, and Cameron revealed that his invitation had really been Maggie Donahue's idea. "She figured it meant a lot more to you than it would to her, so that's how I came to call you up."

"It was certainly nice of her."

"She's a real friend."

Bridget's mind did a double take. "You mean we're going to the studio?"

"That's it. It's going out from the NBC studio right here in Rochester, and we'll be able to see it and hear it."

"Don't we have to have tickets?"

"I got a couple."

"How?"

"It's taken care of."

"From Chloe?"

"Never mind. I got them."

At the look on Bridget's face, Cameron quickly crossed over, took her hand. “Now what's the use of acting like that? Yes, she called me up, and the tickets are there waiting for me. And she will call you up, of course she will. But why would she be calling you in the morning; like she did me? She knows you are never home then. And then another thing, she has probably been busy. I hear they run those singers ragged, rehearsing them, the day of a broadcast. Okay? She will call. Of course, she will.”

“Oh No. She won't call me.”

As Cameron did not know the full details of Chloe's departure from home, his optimism was understandable. He evidently regarded the point as of small importance, for he began to talk amiably, sipping his wine. He said it certainly went to show that the kid had stuff in her all right, to get a spot like that with a big show, and nobody giving her any help but herself. He said he knew how Bridget felt, but she was certainly going to regret it afterwards if she let a little thing like this stand in the way of being there at the kid's first big chance. Because it was a big chance all right. The singers with these big spots are paid well and sometimes, if they had the right stuff, they hit the big time overnight.

Bridget let a wan, pitying smile play over her face. If Chloe wanted this, it was certainly all right with her. Just the same, it certainly seemed funny, the difference between what Chloe might have been, and what she was. Cameron gave her a quizzical smile. “What do you mean by that?”

"Well, it was a pleasure to listen to her. She played all the classical composers. She associated with the right people. They were not my choice in friends, but they were respectable. Her mind was on higher things. And then, after Mr. Taylor, Jr. died, I cannot understand what got into her. She began going around with cheap, awful people. She met that boy. She let Greyson Hobbs poison her mind against me. And now, she is on the Graham Norton show. The Graham Norton show! She went from Beethoven to the Graham Norton show." Bridget sighed. "No, I don't want to go to the broadcast. It would make me too sad."

Truth to tell, Bridget had no such critical prejudice against Graham Norton as her remarks might indicate. If Chloe had called her up, she would have been only too glad to regard this as the first move and gone with delight to the broadcast. But when Chloe called Cameron, and did not call her, it hurt. Also, she hated the idea that Cameron might go without her. She insisted that he take Mrs. Donahue. Cameron stared at her, then mumbled miserably that he guessed he would not go.

Suddenly she asked what advantage there was in going to the studio. He could see it on television. Why not ride with her to Cobbs Hill and hear it there? He could have his dinner, a nice big steak if he wanted it, and then later she would have Mrs. Steele turn it on the television in the dining room and he could hear Chloe without going to a lot of useless trouble.

Bridget could see from the expression on his face he was considering it and at the mention of steak, poor Cameron perked up, and said he had often wanted to see her place at Cobbs Hill.

"Good, then its settled. Go home and change and I'll do the same and I'll pick you up at the usual spot."

"Ah, do you think you should be driving?"

"No, I'll have Jefferson drive us. As for you, call an Uber to get home and we will pick you up at the usual spot.

At Cobbs Hill, Bridget was indifferent to the impending event, and had little to say to the girls, the cooks, and the customers who kept telling her about Chloe's picture in the paper and asking her if she was not excited that her daughter was going to be on television. Cameron, however, was not so reticent. While his steak was on the fire, he held court in the bar, and told all about Chloe, and promised that if hot licks were what it took, the kid had them. When the hour drew near, and Mrs. Steele turned on the big flat screen he had an audience of a dozen around him, and extra chairs had to be brought into the dining room.

It was a strange entourage that gathered with two or three young girls, two married couples, and the rest men. Bridget had intended to pay no attention to the affair at all, but along toward 8:25 that evening, curiosity got the better of her. With Mrs. Steele she went into the dining room and there was a lively jumping up to give her a seat.

The first hint she got that Chloe's performance might not be quite the sentimental singing that Cameron had taken for granted came when Mr. Norton, early in the program, pretended to faint, and had to be revived, somewhat noisily, by members of his staff. The broadcast had started in the usual way, with crazy antics and acts, then Mr. Norton greeted his audience and then he introduced Chloe. When he asked if Chloe was her real name and she said it was, he wanted to know if her voice was unduly piercing. At this someone hit a gong and Chloe said, “No, but my scream is, as you'll find out if you made any more such remarks.” The studio audience laughed, and the group in the dining room laughed, especially Cameron, who slapped his thigh. “She put that one across all right.

Then Mr. Norton asked Chloe what she was going to sing, and she replied, “Habanera.”

“Tell us what it's about.”

“The famous Carmen melody is one of the most popular classic opera songs. It is also known as “L'amour est un oiseau rebelle” (“Love is a rebellious bird”). It expresses mad love that can take a beautiful turn or simply ruins everything.”

“Oh, now I get it.”

Bridget who found the comedy quite disgusting, paid no attention. Then the music began and then Chloe started to sing. Then a chill, wholly unexpected, shot up Bridget's backbone. The music was unfamiliar to her, and Chloe was singing in some foreign language that she did not understand. But the voice itself was so warm, rich, and vibrant that she began to fight off the effect it had on her. While she was trying to get readjusted to her surprise, Chloe came to a little spray of ripping notes and stopped. There was total silence and then the music began, and Chloe sang again, and another chill shot up Bridget's back.

Cold prickly waves of indignation sought to cover the effects of her daughter's voice as she fought hard against her feelings. Some sense of monstrous injustice oppressed her, It seemed unfair that this girl, instead of being chastened by adversity was up there, in front of the whole world, singing and without any help from her. All the emotional assumptions of the last few months were stood on their head, and Bridget felt mean and petty for reacting as she did, and yet she could not help it.

Soon Chloe's pitch changed, and it seemed impossible that anybody could dare such dizzy heights of sound, could even attempt such vocal gymnastics, without making some slip, some dreadful error that would land the whole thing in ruin. But Chloe made no slip. She went on and on, while the audience clapped and the same was happening all around her. At the end, when the last, incredibly high note floated over the finale of the orchestra, Cameron looked up at Bridget. "Jesus Christ, did you hear it? Did you hear it."

But Bridget did not wait for him to finish. She got up abruptly and walked down toward Mrs. Steele's flowers, waving back

Cameron and Mrs. Steele, who called after her, and started to follow. Pushing through the bushes, she reached the bluff overlooking the lake and stood there, lacing her fingers together, screwing her lips into a thin, relentless line. This, she needed nobody to tell her, was no descent from Beethoven to Graham Norton, no cheap venture into a simple love song. It was the coming true of all she had dreamed for Chloe, all she had believed in, worked for, dedicated her life to. The only difference was that the dream that had come true was a thousand times rosier than the dream she had dreamt.

As she stood there allowing herself to calm, she realized something else. By whatever means she would have to take, she knew she would have to get Chloe back.

The resolve was like a fishbone caught in her throat, especially since she was determined to have Chloe make the first move. She tried to put this aside, and drove to Chloe's one morning with every intention of stopping, ringing the bell, and going in. But as she approached the tall apartment building, she hurriedly told Jefferson to drive on without stopping, and leaned far back in the car to avoid being seen, as she had done that morning at Mrs. Witmore's. She felt hot faced and silly, and the next time she decided to visit Chloe she drove the car herself and went alone. Again, she went by without stopping.

Then she took to driving past Chloe's at night, and peeping, hoping to see her. Once she did see her, and quickly pulled in at the curb. Taking care not to slam the car door, she slipped out of the car. Chloe's apartment was on the second floor and like at home, she had stationed her piano in front of the large picture window. Chloe was at the piano playing. Then suddenly the miracle voice was everywhere, going through glass and masonry as though they were air. Bridget listened until the song was finished, then ran back to her car and drove off. But the broadcasts continued, and Bridget's feeling of longing increased, until it became intolerable.

Chloe did not appear again on the witty Graham Norton show. To Bridget's astonishment, her regular spot on the air was now Wednesdays, at three fifteen as part of the Hammond Hour. The show was on WXXI and being offered by the station to Mr. Hammond's pupils to participate. This was the same Joshua Hammond who had once closed the piano so summarily over Chloe's knuckles.

Bridget became anxious each day to be sequestered in her office or at home by three fifteen so that she could listen. It was not easy or always possible, but she managed to catch several of these broadcasts. She drank in Chloe's singing and everything the announcer said about her and soon Bridget had an idea. She would use Mr. Hammond to reach Chloe.

So presently she was in the same old anteroom, With the old vocalizing going on inside, and forced to wait impatiently. She reminded herself repeatedly that Mr. Hammond most likely had been informed she was estranged from her daughter and that would make her presence even less desirable.

Mr. Hammond finally received her, and she had herself under what she thought was perfect control. As he gave no sign of recognition, she told him her name. His reaction was to look at her sharply, then bow, but otherwise made no comment. She then made her little speech, which sounded stiff.

“Mr. Hammond, I've come on a matter that I shall have to ask you to keep confidential, and when I tell you the reason, I'm sure you'll be glad to do so. My daughter Chloe, I believe, is now taking lessons from you. Now for reasons best known to herself, she prefers to have nothing to do with me now, and farthest from my intentions is to intrude on her life or press her for explanations. Just the same, I have a duty toward her, regarding the expenses of her musical education. It was I, Mr. Hammond, who was responsible for her studying music in a serious way, and even though she elects to live apart from me, I still feel that her music is my responsibility, and in the future, without saying anything to her, without saying one word to her, Mr. Hammond, I would like you to send your bills to me, and not to her. I hope you don't find my request unreasonable.”

Mr. Hammond had seated himself, his expression showing that he was not interested in what was being said. He studied his fingernails attentively. Then he stood up. “I am sorry Madame, but that is a subject which I cannot discuss with you.”

“Well, I'm sorry too, Mr. Hammond, but I’m afraid you’ll

have to discuss it with me. Chloe is my daughter, and…"

"Madame, excuse me. I have an engagement."

With quick strides, he crossed to the door, and opened it letting Bridget know the meeting was over.

Bridget sat there and crossed her still shapely legs which said plainly she had no intention of going until she finished her business. He frowned, looked at his watch. "Yes, an important engagement. You excuse me? Please."

He went out, then, and Bridget was left alone. After a few minutes, the little fat woman came in, found a piece of music, sat down at the piano, and began to play it. She played it loud, and then played it again, and again, and each time she played it was louder and still louder. That went on perhaps a half hour, and Bridget still sat there.

Mr. Hammond came back and motioned the little fat woman out of the room. He strode up and down for a few minutes, frowning hard, then went over and closed the door. Then he sat down near Bridget, and touched her knee with a long, bony forefinger, "Why do you want this girl back? Tell me that?"

"Mr. Hammond, you mistake my motives.

"No mistake, no mistake at all. I talked with Chloe. I told her that somebody wants to pay for her lessons now." He paused and leaned over to look directly in Bridget's eyes. "She is not stupid."

"I know that. Do not you think I know that. It doesn't matter whether she knows or not, really…"

"But you said…"

"Never mind what I said."

Mr. Hammond took a deep breath. "Listen, I'll be honest and say I don't care who pays me. But paying for her lessons will not gain you privileges of free admittance to hear your daughter sing."

"I am not looking for any special treatment and really, I think you know that."

"No, I don't know that." He paused, "I'm sure you don't know how special, musically, your daughter is, but if you can sit back and listen, you will learn what I am trying to tell you."

Mr. Hammond again paused attempted a smile and then in a calm voice spoke. "There are different types of soprano voices and the types are based on range, vocal color or timbre, the weight of voice, and dexterity of the voice. Sopranos fall into five categories: coloratura soprano, soubrette, lyric soprano, spinto soprano, and dramatic soprano."

Bridget started to interrupt, but Mr. Hammond raised his hand and she sat back on her chair.

"A coloratura soprano sings pitches at the top of the human vocal range. Although all coloraturas have vocal agility, there are major differences in their range and the exact tonal features of their voices."

Mr. Hammond walked over to a table where there was a pitcher of water. He poured some in a glass, sipped and then continued.

"The music, the Coloratura is an elaborate melody with runs, trills, wide leaps, or similar virtuoso like material and those capable of singing the music are called coloratura. Now within the coloratura category, there are roles written specifically for lighter voices known as lyric coloraturas and others for larger voices known as dramatic coloraturas. Categories within a certain vocal range are determined by the size, weight, and color of the voice. But it is the Coloratura who has a high range and the ability to execute with elaborate ornamentation and embellishment, including running passages, staccati, and trills. The one who has the vocal ability to produce notes above high C (C6) are rare and most sought after. Someone like Cecilia Bartoli, the greatest Coloratura Mezzo Soprano of all times." Mr. Hammond pauses as he reminisce aloud. "I once heard her in person singing from Riccardo Broschi 'Son Qual Nave'. The things she can do with her voice are out of this world almost impossible for the human voice but not impossible for Bartoli."

Mr. Hammond seemed to be elsewhere as he spoke, dreamily, then returning to the present and seeing Bridget's puzzled expression he explained at a level he thought she might grasp. "Mariah Carey and Ariana Grande would probably fall into this category."

Mr. Hammond then started talking again and was telling her a story about snakes, which she had no idea why. Bridget translated what he shared as being Chloe was special, but she knew that all along. "So, you're saying Chloe likes to stand alone. I understand."

"No, no, listen carefully." He was irritated now. "There's no maternal instinct in the reptilian world of snakes. Snake mothers abandon their eggs soon after laying them, never to return. Well in your case, Chloe is the mother snake and will not tolerate any connection necessary to any human being."

Again Mr. Hammond paused and then stood up. "A coloratura soprano is much worse. So madame, my advice to you is to leave this girl alone."

As Bridget sat blinking; trying to get adjusted to the whole scenario, Mr. Hammond paced around the room, then became more animated. He sat down his eyes shining and tapped her knee. "Your Chloe is a coloratura inside, outside, all over. A singer like her comes once in a lifetime."

"Now I understand. I really do understand."

"I think your Chloe has known this most of her life."

"Why would you think that?"

"Let me see. It cost like hell to make a career as a Coloratura and want to be the best at it. First you must rub shoulders with rich people. If they are not rich, they're no good."

"So, she always associated with nice people."

"Nice is fine maybe, but I'm sure they were rich. All coloraturas have what I call 'the gimme' reflect. They always take, never give."

"You don't know her."

Mr. Hammond smiled. "Yes, I do. You spend plenty of money on this girl. What did she do for you?"

"She's a rare child. She can't be expected to…"

“So, she does nothing for you.”

Mr. Hammond tapped Bridget's knee again, grinned. “Let me see. Even as a little girl she sat haughtily erect in her chair, twiddling the ornament of her neck chain and addressing you not as mommy…oh no…she would have a more elaborate address for you.”

“Yes...”

Mr. Hammond dismissed her. “All coloraturas are crazy for rich people, all take no give, all act like a duchess, all are the same, every one of them. All borrow money and study voice or music of some type and never give back or expect to give back a red cent. They’re selfish and hurt the people they should love.” He moved closer. “Make no mistake this girl will gladly let you pay for her lessons, but her actions will only hurt you. If you love her, let her go so you can continue to love her.”

“But she’s my daughter.”

“That means nothing to her. Her mother is music. I spent two hours with her that afternoon when she returned to see me, and I find out she knows more music than I know. I really looked this girl over and I know what I see. I see what comes once in a lifetime, a great coloratura. I go to work. I give one lesson a day, charge her for one a week. I bring her along fast. She learns in six months what most singers learn in five years, seven years. Fast, fast, fast. I remember Malibran was artist at fifteen. I remember Melba, was an artist at sixteen. This girl, was born with a musical soul.”

Bridget, who had listened to this eulogy as one might listen to an opera came to herself with a start, and murmured, “She's a wonderful girl.”

“No, she’s a wonderful singer.”

As she looked at him, hurt and puzzled, Mr. Hammond stepped nearer, to make his meaning clear. “Chloe is a lousy girl and a lousy daughter. All she sees or feels is music.”

Bridget got up. “Well, we're all entitled to our opinion, but I would like it, if you don't mind, if you'd send your bills hereafter to me.”

“No, Madame.”

“Have you any particular objection?”

“For the last two weeks, ever since she appeared on that broadcast to get my attention, she told me her poor dumb mother will try to get her back, and she was right. Here you are offering to pay for singing lessons with an ulterior motive.”

“She…!”

“Yes! If you want Chloe back, you must face her yourself. I will not be the go between.”

Bridget left the studio feeling as though another daughter had died. It took everything she had to make it through the day, but at day’s end instead of taking Mr. Hammond’s advice, she reached a different decision.

She would get Chloe back through Nicholas Lombardi.

CHAPTER 28

Without taking any special effort to do so, Bridget had kept track of Nicholas these last three years, had even had a glimpse of him once or twice, on her way back and forth to Cobbs Hill. He was exactly where she had left him, in the ancestral house, trying to sell it.

The place was in shambles from lack of attention. Paint was peeling and the once well-manicured lawn, now was full of weeds. The two iron dogs at the entrance were now rusty and one of the porch pillars was decaying. Many times, she wanted to offer to help bring the mansion back to glory, but pride kept her from it. You do not make such an offer to someone you have not spoken to in years.

But now she had a plan. This morning she went to the bank, opened her safe deposit box, and made an accurate list of her bonds. She looked at her balances, both checking and savings and with a happy smile, she went on to the next step of her plan.

Bridget, still not comfortable with spending a lot of money on clothing, made a needed trip to Macys and purchased a new dress, and new shoes. The dress was simple, but it was dark blue, and fit her shape in a way that not only slenderized her but made her seem taller and shapelier. She then called an agent, and without giving her name, got the latest asking price on the Lombardi mansion. All this took two or three days.

Just how exact her plan was it would be hard to say. One thing she had learned as a businessperson was that achieving any goal in life is not just about setting clearly defined goals and wanting them badly enough. What it does require is consistent and persistent action. It requires throwing caution to the wind and enduring if necessary tremendous amounts of pain and struggle to reap the rewards desired. Perhaps she herself did not quite know how many steps she would have to take to reach the objective, which was Chloe, not Nicholas.

She finally felt ready and sent Nicholas an email saying she wanted help in picking a house in Pittsford, and would he be good enough to call her around eight that night. Then she sat back and waited for a response.

Thoughts of Nick brought back thoughts of Isabella, though she was now able to look back and not blame herself anymore. Whether she had been home or not, Izzy would have still gotten sick. That she could not have changed either way.

She had come a long way mentally in both the business and

her financial standing. Her next step would be much easier. She tried on her new outfit and liked the results and then carefully hung it up so that it would be ready for her adventure.

She did not have to wait long. That very evening Nick called, and she invited him to join her at the Charlotte branch of her restaurant. Its location and layout showed off her success best but more importantly, she felt comfortable and better able to relax.

When Nick arrived, a pang shot through her at the change in him. He wore slacks, but they were cheap and unpressed. His bald spot was bigger, it had grown from the size of a quarter to the size of a baseball. He was thin and his face lined giving him a hang dog look that was quite different from the jaunty air he had once had. As to how she looked, he made no comment, and indeed indulged in no personal talk of any kind.

She was a little nervous that evening and tried her best to hide it as well as not show her surprise in the change in him. She explained chattily her reason for the call.

"Nick, I simply have to move soon, to a place that is more centrally located, and I think that Cobbs Hill would be convenient for me."

Nick nodded and Bridget continued. "I was hoping, since you know the area, that you would be good enough take me around to see some possibilities."

"Sure, no problem."

"When could we start?"

"How does tomorrow morning around nine sound?"

"Perfect. I'll drive."

That morning he was ready and standing outside when she drove up. Since she had seen the condition of the property before, she was not shocked by it now. Nick climbed in and said he wanted her to see a place on Chadbourne Rd., quite decent, very reasonable. Would she care to drive over there? She said she would love to.

Bridget had done her homework and knew that Nick was sidelining with realtors to get a little money coming in so if all else failed, he would earn something for his time.

She was careful to take notes to show interest as Nick continued taking her from place to place. Shortly after noon and several houses later she announced that nothing quite suited her.

Nick quoted prices and stressed all the highlights of each property, trying to encourage her to decide, but Bridget repeatedly said she just had not seen what she wanted and around five they headed back to his home on Winton Road.

His patience thin, rather curtly, he said goodbye, and got out of the car. He walked up toward the house and stopped. He turned around and saw she was not leaving, so wondering if something was wrong, he stood there a moment, then walked back to the car.

Bridget rolled the window down and Nick leaned over to see she was pensive, sitting behind the wheel and staring at the house. He started to speak, but seeing her cut the motor, then take off her seat belt, he remained silent.

Bridget got out and allowed her eyes to sweep over the estate. “Beautiful, beautiful!”

Nick, always the salesperson, recovered quickly. “It could be, with a little money spent on it.”

“Yes, that's what I mean .... What do they want for it, Nicholas?”

For the first time that afternoon, Nicholas really looked at her. All the places he had taken her to had been quoted around five hundred thousand dollars and were in pristine condition. Evidently it had not occurred to him she could possibly be interested in this neglected property, but he regained his confidence, then said, “Year before last, this place was listed at around four hundred and fifty thousand and worth every cent of it. Last year, three hundred thousand. This year, two hundred thousand, subject to a lien of thirty-one hundred for unpaid taxes.”

She knew all the listings in this area were around four hundred and fifty thousand; at least those in excellent condition, but she knew from her information that Nick’s house could be had for one hundred and fifty thousand, including the tax lien, and she noted ironically that he was a little better salesperson than she had given him credit for. However, all she said was, “Beautiful, beautiful!” Then she turned toward Nick for approval. He nodded and led her up to the door where she stepped over the threshold and glanced around.

It had changed somewhat since her last visit, that night in the snowstorm. All the furniture, all the paintings, all the rugs, all the dust cloths, were gone, and in places the paper hung down in long strips. When she tiptoed inside, the floor was gritty beneath her shoes, but the boards were firm. Keeping up a sort of self-conscious commentary, he led her through the first floor, then up to the second. Presently they were in his own quarters, the same servants' apartment he had occupied before. The servants' furniture was gone, but in its place were a few oak pieces with leather seats, which she identified at once as having come from the cabin at Lake Ontario. She sat down, sighed, and said it certainly would feel good to rest for a few minutes.

He quickly offered tea, and when she accepted, he disappeared into the bedroom. Then he came; out and asked, "Or would you like something stronger?"

"I'd love something stronger."

"I'm out of ice and seltzer, but…"

"I prefer it straight."

"Since when?"

"Oh, I've changed a lot."

The bottle turned out to be Scotch, which to her taste was quite different from rye. As she gagged over the first sip he laughed and said, "Oh you haven't changed much. On liquor I'd say you were about the same."

Bridget grinned at him.

He relaxed and then put on his sales hat again, assuring her the structure was quite solid and the utilities worked fine. She replied,

"Well you don't have to sell me. I am already sold. And you do not have to sit over there yelling across the room at me. There's room over here, isn't there?"

Looking a little foolish, he crossed to the settee she was occupying. Bridget gave him her biggest smile. "You haven't even asked me how I am, yet."

"How are you?"

"Fine."

"Then that's that."

"How are you?"

"Fine."

"Then that's that."

Boldly she touched his hand and was surprised when he pulled it away. "You know, gentlemen in my situation now don't have a great deal of romance in their lives so I'm warning you that the slightest attention might turn me on."

"Oh, that's interesting." She said it as seductively as she could muster.

He looked away quickly and said, "I think we'll talk about the house.

Bridget smiled and switched tactics. "One thing bothers me about it."

"What's that?"

"If I should buy it, as I have half a mind to, where would you be? Would you stay or would I have it all to myself?"

"It would be all yours."

“I see.”

She reached over again to grab his hand and he moved his hand away before she caught it, looking annoyed but then, rather roughly, he put his arm around her. “Is that what you want?”

"Maybe."

But she had barely settled back when he took his arm away.

“I made a slight mistake about the price of this house. To you, it is one hundred and fifty thousand. That will square up a little debt I owe you, of five hundred and twenty dollars, that's been bothering me for quite some time.”

“You owe me a debt?”

“If you try, I think you can recall it.”

He looked like his old self as she said, “Forget it!”

Nick laughed and took her in his arms. He touched the zipper on the front of her dress, and it stayed there for some time as one half of him, said let the zipper alone, while the other half told him it would be ever so pleasant to give it a little pull. Then Bridget felt her dress loosen, as the zipper began to slide. Nick picked her up and she did not resist even when he dropped her on the old iron bed. Then she felt herself, with suitable roughness, being dumped down on the same iron bed, with the same scratchy blankets, she had kicked the beach bag off, years before, at Lake Ontario.

“Damn it, your legs are still immoral.”

“You think they're bowed?”

“Stop waving them around.”

“I asked you a question.”

“No.”

Those were the last words spoken for some time as the familiarities of the past rushed in. She recalled how they spent that first weekend together and how close they had grown in a short period of time. Bridget realized she wanted this man and before she knew it the words came out of her mouth. “Nicholas, I couldn't live here without you. I just couldn't, that's all.”

Nicholas lay still for a long time. Then, in a queer shaky voice he said, “I always said you'd make some guy a fine wife if you didn't live in Irondequoit.”

Growing even bolder now she asked, “Are you asking me to marry you?”

“If you move to Cobbs Hill, yes.”

"You mean if I buy this house.”

“No, it's about three times as much house as you need, and I don't insist on it. But I will not live in Irondequoit.”

“Then all right!”

She snuggled up to him, tried to be impish, but while he put his arm around her, he seemed somber, and he did not look at her. Presently it occurred to her that he might be hungry, and she asked if he would like to ride to Irondequoit with her and have dinner. Nick considered it a moment, then laughed. “You'd better go alone, and I'll open myself another can of beans. My clothes, now, are not quite suitable to dining out. Unless, of course, you want me to put on a dinner coat. That mockery of elegance happens to be all I have left."

"We never had that New Year's party."

"Oh, didn't we?"

Ignoring him she added, "And we don't have to go to Irondequoit."

With eyes closed, Bridget swallowed hard. "Nick, what about us?"

He did not speak right away but when he did it was what she wanted to hear. "I think we are right back where we started."

"What does that mean?"

"I love you Bridget and I don't want to let you go."

Giving it some thought she said, I love you in a dinner coat, Nicholas. If you will put one on, and then drive over with me while I put on my mockery of elegance, we can step out. We can celebrate our engagement. That is, if we really are engaged."

"All right, let's do it."

She friskily smacked him on his lean rump to hustle him out of bed, before jumping out after him.

She was quite charming in such moments, when she took absurd liberties with him, and for one flash his face lit up, and he kissed her before they started to dress. Once clothed they hurried out the house and she drove them to her home and once the car was parked and they had gone inside, Nick was somber again. While she was dressing, he wandered restlessly about, and then put his head in her bedroom and asked if he could use her laptop to send an email. “I'd like Mother to know.”

Surprised, but excited because this meant he was invested in her she asked, “Would you rather talk to her?”

“Sure. I didn’t want to impose.”

“Well, my goodness, do call her. And you can tell her it is all settled about the house, at one hundred and fifty thousand, without any foolish deductions of five hundred and twenty dollars, or whatever it was. If that is what has been worrying her, tell her not to worry anymore.”

“I'd certainly love to.”

He went to the den, and she went on with her dressing. The blue evening dress was long since outmoded, but she had another one, a black one, that she liked very well, and she had just laid it out when he appeared at the door. “She wants to speak to you.”

'“Who?”'

“Mother.”

Despite success, money, and long experience at dealing with people, she felt a chill sweep through her body as she hastily slipped on a robe before taking the cell, to talk to this woman she had never met. But when she picked up the receiver and uttered a quivery hello, the cultured voice that spoke to her was friendship itself. “Mrs. Bitmore?”

“Yes, Mrs. Lombardi.”

“Or perhaps you'd like me to call you Bridget?”

“I'd like that, Mrs. Lombardi.”

“I just wanted to say that Nicholas has told me about your plan to be married. I have never met you, but from all I have heard, from so many, many people, I must approve. I've waited so long for Nicholas to make this move and it makes me happy."

"Well, that's terribly nice of you, Mrs. Lombardi. Did Nicholas tell you about the house?"

"He did, and I do want you to be happy there, and I'm sure you will. Nicholas is so attached to it, and he tells me you like it too and that's a big step toward bliss isn't it?"

"I would certainly think so. And I do hope that some time you'll pay us a visit there."

"I'll be delighted." Then she paused and asked, "And how is darling Chloe?"

"She's fine. She's singing, you know."

"My dear, I heard her, and I was astonished. Not really of course, because I always felt that Chloe had big things in her. But even allowing for all that, she quite bowled me over. You have a very gifted daughter, Bridget."

"I'm certainly glad you think so, Mrs. Lombardi."

"You'll remember me to her?"

"I certainly will, Mrs. Lombardi."

She hung up flushed, beaming, sure she had done very well, but Nicholas's face had such an odd look that she asked, "What's the matter?"

"Where is Chloe?"

Bridget prepared and delivered her story smoothly. "She took an apartment by herself, a few months ago. It bothered her to have all the neighbors listening while she vocalized.

“That must have been hard on you.”

“It was terrible.”

Bridget changed the subject and rushed them out the door thinking, starting out with one more lie was not all that bad.

CHAPTER 29

From that evening things moved quickly, and Bridget did not question or regret the turn of events from her original plan. Within a week, the Lombardi mansion looked as though it had been hit by bombs. The main idea of the alterations, which were under the supervision of Nicholas, was to restore what had been a large but pleasant house to what it had been before it was transformed into a small but hideous mansion. To that end the porticoes were torn off, the iron dogs removed, the brush cleared up, so the original grove of live oaks was left as it had been, without brush overtaking them.

What remained, after all this hacking, was so much reduced in size that Bridget suddenly began to feel some sense of identity with it. When the place as it would be, began to emerge from the scaffolding, when the yellow paint had been scraped off and replaced with a soft whitewash, when green shutters were in place, when a small, friendly entrance had taken the place of the former Monticello effect, she began to fall in love with it, and could hardly wait until it was finished. Her delight increased when Nicholas stated the exterior sufficiently completed and he was about to proceed with the interior, and its furnishings.

Nick seemed bent on pleasing Bridget, and it constantly surprised her, the ways he paid attention to even her smallest likes and dislikes; especially when it came to the house.

About all she was able to tell him was that she liked light and airy; but with this single bone as a clue, he reconstructed her whole taste with surprising expertness. He did away with paper, and had the walls done in delicate kalsomine paint. The rugs he bought in solid colors, rather light, so the house took on a more informal look. For the upholstered furniture he chose bright, coverings. It was all coming together nicely.

He asked permission to hang some of the paintings of his ancestors, as well as a few other small pictures that had been stored for him by friends. However, he did not give undue prominence to these things. In what was no longer an awful room became a big living room, he found place for a collection of Bridget Bitmore, Inc. There was her first menu, her first announcements, a photograph of the Irondequoit restaurant, a snapshot of Bridget in a uniform, other things that she did not even know he had saved all enlarged several times, all effectively framed, all hung together, to form a little exhibit.

At first, she had been self-conscious about them, and was

afraid he had hung them there just to please her. But when she said something to this effect, he put down his hammer and wire, looked at her a moment or two, then gave her a compassionate little pat. “Sit down a minute and I will give you lesson one in interior decorating.”

“I love lessons in decorating.”

“Do you know the best room I was ever in?”

“No, I don't.”

“It's that den of yours, or Cameron's rather, over in Irondequoit. Everything in that room meant something to that guy. Those banquets, those foolish looking blueprints of houses that will never be built, are a part of him. They do things to you. That is why the room is good. And do you know the worst room I was ever in?”

“Go on, I'm learning.”

“It's that living room of yours, right in the same house. Not one thing in it had ever meant anything to you, or him, or anybody until the piano came in, but that was recent. It was just a room.”

Nick seemed far away. “Furnishing a house has to have meaning and the meaning doesn’t have to be rich, like choices in life must be. It does not have to be furnished with Picasso paintings, or Sheraton suites, or Oriental rugs, or Chinese pottery. But it does have to be furnished with things that mean something to you. If they are just phonies, bought in a hurry to fill up, it will look like that living room, or the way this lawn looked when my father got through showing how much money he had. Let's have this place the way we want it. If you do not like the Bitmore display, I do."

"I love it."

"Then it stays."

From then on, Bridget began to feel proud of the house and happy about it, and particularly relished the last hectic week, when hammers, saws, phone dings, and vacuum cleaners mingled their separate songs into one lovely cacophony of preparation. She moved Francine over, with a room of her own, and Jefferson, with a room and a private bath. She engaged, at Nicholas's request, Kurt and Frieda, the couple who had worked for Mrs. Lombardi. Then came the day that they now both looked forward to as they drove downtown, dressed in their finest and got married. It had been decided that it would be a private affair for just the two of them and that was exactly how they did it.

For a week after this quiet courthouse ceremony, she was almost frantic. She had addressed Chloe's announcement herself, and the papers were full of the nuptials, with pictures of herself and lengthy accounts of her career, and pictures of Nicholas and just as lengthy accounts of his career. They had expected this would happen and it was why they opted for the simplicity of the courthouse marriage. Yet, she had expected something to come from Chloe, but there was no call from her, no visit, no text, no email.

Friends called, mostly of Nicholas', who treated her very pleasantly, and seemed offended when she had to excuse herself, in the afternoon to go to work. Cameron called, with all wishes for her happiness, and sincere praise for Nicholas, whom he described as a 'thoroughbred'. She was surprised to learn that he was living with his Mom and Mr. Bitmore.

When she asked about the new arrangements, Cameron said that Mrs. Donahue's husband was offered a big job in Texas, and she joined him there.

Bridget had always supposed Mrs. Donahue a widow, and so apparently had Cameron. Yet the call that Bridget hoped for did not come. Nicholas, aware by now that a situation of some sort existed regarding Chloe, rather pointedly did not notice her mood, or make any inquiries about it.

And then one night at Cobbs Hill, Mrs. Steele appeared around eight in a bright red evening dress, and almost peremptorily told Bridget to close the place, as she herself was invited out. Bridget was annoyed, and her temper did not improve when Archie took off his regimentals at nine sharp and left within a minute or two. She was in a gloomy irritable humor going home, and several times reprimanded Jefferson for driving too fast. Until she was at the door of her new house, she did not notice that a great many cars seemed to be parked out front, and even then, they made no impression on her. Jefferson, instead of opening for her, rang the bell twice, then rang it twice again. She was opening her mouth to say something peevish about people who forget their keys, when lights went up all over the first floor, and the door, as though of its own accord, swung slowly open.

From somewhere within, a voice, the only voice in the world to Bridget, began to sing. Chloe was singing the Bridal Chorus from Lohengrin. She could not breathe as she stood there, holding her chest, and remembering all there was to Chloe. Her dear sweet daughter, singing 'Here Comes the Bride' had once told her that neither song was composed to be performed at a wedding. Rather, German composer Felix Mendelssohn wrote the Wedding March for a 1842 production of Shakespeare's A Midsummer Night's Dream, and 'Here Comes the Bride' was the Bridal Chorus from Richard Wagner's 1850 opera Lohengrin. Bridget prided herself in remembering as she stood there, going from shock to total bliss.

'Here comes the bride' sang Chloe. Bridget floated in, seeing faces, flowers, dinner coats, paper hats, hearing laughter, applause, greetings, as things in a dream. When Chloe, still singing, came over, took her in her arms, and kissed her, it was almost more than she could stand, and she stumbled hurriedly, and let Nicholas take her upstairs on the pretext that she must put on a suitable dress for the occasion.

A few years before, Bridget would have been incapable of presiding over such a party, her commonplaceness, her upbringing, her sense of inferiority in the presence of society people would have combined to make her acutely uncomfortable with no forewarning.

Tonight, however, she was a completely charming hostess and

guest of honor, rolled into one. In a crimson evening dress, she was everywhere, seeing that people had what they wanted, seeing that Archie, who presided in the kitchen, and Kurt, Frieda, and Francine, assisted by Celine and Astrid, from the restaurants, kept things going smoothly.

Most of the guests were Pittsford people, friends of Chloe's and Nicholas's, but her waitress training, plus her years as Bridget Bitmore, Inc., stood her in good stead now. She had acquired a memory like a filing cabinet and had everybody's name as soon as she heard it, causing even Nicholas to look at her with sincere admiration. But she was pleased that he had asked such few friends as she had, Mrs. Steele, and Ida, and particularly Cameron, who looked unusually handsome in his dinner coat, and helped with the drinks. Mr. Hammond was there, and he played while Chloe sang. It was perfect.

Bridget wanted to cry when people began to leave, and then discovered that the evening had hardly begun. The best part came when she, and Chloe, and Nicholas sat around in the small library, across from the big living room, and decided that Chloe should spend the night so that they could catch up with each other.

Nicholas, spiced up the conversation when he asked, “Well goddam it, how did you get to be a singer? When I discovered you, practically pulled you out of the gutter, you were a pianist, or supposed to be. Then I no sooner turn my back than you turn into a fantastic operatic singer.”

“Well, goddam it, it was an accident.” Chloe responded in

kind.

“Then report.”

“I was at the Philharmonic.”

“Yes, I've been there.”

“Listening to a concert. And they played the Schubert Unfinished. And afterwards I was walking across the park, to my car, and I was humming it. And ahead of me I could see him walking along.”

“Who?”

“Hammond.”

“Oh yes, the Neapolitan Stokowski.”

“So, I had plenty of reason for not walking to meet the honorable signer, because I had played for him once, and he wasn't at all appreciative. So, I slowed down, to let him get ahead. But then he stopped, and turned around, and looked, and then he came over to me, and said, 'Was that you who was singing?'

“Well; I must explain that I was not so proud of my singing just about that time. I used to sing Taylor, Jr.'s songs for him, whenever he wrote one, but he used to kid me about it, because I sang full chest, and sounded exactly like a man. He called me the Irondequoit Baritone. Well, that was Hosea, but I did not know why I had to take any kidding off Hammond, so I told him it did not concern him whether I was singing or not, but he grabbed me by the arm, and said it concerned him very much. Then he took a card from his pocket, and a pen, and ran under a light, and wrote his address on it, and handed it to me, and told me to be there the next day at four o'clock, that it was important. So that night I had it out with myself. I knew, when he handed me the card, that he had no recollection he had ever seen me before, so there was no question of kidding. But did I want to unlock that door again or not?"

"What door?"

Nicholas was puzzled, but Bridget knew which door, even before Chloe went on, "Of music. I had driven a knife through its heart, and locked it up, and thrown the key away, and now here was Hammond, telling me to come down and see him tomorrow, at four o'clock. And do you know why I went?"

Chloe was dead serious now and looking at them both as though to make sure they got things straight. "It was because once he had told me the truth. I had hated him for it, the way he had closed the piano in front of me without saying a word, but it was his way of telling me, and it was the truth. So, I thought maybe he was telling me the truth now. So, I went.

And for weeks he worked on me, to get me to sing like a woman, and then it began to come the right way, and I could hear what he had heard that night out there in the park. And then he began to tell me how important it was that I become a musician. I had the voice, he said, if I could master music. And he gave me the names of this one and that one, who could teach me theory, and sight reading, and piano, and I don't know what all."

"Oh yeah?"

"Yeah, and did I get my revenge, for that day when he closed the piano on me. I asked him if there was a little sight reading, he wanted done, and he handed me the 'Die Entführung aus dem Serail'. Seeing the puzzled looks, Chloe explained why this was important.

"By far the lowest and most impossibly galloping romp for a basso in all of opera, Mozart wrote an aria 'Die Entführung aus dem Serail' as difficult as it is for a friend of his, Ludwig Fischer, who had an extremely expansive basso profondo range. The aria occurs near the beginning of Act 3, when Osmin captures Belmonte and Pedrillo, and intends to have them and their lady lovers tortured to death. It goes down to a low D, two octaves below middle C. The very next note, after holding this low D for several measures, is an octave jump."

"The opera is so popular that it has been translated into Italian and Hungarian, among other languages, and the most unbelievable performance of the aria on record belongs to the one and only Ezio Pinza, in Italian, who never learned to read music, but memorized his roles by ear."

Chloe smiling now said, "Well I went through that like a hot knife through butter, and he began to get excited. Then I asked him if he had a job of arranging, he wanted done. He looked puzzled so I told him about Hosea and reminded him we had met at his studio before. He looked at me, looked at the piano and then at the choice of music and sneered and, in that instant I knew, he remembered me."

"All was quiet, and I thought he was going to send me away,

but instead he began what I can only say was a physical examination. He picked up my hands and looked them over and then pinched my nose. He even had a light that he shined in my mouth. But what really confused me was when he began prodding my breast."

Nicholas frowned incredulously and Chloe laughed.

"Yes! Believe it or not, he even dug his fingers into the Dairy." Chloe grabbed her breast for effect. "I didn't exactly know what to think or do." Chloe at this point made a funny face by staring with a weird smile that begin by pressing her lips tightly together and then pressing out the lower lip and then she crossed her eyes.

Nicholas started to laugh. In spite of herself, so did Bridget. Chloe went on, "But it turned out he wasn't interested in love. He was interested in getting the music out. He said it enriched the tone."

"The what?"

Nicholas was out of control as he started laughing harder and coughing at the same time. Just watching him all three of them were howling with laughter, howling at Chloe's Dairy as they had howled at Mrs. Donahue's bosom, that first night, many years before.

Bridget looked around her and told herself that sometimes the best thing you can do is not think or wonder, not imagine and not obsess. Just breathe and have faith that everything will work out for the best and that is what she did. When she went to bed her stomach hurt from laughter, but her heart ached from happiness.

Smiling as she readied for bed, she felt one thing was missing. When she had entered the house, Chloe had embraced her as she had when she was a little girl, only she had not hugged her back. Now she finished getting herself ready for bed and then tiptoed into the room she had hoped Chloe would occupy. She knelt beside the bed as she had knelt so many times in Irondequoit, took the lovely creature in her arms and kissed her. Chloe stirred as Bridget carefully left the room.

Bridget was happy and Nicholas could tell by the way she seemed to dance around the room, as if walking on air. When she finally came to bed, she leaned over him and whispered, "Thank you. Thank you for the best evening of my life."

CHAPTER 30

Bridget now entered days of untold joy, filled with the glory of life and the opera. She entered, the house among the oaks, that her daughter Chloe now shared with them and with her presence came the retinue of admirers, teachers, coaches, agents, and famous people who made life so exciting.

It was the first time Bridget experienced all the facets of theatres, opera houses, broadcasting studios, and other such places, and learned something of the heartbreak they can hold and though it could be fascinating and exciting, it could also be nightmarish.

There was, for example, the time Chloe sang in a local performance of Traviata, given at the Philharmonic under the direction of Mr. Hammond. She had just had the delightful sensation of beholding Chloe alone onstage for at least ten minutes, and at the intermission went out into the lobby. To her furious surprise, a voice behind her, a man's voice, began, "So that is La Bitmore, television's gift to the lyric muse. Why, the girl's simply nauseating. She gargles it over her tonsils in that horrible New York way, she is off pitch half the time, and as for acting did you notice her routine, after Alfredo went off? She had no routine. She planted one heel on that dime, locked both hands in front of her, and just stood there."

While Bridget's temples throbbed with helpless rage, the voice moved off somewhere, and another person obviously in hearing distance of the first was saying, "Well, I hope you all paid close attention to the critique of operatic acting, by one who knows nothing about it. Somebody ought to tell that man that the whole test of operatic acting is how few motions they make, to put across what they are trying to deliver. Take for instance John Charles Thomas and Kirsten Flagstad both highly regarded and champions of less movement.

By now the woman had quite an audience as she continued showing her knowledge of the opera. "Oh yes, and we can't forget Scotti. Antonio Scotti was an Italian baritone, a principal artist of the New York Metropolitan Opera for more than 33 seasons, but also sang with great success at London's Royal Opera House, Covent Garden, and Milan's La Scala." She paused and smiled knowingly. "I guess he was nauseating but he was the greatest of them all. Do you know how many gestures he made when he sang the Pagliacci Prologue? One, just one."

Heads were nodding in agreement and just as they started to walk away, she continued. "This woman, Chloe, if I ever saw one right out of that class, she's it." Joyously Bridget stared at the faces around her that showed they agreed with this wonderful lady. "So, she locked her hands in front of her, did she? Listen, when she folded one sweet little hand into the other sweet little hand and tilted that head at a forty-five-degree angle and began to sing out about the delicious agony of love I felt chills go through my body. Take it from me, this one has the talent of the greats and will be famous." She let out a little laugh, "Since fools like that man judge success by money, she'll have more than enough to shut his face."

Then Bridget wanted to run after the first man, and stick out her tongue at him, and laugh.

Bridget tried not to let anything interfere with their happiness. Since the night Chloe came home, Bridget had little time for Nicholas as she set out each morning to check on her businesses and each evening, she spent either at the opera or going with Chloe to her lessons. She was determined to spend every moment she could with her daughter. Each night she would fall into bed exhausted and several evenings she felt Nick get up and leave the room.

The house still required furnishings, but Bridget was no longer interested and let Nick pick out the furniture himself as she did not have the time. To her great relief, he was okay with that. From then on, he was host to the numerous guests, head of the house, escort to Bridget when she went to hear Chloe sing, but he was not her husband. She felt better about it when she noted that much of his former gaiety had returned.

And there were certain disturbing aspects of life with Chloe, as for example the row with Mr. Levinson, her agent. Mr. Levinson had signed Chloe to a commercial contract singing the background music for some breakfast food. As Chloe explained it, there are two ways singers received payment: session fees plus residuals under the traditional commercials' contracts or through new upfront packages. It would be an off-camera production, so she was to receive $535.40 and additional 50% of that rate, which allows unlimited multi tracking of same vocal parts.

As Bridget was not seeing the problem, Chloe explained that she was sewed into the contract for a year, meaning that during this period she could do no other commercials for anybody else. Bridget calmed Chloe down by telling her that was a fabulous stipend for so little work, and Chloe agreed with her until Nicholas came home one day with John H. Bryan Jr., the president and CEO of Sara Lee Corp. and its predecessor firm, Consolidated Foods. John Bryan had grown Sara Lee into a consumer conglomerate with diverse brands in food and apparel.

Mr. Bryan had decided to spend part of his year in Pittsford and Nick was in high spirits, for they had been best friends in college and had not seen each other in some time. The two men laughed over old times, but when the conversation turned to what each had been up to lately, Nick quickly sidestepped and introduced John to Chloe.

Mr. Bryan met Chloe and Mr. Bryan heard Chloe sing. And Mr. Bryan experienced a slight lapse of the senses, apparently, for he offered her $2,500 a week, a two-year contract, and a guarantee of being mentioned or to be on camera. This of course was on the basis that she would only sing on national commercials for the Sara Lee brand.

Chloe looked at Bridget with a look of disgust because she had not fought against the contract offer before and now was unable to accept, and for some days after that her profanity, her studied, cruel insults to Mr. Levinson, her raving at all hours of the day and night, her monomania on this one subject, were more than even Bridget could put up with amiably.

But while Bridget was trying to think what to do, Patrick Levinson revealed an unexpected ability to deal with such situations himself. He bided his time, waited until a Sunday afternoon, when drinks were being served on the lawn out back, and Chloe chose to bring up the subject again, in front of Bridget, Nicholas, John Bryan, and Joshua Hammond.

Patrick Levinson was among the most powerful people in the entertainment industry. He was responsible for representing and negotiating deals for his clients, so that they got the best jobs available. Of course, popularity was not their forte as being a lawyer in this business was a cutthroat, dirty business. So being disliked or blamed rolled off his back.

He listened with half closed eyes. Then he said, “Okay, now take it back. Take back all the crazy, uncapable thoughts about me that you are having. And, while you are at it, get ready to apologize and say you are sorry.”

“I? Apologize? To you?”

“Yes, I got a better offer for you.”

“What offer?”

Patrick let the suspense build. He slowly gazed at each person in the before finally allowing his eyes to fall on Chloe. He saw exactly what he hoped. Her anger apparent on the surface, her body reacting in stiffness and so he decided to hold back a little longer.

“Let’s have a little fun, shall we.” Chloe looked angry enough to shoot him. He sneered and said, “The performing has a large symphony-sized orchestra, a chorus, children's choir, and many supporting and leading solo singers.”

He paused staring directly at Chloe. “Nothing? You’ve got nothing?”

“Okay, the company employs numerous free-lance dancers, actors, musicians and other performers throughout the season.”

Again, he paused. This time he noticed a slight change in Bridget’s face which was more noticeable on Chloe’s. So, he quickly said, “The roster of singers include both International and American artists and while many singers appear periodically as guests with the company, others maintain a close long-standing association…"

"The Met; you got me in the Metropolitan Opera house?" Chloe was choking on the words as they came out of her mouth. "That can't be it!"

"Well, if you like, I'll cancel the performance."

Never more animated, Chloe seemed unable to stand still as she hugged herself and danced around the room.

"Take it easy. Take it easy. I've told Hammond and he says you have a lot of work to do…a lot of work."

"I don't care. I will do it. I'll do whatever it takes." Then she did something so out of character for Chloe. She said thank you and meant it.

Chloe could not breathe. The Metropolitan Opera, or the Met was the American opera company in New York City, and it was in Lincoln Center. It was the venue for showcasing artistic greatness and a proving ground for emerging artists. Was she ready for this?

"Well, Chloe, I have to get the ball rolling."

"That's crude language when referring to the Met. There is no ball to roll as I accept."

"Great, but there is more. I have to work out the terms…if you know what I mean."

Mr. Levinson knew how hard it was for Chloe to say anything at all about terms, for the Metropolitan Opera was a singer's paradise. They had fault many a fight over what was expected of her and how much money she would earn. Sometimes it even embarrassed him to present her decision.

“I don’t care. I accept.”

He had one more bomb to drop. He squinted as though he couldn’t see her and said, “Not so fast. They will take you or they will take Lucas and it is my choice. I handle you both, and Lucas does not cuss me out. She's nice.”

Chloe’s head swiveled so fast they heard it snap. “A contralto's no draw.”

“They asked me to supply my best client and I said I will. The Contralto gets it if you don't apologize.”

There was silence. “I said thank you.”

“Thank you is not an apology.”

Chloe pressed her lips together tightly, then thoughtfully allowed her lower teeth to cover her upper lip. She remained silent as her face went through several contortions until finally, she said, “Okay, Levy. I apologize.”

Mr. Levinson looked up, walked over to Chloe, and slapped her hard on the cheek. Nicholas and Mr. Bryan jumped up, but Mr. Levinson paid no attention. With his soft, pendulous lower lip hanging down, he spoke softly to Chloe, “What do you say now?”

Chloe's face contorted as she fault hard to not raise her hand to her burning cheek. Her eyes snapped as she stared at Mr. Levinson and at that moment Bridget was afraid for Mr. Levinson. He had likened her to someone she felt was beneath her and that meant she had to defend herself. On more than one occasion she had risen to hostility and took out her anger on everyone around her.

As she stared at her daughter, she saw her face soften and after another dreadful pause, Chloe said, "Okay."

"Then okay. And let me stress it now, Bitmore. Don't start nothing with Pat Levinson." Before sitting down, Mr. Levinson turned to Mr. Bryan who had been listening patiently.

"Well, Mr. Bryan."

He knew what to say but stared innocently at Levinson. Earlier John and Pat had discussed the matter thoroughly and though Pat Levinson had an odd way of showing it, he was looking out for Chloe. John's offer was sincere and a good one, but he knew it was no match to Pat's and had thoroughly agreed he did not want to step in the way of her advancing her career. Now he smiled and said, "Consider the offer withdrawn."

Chloe mouthed, "Thank you" at John Bryan and then hearing Pat speak, turned toward him.

"Listen my client, Jennifer Lucas, is available. She's a great Contralto, really." He stared in Chloe's direction.

"No, that's all right. I'm fine with our current commercial for now."

Pat resumed his seat. Nicholas and John resumed their seats, but Mr. Hammond poured himself another glass of the red wine. He was not sure what he should say or do so decided not to utter a word.

CHAPTER 31

For the rest of the summer Bridget spent as much time as possible with Chloe who began early preparing for her appearance at the Met. There were innumerable trips to buy clothes, apparently a coloratura could not merely buy a dress, and let it go at that. She tried to explain to Bridget that she had to wear something with visual interest, but not so much that it detracted from her performance. Bridget would nod and pick out something and Chloe would say, with dismay. “If I choose to wear something sparkly, it has to be sparkly on one area of the clothing. I do not want sparkly. I want it to shimmer.”

From then on, she just gave her opinion and let Chloe pick out the clothes. One day they went to buy pantyhose and Bridget felt capable of handling that on her own, so she left Chloe searching for a pair of jeans. When she returned, they left the store and headed toward home.

They were seated in the kitchen and Chloe was all up in her head when Bridget, wanting to have a conversation said, "So, what does your schedule look like today?"

Chloe was thoughtful and then said, "Well, it was to practice first and then maybe go to the lake for a bit, but that's out."

"Why?"

"Well, mother, I have to get a pair of pantyhose is why."

Bridget stared, puzzled by this, but she was not waiting long. Chloe's face drew up into an awful sneer. "The pantyhose you got have a sheen. You do not wear pantyhose with a sheen. The stage lights will reflect off them and make your legs appear bigger than they are." Chloe took a deep breath as she stared at her mother as if she were a child. "I've told you repeatedly that all sorts of things have to be considered. Such as whether the material takes up light; from the spots or reflects it. It cannot give off light and it cannot absorb it. Why can't you get that through your thick head!" With that she stumped out of the kitchen.

Bridget was more embarrassed than angry as she gave it one more try. They had exhausted every store trying to find that one dress above all dresses, so Bridget decided that it was time to go to a pro. One afternoon she went to see a dressmaker she knew in Irondequoit who lived off Portland Avenue. This woman was known for not only making the outfit but offering the right suggestions for the style and design. Mary knew Chloe and had made a few choice outfits for her so she could take care of it. "If she needs any adjustments, just have her stop by later."

So as the days passed and Chloe grew more frustrated, Bridget kept reminding herself it would soon settle down. The day she got the call, she went over and picked up the dress. When Mary brought it out of the back room, Bridget knew this was the one. The gown looked professional and comfortable to sing in. She could tell that it allowed for ease of movement.

Mary turned on a side lamp that shown on the fabric and it looked good under lights. "I made sure she had room to breathe. I also built in an inner corset, added extra padding and elastic in the places I think will flatter Chloe's figure."

"It's perfect. I think it's perfect."

"Let's hope Chloe will feel the same. I like for people to come to me and leave with a smile and a gown!"

It was exquisite and when she showed it to Chloe, Chloe had a hard time keeping from jumping up and down with joy. The dress was bodice fitted with her arms and upper chest bare. The black upper dress was a deep grayish black that worked well in the light and it was mini length in front that slowly went down to floor length in the back. The highlight of the dress that made it beyond special was the flouncy petticoat design of the layers and layers of pink net, forcing it to move away from the body. Chloe tried it on a dozen times, unable to make up her mind whether it was right, or she was in love with it. In the end, she decided it was perfect and Bridget let out a sigh of relief.

Bridget knew this was only part of the preparations that Chloe was dealing with beyond practicing. There was the question of the publicity, and how it should be handled. Here again, it seemed out of the question merely to call up the editors, tell them a local girl was going to appear, and leave the rest to their judgment. Chloe did a great deal of telephoning about the 'releases,' as she called them, and then when the first item about her came out, she went into a rage.

At the end of an afternoon in which she tried vainly to locate Mr. Levinson, that gentleman arrived in person, and Chloe marched around in a perfect lather, "You've got to stop it, Levy, you've got to kill this society girl stuff right now! And the Pittsford stuff! What do they want to do, kill my draw? And get me taunted off the stage. We are not dealing with society people in this town. And how many Pittsford people go to concerts, or Irondequoit people, just to see a local girl? It won't be enough."

Chloe took a breath as she pranced around the room. "Saying I studied right here in Irondequoit will kill me. The Metropolitan Opera House has a massive seating capacity of 3800. It is the largest repertory opera house in the world. If you didn't know that you should have asked me or Mr. Hammond."

Chloe remained indignant feeling he was trying to make her into a little kid from upstate New York; even worst, born and raised in Irondequoit. That was bad, but worse was saying she had all her training there and had never been to Europe or any other exotic place for training. At one point Bridget started to go to Chloe and console her, but Mr. Levinson stopped her.

And then she witnessed it. She witness the change as different as a caterpillar is from a butterfly. Chloe paused, turned and with the sun shining through the window to aid in the transformation, Chloe glowed. Mr. Levinson you are right. Let's play it up that way. Let me be the shining light.

Bridget had no idea what was happening. She was only glad the battle had ended.

CHAPTER 32

Bridget had always prided herself in knowing her daughter better than anyone, but now she was a stranger. She knew Chloe's emotions were literally light switches that flopped on, off, on, off, going from high on life to Darth Vader in a matter of seconds if what she heard was not what she desired. Now, she did not care to know this stranger who gave her the smallest measurable unit of human connection, but for Bridget it still contained powerful emotional nutrients that alleviated the symptoms of feeling alone. So now she stood back with disregard knowing that anything she did or said would not phase Chloe one way or the other.

Bridget, despite her worship of Chloe, felt indignant that she should now claim Irondequoit as her own, after all the mean things she had said about it. That sense of not caring only lasted a day as she abandoned herself to preparing for the concert.

She gave no thought to cost as she reserved three boxes,

holding four seats each, feeling sure that these would be enough for herself, Nicholas, and such few people as she would care to invite. But then the Met called to say they had another lovely box available, and she began remembering people she had not thought of before. In a day or so, she had asked Mom and Mr. Bitmore, her mother and sister, Harry Temple and William, Ida and Mrs. Steele, and Cameron. All accepted but Mrs. Steele, who rather pointedly declined. Bridget now had six boxes, with more than twenty guests expected, and as many more invited to the supper she was giving, afterwards.

Being that going to New York City was a four-hundred-mile trip, she arranged not only transportation, but for those who wanted, a hotel room for the night.

At the advice of Hammond, two days before the concert, Chloe and Bridget left for New York City. They would be staying at the Manhattan Club that was in walking distance to the Met. While Chloe spent her time rehearsing, Bridget filled her time walking to Time Square and the Museums in Central Park. She ate most meals alone, but that suited her fine. It brought out an awareness of how little of the world she had experienced, especially at the airport as she stared at the arrival and departure screens showing destinations to places, she had never seen and probably never would before she died. It was just like she felt looking at the map of Central Park listing all the areas she could go and on each was an arrow pointing out 'you are here'.

On the day of the opera, Chloe was beside herself and impossible to be around as she tore the place apart, gathering her things and putting them in a chic valise Bridget had purchased for the occasion. That, along with a matching garment bag had set her back a pretty penny, but like all the expenses, she felt at ease.

Family and friends started arriving and Bridget was busy playing host until it was time to go to the Met. Some went by car, while others joined Bridget and Cameron who opted to walk.

The closer they got, the more people they saw, heading in the same direction and as she looked around her, she was filled with the realization that each random passerby was living a life probably more vivid and complex then her own; populated with their own ambitions, friends, routines, worries and craziness and she felt a kinship.

Weaving their way through the crowd, they were soon being chaperoned to their box where they took their seats and Bridget did an eye count to see if everyone had made it. She leaned back content when everyone was accounted for. Since they walked, the others were already seated.

Cameron, who sat on the edge of her box unabashedly took her hand, "Bridget, look at this. You did a magnificent job of promoting. The event is a sellout."

She had never dreamed she would be here at the Metropolitan

Opera House or anywhere near Lincoln Center at Lincoln Square in the Upper West Side, but here she was, watching as nearly four thousand people worked their way to their seats and some filed in to fill the almost three hundred standing places at the rear of the main floor and the top balcony.

At the entrance she had watched as people were pouring through all entrances, and now Cameron pointed to the upper tiers of seats, already filling up. Bridget had wanted to come early, so she would not miss anything, particularly the crowd that had come just to hear her child sing, but that had not happened.

The lights had been lowered when Nicholas, who had driven Chloe, slipped into the box and shook hands with Cameron. Then the orchestra filed into the shell, and for a few minutes there was the sound of tuning before the lights went up, and the orchestra came to attention.

Over the recent years Bridget had prepared herself for this moment of seeing her daughter perform at a concert hall, but not in her wildest dreams would she have guessed it to be the Met.

While she listened to Chloe sing at rehearsals, she had plenty of time to mentally prepare for the event. She knew that The Metropolitan Opera had engaged many of the world's most important artists and one, Enrico Caruso had sung more performances with the Met than with all the world's other opera companies combined. This opera house was the best of the best and no one could disagree with that.

She had read that each season, the Met stages more than 200 opera performances in New York. More than 800,000 people attend the performances in the opera house during the season, and millions more experience the Met through new media distribution initiatives and state-of-the-art technology. So, if all went well, Chloe was about to become famous.

She had placed the family perfectly, having read about the acoustics being excellent, but that the best sound was in the balcony and family-circle levels. She also knew that the Opera could be a bit intimidating if you have never been to one so she did her research so that she would not miss anything. There was so much she needed to learn and understand and the last thing she wanted was to appear an idiot at the after party.

Then there was a crackle of applause, and she looked around in time to see Mr. Hammond, who was to conduct, mounting his stand, bowing to the audience and to the orchestra. Without turning around, Mr. Hammond raised his hand. The audience stood. Cameron and Nicholas stood, both very erect, both with stern, noble looks on their faces. Bewildered, Bridget followed suit.

She was not sure what was going on and that was her first inclination she might be in for some surprises. As her mind raced and her confidence dropped, there was silence and then the orchestra began playing the Star-Spangled Banner, and the audience sang.

Once seated again, several moments of silence followed and then the spotlight shown on the tiny figure onstage, and the room filled with applause that echoed in every corner until Mr. Hammond raised his wand. Total silence blanketed the hall and there was only the sound of the orchestra followed by the voice of an angel. In that instance, Bridget totally understood why Mr. Hammond had done his physical exam of Chloe that day and announced to her with confidence, she could do this.

The songs Chloe now sang were well known to Bridget only they sounded richer, and she drank in the image of her daughter and the sound of her voice.

Bridget was aware that Hammond had played on Chloe's age and the age of the audience that would come to see her. Everyone, but Bridget was in for a surprise.

The first number was 'Good Morning Starshine' from Hair. From that she sang 'Take a Chance on Me' by Abba, followed by 'Dancing Queen' and 'Winner Takes it'.

There was a slight break and Bridget who did not want to leave her seat, did so just so she could hear the comments. People could not praise the music, the singer, the whole performance enough as they talked amongst themselves.

After the thunder of applause, Chloe left the stage, and they were entertained by the orchestra. Mr. Hammond was still acknowledging his applause, when the lights were slowly lowered and then went up and for a long time there was a murmur like the murmur of the ocean. Then the murmur died off a little and catching the crowd by surprise, Chloe was in the center of the stage before they recovered. She was dressed in suede from head to toe and had a parasol open as if shading herself from the sun. Then behind her a screen was lowered and there was projected on it animated animals and then she sang, ‘The Lion Sleeps Tonight’. Chloe was recalled for several bows. Cameron was saying it was none of his business, but in his opinion that conductor could very well have allowed Chloe to sing an encore after all that applause. Nicholas, not much more of an authority in this field than Cameron was, but at least a little more familiar with the opera, said it was his impression that no encores were ever sung.

That ended Chloe’s segment and another singer came on stage doing a number that was quite long, was in fact the longest number Bridget had ever heard, but she had a beautiful voice and the audience enjoyed it. One more singer came on stage before the concert ended with each performer returning to take a bow.

As they filed out, Bridget listened. She needed to hear firsthand what people were thinking. Someone in the crowd was saying, “For opera, the emphasis is on the music and singing. If you find yourself getting lost in the music or an impressive aria it’s working.”

“Yes, it’s all about finding your own enjoyment in opera and being present in the music and its emotion and that first singer had captured my every emotion with her voice.”

Not one negative comment did she hear, and Bridget was walking on cloud nine as she hurried back to the hotel.

Bridget was so thrilled that little quivers went through her, and they kept going through her the rest of the night, during the supper party. She would always remember that moment when Chloe came out for bow after bow, and presently, after her dozenth or so reappearance, she came out followed by Mr. Hammond, and without any encumbrance, just a simple, friendly little girl, hoping to be liked.

At the party when a gentleman with a flute stepped forward, carrying a chair, and camped near Chloe she went over and shook his hand. Then Mr. Hammond accompanied her on the piano that had been requested be in the room and Chloe, so unlike herself said, "May I sing a song just because I want to sing it?" As the audience broke into amiable applause, Nicholas looked at Bridget, and she sensed something coming. Then Mr. Hammond played a short introduction, and Chloe began to sing 'Memory' that had been Bridget's favorite back in the happy days when she used to come home for her rest, and Chloe would play the numbers she liked to hear.

It was all for her.

Chloe sang to Bridget and whether the guests knew it was her she was singing to; it did not matter. When she thought about that evening, this would be the highlight for her. Later when the last guest had left and she and Cameron had tried to put some semblance of order back in the room, she sat down with him.

Cameron was happy, but sad at the same time. He almost told Bridget of the secret he had been keeping for some time, but to tell her was only so he could relieve his soul. He could not do it to her.

When Nick arrived, Cameron said goodnight to them both and she went to the bedroom. As she undressed, she recalled those dark dreary days when she did not know where the next nickel would come from and how hearing Chloe sing that song had made her feel, back when she was practically penniless and then when Cameron was gone, it took on even a sadder reflection causing her to want more. That verse, 'I must wait for the sunrise, I must think of a new life, And I mustn't give in. When the dawn comes, tonight will be a memory too, And a new day will begin.'

"So powerful," Bridget said as she climbed into bed and tried to sleep, but she was so wound up she lay staring at the ceiling thinking, this was the climax of Chloe's life, but it was also the climax of hers.

CHAPTER 33

It would have been so perfect if it had not crested into a financial catastrophe that had been ongoing since the day, she so blithely agreed to take the house off Mrs. Lombardi's hands.

When she made the arrangement, to do a major part of the financing through the Federal Homes Administration, about which she had heard good things, she received her first jolt. She was told they could only lend funds up to $150,000. She did not foresee this as a problem, but she was hoping for a little more so that she did not have to stress her business accounts by lending herself money.

Bridget recalled going to her bank and receiving another shock when she learned she did not have enough cash unaccounted for by the businesses. She could not believe it.

She had stood at the desk in the lobby when the second jolt brought her back to reality. The truth was that she used to be careful with her money, but lately she had started spending as though the well was endless.

She stood there for some time trying to decide and finally, ignoring all the little whispers in her head to stop now before she dug a deeper hole, she asked for the bank manager.

Bridget had sat down with the bank manager and talked through her current needs. The bank manager listened, then said they would issue the loan once the property had been sufficiently repaired.

He did not budge on the issue and Bridget did not budge either. She hesitated a day, before making up her mind to go ahead with the project.

Up to then, she had known there would be outlays, but thought of them vaguely as a couple of thousand to put the place in order, and a few thousand to furnish it. After the bank's report however, she had to consider whether it would not be better to give the place a complete overhaul that the bank would approve. Bridget called in a contractor who hired licensed people to take care of the water main, electrical, and other major structural needs of the property. When the work had been inspected and approved, she got her loan.

That was when she called on Nicholas for help. She did not tell him about the financial problem, but she was delighted when he hit on the plan of restoring the house to what it had been before Lombardi, Sr., put into effect his bizarre ideas for improvement. But while this satisfied the bank, and qualified her for the loan, it cost upwards of $300,000, and cleaned out her personal accounts.

For the furnishings, she had to sell bonds.

Money was flowing out the door faster than it was coming in, but she ignored it. When she married Nicholas, he had to have a car, or she thought so. That represented twenty-four thousand and she had taken that out in a loan. He needed it, she told herself. Only the more she spent, the easier it became to justify unnecessary expenses.

To get money to cover a few other things that had come up by then, she dipped into the reserves of the corporation. She drew herself a check for five-hundred thousand dollars and marked it as a loan. But she did not use a check from the big checkbook used by Miss Thompson, the lady she employed to keep the books. She used one of the blanks she always carried in her handbag, in case of emergency. She kept saying to herself that she must tell Miss Thompson about the check, but she did not do it. Then, in December to take care of Christmas expenses, she gave herself another advance of fifty-five hundred dollars, so that by the first of the year there was a difference $505,500 between what Miss Thompson's books showed and what the bank was actually carrying on deposit.

But these large outlays were only part of her difficulties. The bank, to her surprise, insisted on amortization of her loan as well as regular interest payments, that were a great deal more. Then Nicholas, put her to somewhat heavier expenses in the kitchen than she had expected. Then the endless guests, all of whom seemed to have the thirst of a caravan of camels, ran up the bill for household entertainment to an appalling figure. The result was that she was compelled to increase her salary from the corporation. Until then, she had allowed herself a weekly salary of a thousand dollars from the corporation's four component parts, the Food Truck, the Lake restaurant, the Irondequoit restaurant, and the Cobbs Hill restaurant.

This was far more than she needed for her living expenses, but she had seen it as a way to plan for a rainy day. As for the business accounts, they too carried a tidy reserve of cash after all expenses were paid.

But then she hiked her salary to five thousand dollars a week and the business reserve eventually ceased growing. In fact, Miss Thompson, with stern face, several times notified her that it would be necessary to transfer money from the Reserve. These transfers would be necessary to cover her salary increase to five thousand a week.

Bridget was embarrassed, but she needed the money so okayed the transfer. She had spent enough time with Miss Thompson setting up the books for the business, to know this was not a good idea, but she felt there was no other alternative. When she left the accountant's office, she avoided looking in Miss Thompson's eyes. She could not help feeling like a thief. This was the corporation's money, not hers.

The Reserve was a sort of sacred cow that was maintained for many purposes, such as debt service or maintenance. Accountants must maintain these accounts accurately to report these amounts to internal and external stakeholders, which luckily, her business did not have.

In March, when Miss Thompson made up the income statements, and took them down to the notary and swore to them, and left them, with the tax checks, for Bridget's signature, Bridget was in a cold sweat. She just could not face Miss Thompson and tell her what she had done. So, she took the statements to another accountant, and swore him to secrecy as she told him what she had done and asked him to get up another set of forms, which she herself would swear to, and which would conform with the balance at the bank.

He seemed hesitant, and asked her a great many questions, and took a week making up his mind that nothing unlawful had been done so far. But he emphasized 'so far', in an accusing way. He charged five hundred dollars for his services, an absurd sum for what amounted to a little recopying, with slight changes. She paid him, and had him file the paperwork and the checks, and told Miss Thompson she had mailed them herself.

Two days later Bridget could not pay her food bill. Bills of all kinds, in the restaurant business, are paid on Monday, and failure to pay is a body blow to credit. Her meat supplier listened to Bridget as she pleaded for a little more time. Expressionless he agreed to deliver meat until she straightened this out. But all during the following week, Archie was complaining about the inferior quality of the top sirloins, and Mrs. Steele had to be restrained from calling Mr. McHale personally.

Bridget was asking for time in paying bills and the pressure was building. And then one day Greyson Hobbs strolled into the restaurant.

"Hi Greyson. It's so good to see you."

"Not so good, Bridget. Not so good."

At that point he pointed to her office and like a child about to be punished she followed him.

"Close the door."

Obediently, Bridget closed the door and sat down.

"We need a little conference, Bridget. I've been retained by several of your creditors and I'm hoping we can make short order of this." He went over the list of creditors and the amounts and handed a copy to Bridget. There was a litigation against Cobbs Hill that stood out.

"Listen, Bridget, I want you to review that list with the accountant and we will meet with the creditors at your Cobbs Hill restaurant tomorrow night. We could have dinner and talk things over."

That was the night Chloe was to be at the Eastman Theater. Bridget shrilly said it was impossible, she had to be at the Eastman Theater; nothing could interfere. Then, said Greyson, "How about one-night next week?" He paused. "How about Monday?"

The delay made matters worse, for Monday saw more unpaid bills that now included the three wholesale grocers, and several small fry market men who had previously been flattered if she so much as said good morning.

On the designated rescheduled date, Bridget arrived expecting the worse. Greyson, however, kept everything on a courteous plane. He had assembled a small group and they also remain courteous, avoiding the matter in hand while dinner was being served. He insisted that Bridget give him the check for the creditors' banquet, as he somewhat facetiously called it. He encouraged her to talk, to lay her cards on the table, so something could be arranged. He kept reminding her that nobody wanted to make trouble. It was to the interest of all that she get on her feet again, that she become the A1 customer she had been in the past.

Yet, at the end of two or three hours of questions, of answers, of figures, of explanations, the truth at last was out, and not even Bridget's stammering evasions could change it. All four units of the corporation, even the Cobbs Hill restaurant, would be showing a profit if it were not for the merciless milking that Bridget was giving them to keep up the establishment in Cobbs Hill. Once this was in the open there was a long, grave pause, and then Greyson said, “Bridget, you mind if we ask a few questions about your home finances? Kind of get that a little straightened even though it is nobody's business but mine, as far as that goes. If we just went by what was our business, we would have gone to court already, asked for receivers, and strictly kept our questions to ourselves. We did not do that. We wanted to give you a break. But looks like we are entitled to some considerations, too don't you think? Looks like we could go into what we think is important. Maybe you do not think so. Maybe that's where the trouble is.”

“What do you want to know?”

“How much does Chloe pay in?”

“I don't charge my own child board.

“She's a big expense though, isn't she?”

“That’s none of your business.”

He ignored her reply. “How much do you think she’s making? Do you have any idea?”

“I don't keep books on her.”

“This is what we need to discuss because I know how much she’s making. Chloe makes more a week than you do. If she keeps on the same schedule, even without signing up any new performances or commercials, she will bring in seven figures.”

Bridget was astonished, but she tried her best to hide it. She had no idea. Chloe never once offered to pay for anything, and she had to know they were in trouble financially. So, she replied, “But she has major expenses. You don’t know how much she has to pay for her career."

"Sure, I do. She pays them with your money and uses hers to support her image. All I am saying is it would be justified in deducting an amount to pay for her keep? If you did, that would kind of ease the pressure."

Bridget opened her mouth to say she could not do any deducting of money she gave to Chloe. That was a personal matter between her and her daughter. Then, looking closer at Greyson who reacted badly when his ideas were dismissed, she noted something familiar, something cold. Her heart skipped a beat, she knew she must not fall into any traps, must not divulge any more details about her personal life. She stalled. "Listen, gentlemen I need to give this matter some thought, since I hadn't considered it before. I need to check the legal issues involved before I make my decision."

If she had learned anything during her lifetime, it was to be careful and alert. She knew better than this. She knew she must be on her guard. There was more going on than being discussed here.

Being more observant she began concentrating deeply. The first thing she identified was his choice of men to bring to the table. They were the two people who she owed the biggest debt. Besides that, they had never befriended her beyond the level required to keep her business. Bridget mentally shook the cobwebs out of her brain and stopped feeling victimized. It was then she happened to catch a look between Mr. Huss, the friendly chicken farmer and Mr. McHale, the person supplying the steaks at her Charlotte restaurant. Neither gentleman seemed very interested in the exchange going on between Bridget and Greyson. They were merely props. At first, she was puzzled by this transfer, but then her mind played catch up and she knew what this was about. Greyson was engineering a deal.

Feeling her confidence returning, Bridget thought hard, and a light went off. This was not about her or her lack of finances at all. This meeting had one purpose and that was how they could get at Chloe's money. She should have known Greyson was more aware of how much Chloe made and he knew how much she had been squeezing out of the business to use for Chloe's benefit. Of course, Greyson had done his homework and before setting up this meeting had already discussed the details with the creditors.

They had tried to blindside her. The creditors were to get their money, the corporation was to be placed on a sounder basis, and Chloe was to foot the bill.

Bridget was filled with rage. It did not occur to her that there was an element of justice in this arrangement, that the creditors had furnished her with goods, and were entitled to payment; that Chloe earned large sums and had run a lengthy bill. At that moment there were no business arrangements on her mind. Instead, she saw this moment as her actions hurting the one child she still had and as a mother she had to protect her. No crafty actions or methods were considered as she allowed her anger to come to the surface. "No child of mind is going to be made the victim of any such arrangement. Not if I have anything to do with it."

Greyson had expected some reluctance, but not this. “Looks like we need to go into what we think is important. Maybe you do not think so. Maybe that's where the trouble is.” Taking on a superior stance he continued. “It's you Bridget, that's behind the eight ball, not us.”

That is when it occurred to her. Bridget’s excitement was boiling over, so she slowly pushed her chair back and stood. She remained silent as she mulled over the matter so that she would present the details properly. When she finally spoke, words came out of her mouth calmly and reflective of her confidence.

“I don't believe you or anybody has any right, even any legal right, to take what belongs to me, or what belongs to my child, to pay the bills of this business.” Turning her body so that she addressed Greyson with eye contact she added, “Maybe you've forgotten, Mr. Greyson Hobbs, that it was you that had me incorporate. It was you that had the papers drawn up and explained the law to me. And your main talking point was that if I incorporated, then my personal property was safe from any and all creditors of the corporation. Maybe you have forgotten that, but I haven't.”

“No, I haven't forgotten it.” Bridget was taken aback at how calmly he spoke those words. She thought she had taken control of the matter and that should have shaken Greyson and the men at the table. It did not.

Trying to retain her composure she watched as Greyson's chair scraped against the floor as he stood to face her, where she was already standing, a few feet back from the big round table. “I haven't forgotten it, and you're quite right, nobody here can take one dime of your money, or your personal property, or Chloe's, to satisfy the claims they have. Makes no difference how reasonable the claims may be. They cannot touch a thing; it is all yours. All they can do is go to court, have you declared bankrupt, and take over. The court will appoint receivers, who will act as custodian of your property, finances, general assets, or business operations.”

“Okay.”

Now it was time for Greyson to be stunned. Not sure she understood he added, “The bottom line is you'll be out.”

“All right, then I'll be out.”

Again, Greyson was speechless, but he was sure of himself. He had the ace and Bridget was only putting up a smoke screen.

Now Greyson landed his bombshell. “You'll be out, and Ida will be in.”

It was like someone had slapped her. “Who?”

The word came out thick with emotion. She spoke coldly; uneasy and suspicious. Greyson observed the effect of his announcement and waddled in it.

“You didn't know that did you?”

“That's a lie. She wouldn't…”

Greyson was enjoying this as he interrupted her. “Oh yes she would. When I approached her, Ida, she cried, and said at first, she would not even listen to such a thing, she was such a good friend of yours. But she could not get to you, all last week, for a little talk. You were too busy with personal commitments, which of course included Chloe's concert. Maybe that hurt her a little. Anyway, now she will listen to reason, and we figure she can run this business as good as anybody can run it. Not as good as you, maybe, when you have your mind on it. But better than a woman who has replaced her business sense with her mother hat. A woman who now redirects funds from the business to her child with no consideration to the fact she is putting her business in jeopardy."

Bridget could hear his words, but her mind had stalled. Ida was her friend and her business partner. She just would not stab her in the back. That news stung Bridget to her core, and she was unable to stop the tears that welled in her eyes. Quickly she turned her back on Greyson so that he would not see her tears.

Only Greyson was not done yet. In a cold, calculating voice he continued. "Bridget, you might as well get it through your head, if you want to keep your business you have to do three things."

Slowly Bridget turned around. "And what is that?"

"You've got to cut down on your overhead, so you can live on what you make. You must raise some money. It needs to come from Chloe, or from the Bitmore Drive property, or from somewhere, so you can square up these bills and start over."

"Is that it?"

"And you've got to cut out this running around and get down to work."

Greyson looked Bridget in the eye and saw her pain. "Now, as I said before, there's no hard feelings. We all wish you well. Just the same, we mean to get our money. You show us some action by a week from tonight, and you can forget what has been said. You don't, and we'll have to take action ourselves."

It was around eleven when she drove up to the house, but she tapped Jefferson on the shoulder and stopped him when she saw the first floor brightly lit, with five or six cars standing outside. She was on the verge of hysteria, and she could not face Nicholas, and eight or ten golf players, and their wives. She told Jefferson to call Mr. Lombardi aside, and tell him she had been detained on business, and would not be in until quite late. Then she moved forward, took the wheel, and drove out again.

It was almost automatic with her to turn left at the traffic circle, continue over the bridge, and level off for Irondequoit and Cameron. As she pulled up in front of his mother's house there were no lights on, but she felt sure he was home. Just in case, she hurried up the drive and peeked in the garage and saw the car. He was the only one who drove it now.

Quietly she walked around the house to the back bedroom that she knew Cameron occupied. Using the tips of her fingers, she tapped softly and in seconds, Cameron's face appeared.

Cameron raised the window started to ask what was up but stopped when he saw her wild-eyed expression.

"I'll be right out." He pointed with his hand to the front of the house.

Bridget nodded her head and headed back to the front and when she got there, Cameron was already on the porch.

His eyes were on her as she came up on the porch. He stood there in his familiar, battered red bathrobe and then moved forward to meet her. Cameron reached out and gently put his hand under her chin, lifting her head up.

"Goddam it this is no place to talk. I cannot take you inside and talk either because Mom and Pop are watching television and will be hollering, wanting to know what is going on. Please, give me a minute Bridget. I need to get some clothes on, and I will be right back. Promise me you will not go anywhere. Please?"

Bridget nodded. Not knowing what else to do, she walked back to her car and sat. Her mind was empty of all thoughts as she sat there. Just seeing Cameron seemed to comfort her because she knew he was on her side. She needed someone on her side.

Cameron was back in minutes. She turned, sensing he was there by the car before she saw him and managed a weak smile.

"Want me to drive, Bridget?"

Again, rather than speak, Bridget nodded and mechanically opened the car door, stepped out and walked across the front of the car to the passenger side.

"Fasten your seatbelt Bridget."

She did and once they were strapped in, Cameron pulled away from the curb in the easy, grand style that nobody else quite seemed to have. Whether it was their old SUV or this, her expensive Mercedes, he had the skills and expertise required for getting behind the wheel and in an instant become as one with the automobile. She liked that about him; that and his strong focus on the task, to the point that he would get defensive when others interfered with his driving.

Bridget leaned back against the seat. She trusted him and had confidence in the thought he was going to figure out what to do about everything. She gave him a wan smile.

They headed north on List Avenue toward Old North Hill and turned left onto Pinegrove Avenue. He continued and turned right onto St. Paul Blvd. Neither spoke. Cameron turned again onto Colebrook Drive then made a right onto Lake Shore Blvd where he pulled into the parking lot that allowed them to look down at Lake Ontario.

Shutting off the car, Cameron turned toward Bridget. “Shall we get out?”

Bridget again only nodded, and they got out of the car. They met at the front of the car and walked across the blacktop drive to the grassy area beyond. There they stood quietly gazing across the lake. Bridget felt her body relax and her facial muscles untighten as the frustration drained out of her and she allowed herself to enjoy the tranquility of that moment.

When Cameron felt she was calm, he guided her back to the

car and they drove toward Kings Highway turning left, then right onto Titus Avenue and another right onto Cooper Road to merge onto St. Paul Blvd again.

Bridget did not question him or care to know where they were going. She only stared out the window glad to let him take over. She watched as they turned onto Thomas and headed toward the Colonel Patrick O'Rorke Bridge that spanned the Genesee Riverway Trail.

As they approached the bridge, Cameron, trying to take her mind off her problems asked, “Bridget, do you remember the original name of the bridge?”

“What?” She had been allowing herself to just drift in empty thoughts and now she straightened and said, “Oh, yes, the Stutson Street Bridge.”

“Yes, that’s right.” Cameron was trying to bring her back, out of her head so that they could talk about what was bothering her. To keep her with him he said, “That’s right Bridget. They renamed it to the Colonel Patrick O'Rorke Memorial Bridge in honor of this Civil War hero who grew up in Rochester and led the New York 140th Infantry at the Battle of Gettysburg.”

This was another quality she liked about Cameron. He knew to say “calm down” would be counterproductive and invalidating her feelings would only lead to resentment. Instead, he had his way of getting her to the point she could face the matter and share it with him.

Across the bridge they turned right onto Lake Avenue and

Cameron finally pulled into the parking lot of one of the many restaurants and bars along the way to Ontario State Park. He turned to Bridget. “Thought you might like a drink.”

“Thanks. I do.”

Together they went into the restaurant and Cameron was glad to see it was quiet and empty. Once seated Bridget was ready to release the pain and anguish as she broke down in tears. Cameron gave her the time she needed and during that breakdown, Bridget was able to put it all in words. She told the whole story, or at least the whole story beginning with Chloe's return home. What she did not share was the financial situation with Nicholas and particularly the unusual circumstances of her marriage. All of that she conveniently left out. But as to recent events she was flagitiously frank, and even told him about the two checks, yet undiscovered by Miss Thompson.

Cameron let out a low release of whistling air through his lips, after which there was a half hour interlude, while he went into all details of this transaction. Bridget spoke in frightened whispers and ended by informing him that she had to take some action by the end of the week.

Once she had divulged it all, she felt a queer spiritual relief. She felt like Cameron had told her he felt when he confessed his sins. Not being Catholic she could not understand why Catholics did this and he said that it was God’s plan for people to face their sins, acknowledge the wrong they have done, and seek forgiveness from a priest, who represents God and has authority from Christ. Cameron was not God or a priest, but he had a way of helping people.

Cameron listened intently, not allowing his face to give a hint of what he was thinking. She had come to him because she knew of any other person in the world, he would understand. He was good at understanding others. He could pick up her emotional cues, often from body language, tone of voice, and other non-verbal elements of communication. So now he listened to not only the words, but their deeper meaning.

For many years he had watched their daughter manipulate Bridget to the point of tears and tried to help her see Chloe for what she was, a self-centered and cruel spirit. She was a sociopath.

Finished telling Cameron her tale of woe, Bridget sat back, staring at him; waiting for him to tell her what to do. He wished he could tell her, and she would see that all her problems started and ended with Chloe. Chloe manipulated her, especially because she loved her and felt she owed her something, but it was hopeless. Chloe had a profound lack of conscience hidden by her charming demeanor. Instead, he leaned across the table and patted her hand.

"There's no legal border between you and your company so you're free to spend money as you choose. Keeping your personal and business finances separate, though, makes it easier to track business expenses and easier to prove to the IRS they were business expenses."

Bridget heaved a sigh of relief. The stressful, unpleasant feeling was gone as she gave Cameron a weak smile.

He allowed her to enjoy that feeling before solemnly he added, "Not saying it wasn't pretty damn foolish."

"I know it was foolish."

"Well then…"

Cameron leaned back on his seat, giving her time to think about it and when she leaned across the table and reached out, he moved forward and placed his hand in hers. She kissed it, then looked up at him with a sad smile. At that moment he knew she was aware of what she had to do. She understood that the only way to solve this situation was through Chloe, only her heart fought against her accepting it.

Cameron downed his second drink, trying to delay the inevitable. Even though he was sure she understood, he also was sure she could not say it aloud, but she had to hear it. "She's the one that's costing you money, and she's the one that's making money. She's got to pay her share."

"She's our child, Cameron, not our bank account. I never wanted her to feel obligated."

"I never wanted her to know we were having marital

problems, but she found out just the same." Then with a cautious air he added, "Especially when you threw me out."

He had not meant to say that, but it was too late to take it back. His neck snapped as he looked across the table and saw the expression on Bridget's face. All the sympathy in the world would not erase the damage those words had done, but he had to think quickly. He had to at least turn her mind away from that and he figured out what to say. "Listen, Bridget, if she'd had money when Bitmore Homes began to go under, and I'd taken it, Bitmore Homes would still be ours and as a result not only us, but Chloe would have been better off."

It worked. Bridget pressed Cameron's hand, and sipped her wine, then she held his hand tightly. "Thanks Cameron." She had not let herself realize until then that Cameron had been through all this himself, that she was not the only one who had suffered.

"Bridget, think about all you've done for her. Who the hell put that girl where she is today? Who paid for all that music? And that piano? And that car? And those clothes? And…"

"You did your share."

"Mighty little."

"You did a lot." Bridget paused and with sincerity continued. "You did plenty. We lived very well before the bottom dropped out, Cameron. Chloe was eleven years old when we broke up, and she is twenty now. I've carried on nine years, but it was eleven for you."

With a knowing twinkle in his eyes he replied, "Eleven years and eight months."

Bridget lifted his hand to her cheek. "All right, eleven years and eight months, if you must bring that up. And I am glad it was only eight months, how do you like that? Any woman can have a child in nine months after they marry." She said with laughter in her voice.

Getting in on the fun, Cameron winked and added, "But when it was only eight, that raised eyebrows, didn't it?"

A comfortable silence lingered before Cameron said, "You want me to talk to Chloe?"

"I can't ask her for money, Cameron."

"Then I'll do it. I will drop over there this afternoon, and bring it up friendly, and let her know what she must do. It's just ridiculous that you should have your back to the wall, and she lives the good life at your expense."

The more the idea became a reality, the more Bridget held back. "No, No. I'll mortgage the house in Irondequoit."

Cameron's eyes widened; his mouth twisted as he absorbed what Bridget had suggested. He had to calm down and when he did, he found the words to change her mind. "And what good will that do you? You raise maybe a hundred fifty thousand and you square up some for a few weeks, and then you are right back where you started. She's got to help and keep on helping."

She knew he was right, but she did not want to accept it yet. There had to be another way. If they concentrated, they might come up with an alternative way of solving this dilemma. "Let's say we go for a walk on the boardwalk."

"Great idea."

Bridget paid the bar tab and then they went out into the night. Cameron had her climb back in the car even though it was a short distance to the boardwalk. He drove to the beach parking area where he shut off the engine and they prepared to get out.

They walked swiftly through the lot as if trying to beat the cold night air as they made their way to the boardwalk that would take them out over the lake. When Bridget's foot stepped over the edge of the walkway across the late, she paused, looking up at the sky and feeling the chill going through her thin coat. She told herself this was ridiculous.

But then she saw shadows of others who were out there heading down the pier, barely visible in the darkness of the evening. She stepped forward and felt, rather than saw Cameron beside her as they made their way.

The quiet was broken now and then by the sound of a wave gently lapping against the sides of the pier, or a whisper between two lovers as they all headed in the same direction. Except for the marker out at the end, there is nothing on the pier other than cable guard fences on each side and occasionally there might be a puddle or two on its smooth even surface.

Many people, Bridget recalled, used the sound of waves to sleep and relax and she understood perfectly why. It had a peaceful and calming effect and as they continued down to the end of the pier, she felt comfortably warm, no longer having thoughts of the cold or how her world was so out of balance.

When they reached the end of the pier, they paused briefly to stare across the smooth surface of the water before turning back around and heading toward the parking area. By the time they reached the car they were chilled through and Cameron turned on the heat, full blast.

"This will warm you up," he said as they sat a moment enjoying the first flow of heat entering the car. Several minutes later, they were leaving the parking area and turning onto Lake Avenue.

They were stopped at the light before their turn onto the bridge when it all came back to her so strongly that her head snapped back against the seat and she felt actual physical pain in her shoulders. She was remembering it all and as if their minds were threaded together, at that instance Cameron blurted out, "Bridget, you've got to do it yourself. You have got to talk to Chloe. It can't come from me."

Shocked by his words, it took her a minute to catch up and when she did, she replied, "Why?"

"Because you've got to do it tonight."

"'Tonight? It is too late to do it now. Besides, I want to figure out what to say." Bridget paused and sensing he was not buying it she practically whispered, "I can't, it's late, she'll be asleep."

"It doesn't matter how late it is, or whether she's asleep, or she's not asleep. You've got to tell her now."

"What brought this on, huh, Cameron. I thought you were going to tell her for me. I don't understand this change of heart."

"I'll tell you what brought it on. It is the fact that you forgot, and I forgot, and we both forgot who we are dealing with. It's not just Chloe." He swallowed then through pursed lips expelled air before continuing. "Bridget, you can't trust Greyson Hobbs, not even till the sun comes up. He is a cheap, chiseling little crook, we know that. He was my friend, and he crossed me, and he was your friend, and he crossed you…"

Again, he paused as if afraid to speak the words aloud and reached over to grab Bridget's shoulder. "But listen, Bridget, he was Chloe's friend too. Maybe he's getting ready to cross her."

"But what could he do to Chloe?"

Cameron swallowed hard, remembering and then after giving it some thought said, "There is lot he could do but consider that he's trying to get her money. Not for you, but for himself."

"That's ludicrous. There is no way he has the power or control. Besides, he cannot, not for corporate debts."

"How do you know."

"Why, he…"

"That's it, he told you. Greyson Hobbs told you and Greyson Hobbs wrote up the contracts too. You believe everything he says? You believe anything he says? Maybe that meeting tonight was just a phony. Maybe he is getting ready to compel you to take over Chloe's money, as her guardian, so he can attach it. Maybe you, I, and Chloe will all have papers slapped on us tomorrow."

She stared at him in disbelief, then slowly she allowed herself to accept the fact he was not involved, but he was right. He was so right. "What do we do."

"You're going to see Chloe tonight and by whatever means you can come up with you're getting her out of that house, so no process server can find you. You're meeting me at the restaurant in Irondequoit for breakfast, and by that time it'll be busy."

"I don't understand. He'll look for us there."

"Doesn't matter. There'll be four of us at that table, and the other one will be a lawyer."

"Oh my god. You are the best Cameron. The absolute best."

Cameron smiled. He knew she meant it and not in a selfish way and that made him feel good about himself. He needed to feel noble after all he had put her through. That he had hurt her had always played on his conscious. But it was not until recently he realized how much of the way Chloe treated her was his fault. His daughter's lack of respect for her mother was his fault indeed.

He knew that Chloe had a serious deficiency, but he had ignored it. That willingness to disregard what her mother said he learned was at the base of their family conflicts, as she fought to dominate them so she could get things from them. He actually thought it was cute until she got older and the need to take became more prominent. At first, he thought it was because she liked the feeling of power and control, but over the years she had taken money, sex, business partners, homes, cars, investments and even their reputation. What finally brought him to understanding his daughter was the fact that she lacked a conscience and would do anything to get what she wanted. Hadn't he known that all along. Hadn't he held tight to her secret, not telling Bridget, or even letting Chloe know he knew. He understood it, because in some ways he was exactly like her.

CHAPTER 34

Bridget dropped Cameron off at his parents' home and giving her one last bit of encouragement said, "You can do this, Bridget, you can do this."

Bridget smiled, waving as she pulled away from the curb and headed toward home. It was hard to use that word to describe where she lived. It was not home. How she wished she still lived on Bitmore Street where her life was less complicated. She could feel herself weakening and quickly turned her thoughts back to the present, replaying the words spoken by Cameron. By the time she reached the house in Cobbs Hill, she was ready.

Bridget pulled up in the drive and glanced at the clock in the car. It was after three and the house was dark, except for the hall light downstairs which meant they were probably in bed, asleep. That was good.

Not wanting to chance waking anyone up she turned off the

headlights and pulled the car up to the front door. She sat for a moment listening and not hearing anything she opened the car door and practically tiptoed over the driveway to the grass to make as little sound as possible. Again, she paused to listen before forcing her hand out to turn the doorknob. As she knew it would be, it was unlocked. That was Nick's way of course. He wanted to make sure when someone came to visit him, they were not blocked by a door. When she had protested, he had said, "The only people coming up that drive are people I know, so why lock them out?"

Bridget was used to locking windows and doors before turning in at night. During the day she used to keep the back door unlocked when she was in the kitchen, but only then. But they had enough to argue about and doors became less important.

Once inside she felt all the pressures of her life and they helped carry her up the staircase. She walked with determination down the long hallway until she stood in front of Chloe's bedroom. Bridget looked down the hall and then turned and tapped on Chloe's door. There was no answer. She tapped again, using the tips of her fingers, to make only the softest sound. Still there was no answer. "Chloe," she whispered, then waited for a response. Nothing.

Bridget turned the knob slowly and stepped inside. It was dark in the room and she stood waiting for her eyes to adjust before venturing further. Not wanting to startle her daughter, she left the light off and tiptoed slowly across the room until her shins hit the edge of the bed. There she bent down and reached out to gently touch Chloe, careful not to startle her awake.

Her hand sunk down to the blanket and her eyes, adjusting to the darkness realized there was only a pillow where her hand had come down. She padded the bed in several places and then stood up. It was obvious Chloe was not in her room.

Quickly she snapped on the bed side lamp and looked around. Nobody was in the room, and from the smoothness of the bed itself, it had not been slept in. Bridget's heart started to race, and she took a deep breath to settle her nerves. She walked across to the dressing room. Empty. She went into the en suite. Empty. Feeling foolish, she went into the walk-in closet and found it empty too.

"Oh my god, she's gone. They got to her before I could." Shaking her head back and forth, she sat down on the edge of the bed and lowered her head into her hands as she whispered softly. "Pull it together Bridget. Don't you cry, don't you cry." She sat there for several minutes until finally she had herself under control and stood. Without thinking why, she returned to the closet and flipped on the light, then turned around checking it out. She let out a sigh. Chloe's things were there, even the dress she had worn that night.

So, Chloe had been there that evening and must have changed into her night clothes. She had been there, but where was she now.

Another idea entered her head and Bridget hurried back down the hall to her own room, on the chance Chloe had gone there to wait for her, and fallen asleep, or something. She was smiling as she opened the door to her room and walked in silently, not turning on a light until after she had taken in every space within and not seen Chloe.

"Where is she. Where is she," she repeated as she hurried down the hallway swinging open doors and checking every room as she went until she reached Nicholas's room. There she paused, a sense of dread causing a lump in her throat, making it hard to swallow. Her tempo was quickening now, and it was no finger rap this time. This time she balled her fist and knocked sharply on his door. There was no answer. She knocked again, insistently, and when there was no answer, she kept on knocking, then tried the door. It was locked.

Pressure built behind her eyes as her mind raced with unpleasant thoughts. This was the man who liked to leave doors unlocked so why did he need to lock his bedroom door. "Nicholas," she yelled. "Nicholas!"

Finally, he answered her in a voice repressed with sleep or too much to drink. "What's the matter with you. What do you want?" She could hear the irritation in his voice, and she did not blame him; that is yet.

"Nick, the door is locked. Let me in. I need to talk to you."

"Go away Bridget." He paused, his voice growing stronger. "Go to bed. We can talk in the morning."

"I'm not going anywhere."

She listened and fearing he had fallen back to sleep, she knocked on the door again. "Let me in Nick. I need to talk to you about Chloe."

The words hung in the silence as she waited for him to say something or do something. She started to knock again but stopped. She heard movement in the room and waited. She could trace his steps in her mind as he walked across the floor, then stopped at the entrance. "Nick?"

"Yes, yes," he said, and she heard the door being unlocked and slowly opened. It was dark inside, and he only had the door opened slightly and when she started to slip through, he stopped her. "Okay, fine, we can talk here. Chloe is missing."

"For God's sake, is that what this is about? She's not an infant."

"Where do you think she is?"

"This is a big house; she could be anywhere." He paused then spoke harshly. "Did you check the kitchen? Maybe she got hungry and is in the kitchen."

Bridget's head bobbed up and down. She should have checked the kitchen. "Right, I'll check the kitchen." She started to turn around, then turned back. "Suppose she's not there, what do I do then?"

"I don't know Bridget. Do whatever you want. I'm going back to bed."

"But you saw her this evening."

Trying to be patient he said, "Yes, until I went to bed. I don't know what she did." Annoyance building, he converted to sarcasm. "Maybe she went somewhere. Maybe she had a blowout. Maybe she is looking at the moon. It's a free country."

"She didn't go anywhere."

"How do you know?"

"Her dress is here."

"Couldn't she have changed it?"

"Her car is here."

"Couldn't she have gone with somebody else?"

This simple possibility had not even occurred to Bridget. She was about to apologize for her rude intrusion when she became aware of Nicholas's arm. He stood there at the half-opened doorway with one hand acting as a doorstop against any pressure she put on it and the other hand had reached across the opening and was pressed against the door frame.

Bridget stared closely at Nick's face and knew he was keeping something from her. Before he could stop her, she slipped her hand through the door opening and it seemed luck was on her side when it rested on the light switch. She pressed it up and light flooded the room.

Her eyes darted quickly around the room and suddenly stopped. Chloe was looking at her, from the bed.

CHAPTER 35

Nick moved back from the door, allowing Bridget to come all the way in. He went over and sat down on the other chair in the room; the color draining from his face. Bridget just watched him as he slumped back, his body language already telling her what he was about to say. What she thought was going on, was true. He was guilty. Bridget leaned her head against the wall for support and not hearing anything from Nick she closed her eyes and told herself she could handle this. She felt a surge of confidence flow through her body and looking directly at Nick she spoke. "I said, have you been having an affair with my daughter?"

The words floated in the air between them, and she heard Nick sigh. He shook his head "I guess I should say I'm sorry. I never meant this to happen."

"Just tell me everything, Nick. Do not try and lie. Just tell me straight." Her knees seemed to weaken as her body shook as if she were chilled. To keep from falling, Bridget plopped into the nearest chair and at that moment, there was only her and Nicholas in the room.

Nicholas' voice rambled on incoherently as he squeezed as many words as possible out of his mouth in one breath. Each word he uttered spoke realms on the pointlessness of his life that ended in a hysterical denunciation of Bridget. He said she had used him for her purposes since the first time they met. He said she was too busy to consider what she was doing to the people she said she loved and who loved her. He went on to say he knew she begrudged having to give him money but if the shoe were on the other foot, he would have given it to her freely. He worked down to their marriage, and correctly accused her of using him as bait to help control Chloe. And then he bunched it all together saying, "I am human, Bridget and I need to be loved. Chloe was willing to love me, and we fell in love."

Bridget started to speak, but he cut her off. "How does that grab you dear. You played your hand and dropped me right into Chloe's arms. I needed to be independent of you and I am, but only by falling in love with your daughter."

Bridget was beyond listening as she sat in the upholstered chair, near the door, her feet turned in, and staring at the floor as she tried to make sense of it all. But while her eyes were on the floor, her mind was on her lovely daughter in her husband's bed, and she was physically sick at what Chloe's presence there meant. It was too much to take in, but she tried to remain calm.

And then, Chloe interrupted the silence saying to Nicholas, "Darling! Let's not get bottled down with explaining ourselves. She has been such a pest to me. I literally cannot open my mouth in a theater, or a studio, or anywhere, that she is not there, rushing down the aisle, embarrassing me. But what do I do? I remain calm while I scream inside. That is what I do, and it works."

Bridget was listening to all of this, her breathing heavy as though she had just jogged a mile, making it impossible for her to speak. All she could do was watch as Nicholas got up and began pacing the floor in his boxers and when he figured out what to do next, he headed to his closet and pulled out clothes that he put on.

Bridget followed him with her eyes, viewing it as though she was seeing it on the big screen. When Nicholas finished dressing, she allowed her eyes to fall on her daughter. Chloe was smiling and Bridget watched as she got out of the bed and went to the dresser where she picked up a hairbrush and began brushing her hair. Chloe was stark naked.

Chloe hummed as she brushed and was still humming when she headed for the door and as she passed by Nicholas, he handed her the kimono, from the foot of the bed. Bridget watched and absorbed every hurtful minute as it played out in front of her, but when Chloe started toward the door, she finally snapped.

It was then that Bridget sprung from the chair and it was not at Nicholas that she vaulted, her husband, the man who had been untrue to her. It was at Chloe, her daughter, the girl who had done no more than what Bridget had once said was a woman's right. With fire blazing in her eyes, she saw Chloe for what she was, a ruthless creature seventeen years younger than herself, with a thin waist and a generally feminine shape. But she had fingers like steel from playing the piano, and broad muscular shoulders and powerful legs from riding, swimming, and all the recreations that Bridget had made possible for her. Yet this athlete was crushed by a panting, little thing in a black dress, and a string of beads that broke and went bouncing all over the room.

Bridget was beyond understanding now as she fought her daughter, wildly swinging at her, wanting to hurt her like she had been hurt. Somewhere in the distance she heard Nicholas yelling at her and felt him trying to drag her away from Chloe, but in her current state of mine she was stronger than him."

Chloe fought back. She scratched at her eyes, at her face, and Bridget could taste blood trickling into her mouth. But nothing stopped her as she knocked Chloe onto the floor and climbed on top of her. She grabbed the throat of the naked girl beneath her and squeezed hard. Nicholas managed to grab her arm and pull one hand from around Chloe's neck, but Bridget wrenched the hand free of Nicholas, and squeezed with both hands. She watched as Chloe's face turned red and then purple. Chloe's tongue popped out of her mouth and her eyes began to lose expression. Yet Bridget squeezed harder.

Nicholas finally managed to pull Bridget off Chloe by administering several blows to her head. When he dragged her back away from Chloe she sat on the floor, beside the bed, her head throbbing from the heavy blows.

Across the room, draped in the kimono now, huddled with both hands holding her throat, was Chloe. She was gasping, and Nicholas was talking to her, telling her to relax, to lie down to take it easy. But Chloe was not listening. She got to her feet and staggered toward the door.

Bridget misread her actions and taking her evil nature for granted, managed to claw herself up and lurched for her.

Nicholas was pleading for an end to this nonsense, as he followed Bridget out into the hall where they came face to face with Francine and Frieda standing in the hallway in their night gowns and haphazardly pulled on robes. Frieda was missing one slipper but did not seem to notice.

Chloe paused to stare at them. It was evident that the commotion coming from Nick's room had been loud enough to wake the dead and the frightful stare on their faces let them know how vicious they sounded. But Chloe continued her way, leading them down the big staircase. They were a ghastly sight, Bridget with her dress ripped and in disarray, and Chloe, barely covering her naked body with the kimono. Of the three, Nick looked put together, but all three had the same expression on their faces, their mouths and face twisted in a way that showed hatred and pain.

Upon reaching the main floor, Chloe headed toward the living room, her gait and balance off kilter as she made her way to the piano. Using one hand to support her, Chloe reached down and the silence in the room was replaced by the piano key pressed, and immediately lifting off the string, allowing the string to sound.

No one moved as Chloe tried to relax by straightening her frame. She pressed the key again and only its sound hung in the air. She knew Chloe was trying to sing.

Her mind flashed back to a day when Isabella was to sing. She had a small, solo part in a school play and during practice she suddenly could not sing. Little Izzy tried and tried and soon was sobbing so hard, the teacher was scared she would make herself sick, so they called Bridget to come to the school.

One look at her daughter and she knew that the thought of singing on stage alone, finally dawned on her and her throat closed. But it was not what Bridget said that helped her daughter then. It was what her teacher had said.

When Izzy sobbing in her mother's arms said, "I can't do it mommy." The teacher had gently turned Izzy toward her, smiled and spoke. "Here's what you do. Take in deep breaths of air and keep your mind on doing that Izzy". Izzy did that.

"Do you feel relaxed?" Izzy nodded.

"Okay, now think how cool it would be if a little bird was flying around your head and when you feel yourself start to smile, let yourself relax and sing."

It had worked.

Bridget forced the memory back as she watched the drama in front of her. She knew this was far worse than that time so long ago. It was worse on many levels. Tears were rolling down her cheeks and her legs suddenly went weak, forcing her to grab hold of Nick for support. Startled, she watched as Chloe's body jerked forward as if she were about to vomit but nothing happened. Chloe pressed the key again and it seemed her whole body shook with the effort to get a sound to come out of her mouth.

It was a battle of body over determination going on as Chloe pressed the key again and this time a gurgling croak, rising in pitch and seeming to come from the back of her throat filled the room. Chloe raised her head and with eyes as big as saucers and her mouth wide open, she fell in a heap, her body writhing hopelessly on the floor.

Bridget started toward her and this time Nick did not stop her. When she stood over her daughter, she reached down and touched her back. Chloe looked up frightfully and scampered on all four until she was under the grand piano.

Wracked with guilt Bridget sat down on the bench, pained by the realization of what she had done. She had managed to turn a civil discussion into a senseless battle that no one could win. She had over reacted, not because she loved Nicholas and did not want to lose him. No, that love was no more, and she doubted it ever existed. It was because it was all about Chloe as every fight or argument in her life had been. But this time it was different because she knew what a monster her daughter had become, and she let herself express her anger.

Allowing herself to release her feelings sent her head spinning backward and a memory surfaced so clearly, as if it were happening right at that moment. It was of Chloe, standing at the corner of the garage with something in her hand. She saw herself hurrying out to see what Chloe was doing and had been shocked beyond words. Her beautiful daughter held a bird in her hand and holding its wing, she was struggling to rip it off. She had screamed at her and Chloe had said she was sorry, but just so mad.

Bridget had never told anyone, not even Cameron, what she had witnessed that day. Now, for the first time Bridget allowed herself to think about the bird wing that Isabella had found. She allowed herself to remember.

Bridget's attention was drawn to Nicholas who began to weep hysterically and to shout at her, "What have you done! What have you done?"

CHAPTER 36

It was Christmas again and snowing. Rochesterians know snow. From the first light fall to the branches of the trees bowed with the heavy load they will carry, everything glistens, and the world becomes a fairyland. Colors appear bright against the white blanket that spreads as far as the eye can see and houses become works of art, decorated with snowy roofs and hanging icicles. Winters can be harsh, unpredictable, and unforgiving but Bridget cannot stop marveling at the quiet beauty of snow-covered trees, and the first snowfall sprinkled on the porches. To her it was like the sky was washing away all sins and allowing for a fresh start.

Bridget after the most crushing period of her life, was beginning to live again, to hope that the future might hold more than pain, or even worse, shame. It was not the collapse of her world that had paralyzed her will, it was the feeling of losing people in her life that she thought of as friends that broke her heart.

That feeling lingered. It was a desperate feeling in her gut that did not leave no matter where she went or what she did.

It happened all at once and went for months in one stifling heap of madness. The loss of Bridget Bitmore, Inc., had been intensely painful, like losing a child. Bridget felt the stress of being a failure and tried to soften the blow by telling herself that this was a window of opportunity to reinvent herself. But no matter how many times she tried telling herself that it was just uncertainty she feared, she could not sleep, and the stress continued to build. She felt numb.

Cameron tried to console her, reminding her she had maneuvered through a lot trying to create a meaningful future for the business and for her family. So, what, Bridget thought. That was then and this was now. Now she needed to feel that she was productive and adding value to her life and those who depended on her, but the reality was that the foundation of her life had fell out from under her and she had no idea how to get it back, or if she wanted to get it back.

There was more to it than the loss of the business that prayed heavily on her mind. She had let her guard down and suffered the consequences. She knew Greyson was not to be trusted and yet she had not kept a close eye on him. She also knew if he had not been so brutal it could have all ended differently. And then there was Mrs. Lucy Steele, the woman whom she had loved and trusted as a friend for those many years. If Mrs. Steele had been a little more loyal, and not gone off on her four-day drunken binge after being forced to decide about her job and her income. And if her husband, Ashton had not run off with some bimbo, the winds might have shifted another way.

Uncertainty affects different people in different ways. Bridget felt uncomfortable with it and needed more certainty in her life. She had fought hard and lost herself in the process, so she went to Reno to do meditation in a private resort and at the same time, divorce Nick. Should she move? What were her options now? She had tried breathing methods, swimming as she tried to discover herself. She stayed in Reno for six weeks in a fever dream, listening to the news from home, afraid not to. Then came the wilting discovery that she could no longer do business under her own name. That, it turned out, was still owned by the corporation. When she returned to Rochester it was all waiting for her.

But the worst was yet to come. On her return a deeper wound surfaced when she received a call, she was expected to attend a meeting. It lasted barely an hour, that painful session with a stenographer and a pair of attorneys.

Two weeks of persistent hoarseness and a noticeable change in her voice was first ignored by Chloe, figuring as soon as her throat healed, she would be fine. But when she tried to sing and a raspy, breathy sound came out, she started to worry. What she did not realize was that because of the strangulation a growth was developing on her vocal cords.

Chloe turned to Nick for advice, and he told her to just give it some time and her voice would come back. Chloe not one to wait for anything, gave it a few days and tried again. In tears she ran to Nick.

"Chloe, just like your legs can get tired from running, your voice can get tired when you use it for a long time. You need to rest the vocal cords and rest your body and mind."

She trusted Nick and felt he knew what he was talking about, but she became impatient and soon was sure it was more than tired vocal cords, so she placed a call to her doctor.

Chloe's doctor gave her a complete examination, paying special attention to her throat. He could not find anything wrong but told her she should see an ENT for further evaluation. Seeing her puzzled expression, he explained that an ENT is an ear, nose, and throat doctor. He would be better equipped to figure out what was going on.

Chloe's mind was in a spin on what to do, so she called Greyson and together they went to the appointment with an ENT. It would be necessary to have it on record.

In the consultation, Greyson made sure the ENT knew what had happened and that Chloe made her living by singing.

The doctor performed a laryngoscopy exam, informing Chloe that he would get a close view of her larynx and collect samples and if he saw any obstructions, remove them.

Greyson was sent to the waiting room and Chloe was taken down the hall to an examination room where she was given a shot. She watched as they prepared a tray with instruments and tried not to get scared. But soon she was under and when she woke, she could not remember anything.

Greyson stood across the room with a worried expression on his face. Chloe tried to speak but could not. "Chloe don't try to talk. We found a growth on your vocal cords; Chloe and it requires surgery." Chloe started shaking her head back and forth. "I'm sorry, Chloe. Many of these growths can be treated without surgery if they are detected early. But you have waited too long."

Chloe looked up as if pleading with him. "I promise it will be okay, but you need the surgery. Afterwards you will require therapy and it is important that you not skip it. You exerted a great deal of energy to produce your voice and that caused you to use the muscles in your neck to help produce sound, leading to muscle strain on top of everything and you need to relearn how to relax these muscles during vocalization." The doctor paused and stared directly at her. "Are you listening to me, Chloe. I know you had a busy schedule, but if you don't follow these instructions, this could end your career."

Chloe nodded furiously. “Good. I’m glad you understand.”

So, Chloe had the surgery and tried to keep to the schedule of no singing until the voice therapist released her. She had been assigned voice therapy appointments consisting of one 45-minute-long session per week for four to six weeks. After just a few sessions, she felt good, and she was sure she could handle a rehearsal for the Sara Lee Corp.

She arrived at the studio and representatives from Sara Lee were there at the rehearsal. But Chloe was confident. She was in her element and it would be fine. She opened her mouth to sing. But a rough unpleasant sounding voice was the best she could do, and the rehearsal was called off.

Chloe was devastated. This was a big contract and she assured Sara Lee she was willing and able to go through with her contract. Only they did not listen. In a matter of days, Sara Lee Corp went to court to have the contract annulled, on the ground that Chloe was no longer able to fulfill it. Chloe's attorney who was the brother of Mr. Levinson, her agent, acted quickly and felt it necessary to prove that Chloe's vocal condition was due to no fault of her own.

CHAPTER 37

Thus, it was that Bridget, after moving out of the Lombardi mansion and advertising it for rent, after returning from Reno where she had gotten her divorce, had to face yet more frustrating pain. She had to give a deposition, talking about the quarrel, and how she had choked Chloe, causing her to lose her voice. This was painful enough, even though neither attorney pressed her for an exact account of what the quarrel was about and let her ascribe it to "a question of discipline."

But the next day, Chloe's popularity led to headline news of the owner of Bridget Bitmore Corp, trying to kill her only daughter and calling it a matter of discipline.

It was another devastating blow and not knowing what else to do, Bridget took a plane back to Reno to try and find some peace.

It was peace that she sought, but she felt she gained much more when Chloe followed her to Reno, and elaborately forgave her. Bridget did not take notice of the photographers, nor let the pictures and the stories in the papers bring her down. None of that mattered. What did matter to her was that Chloe said she forgave her.

It was a strangely different Chloe who settled down with her at the hotel. This wan, smiling wraith who talked in whispers, on account of her throat condition seemed more like the ghost of Chloe than Chloe herself.

At first Bridget felt that Chloe came to see her, not to offer her forgiveness, to make her suffer knowing that she had turned her own daughter's life upside down. She had done Chloe a wrong by allowing her temper to get the best of her, but before coming face to face with her daughter, she had learned to accept it and allowed herself to share the blame with Chloe. But seeing her, all that changed. All Bridget could digest was that she had hurt Chloe both mentally and physically, and there was but one way to correct the wrong. Since she had deprived Chloe of her voice, her means of making a living, she must provide for her.

From seeing her lovely daughter's face, Bridget was backed into her familiar emotional pattern, only with new excuses.

She was not alone in her thinking. Cameron felt about the same as she did. Though he would never come out and verbally blame her, she knew that was how he saw it. But she knew Cameron still had feelings for her and he was the only one who could see through Chloe's manipulation, if that was all it was. Talking with him would be a blessing and so Bridget reached out to him and asked him to come to Reno. Cameron said, 'yes', he would come so Bridget sent him money for a ticket, and he came to Reno. He understood why she did not want to face people she knew in Rochester, just yet.

That first day, Bridget picked Cameron up at the airport and knowing he had never been in the area, she took him on a tour. They went to see the house where Mark Twain freeloaded off his brother in the early 1860s. From there they went to the home where George Ferris, the inventor of the Ferris Wheel, grew up and then on to the location where John Wayne filmed his last movie, "The Shootist"; all this they took in as they walked along the Kit Carson Trail, along tree-lined neighborhoods in the city's west end.

From there they stopped at a little café to eat and then on to South Lake Tahoe and the serene setting of St. Francis of the Mountains. Italy has its Sistine Chapel. New York is known for its St. Paul's Chapel. And for Lake Tahoe, it is St. Francis of the Mountains. She had found it so very peaceful the first time she came. No matter what faith, you could appreciate the unique architectural beauty of the stone structure, tucked away in a grove of Aspens.

It seemed the perfect spot to talk. They found a bench where they could sit and take in the area and Bridget talked. Since it had all happened, she had not allowed herself to tell her side of the story because no one wanted to hear it. So now, she told Cameron everything from beginning to end. When she finished, she leaned back against the bench feeling surprisingly empty of the pain, and more aware of the circumstances that had led to it. She ended with, “And, Cameron, Chloe followed me here and said she forgives me.” She paused. “It’s not our Chloe though.”

“What do you mean?”

“You’ll see when we get back.”

Cameron was greatly moved, learning that Chloe had forgiven her mother. “Goddam it,” he said, “but that makes me feel good.”

He leaned back against the bench and sat quietly bathing in the comfort that they had always felt when they were together. “Bridget, I think that we should provide Chloe with a home; a real home.”

Bridget was not surprised, nor did he expect she would be. “So, you are saying you want us to be a family again?”

“Yes, and I’m asking you to marry me again.” He paused and putting his hands on either side of her face so that he could look directly into her eyes he added, “I’m asking if you still love me because I love you.”

He started to go on, but Bridget stopped him. “Yes, I’ll marry you. My God, Cameron, you have to know I still love you.”

So, with her divorce finalized, she was no longer Bridget Lombardi. When they arrived back at her hotel, they told Chloe of their plans and she seemed elated. It was not until shortly before the day they went to the courthouse to marry that they found out she had called her agent who in turned had relayed the information to her lawyer, Mr. Levinson, who arrived at the courthouse saying he happened to have business in town.

Bridget left the courthouse feeling confident and happy.

CHAPTER 38

The days after Thanksgiving seemed bleak and empty as she mourned the loss of her businesses and running out of important things that she needed to do left her too much time to think. She could not go anywhere as money was tight and every penny was accounted for.

Bridget had mortgaged the house on Bitmore Drive, into which she had now moved after leaving the Cobbs Hill residence and the money she got from the sale had mostly been spent in Reno, and the rest of it was rapidly vaporizing. Yet she had resolved they were going to have Christmas, and bought Cameron a new suit, and Chloe a photograph shooting and several CDs.

It was recklessness but it made her feel more like her old self. Since returning to Rochester, she had been sad. She had Cameron and Chloe, but she missed her friends and the excitement of the restaurants during the holidays. Being able to put gifts under the tree restored her hope in the future.

Francine, who had stayed on with the Bitmores was a familiar and comfortable face and Bridget constantly thanked her for sticking by her until Francine finally told her that she knew she appreciated her, but her constantly telling her was making her feel awkward.

It was Francine who forced her to go out. "You can't just hide in the house and think no one knows you're here. They know, so why not show them you want to be friendly."

It was good advice and Bridget took it and the best that could happen, did happen on one of her outings. After dinner that night Cameron had made eggnog, and as the three of them went back to the dining room together. That is when she shared her news.

"Guess what?"

"What?"

"I bumped into Jordan, one of my old customers who owns several restaurants, and he was furious at the pies that were being delivered to him by Bridget Bitmore, Inc. He could not believe it when I told him I had nothing more to do with it, but when I asked him how he would like to have some of my pies, he almost, kissed me, saying, yes, yes anytime. Bring in apple and lemon pies. Pumpkin too if you have time." Bridget paused and with a dreamy look on her face added, he said, "You are the pie lady!"

In the midst of drinking the eggnog, Cameron flung his head back, forcing the liquid down the wrong pipe and was caught in a fit of coughing. He tried to speak but could not. Francine, trying to control herself, could not hold back any longer and started laughing; forcing the milky drink to shoot out her nose and mouth. Then Bridget, taking in the scene stopped biting her lip and joined in. All four laughed until their sides hurt.

It was Cameron, finally able to talk who said, "Bridget, what a great idea. If you want to make pies, I mean if you feel like it, go for it. I'll help sell them."

Chloe, still having problems with her throat whispered, "And I'll eat them."

It had been too long since they had all been under the same roof and enjoying each other's company. Bridget did not want it to end. She wanted to hug and kiss her daughter, but she held back and settled for giving her a smile.

The doorbell rang and Francine grabbed a napkin to wipe her face and the front of her dress before going to answer it. When she returned, she had a puzzled expression on her face. "There's an Uber guy at the door, Mrs. Bitmore."

"Uber? I didn't order any Uber driver."

"I didn't think so. I'll tell him."

Chloe stood up and grabbed Francine's arm as she whispered, "I ordered it."

Stunned, Bridget stood and asked, "You ordered it?"

"Yes, Mother."

Chloe calmly faced Bridget. "I decided some time ago that

the place for me is New York, and I'm leaving in a little while for the airport. I meant to tell you."

Bridget could hear her voice as she no longer whispered. She also saw her eyes that were now cold and calculating, the eyes of the old Chloe. Bewildered Bridget blinked, but the sweet child of just moments ago was gone and in her place was the old Chloe. And Bridget knew. She knew but had to ask.

"Who are you going with?"

"Nicholas."

"Nicholas Lombardi?"

Oh, the little things lovers neglect to mention and how blind she had been. All the time that Chloe had spent with Nick and she had thought it wonderful they got along so well. Never had it crossed her mind how it all had been arranged.

Stunned, she froze while all sorts of visions flitted through her mind, and slowly the pieces fell together. Greyson had played his hand well from first destroying Cameron and then gone on to her before grabbing the peach he was after. She had always felt there was something behind those eyes that bothered her and now she knew what it was.

Her mind could not stop now as her eyes were opened. She played out scenes and conversations between Hosea Taylor, the wonderful instructor who Chloe had showed more than a passing affection at his death. She had thought Chloe was becoming more sensitive. In a way she was.

It had all been right there in front of her, starting with the that staged confrontation between Pat Levinson and John Bryan. Twenty-five hundred a week for a newbie in the industry! Just reading their body language it was apparent that money was buying more than a voice. Was Mr. Hammond in on it too or was he an innocent like herself.

She tried to breathe deeply and choked as she recalled all the rich friends that Nick had so casually introduced Chloe too, but refused to have her meet them. And then there were Nick's parents who he told her were rich and supported him; especially after his golf career fell flat. The infamous parents that he would not introduce her too, and, oh my god, even after seeing the mansion in such shambles she had not figured it out. Were they even alive?

The world went silent for a moment while scenes of a silent movie played back in her head. Bridget's forehead wrinkled when it dawned on her the real reason that Lucy had betrayed her. She had thought it was because she was at a low point and vulnerable, but though devastated finding out her husband had cheated on her, was only part of it. It was not that he had cheated, it was with who.

Chloe had learned from the expert how to manipulate and get what she wanted, and he had taught her well. That is how she was able to get the surgeon to say she had surgery for an obstruction in her throat.

All that had passed between them, all the hate and frustration surfaced now as she cringed at how easily this daughter had manipulated her, believing she was sorry when she had followed her to Reno so that the bloodhounds sniffing around were taken off track, which explained the appearance of Mr. Levinson at her wedding. It was all there in clarity now.

Bridget stared at her daughter, allowing herself to admit she had been fooled once again as she swallowed the lump in her throat so that she could tell Chloe.

Finally, she was able to take a deep breath and speak, only she did not direct her words at Chloe, but instead to Cameron as if she needed to catch him up on what was really happening.

"I see it now Cameron .... Chloe did not lose her voice at all. She just thought faster than anybody else, that night. Amongst other things, she wanted out of her contract with Mr. Bryan." Seeing his puzzled expression, she stayed on the surface of that issue, trying to make it, make sense. "She used to sing full chest, like a man, and she was able to do it again. So, she did, and she made me swear to choking her, which I did, and she orchestrated a surgery for a court record, so the news could print it. But then she found out she had gone a little too far. The news did a little digging and found out about Nicholas, and that was not so good for her image. So, she came to Reno, and had pictures taken with her loving mother holding her. And at my wedding, to you, Cameron she made sure there were no pictures to contradict what she wanted to erase."

Bridget looked at her daughter's face and continued. "And it was not by accident, that Patrick Levinson, her lawyer showed up at our wedding, was it Chloe. Anything to cover up, to hide what had really been going on, the love affair she'd been having with her mother's husband, with her own stepfather."

How greatly mortals need stability, equanimity, poise, to remain unshaken by events which befall them. This was not through mortal will-power that this creature before her seemed untraumatized. She had a cold heart and was not shaken in mind or spirit. Bridget had expected that once she realized her mother knew how she had been played, she would show a little humility, but this stolid indifference was too much to swallow. Bridget started to react, but Chloe cut her off.

"What does it matter, anyway, I'm leaving."

"Oh daughter, it matters. It matters to me and to your father even before I clarify every stinking detail of your betrayal. And yes, it was a betrayal." She said this with a dramatic sweep of her hand.

Bridget's voice stressed her anxiety as she spoke, and Chloe's hand involuntarily went to her throat. But this time it was only her voice that was out of control.

Cameron managed to bring himself around to all that had

happened, and the pain went so deep he had remained silent. Now he spoke. "When you were growing up, I saw myself in you and I thought that to be a good thing. Every parent has a favorite and Isabella was your mother's, and you were mine."

Cameron paused and looking up saw the smile that eased Chloe's expression. "But now, I have changed, and I see through you what I was and it's ugly. But it still hurts to know you are loss to me. It's like the death of another child." He lets out a choking sob. "When someone loses their spouse, they are called a Widow or Widower. When a child loses a parent, they are called an Orphan. But when a parent loses a child, there is no word, because it should never happen."

He stepped forward and Chloe, sensing it was safe, went to her father and kissed him. Cameron kissed her back; but his eyes were averted and cold as he gazed at Bridget. He whispered in her ear, "I have never told anyone about the birds." He moved back and grabbed her hand.

"It's good you're leaving, and I expect never to see or hear from you again. I do not want to know anything about you or your life and I," he turned toward Bridget, "nor your mother will ever be there for you. You are dead to us and we have practice on how to deal with the loss of a child."

Together they watched as Chloe turned and headed for the door. They remained silent when she paused while turning the door handle and Bridget thought, maybe, just maybe she would apologize. Only she did not. Without turning back around she stepped over the threshold and slammed the door behind her.

The sound of the door slamming shut was too much for Bridget and she released Cameron's grip and ran down the hallway to her bedroom where she flung herself on the bed and cried. She cried long and hard as she faced the fact, she was a forty-seven-year-old woman. She cried because she had lost everything she had worked for, over long and weary years. She cried for the loss of Isabella and the loss of Cameron, who through all of it had remained by her side. And finally, she cried for the death of Chloe who she had loved so deeply even though she had turned on her repeatedly, with tooth and fang, and now had left her without so much as a kiss or a pleasant goodbye.

She felt the pressure on the bed and turned over to see Cameron. He had a decisive look in his eye and a bottle of wine in his hand. As she gazed at him, she felt his love intermingle with her own and knowing him so well, she knew he wanted to end this pain and misery.

"Bridget?"

"Yes?"

"To hell with her."

Bridget stared at him feeling her throat close as a lump blocked her voice. And the tears flowed from her eyes silently until she could finally let out a wail. That is when Cameron dropped the bottle on the bed and pulled her up and grasped her close in his arms. When he sensed she was somewhat in control, he held her back at arm's length and lightly shook her. "It's you and it's me forever. I say to hell with her!"

Those words shocked her to the core, and she stopped crying. She looked up into the face that had endured a lifetime of sorrow, but somehow, they had managed to end up back where they had started. Just the two of them. Now she had to draw that knife across the umbilical cord and God alone knew how hard that would be. But she did it.

Cameron felt her arms come up and hug him tightly and he reached down and lifted her face so that he could look in her eyes. Bridget swallowed. "Yes, I'm with you. To hell with her!"

"Goddam it, that's what I want to hear! Come on."

"Where are we going."

"We are going to celebrate…celebrate us."

Bridget turned and stood while Cameron grabbed the bottle. With it in one hand, he wrapped the other arm around Bridget's waist, and they headed down the hallway, side by side. They went into the kitchen and he seated her on one of the breakfast stools while he got them a couple of glasses. Her mind empty of all thoughts now, she smiled and watched as he opened the wine and poured some in each of their glasses, before sliding one over in front of her.

She brought the glass up to her lips and started to take a sip. At that moment there was a knock at the door. "Who could that be. She wouldn't dare…"

Cameron told her to relax. He would get it.

Bridget sat, rubbing the sides of the wine glass, and waiting. She heard voices but could not make out what was being said. Finally, she heard footsteps. She looked up and Cameron stood with two police officers.

Bridget started to stand, but felt her legs giving out so sat back down.

"What…what is it? Cameron, did something happen to Chloe."

"No, not really. Get your coat, Bridget."

Those would be the last sane words spoken to her. Bridget followed Cameron and they went out to climb into the police car. They road silently to the station and when they arrived, she saw Nicholas standing near the entrance. "What's going on, Cameron." Cameron just shook his head and frowned.

They were taken to a conference room where Cameron's parents, along with Nicholas were now seated and after a few minutes Dr. Crawford joined them.

Bridget had thought she had faced the worse, but she had not. Slowly the doctor told them that they had finally figured out what had happened to Isabella. She had been poisoned. Someone had been giving her arsenic. Once they had discovered it, they had called the police and a thorough investigation had begun. It had taken them till now to find out who was at the bottom and when they did, they had taken Chloe into custody.

Bridget jumped up out of her seat, frantically looking around. “No, it’s got to be a mistake…” She stared at Cameron who stood and pulled her close. “There’s been no mistake, madam. Once we had the evidence and confronted her with it, she admitted that she had put antifreeze in Izzy’s pretend drinks at first and then later in anything else she could hide it. She said she just wanted to make her sick enough so that she did not force all the attention on her.

Then the officer looked at Bridget and spoke. “What got me was when she said to me, “I can’t understand why you are making such a big deal out of this.” That is what she said.

ABOUT THE AUTHOR

Juanita Tischendorf is an author of both fiction and non-fiction books. Her genre goes the gamut, from crime mystery, action adventure, fantasy, and romance and for teens a self-improvement book. She was born in Philadelphia, PA, spent her adolescence in New Jersey and has lived most of her life in Rochester, New York. When not writing, she can be found walking around the Irondequoit area, sewing, mainly now to provide free face masks, and reading.

To learn more about the books by Juanita Tischendorf go to https://www.facebook.com/nitatischen/

or https://www.amazon.com/author/juanitatischendorf

www.ingramcontent.com/pod-product-compliance
Lightning Source LLC
Chambersburg PA
CBHW052345020726
47503CB00001B/117

* 9 7 8 1 7 3 5 0 7 1 2 4 4 *